THE CONSOLATION OF PHILOSOPHY

BOETHIUS

THE CONSOLATION
OF PHILOSOPHY

With an Introduction
and Contemporary Criticism

Edited and translated by SCOTT GOINS
and BARBARA H. WYMAN

Ignatius Critical Editions Editor
JOSEPH PEARCE

IGNATIUS PRESS   SAN FRANCISCO

Cover art
Allegory of Philosophy, Raphael, 1511
Stanze of Raphael, Vatican

Photo Credit: Scala/Art Resource, N.Y.

Cover design by John Herreid

©2012 by Ignatius Press, San Francisco
All rights reserved
ISBN 978-1-58617-437-8 (PB)
ISBN 978-1-68149-476-0 (eBook)
Library of Congress Control Number 2011940927
Printed in Italy ∞

Tradition is the extension of Democracy through time; it is the proxy of the dead and the enfranchisement of the unborn.

Tradition may be defined as the extension of the franchise. Tradition means giving votes to the most obscure of all classes, our ancestors. It is the democracy of the dead. Tradition refuses to submit to the small and arrogant oligarchy of those who merely happen to be walking about. All democrats object to men being disqualified by the accident of birth; tradition objects to their being disqualified by the accident of death. Democracy tells us not to neglect a good man's opinion, even if he is our groom; tradition asks us not to neglect a good man's opinion, even if he is our father. I, at any rate, cannot separate the two ideas of democracy and tradition.

—G. K. Chesterton

Ignatius Critical Editions—Tradition-Oriented Criticism for a new generation

CONTENTS

INTRODUCTION

Scott Goins and Barbara H. Wyman
McNeese State University

The name Boethius (A.D. 480–524) is little recognized today, a fact we should lament. For he has a singular importance in history,[1] and the lessons from his *Consolation of Philosophy* are arguably more important now than ever. Born a mere four years after the fall of Rome and its Western Empire, he was uniquely placed to make a difference in a world that was crumbling around him. Classically educated in the finest Roman tradition, Boethius rose to political importance as consul of Rome in 510 under Theodoric, the Ostrogothic king. Theodoric, who gained power by the brutal murder of Odoacer in the latter's palace at Ravenna, had realized the expediency of retaining government positions for the Roman aristocracy, which would provide experience and stability during such a period of political upheaval. Though Theodoric left in place a veneer of Roman culture and governance, he retained the power. And so it was natural that Theodoric would use the talented and respected Boethius to enhance his political image. It was evident to Boethius that things once honored by many were increasingly disregarded and unappreciated in the new era of

---

[1] See, e.g., Frederick Copleston, *Medieval Philosophy*, pt. 1 of *A History of Philosophy* (Garden City, N.Y.: Image, 1962), 2:116–20, and H. Liebeschutz, "Western Christian Thought from Boethius to Anselm", in *The Cambridge History of Later Greek and Early Medieval Philosophy*, ed. A. H. Armstrong, pp. 538–55 (Cambridge: Cambridge University Press, 1967). On Boethius' life and general contribution, see Henry Chadwick, *Boethius: The Consolations of Music, Logic, Theology, and Philosophy* (Oxford: Oxford University Press, 1981); Gerard O'Daly, *The Poetry of Boethius* (Chapel Hill: University of North Carolina Press, 1991), pp. 1–29; and John Marenbon, ed., *The Cambridge Companion to Boethius* (Cambridge: Cambridge University Press, 2009).

Gothic Rome, despite Theodoric's apparent sympathies. This husk of the fallen empire would eventually dry up and blow away as the center collapsed.

Theodoric, it had been rumored, was illiterate, but it is a point of historical fact that he was educated in Constantinople and knew some Latin; he had an appreciation for Roman culture and law and for the ornamentation of ceremony, but he had no intention of fusing the two cultures, Roman and barbarian. As a Goth, Theodoric adhered to the nontrinitarian theological system of the heretic Arius, which may have contributed to his eventual suspicion of the orthodox Boethius. For a while, there remained a friendship of sorts between the two men; Theodoric was aware of his handicap as a Gothic invader among Roman patricians, and he was astute enough to realize that by virtue of a friendship with Boethius, he might more easily succeed in his new kingdom.[2] What Boethius could not have known was that the same Theodoric, the friend who asked him to design and build a water clock as a gift for the Burgundian king,[3] would later, by means of ambiguous evidence regarding supposed treason, have him brutally tortured and executed.[4]

[2] See Chadwick, *Boethius*, chap. 1, pp. 1–68; see also John Matthews, "Anicius Manlius Severinus Boethius", in *Boethius: His Life, Thought and Influence*, ed. Margaret Gibson (Oxford: Basil Blackwell, 1981), pp. 15–43.

[3] See S. J. B. Barnish, trans. and ed., *Variae*, by Cassiodorus (Liverpool: University of Liverpool Press, 1992), pp. 38–43. These *Variae* of "Magnus Aurelius Cassiodorus Senator; The Right Honourable And Illustrious Ex-Quaestor of the Palace, Ex-Ordinary Consul, Ex-Master of the Offices, Praetorian Prefect and Patrician, Being Documents of the Kingdom of the Ostrogoths in Italy, Chosen to Illustrate the Life of the Author and the History of his Family" are the actual documents written by Cassiodorus, Boethius' contemporary, who wrote state letters at the behest of King Theodoric. In several of these letters, King Theodoric asks Boethius to make not only a water clock but also a sundial for Gundobad, king of the Burgundians. Theodoric requests in another letter that Boethius help him select a cithara player, since Boethius wrote a treatise entitled *De institiutione musica*. However, Theodoric mistook what *De musica* is all about: it has nothing at all to do with playing musical instruments and instead has everything to do with Pythagoreanism and cosmic harmony.

[4] On Boethius' fall, see Chadwick, *Boethius*, pp. 54–56, and John Moorhead, "Boethius' Life and the World of Late Antique Philosophy", in Marenbon, *Cambridge Companion to Boethius*, pp. 18–22.

Nor could Boethius have known that the philosophical work he wrote while in prison awaiting his eventual execution would become one of the most influential works of Western civilization. *The Consolation of Philosophy*, which grapples with the existence of evil in a world controlled by a loving God, is made all the more poignant when one realizes that Boethius was in reality dealing with this very problem; he was all alone, imprisoned because of the whims of the tyrant Theodoric, with little recourse but to his own *fides et ratio*. A work of genius composed without the aid of any books, the *Consolation* has kept scholars busy to this day. This "dazzling masterpiece"[5] was the inspired outpouring of a brilliant mind and a gentle soul who, when gazing out of his prison window, found solace by watching the stars, which kept their "ancient peace" pointing to the "Amor quo caelum regitur",[6] the Love that ruled not only the heavens but also the lives of men.

Boethius had grasped the gravity of the situation of the world in which he was living. As former consul in good standing with the court (before the falling out with Theodoric), he turned his eager mind and ample talents to preserving classical learning. We know now that, but for Boethius, much of this ancient thought would have been lost to a world descending into the age referred to ever after as "dark". Boethius' prescience showed him the path to take during this confusing time; he therefore set about to preserve the foundations of education, especially in the areas of dialectic and the four mathematical disciplines: geometry, arithmetic, astronomy, and music. He coined the term "quadrivium"[7] for these mathematical disciplines, which he considered an indispensable path to abstract knowledge; the quadrivium, in conjunction with the

[5] Chadwick, *Boethius*, p. v.

[6] Edmund T. Silk, "Boethius' *Consolatio philosophiae* as a Sequel to Augustine's *Dialogues* and *Soliloquia*", *Harvard Theological Review* 32 (1939): 17–39.

[7] See Chadwick, *Boethius*, p. xii. For a full treatment of Boethius' development of the quadrivium, see ibid., pp. 70–117, and Alison White, "Boethius in the Medieval Quadrivium", in Gibson, *Boethius*, pp. 162–205.

trivium,[8] subsequently became the foundation of liberal arts education throughout the Middle Ages and the Renaissance. Boethius also wrote the standard treatises in each of these disciplines. Although his works on geometry and astronomy are lost, *De institiutione musica* and *De arithmetica* have survived, and both were considered indispensable textbooks for many centuries.

Boethius also provided an invaluable link to Plato and Aristotle for medieval and Renaissance readers. The Latin West in the age of Boethius had little Plato; all that existed was half of the *Timaeus* in a version from Cicero. Even less Aristotle was available. It was Boethius' fear that the irreplaceable knowledge and learning of these philosophers would be lost for want of translation.[9] So he set for himself the task of translating all that he could of both philosophers. Since he realized that Aristotle would be little understood, he also planned to provide commentaries. But this project was halted by his imprisonment and execution. What translation he managed to complete included Aristotle's writing on logic, prefaced by Porphyry's *Isagoge*. Along with two commentaries on Porphyry, he completed one commentary on Aristotle's *Categories* and two on Aristotle's *De interpretatione*. It is solely through these works that the early medieval world knew Aristotle. During his short life, Boethius also managed to write *De differentiis topicis* (a commentary on Cicero's *Topics*) and several original treatments of certain problems in logic. In what were to be his last years, he completed four theological tractates, the *Opuscula sacra*, and two theological treatises, *De fide catholica* and *De disciplina scholarium*. Boethius' importance in Western thought was most firmly established by his final and most influential work, *The Consolation of*

[8] The trivium, a term coined in medieval times, comprised the three subjects taught first: grammar, logic, and rhetoric. After the development of the quadrivium, the trivium became a preparatory for the quadrivium. See Miriam Joseph, *The Trivium: The Liberal Arts of Logic, Grammar, and Rhetoric* (Philadelphia: Paul Dry Books, 2002).

[9] See Chadwick, *Boethius*, p. x.

Philosophy.[10] Lorenzo Valla was truly right to call Boethius the "[l]ast of the Romans, first of the scholastics".[11]

Boethius' influence on subsequent ages can hardly be exaggerated, especially in respect to the *Consolation.* As C. S. Lewis has remarked of this work, "Until about two hundred years ago it would ... have been hard to find an educated man in any European country who did not love it."[12] Saint Thomas Aquinas refers to Boethius by name 135 times in the *Summa theologica.*[13] Dante places Boethius in *Paradiso* (10.124–29), and Boccacio and Jean de Meun draw heavily on Boethius. He is widely recognized as a major influence on Chaucer, whose discussion of fate and divine providence in several of the *Canterbury Tales* and in *Troilus and Criseyde* comes directly from the *Consolation.* Chaucer also translated the *Consolation* into English, as had King Alfred the Great before him. Indeed, no properly equipped library in Europe was without Boethius' *Consolation, De musica,* and *De arithmetica.*[14] Studies in manuscripts have demonstrated the general availability of these works, the surviving examples of which equal the works of Saint Augustine and the Bible in their extent, number, age, and completeness.[15] Boethius' arguments on the matters of providence and free will were so important that the medieval world considered him an authority as important as, but more

[10] On the importance of Boethius' philosophical works and the theological tractates, see, e.g., Chadwick, *Boethius,* pp. xi–xv, and Marenbon, *Cambridge Companion to Boethius,* pp. 1–5.

[11] Quoted in Chadwick, *Boethius,* p. x.

[12] C. S. Lewis, *The Discarded Image: An Introduction to Medieval and Renaissance Literature* (Cambridge: Cambridge University Press, 1964), p. 75. For other discussions of Boethius' influence during the Middle Ages, see Howard Rollin Patch, *The Tradition of Boethius: A Study of His Importance in Medieval Culture* (New York: Oxford University Press, 1935), and Winthrop Wetherbee, "The *Consolation* and Medieval Literature", in Marenbon, *Cambridge Companion to Boethius,* pp. 279–302.

[13] See Ralph McInerny, *Boethius and Aquinas* (Washington, D.C.: Catholic University of America Press, 1990), p. 10.

[14] Patch, *Tradition of Boethius,* p. 21.

[15] James Collins, "Progress and Problems in the Reassessment of Boethius", *Modern Schoolman* 33 (1945): 8.

versatile than, the Church Fathers.[16] In the Middle Ages, scholars relied on the mathematical teachings of Boethius' quadrivium,[17] and their arguments on divine providence derived directly or indirectly from the *Consolation*.[18] In the twelfth century, the Christian humanism flowering at Chartres was based on Boethius' Pythagoreanism and Platonic heritage.[19]

Enthusiasm for the *Consolation* continued in the sixteenth and seventeenth centuries. Boethius' most famous translator in the Renaissance was none other than Queen Elizabeth I.[20] There is little doubt that Saint Thomas More, Shakespeare, Milton, and many others, including George Herbert,[21] read and drew from Boethius, as Boethian imagery has been noted and catalogued in their works.

One of the most enduring of all Boethian images, from the Middle Ages to the present, is the *Rota Fortunae* or Wheel of Fortune. The goddess Fortuna had been around since antiquity, but the conventional portrait of fickle Fortune spinning her wheel and deciding fate with the flick of her wrist is a direct legacy of Book Two of Boethius' *Consolation*. The Wheel of Fortune motif was used significantly in the famous *Carmina Burana* of the thirteenth century, a work which was resurrected in the twentieth century when the classical composer Carl Orff set selections of it to new music. Fortuna was also used by John Kennedy Toole in his 1981 Pulitzer Prize winning novel, *Confederacy of Dunces*; the main character, Ignatius J. Reilly, continually refers to the goddess Fortuna as having spun him downwards on her wheel of luck. Throughout this quirky novel, Ignatius makes many references to Fortuna and to Boethius himself. An admittedly trivial but nevertheless familiar use of the Wheel has found its way into modern popular culture through the ever popular (and long

---

[16] Chadwick, *Boethius*, pp. xiii–xv.
[17] See White, "Boethius in the Medieval Quadrivium", pp. 162–65.
[18] See Patch, *Tradition of Boethius*, p. 25.
[19] Collins, "Progress and Problems", p. 10.
[20] On Boethius in the Renaissance, see Patch, *Tradition of Boethius*, pp. 75–81.
[21] See Barbara Hart Wyman, "Boethian Influence and Imagery in the Poetry of George Herbert", *Studies in Philology* 97 (2000): 65–68.

running) game show, Wheel of Fortune, where contestants win or lose money determined by the random spin of a wheel.

An introduction to the *Consolation* would be incomplete if mention were not made of the so-called "vexed question"[22] of Boethius' Christianity. For a time it was held that Boethius' execution was a religious issue and that he was in fact a martyr for the faith.[23] Some critics in the modern era, however, challenged this claim and further complicated the issue by the suggestion that Boethius was not even Christian, because Christ, forgiveness, and salvation are not specifically mentioned in the *Consolation*. The authenticity of Boethius' authorship of the theological tractates was also questioned, discounting these overtly Christian works as evidence of Boethius' Christianity.[24] The last word for many, although not all, was the discovery in 1877 of a letter of the historian Cassiodorus, Boethius' contemporary, which mentions the treatise *De Trinitate*, and Boethius' other theological works, ascribing authorship to Boethius. Cassiodorus, a Roman senator and himself a former consul, served in various high offices from A.D. 505 to A.D. 538 under several Ostrogothic kings, including Theodoric. Cassiodorus became the chief publicist during this time and the meticulous state papers which he compiled are a major source for historical information not only on the Roman government, but for the culture and politics in the early years of Ostrogothic Rome. This is strong evidence for Boethius' Christianity.[25] And

[22] Silk, "Boethius' *Consolatio philosophiae*", p. 19. The absence of overt references to Christianity seems so striking to some that one modern critic, Joel C. Relihan, has argued that Boethius intentionally subverts the arguments of Lady Philosophy, thereby exposing the demerits of ancient thought in comparison with Christian contemplation. Joel C. Relihan, *The Prisoner's Philosophy: Life and Death in Boethius' "Consolation", with a Contribution on the Medieval Boethius by William E. Heise* (Notre Dame: University of Notre Dame Press, 2007).

[23] Boethius was canonized by Pope Leo XIII in 1883 and has a cultus at Ravenna. His feast day is October 23—Saint Severinus Boëthius, Martyr; catalogued in the Roman Martyrology.

[24] Gerald Vann, *The Wisdom of Boethius*, Aquinas Society of London 20 (London: Blackfriars, 1952), p. 3.

[25] For a thorough treatment of the religion of Boethius, see Chadwick, *Boethius*, pp. 247–53.

then there are many whose opinions count: Pope Benedict XVI,[26] C. S. Lewis,[27] and Henry Chadwick, among others, who argue that, although Boethius might have written as a philosopher, he believed as a Christian.

Does Boethius' *Consolation* still have value for readers today? The answer is a firm yes, for there are many troubling parallels between Boethius' world and ours. Today's world is under attack by a different type of barbarian, highly educated ones: relativists who think that the only truth is that which can be proved by the physical sciences. As a result, our modern world seems ever more intent to push science to the limit, testing boundaries of morality and ethics. Indeed, practical science has become exalted as the supreme exercise of the intellect, used to master nature and gain power, with little concern for moral obligation. Materialism and consumerism are results of this disregard of core values based on natural law, as humans strive to fulfill their inner emptiness with the false gods, the *falsa bona* about which Boethius warned. The timeless truth of Western tradition, which exalts the dignity of every human person, is in greater danger of being lost today than it was over fifteen hundred years ago when the Goths sacked Rome. The new barbarian is far more dangerous. These barbarians have neither belief in natural law nor morality and are practitioners of a different and more subtle kind of sacking. We are in desperate need of a corrective.

For Boethius, philosophy was the love of wisdom based on the knowable reality of truth.[28] He taught that this kind of

---

[26] Benedict XVI, "Boethius and Cassiodorus" (general audience, Paul VI Audience Hall, March 12, 2008), http://www.vatican.va/holy_father/benedict_xvi/audiences/2008/documents/hf_ben-xvi_aud_20080312_en.html.

[27] See Lewis, *Discarded Image*, pp. 76–79, for a defense of Boethius' Christianity and his choice to limit himself to philosophical arguments while in prison. A similar approach is taken by Danuta Shanzer, who argues that the *Consolation* might have avoided overt references to Christianity because Boethius had a philosophical audience in mind that was not necessarily Christian. See Danuta R. Shanzer, "Interpreting the *Consolation*," in Marenbon, *Cambridge Companion to Boethius*, p. 244.

[28] Vann, *Wisdom of Boethius*, pp. 6–7.

wisdom is a living word which illuminates the mind of man. Therefore, the possession of true knowledge (as opposed to so-called scientific fact) leads to the highest Good, the *summum bonum*, which cannot be taken away and does not disappear if one is imprisoned. This Truth which is real and knowable needs to be proclaimed again to our world, which is tumbling into darkness.

Perhaps then we shouldn't be surprised that Boethius (along with Cassiodorus) was the subject of Pope Benedict XVI's general audience in March of 2008.[29] The Pope finds the lessons of the *Consolation* invaluable for the world: that life is transient and full of suffering; that against Wisdom, evil will not prevail; that the existence of evil is not contradictory to a world governed by a loving God. In the *Consolation*, Boethius' intent was to bring man to encounter and love God as an act of the will, not relying on irrational human feelings. He sought to engage the reader in his own personal struggle, and in so doing, to instruct. Through the study of mathematics, astronomy, music, and philosophy, Boethius saw perfect harmony and order in the created universe and loved the Creator in response. As we read the *Consolation*, we experience the pilgrimage of every man who wishes to find peace and who discovers that it is to be found in the submission of the will to the perfect will of God.

[29] Benedict XVI, "Boethius and Cassiodorus".

A NOTE ON THE TRANSLATION OF
THE *CONSOLATION*'S POETRY

Boethius was a torch shining throughout the Middle Ages. Yet, as H. R. Patch remarked, "What name of equal distinction has suffered such wane?"[1] This being so, we hope that this new translation of *The Consolation of Philosophy* will help introduce Boethius to those who have not yet met him.

The *Consolation* is a prosemetric composition, a combination of prose and poetry, the form of Menippean satire. It is not uncommon for someone assigned to read the *Consolation* to pick up the work, confront the poetry, skip it, and go on to the prose. This is a shame because the poems do a nice job of augmenting the lessons taught in the prose. Perhaps readers do this because the translation of the poetry has often taken second place to the translation of the prose. So how *does* a translator best translate poetry from one language to another? Does he try to be completely literal and go so far as to make prose translations of poems? Is it more important to get across the sense of the poem and worry little about form?

Of course, it is true that something is "lost in translation". Imagine Shakespeare in Italian. It really would not be Shakespeare but something else altogether. And that is the point—a translator is a cocreator. He must attempt to understand and then re-create a work from one world so that it exists in the next. This can be daunting. What is more, works need to be retranslated as the English language, as well as styles and tastes, changes.

With this in mind, we have taken a few liberties with the translation of the poetry. The goal of this translation was simply to create clear and pleasing lines that present Boethius'

[1] Howard Rollin Patch, *The Tradition of Boethius: A Study of His Importance in Medieval Culture* (New York: Oxford University Press, 1935), p. 1.

imagery in such a way that they are recognizable and able to be understood, a goal that necessitated at times simplifying a line. The poetic line in Latin is counted and measured differently from the English poetic line, each driven by the structure of the language. Latin poets will often pile on adjectives so as to make the meter work, but in English, this would seem redundant. Since Boethius' poetry did not rhyme, the poems in our translation are in free verse, with the hope that the beautiful Boethian imagery might come across unencumbered by the constraints of regular meter or unnatural end rhyme. End rhyme can become tedious in a translation; one soon wearies of reading it. We have chosen to focus on word choice—finding words that would most accurately reflect the mood and the intent of the poem. What we tried to convey across the abyss of time and language is Boethius' personality, so evident in his imagery. He looked into the night sky and was comforted by multitudes of quiet stars keeping their "ancient peace" (4.met.6), perceiving God in the deep but dazzling darkness. He was the gentle scholar who, from his cell, recalled gathering violets in a spring wood and thought of a little "tree-loving" bird who was saddened when she caught a glimpse of her tree from within a cage (3.met.2).

There are many translations of the *Consolation*. Our hope is that the simpler poetic lines will allow a modern reader to enjoy the poems, so that they might be what Boethius intended—a "refreshment" and a "sweetness" to break the often-dense philosophical message he sought to convey in his prose. But above all, our hope is that both the poetry and the prose are accessible and bring Boethius *the person* to the reader, that what is lost in translation may be regained through transformation.

Translators' Acknowledgments

We would like to thank Dr. John Wood, whose encouragement and enthusiasm have set so many on the path of discovery. We would also like to thank Dr. Robert Benson, professor of English at the University of the South. Dr. Benson first introduced Scott to the *Consolation* and kindly commented on an early version of part of our translation. We are also grateful to our institution, McNeese State University. McNeese has been supportive of our efforts both to translate the *Consolation* and, more important, to make the classical tradition available to our students.

The Text of

THE CONSOLATION

OF PHILOSOPHY

Book 1

metrum 1[1]

> I once composed verses with joy!
> Forced by grief,
> melancholy measures I now collect.[2]

---

[1] metrum 1: Boethius' first poem, or *metrum*, is in elegiac meter, which was often used in antiquity for mournful verse. Scholars have noted in this poem echoes from Ovid's poetry written when he (like Boethius) was exiled under imperial disfavor. See, e.g., *Tristia* 5.1.5–6: "Just as our condition is mournful, so will our poetry be,/with words fitting the subject at hand." (All translations of primary sources found in the notes are our own unless otherwise stated.) For further examples and discussion, see Joachim Gruber, *Kommentar zu Boethius, "De consolatione philosophiae"*, 2nd ed. (Berlin: Walter de Gruyter, 2006; originally published 1978), pp. 54–55; Anna M. Crabbe, "Literary Design in the *De consolatione philosophiae*", in *Boethius: His Life, Thought and Influence*, ed. Margaret Gibson (Oxford: Basil Blackwell, 1981), pp. 244–51; and Gerard O'Daly, *The Poetry of Boethius* (Chapel Hill: University of North Carolina Press, 1991), p. 38.

[2] *I once composed verses . . . melancholy measures I now collect*: These lines are reminiscent of the close of Virgil's *Georgics* (4.563–66):

> At that time sweet Parthenope nourished me,
> Virgil, as I enjoyed the pursuit of inglorious leisure
> and toyed with songs of shepherds, and in the boldness
> of youth sang of you, Tityrus, under the shade
> of the spreading beech tree.

Some scholars have also connected Boethius' lines with the pseudo-Virgilian opening of the *Aeneid* (1.1.a–b):

> I am he who once tuned my song on a slender reed,
> then, leaving the woodland, constrained the neighbouring
> fields to serve the husbandman, however grasping—
> a work welcome to farmers.

(For the pseudo-Virgilian lines and their translation, see Virgil, *Eclogues; Georgics; Aeneid 1–6*, trans. H. Ruston Fairclough, Loeb Classical Library 63 [Cambridge: Harvard University Press, 1935].)

Like Virgil, Boethius writes of his change of literary genres, in Boethius' case from happy bucolic poetry to elegy. We do know from the *Anecdoton Holderi* (see S. J. B. Barnish, trans. and ed., *Variae*, by Cassiodorus [Liverpool: University

Torn Muses[3] bid me write—
elegies drench my face.
Terror no more prevents
these songs, my final companions,
from brightening my path.
Poems, once the glory of my green youth,
console me now in old age's gloom.[4]
Old age came unsought:
hastened by evil, commanded by pain.
With hair whitened, and skin trembling loose,
my worn frame quakes.
Death, sorrowful in sweet years,
called in sadness is welcomed.
He shuns my wretched cries,
refuses to close my weeping eyes.
This dismal hour engulfing my head
came while Fortune favored me.

---

of Liverpool Press, 1992], pp. xxxv–xxxvii) that Boethius once wrote bucolic
poetry. For a discussion of this passage, see Crabbe, "Literary Design", pp. 244–
51, and O'Daly, *Poetry of Boethius*, pp. 32–38. It should be noted that Boethius
might not have known of the pseudo-Virgilian passage, since it was not part of
most of the early manuscripts. It is possible that he knew of the passage from the
grammarian Priscian, who wrote treatises dedicated to Boethius' father, Symmachus. Priscian cites the pseudo-Virgilian passage.

[3] *Torn Muses*: "Torn Muses" are the sorrowful Muses of elegy, which Boethius
will eventually see as destructive.

[4] *old age's gloom*: Boethius is actually only about forty-five; he is exaggerat-
ing, or perhaps sorrow has made him feel older than he really is. Gruber, *Kommentar zu Boethius*, p. 55, compares Ovid's *Epistulae ex ponto* (1.4.20), likewise
written in exile. See also Jo-Marie Claassen, *Displaced Persons: The Literature of
Exile from Cicero to Boethius* (Madison: University of Wisconsin Press, 1999),
p. 249.

Cf. also *Pearl* 33: "In bliss you abide and happiness,/And I with woe am worn
and grey;/Oft searing sorrows I possess" (*Pearl*, in *Sir Gawain and the Green Knight,
Pearl, and Sir Orfeo*, trans. J.R.R. Tolkien [Boston: Houghton Mifflin, 1975]).
On *Pearl* as a poem in the tradition of the *Consolation*, see Michael H. Means,
The "Consolatio" Genre in Medieval English Literature (Gainesville: University of
Florida Press, 1972), pp. 49–55, and Michael D. Cherniss, *Boethian Apocalypse:
Studies in Middle English Vision Poetry* (Norman, Okla.: Pilgrim Books, 1987),
pp. 151–68.

She changed her cheating face;[5]
now wicked days drag forward endlessly.
My friends! You boasted my happiness!
How faltering was that life
of a man now fallen.

1. Silent and alone, I was thinking about these things and began to record my tearful complaint, when it seemed to me that a woman appeared, standing over my head.[6] She had a holy look,

---

[5] *She changed her cheating face*: The deceit and treachery of Fortuna will be much more fully developed in book 2. For Boethius' wording, cf. Seneca, *Octavia* 377–80:

> Why, mighty Fortune, did you encourage me with your false face,
> and lift me up high when I was content with my lot,
> and then make me fall all the more heavily, as I looked
> down from my citadel and saw so many fears?

[6] *a woman appeared, standing over my head*: The epiphany of Lady Philosophy has many classical literary antecedents. The origin of such scenes goes back to Homeric poetry. See especially *Iliad* 1.194–222, when Athena convinces Achilles not to kill Agamemnon; *Odyssey* 6.14–81, when Athena advises Odysseus on his conduct among the Phaeacians; and *Odyssey* 14.187–440, when Athena advises Odysseus on how to act among the suitors when he returns to Ithaca. Athena was, of course, the goddess of wisdom and philosophy and so is a particularly good pattern for Lady Philosophy.

Boethius was perhaps influenced by Martianus Capella, *De nuptiis Philologiae et Mercurii* (*On the Marriage of Philology and Mercury*) 2.127. *On the Marriage of Philology and Mercury* was a long Neoplatonic allegory inspired by the story of "Cupid and Psyche" in books 4–6 of Apuleius' *Metamorphoses* (or *Golden Ass*). Proposed dates for the poem vary, so it may not have been written before the *Consolation*. See Gruber, *Kommentar zu Boethius*, p. 17.

See also the opening of Augustine's *Soliloquies*: "As I had been revolving with myself matters many and various ... suddenly some one addresses me, whether I myself or some other one, within me or without, I know not" (Augustine, *Basic Writings of Augustine*, ed. Whitney J. Oates, vol. 1 [New York: Random House, 1948]).

Cf. also Jean de Meun, *Romance of the Rose* (4221–24): "While I raved thus about the great sorrows I was suffering, not knowing where to seek a remedy for my grief and wrath, I saw fair Reason coming straight back to me; as she descended from her tower she heard my complaints" (Guillaume de Lorris and Jean de Meun, *The Romance of the Rose*, trans. Charles Dahlberg, 3rd ed. [Princeton: Princeton University Press, 1995]).

For further references, see Joachim Gruber, "Die Erscheinung der Philosophie in der *Consolatio philosophiae* des Boethius", *Rheinisches Museum für Philologie* 112

and her eyes showed fire and pierced with a more-than-human penetration. One could hardly guess her age; her face was vital and glowing, yet she seemed too full of years to belong to this generation. Her height was hard to tell; at one moment it was that of any ordinary human, but at another she seemed to strike the clouds with the crown of her head.[7] Indeed, when she lifted her head higher, she could no longer be seen by mortal eyes.

Her clothes were made of the finest thread, skillfully woven and imperishable—woven by the woman herself, as I later learned from her. Yet a film grown dark with age, looking like soot covering a statue, obscured her dress.[8] On its bottom hem was woven the Greek letter *pi*, with a series of steps ascending to a *theta* that rose above it.[9] But this same garment had been

(1969): 168–86; Gruber, *Kommentar zu Boethius*, p. 62; and Pierre Courcelle, "Le personnage de Philosophie dans la littérature latine", *Journal des Savants* (1970): 209–52.

[7] *Her height was hard to tell . . . crown of her head*: Bernard Jefferson compares the description of Fame in Chaucer's *House of Fame* (1369–75):

> Me thoughte that she was so lyte
> That the lengthe of a cubite
> Was lengere than she semed be.
> But thus sone, in a whyle, she
> Hir tho so wonderliche streighte
> That with hir fet she erthe reighte,
> And with hir hed she touched hevene.

(Bernard L. Jefferson, *Chaucer and the "Consolation of Philosophy" of Boethius* [Princeton: Princeton University Press, 1917], pp. 140–41.)

[8] *Her clothes were made . . . obscured her dress*: Henry Chadwick notes that the description of Lady Philosophy's garment is based somewhat on Athena's *peplos* at *Iliad* 5.734–35: "[Athena] slipped off her elaborate/dress which she herself had wrought with her hands' patience" (Henry Chadwick, "Theta on Philosophy's Dress in Boethius", *Medium Aevum* 49 (1980): 175; *The "Iliad" of Homer*, trans. Richmond Lattimore [Chicago: University of Chicago Press, 1951]). According to Chadwick, the Neoplatonists "liked to meditate" on the garment's "allegorical significance". Of course, the film on Lady Philosophy's garment and the film we will later see covering Boethius' eyes refer symbolically to obscured wisdom and diminished perception.

[9] *On its bottom hem . . . theta that rose above it*: The *pi* and *theta* refer to practical (*practikê*) and theoretical (*thêorêtikê*) philosophy. Practical philosophy includes ethics and political science. Theoretical philosophy includes Boethius' quadrivium (arithmetic, geometry, music, and astronomy). These studies, in focusing on

ripped by the hands of some violent men, who had torn away
from it what bits and pieces they could. The lady held books
in her right hand and in her left a scepter.

As she caught sight of the Muses of Poetry standing by my
bed, giving me words to suit my tearful mood, the Lady was
angry for a moment and her eyes flashed with savage fire.[10]
She spoke: "Who let these whorish stage girls come to see a
sick man? It's more pain they bring than remedies. No, they
make things worse with their sweet-tasting poison. These are
the kind of women that choke off a mind's rich fruit, wrapping it up in sterile thorns of passion. They make a mind more
used to disease, instead of setting it free from pain. If you were
trying to seduce a common man with your enticements, as you
usually do, it wouldn't bother me so much. Then you would
not be damaging my work—but a man weaned on Eleatic and
Academic philosophy?[11] Now go, you Sirens,[12] sweet until you

---

the divine harmony in the created order, "constitute in Neoplatonic epistemology a ladder of ascent between the physical sciences and metaphysics or theology" (Chadwick, "Theta on Philosophy's Dress", p. 176).

[10] *As she caught sight . . . eyes flashed with savage fire*: Lady Philosophy has no
use for the destructive self-indulgence of the poetic Muses. Crabbe, "Literary
Design", p. 255, compares Augustine's vision of Continence, who gives him the
strength to overcome the voices of earthly attachments (*Confessions* 8.11). For
other passages in Augustine that point out the dangers of pagan literature, see
Confessions 1.16; *City of God* 2.14; and *De doctrina christiana* 2.18.28.

[11] *Eleatic and Academic philosophy*: "Eleatic philosophy" refers to the thought
of Parmenides (fl. 475 B.C.) and Zeno (fl. 460 B.C.), both of Elea, a Greek colony
on the southern coast of Italy. These two philosophers contributed to the development of the dialectical method essential to subsequent philosophy. "Academic philosophy" refers to the thought of Socrates (469–399 B.C.) and Plato
(429–347 B.C.).

[12] *Sirens*: The Sirens were dangerous singers in ancient myth who lured sailors to their shores with their enchanted music. In some versions of the myth,
sailors never want to leave the island of the Sirens; in others, the ships crash
on the island's rocky coast. The earliest and most famous account of them is
Odyssey 12.153–200. The Sirens figured prominently in the Neoplatonic allegory of the *Odyssey* (Robert Lamberton, *Homer the Theologian: Neoplatonist
Allegorical Reading and the Growth of the Epic Tradition* [Berkeley: University
of California Press, 1986]). O'Daly, *Poetry of Boethius*, p. 39, suggests that Boethius is contrasting the "Muse of Pleasure" of Plato's *Republic* (607A) with the
"Muse of Truth" of the same work (548B). For a brief summary of the allegoric

bring destruction; leave him to my Muses to be cured and made whole."

Chastised by her words, they lowered their heads in sadness and by their blushes confessed the truth of her accusations. They withdrew from my room in sorrow. But my eyes were so bathed with tears that I could not recognize who this woman was that had shown such authority. I cast my gaze upon the ground and quietly waited to see what she would do next.

Then she approached the edge of my cot and sat. Looking at my face, worn with grief and dejected with sorrow, she bitterly mourned my mind's confusion:

metrum 2

> "The mind is blunted when worry grows
> swollen by earthly winds.
> Drowned in darkness,
> stretching into outward abyss,
> its light is left behind.
> This man was once free to walk
> under open heavens, familiar
> with celestial courses; he viewed
> the sun's light, the icy moon, and
> wherever stars on wandering returns
> danced through changing circles.
> All these he possessed—
> mastered with numbers.[13]

---

significance of the Sirens in classical and Christian thought, see D. W. Robertson, *A Preface to Chaucer: Studies in Medieval Perspectives* (Princeton: Princeton University Press, 1962), pp. 143–44.

[13] *This man was once free . . . mastered with numbers:* In Pythagoreanism and Neoplatonism, the study of astronomy, musical harmony, and mathematical theory enabled man to catch a glimpse of divine intelligence. Boethius' devotion to these studies is shown in his authorship of treatises on music and arithmetic. See Henry Chadwick, *Boethius: The Consolations of Music, Logic, Theology, and Philosophy* (Oxford: Oxford University Press, 1981), pp. 69–107. Lady Philosophy, of course, laments that Boethius' brilliant mind has lost contact with the truth it had grasped.

He understood many causes:
of noisy gales disturbing the tide,
what breath tumbles the earth,
why the sun falls into the western sea
to rise in the east,
what regulates spring's hours
that blossom the earth,
and who made fertile autumn
flow with full grape.
He pried into hidden nature's secrets.
This man now lies,
his mind light-forsaken,
neck pressed with chains,[14]
face cast down,
forced to discern nothing
but the ground.

2. "But now is the time for remedies[15] instead of tears," she
said. She then continued, looking straight into my eyes: "Are

---

Cf. George Herbert's "Vanity":

> The fleet Astronomer can bore
> And thread the spheres with his quick-piercing mind:
> He views their stations, walks from door to door,
>   Surveys, as if he had design'd
> To make a purchase there: He sees their dances,
>   And knoweth long before,
> Both their full-ey'd aspects, and secret glances.

(1–7)

[14] *his mind light-forsaken, / neck pressed with chains*: Chadwick, "Theta on Philosophy's Dress", p. 176, argues that the "chain may be literal as well as symbolic." Of course, the symbolism of the mind being dragged down by chains is in keeping with the Platonic idea of the body as the prison of the mind. Similar overtones are present in the "mind light-forsaken". The inhabitants in the cave in Plato's famous "Allegory of the Cave" are chained by the legs and neck so that they cannot see the light (*Republic* 7.514).

Cf. also George Herbert's "Affliction (I)", lines 1–12, 19–29. Herbert's autobiographical poem seems to be echoing Boethius' lament (1 *metrum* 2 and 1 *prosa* 1). See Barbara Hart Wyman, "Boethian Influence and Imagery in the Poetry of George Herbert", *Studies in Philology* 97 (2000): 61–95.

[15] *remedies*: The remedy in question is for Boethius' lethargy, a classical and medieval term for a condition in which the patient has no will to take action.

you the one who was nursed on my milk and ate at my table until you gained manly strength of mind? Did I not give you all the weapons you needed, ones that would have kept your mind safe from harm? At least they would have, if you hadn't thrown them away. Do you recognize me? Why don't you say anything? Is it shame or confusion that leaves you silent? If only it were shame! But I can see it's confusion that overwhelms you."

When she saw that I was not just silent but totally speechless and completely unable to talk, she gently laid her hand upon my breast and spoke. "There's no real danger here. He's simply dazed, as one would expect of a man suffering under delusion. He's forgotten who he is for a moment. He'll easily remember again soon—that is, if indeed he ever knew me. But first we'll have to wipe away the cloud of mortal cares that darkens his eyes." [16] Saying this, she folded her gown, and with it wiped my tear-filled eyes.

metrum 3

>Then with night scattered,
>shadows left me, and
>to my eyes returned their first strength.
>As when the violent west wind gathers stars,
>stormy rains persist in the sky,

See Wolfgang Schmid, "Philosophisches und Medizinisches in der *Consolatio* des Boethius", in *Festschrift Bruno Snell*, ed. Thomas B. L. Webster, pp. 113–44 (Munich: C. H. Beck, 1956), and W. Schmid, "Boethius and the Claims of Philosophy", *Studia Patristica* 2 (1957): 368–75 (the 1957 article is an abbreviated version in English of the 1956 article).

[16] *But first we'll have to wipe away . . . darkens his eyes*: The concept of removing a mist that prevents mortal eyes from seeing the divine occurs in the *Iliad*, when Diomedes is allowed by Athena to see what gods are fighting in battle (5.127–28) and when Poseidon clears the mist from Achilles' eyes (20.341–42). When the image occurs at *Aeneid* 2.604–6, Venus clears the mist from Aeneas' eyes so that he can see the actions of the gods in the fall of Troy. In the *Aeneid* and the *Iliad*, the image has clearly acquired Platonic overtones. The clouded eyes suggest a lack of perception, just as the limited vision in Plato's cave suggests limited understanding. See *Republic* 7.514.

the sun lies hidden,
no stars are yet in the heavens—
night is poured on the earth from above.
If the north wind should flog this dark,
this night released from a Thracian cave[17]—
its force would unbar the day, once closed.
The sun now launched,
shines with sudden light, and
strikes wondering eyes with its rays.

3. In just this way the clouds of my sorrow were dispelled. Now my eyes drank in the bright light of heaven, and I could recognize the face of the one who was healing me. When I cast my eyes upon her and fixed my gaze, I saw it was the one whose home I had visited since my youth—the Lady Philosophy, my nurse. "Why have you come down from on high to see me in the loneliness of my exile, O lady of all virtues?[18] Do you wish to stand on trial with me and face the charges they have falsely laid against me?"

"Would I desert you, my child?" she replied. "Wouldn't I help you carry this burden of ours that has been laid upon

[17] *Thracian cave:* According to mythology the north wind (Boreas in the original) lived in a cave in Thrace (in Northern Greece).

[18] *Why have you come down . . . O lady of all virtues?* This is surely the inspiration for Dante's lines in *Inferno* (2.76–84), where Virgil asks Beatrice why she has come down from Heaven to seek his aid in guiding Dante through the underworld.

> O Lady of power through whom alone the human
> race rises above all the contents of that heaven whose
> circles are smallest [the changeable, sublunary heaven],
> so pleasing to me is your command that obeying,
> had it already taken place, is slow; no more is
> needed than to unfold your desire.
> But tell me the reason why you do not shrink
> from coming down here, into this center, from the
> spacious place where you desire to return.

(*The "Divine Comedy" of Dante Alighieri*, vol. 1, *Inferno*, trans. Robert M. Durling and Robert L. Martinez [New York: Oxford University Press, 1996].) See, e.g., Means, *"Consolatio" Genre*, pp. 44–48. Of course, the dramatic situation of the *Consolation* inspired Dante's concept of a man guided by figures of human and divine wisdom (Virgil and Beatrice).

your shoulders by those that hate me? It would not be right for Philosophy to let an innocent man walk his path alone. To think that I would be afraid to face an accusation or tremble in fear—as if such charges were new to me!

"Do you think this is the first time that wicked men have made assaults against the walls of wisdom?" she said. "Didn't we often have to engage in battle against rash folly in the old days, before the time of my Plato? And while Plato lived, didn't I stand beside his Socrates as he won victory by death, a death he did not deserve?[19] And after that, the Epicurean and Stoic herds and all the rest tried to snatch his legacy, every man for himself. They grabbed me, too, as their prey while I shouted and struggled against them, and they ripped this garment of mine, which I had woven myself.[20] As they went away with some little shreds torn from it, they thought that I had yielded myself completely to them. Since these men were seen with little bits of my clothing, they were foolishly assumed to be my friends. How many of them were destroyed by the errors of the crowd!

"But even if you don't know about the older examples, like Anaxagoras' flight, the poisoning of Socrates, or Zeno's tortures,[21] surely you could have thought about men like Seneca,

---

[19] *Socrates . . . a death he did not deserve*: The story of Socrates' trial and martyrdom for allegedly corrupting the youth of Athens and for teaching against the traditional religion is told in Plato's *Apology, Crito*, and *Phaedo*.

[20] *And after that . . . I had woven myself*: Lady Philosophy's point seems to be that various philosophical groups claimed to teach the truth when they were teaching only a portion of it. In their rapacious desire to lay claim to wisdom, they snatched whatever they could get from Philosophy's garment.

The Stoics advocated the strict following of duty without allowing the individual to take account of his emotions and desires. The Epicureans advocated attempting to rid one's life of pain through the avoidance of anxiety about the afterlife and about worldly ambitions. Unlike the Stoics, the Epicureans believed that one should avoid the political life. Although Boethius inclines toward the Stoics, he may have learned the value of Epicurean teachings on the latter point! In the *Consolation*, Boethius quotes very often from the Stoic author Seneca, and he occasionally seems to allude to the Epicurean poet Lucretius.

[21] *Anaxagoras' flight . . . Zeno's tortures*: Anaxagoras (c. 500–428 B.C.) died while he was in flight from Athens on charges of impiety, after he taught that the sun

Canius, or Soranus[22]—such examples are hardly ancient or obscure. These men died simply because they were trained in my ways and had no taste for the pursuits of wicked men. So don't be surprised if we're tossed about by storms on the sea of life, when we ourselves have chosen to be displeasing to the wicked. Indeed, we must despise their army, even if it is a large one, since no general directs it. Instead, it rushes about, carried here and there by a flood of error. If this army should set itself into ranks and attack us fiercely, we have a leader who will draw us into her fortress, while our enemies spend their time searching for their little bags of plunder. Yet we, untouched by their mad confusion, look down and laugh as they grab at every worthless thing they can find. Their cunning folly cannot climb the walls that keep us safe.[23]

---

was only a hot stone and that the moon reflected its rays. Socrates was forced by the Athenians to drink hemlock. Zeno of Elea (c. 490–430 B.C.), mentioned above (see p. 7, footnote 11), was tortured under the instruction of the tyrant Nearchus.

[22] *Seneca, Canius, or Soranus*: Canius was a Stoic who opposed the Roman emperor Caligula (ruled A.D. 37–41), who had him killed. Both Seneca and Soranus were killed by Nero (ruled A.D. 54–68), who is portrayed in the *Consolation* as the archexample of a tyrant, like Theodoric. Just as the philosopher Boethius had served Theodoric as advisor, so Seneca had been a close advisor and in fact the tutor of Nero. See Tacitus, *Annals*, books 12–16.

[23] *If this army . . . walls that keep us safe*: Cf. Seneca, *Epistula moralis* 82.5 (quoted by Gruber, *Kommentar zu Boethius*, p. 114): "Philosophy should be surrounded by an impregnable wall that Fortune cannot cross as she tries to shake it with her many siege engines. The mind that has deserted things outside itself stands on a spot that cannot be overcome, and it secures victory from atop its tower; all weapons fall below it."

Similar in tone to Boethius' image is Lucretius, *On the Nature of Things* 2.7–13:

> But nothing is sweeter than to dwell in peace
> high in the well-walled temples of the wise,
> where looking down we may see other men
> wavering, wandering, seeking a way of life
> with wit against wit, line against noble line,
> contending, striving, straining night and day,
> to rise to the top of the heap, High Lord of Things.

(Lucretius, *The Nature of Things*, trans. Frank O. Copley [New York: Norton, 1977].)

metrum 4[24]

> The virtuous man,
> calm in his orderly life,
> stares Fortune in the face
> and drives proud Fate beneath his feet.
> He holds high his unconquerable head!
> Nothing shall move that man—
> not the madness and menace of the sea
> disturbing the tide,
> nor Vesuvius' broken furnace
> hurling rock,[25]
> nor the bolts of heaven's fire
> striking towers.[26]
> Why do miserable men wonder
> at raging tyrants
> with no true strength?

[24] metrum 4: Cf. the lines of *metrum* 4 with Horace's description of the Stoic wise man, *Ode* 3.3.1–8:

> The man who is just and firm in his intent
> is not shaken in his resolute mind,
> whether by the zeal of the crowd
> as they bid him do evil
>
> or by the face of the tyrant looking on,
> or by the stormy wind that swells
> the Adriatic and lifts it up,
> or by the mighty hand of Jove.
>
> If the world should break and fall,
> the ruins would cause no fear
> as they fell upon his head.

[25] *Vesuvius' broken furnace / hurling rock*: Vesuvius, the only active volcano on mainland Europe, is in southern Italy near the Bay of Naples. Pliny the Younger described its eruption in A.D. 79, when it destroyed Pompeii and Herculaneum.

[26] *bolts of heaven's fire / striking towers*: The idea of lightning striking lofty towers perhaps comes from another Horatian ode (*Ode* 2.10.10–12): "Lofty towers crash with a heavier fall, and lightning strikes mountains on their peaks." Horace's lines suggest the avoidance of divine anger by following the golden mean (moderation, knowledge of man's limitations), while Boethius' verses praise the fearlessness of a brave man in the face of the dangers of nature.

Fear not, hope not;[27]
this impotent wrath you will disarm.
The anxious man dreads and desires;
he cannot be firm,
under his own authority.
He abandons his shield, his post,
and fastens the chain by which
he can be dragged.[28]

4. "Do you understand this?" she said. "Have my words sunk into your heart? Or are you simply 'like the ass that heareth the lyre'?[29]

"Why are you crying? Why cover your face with tears? 'Speak forth thy mind!' as the poet says.[30] You can't expect the benefits of treatment if you won't uncover your wound."[31]

---

[27] *Fear not, hope not*: The abandonment of fear and hope would be in accord with Stoic thought. Unlike Christians, who regard hope as a virtue, the Stoics felt that relying on hope made one's mind vulnerable, since hope could be baseless. In general the ancients often felt that hope was not necessarily a good thing.

[28] *fastens the chain . . . he can be dragged*: Again, one sees the image of the soul in bondage. Gruber, *Kommentar zu Boethius*, p. 119, compares Plato, *Phaedo* 82E. See similarly Augustine, *Soliloquies* 24.

[29] *like the ass that heareth the lyre*: Our pseudo-Elizabethan translation is an attempt to reflect Boethius' use of Greek in his original. "Like the ass that heareth the lyre" is a Greek proverb, suggesting a person too dull-witted to appreciate higher things. Boethius was one of the few Latins of his day who knew Greek.

In *Troilus and Criseyde*, a work that is strewn with Boethian allusions, Chaucer borrows from this passage. Pandarus is chiding Troilus, who is in a lethargy because of his love of Criseyde:

> What! Slombrestow as in a litargie?
> Or artow like an asse to the harpe,
> That hereth sown whan men the strynges plye,
> But in his mynde of that no melodie
> May sinken hym to gladen, for that he
> So dul ys of his bestialitie.
>
> (1.730–35)

According to Robertson, *Preface to Chaucer*, p. 129: "One of the most common iconographic devices for showing deafness to celestial harmony throughout the Gothic period was to represent an ass seated before a harp."

[30] *'Speak forth thy mind!' as the poet says*: This is a quotation from Homer, *Iliad* 1.134, when Thetis is consoling Achilles, after Agamemnon has insulted him.

[31] *You can't expect . . . uncover your wound*: Cf. *Troilus* 1.857–58 (Pandarus speaking): "For whoso list have helyng of his leche, / To hym byhoveth first unwre his wownde."

So then I collected my strength of mind and replied, "Do I still need to explain my bitter sorrow? Isn't it clear enough how Fortune has raged against me? Doesn't this very place cause you pain? Is this our library[32]—a place that you yourself chose long ago as a sanctuary in our house, where you would safely teach me the wisdom of God and man alike? Was this the way I used to look? Was this the way I dressed when I was delving into nature's secrets, when you charted out for me the course of the stars, when you taught me how to live and what life meant, by seeing the heavens as patterns of reality? Is this the reward I get for following you?

"Weren't you the one who hallowed the words of Plato when he claimed that the Republic would be blessed if lovers of wisdom ruled it or if its rulers happened to love wisdom? You used the words of that very man to argue that this is why the wise must take a part in public affairs, so the helm of state won't fall to wicked and criminal men, who would bring ruin and destruction to the good.[33] And so I followed this advice and chose to apply to public affairs what I had learned from you in our quiet hours together. You and the God who planted

[32] *library*: Boethius was confined from his home, probably in Pavia. There is considerable debate as to the conditions of Boethius' imprisonment and in particular as to what kind of access, if any, he would have had to books. Pierre Courcelle argues that Boethius was likely under house arrest only and that he would have had access to books (Pierre Courcelle, *"La consolation de philosophie" dans la tradition littéraire: Antécédents et postérité de Boèce* [Paris: Études augustiniennes, 1967], p. 323; see similarly C.S. Lewis, *The Discarded Image: An Introduction to Medieval and Renaissance Literature* [Cambridge: Cambridge University Press, 1964], p. 77). Chadwick, in "Theta on Philosophy's Dress", p. 176, and *Boethius*, pp. 225–26, argues for the likelihood of a stricter imprisonment. He contends that Symmachus, Boethius' foster father and father-in-law, might have bribed a jailor into letting Boethius have a few books. In any case, we can be sure that Boethius had an exceptional memory with regard to literature.

[33] *this is why the wise . . . destruction to the good*: For Plato's concept of the philosopher-king, see *Republic* 473D: "Unless . . . either philosophers become kings in our states or those whom we now call our kings and rulers take to the pursuit of philosophy seriously and adequately, and there is a conjunction of these two things . . . there can be no cessation of troubles, dear Glaucon, for our states, nor, I fancy, for the human race either" (Plato, *Republic*, trans. Paul Shorey, 2 vols., Loeb Classical Library 237, 276 [Cambridge: Harvard University Press, 1935, 1937]).

you inside the minds of good men can bear witness that I only took part in public life for the sake of benefiting all good men. But because of this motive I have endured grim and irreconcilable quarrels from the wicked, and for the sake of keeping my conscience clean I have preserved the law and never been afraid to offend the powerful.

"How often I stopped Conigastus and prevented him from robbing the wealth of every powerless man! How often I cast down Trigguilla,[34] the Prefect of the Palace, when he had planned to harm someone, indeed even when he had already carried out his plans! How often I risked myself by using my authority to protect the unfortunate, as they suffered countless attacks from the unchecked greed of the barbarians! I never strayed by choosing wrong over right. I grieved equally with the provincial families when their estates were swallowed up by private greed and public taxation. When the famine occurred in Campania, and it seemed threatened with ruin by a ridiculous taxation to provide for the army, I took my stand against the Praetorian Prefect.[35] I favored the common good of the people and opposed him in front of the King; I won.

---

[34] *Conigastus . . . Trigguilla*: Very little is known of Conigastus or Trigguilla. Cassiodorus, who was apparently related to Boethius and who would succeed him as *magister officiorum* (master of offices), wrote a letter for the Ostrogothic king Athalarich to Conigastus. See Barnish, *Variae*, p. 106. Both Trigguilla and Conigastus were Goths. As J. J. O'Donnell notes, "No Goths appear in a good light in the *Consolatio*, for Boethius had given up currying favor by this time." The aristocratic Romans like Boethius would have had great disdain for the Goths, whom they regarded as half-civilized. As prefect of the palace, Trigguilla was "in charge of the royal household and thereby able to exercise influence over many spheres of activity" (J. J. O'Donnell, ed., *Consolatio philosophiae*, vol. 2, Bryn Mawr Latin Commentaries [Bryn Mawr: Thomas Library, Bryn Mawr College, 1984], p. 11).

[35] *it seemed threatened with ruin . . . against the Praetorian Prefect*: Boethius opposed the imposition of a *coemptio*, which would have required farms to sell produce at less-than-market prices. Campania was an area of large farms owned by Roman aristocrats, whom Boethius may have seen as being "land poor" and gravely threatened by such taxation.

The praetorian prefect was originally the leader of the Praetorian Guard, the emperor's official bodyguard. Later the office was somewhat like that of a secretary of state or prime minister. See Barnish, *Variae*, p. 186, and O'Donnell, *Consolatio*

"When those ambitious palace dogs had nearly devoured the wealth of Paulinus, a man of consular rank,[36] I snatched him out of their gaping jaws. I endured the hatred of the informer Cyprian, who had tried to destroy Albinus,[37] seeking to pronounce him guilty without a trial, though he, too, was a man of consular rank. Didn't I pile up quite enough ill will against myself? But surely other men should have kept me all the more safe, since my love of justice kept me from making any provision for my safety by favoring the palace courtiers.

"And who are the informants that have caused my downfall? Basil,[38] for one, a man once dismissed from serving the King, who now is forced by his debts to lay a charge against me. Opilio and Gaudentius[39]—both banished for countless, cunning frauds, who then refused to go and instead took refuge in a sanctuary.[40] When the King learned of their conduct he decreed that they had to leave Ravenna by a certain day or else be branded on the forehead and driven out. What harsher condemnation could have been added to that? But on that very day an accusation was made against me by these same men. Tell me, is that the reward I earned for my virtue? Did my prearranged conviction somehow make them just

<hr />

philosophiae, p. 12. O'Donnell suggests that Boethius may have been master of offices at this time.

[36] *Paulinus, a man of consular rank*: As a man of consular rank and a patrician, Paulinus (consul in 498) represented the old Roman nobility and thus, in Boethius' mind, well-deserved protection from the Goths and the timeserving Romans (like Cyprian below) in league with them.

[37] *Albinus*: Albinus was a consul in 493. Around 523 he was charged with treason against Theodoric because he allegedly wrote letters in support of the Eastern emperor Justin. See Chadwich, *Boethius*, pp. 48–49.

[38] *Basil*: Basil was a senator and the father-in-law of Opilio (see the next footnote).

[39] *Opilio and Gaudentius*: Opilio was the brother of Cyprian; Gaudentius was a senator. O'Donnell notes that Opilio and Cyprian "remained fiercely loyal to whatever Gothic regime held power, and prospered after Boethius's death" (O'Donnell, *Consolatio philosophiae*, p. 13).

[40] *took refuge in a sanctuary*: The tradition that a temple afforded sanctuary was also applied to Christian churches. O'Donnell notes that "clearly a Christian church is implied. The etiquette of Late Latin style encourages writers like Boethius to avoid neologisms like *ecclesia*" (ibid.).

accusers? Shouldn't Fortune have been ashamed—if not at the innocence of the accused, at least at the worthlessness of the accusers?

"Do you want to know the substance of the charge against me? That I wanted to preserve the Senate.[41] In what way? I am charged with preventing an informer from introducing documents accusing the Senate of treason. So what do you think, my teacher? Shall I deny the charge, so that I don't bring shame upon you? But I did want to keep the Senate safe, and I will never stop wanting to do so. Should I confess, then? There is no chance now to stop my accusers. Perhaps I should say that I was wrong in wanting to keep the Senate secure. Indeed, by passing decrees against me the Senate did act disgracefully. Yet foolish self-deception never changes the true worth of anything. Agreeing with the advice of Socrates, I think it would have been wrong to hide the truth or give in to falsehood.[42] But I will leave it to you and to the judgment of the wise to decide whether or not I have told the truth. To the pen and human memory I have entrusted the substance and account of this charge so future generations will not be fooled.[43]

"And what good does it do to speak of the forged letters that suggest I was hoping for Roman liberty? The lies of my accusers would have been obvious enough if I could have used their confessions.[44] This always carries the most weight in such

[41] *I wanted to preserve the Senate*: Boethius' enemies apparently told Theodoric that Boethius was conspiring with the Eastern emperor to oust him. Theodoric apparently suspected the Senate of taking part in Albinus' supposedly treasonous activities. Boethius spoke in support of both Albinus and the Senate as a whole and was accordingly also viewed as a conspirator. See Chadwick, *Boethius*, pp. 48–49.

[42] *Agreeing with the advice of Socrates . . . give in to falsehood*: See Plato, *Theaetetus* 151D (Socrates speaking): "In no way does it seem to me to be right to give in to falsehood and to hide the truth", and *Republic* 485.

[43] *To the pen . . . future generations will not be fooled*: Perhaps Boethius had previously written some type of document stating his innocence.

[44] *The lies of my accusers . . . used their confessions*: Gruber, *Kommentar zu Boethius*, p. 129, suggests that Boethius means he could have proven that the informers were lying if he had been given the opportunity to cross-examine them. We

cases. But what freedom can be hoped for now? I only wish there were some. Then I would have used the words of Canius, when Caligula accused him of complicity in a plot against him: 'If I had known of it, you would not have.'[45]

"In this situation I am not made so dull by grief that I complain about wicked men contriving evil against virtue. What astounds me is that they have carried out their wishes. I suppose it is a common fault to lean towards evil, but it is almost monstrous that every wicked man accomplishes his plots against the innocent, while God looks on. That's why one of your followers rightly wondered, 'If God exists, what is the source of evil? But what is the source of good if He does not?'[46] I can understand if wicked men who seek the blood of the Senators, and indeed of all good men, should wish to destroy me, too, since I am fighting for these very causes. But surely I didn't deserve this from the Senators themselves?

"You remember, I'm sure—for you yourself were always right beside me, directing me what to do or say—what I did at Verona[47] when the King, in his eagerness for the ruin of the Senate, laid against it the same charge of treason that had been leveled against Albinus. Surely you recall how I defended them all with no regard for my own security. You know that I'm saying these things strictly out of regard for the truth, that I've never wanted to boast. For when a man displays his own

---

will learn later that Boethius was convicted without being allowed to attend his own trial. (See 1 *prosa* 4, paragraph 11, p. 21 below.)

[45] *words of Canius . . . 'If I had known of it, you would not have'*: The death of Canius, a Stoic, is given in Seneca's *Dialogues* 9.14.4–10. Canius' clever retort is not recorded by Seneca or any known source, but Seneca records a similar incident. When a centurion came to Canius' house to take him away for execution, he found Canius playing a board game with a friend. Before Canius was led away, he counted his tokens and said to his friend, "After I'm dead, don't lie and say you defeated me." The Stoic Seneca, of course, sees Canius' carefree attitude as the proper one in the face of death.

[46] *If God exists . . . if He does not?* The exact source of this quotation is unknown. See O'Donnell, *Consolatio philosophiae*, p. 14. Boethius will later see that evil does not truly exist, since it is only the absence of good.

[47] *Verona*: The Ostrogothic kings often held court at Verona, as well as at Pavia and Ravenna (O'Donnell, *Consolatio philosophiae*, p. 15).

good deeds and then reaps the reward of praise, he lessens in some way the satisfaction of a peaceful conscience, by trying to justify himself.[48] But you see what results my innocence has brought. Instead of receiving the rewards of true virtue I suffer the penalty of a crime I didn't commit. Even when a crime was openly confessed, has there ever been a time when it was met by judges so severe that none were moved by an awareness of man's weakness or by the tricks of Fortune that affect everyone? If I were accused of wanting to set fire to a temple, of wickedly putting priests to the sword, of planning the slaughter of all good men, a sentence would be passed against me—but in my presence, after I had confessed or been found guilty. Now, five hundred miles away,[49] without defense or the opportunity to say a word, I am sentenced to death and condemned for favoring the Senate too much. How unworthily these Senators have repaid my efforts! Little do they deserve that anyone should take such risks for them!

"The very ones who fabricated this charge know its value, an accusation they have further blackened by inventing the lie that I committed sacrilege in order to gain office.[50] But you yourself, who are planted deep inside me, have driven from the depths of my heart any desire for transitory things, and under your gaze there could be no place for sacrilege, for you daily instilled in my ears and thoughts that Pythagorean

[48] *For when a man . . . trying to justify himself*: Cf. Cicero, *Tusculan Disputations* 2.64: "All things seem more praiseworthy to me, when they are done without promotion or public witness—not that we must avoid these, since we want to bring good deeds to light—but still, virtue has no greater theater than the conscience."

[49] *five hundred miles away*: Boethius was probably being held at Pavia, five hundred miles from Rome.

[50] *the lie that I committed sacrilege in order to gain office*: Boethius' political success and extensive scientific and philosophical knowledge might have seemed eerie to some. (For instance, he was asked by Theodoric to construct a water clock for the king of the Burgundians; see the introduction, p. x, footnote 3.) In 510/511, a little over ten years before Boethius was imprisoned around 523, two senators had been convicted and executed on charges of black magic. See O'Donnell, *Consolatio philosophiae*, p. 16, and Gruber, *Kommentar zu Boethius*, p. 134.

precept: 'Follow God.'[51] And it would not have been fitting for me to look for the aid of inferior spirits, when you had endowed me with virtue in order to make me become like God. Besides this, the purity of my home, my companionship with honorable men, and my relationship with my father-in-law[52]—a holy man, as worthy of reverence as you yourself—should argue against any suspicion that I might have committed such a crime.

"It's unspeakable that these wicked men will gain credence for their charge because of my closeness to you. I will seem to be implicated in evil, simply because I have been steeped in your teachings and governed by your ways. It's not enough that my reverence for you has provided me no help; you too have to be ripped apart because I am assaulted. Indeed, what adds one more trouble to all the others is that most men look not at the merit of a charge but rather at its outcome. They judge that a man has acted rightly only when things turn out well for him. And so it always happens that the first thing an unfortunate man loses is his reputation. It causes me pain now to hear the rumors spread by the people and to imagine how confused and contradicting their judgments are. I would say that this is the ultimate burden of misfortune: a wretched man is believed to deserve all that he suffers, even when the charge against him has been made up. Such is the case with me. Deprived of possessions, stripped of honors, and disgraced in the eyes of man, I have suffered punishment for doing good.

"I seem to see on the other hand, workshops of unspeakable crimes, places where scoundrels happily wallow in their pleasure, each desperate man threatening others with fraudulent charges trumped up by informants, dashing to the ground good men, frightening them by our example. Each scoundrel boldly

---

[51] *Follow God*: Again, we cannot trace the original source, but this or similar expressions were common among ancient philosophers. See, e.g., Iamblichus, *Life of Pythagoras* 18.86; Seneca, *Dialogues* 7.15.5; and Seneca, *Epistula moralis* 16.5. Pythagoreanism, in which numbers and numerical relationships demonstrate the order inherent in the world, is central to Boethius' thought.

[52] *my father-in-law*: Symmachus, who was much loved and respected by Boethius, was Boethius' father-in-law and also his foster father. Symmachus was one of the great minds of the period.

undertakes crimes with impunity, indeed is induced by rewards
to accomplish them. The innocent, on the other hand, are
deprived of their safety and defense. And so I cry:

metrum 5[53]

> O Builder of the starry universe!
> Sky spinner, star whirler,
> You are the commander.
> All obey Your laws:
> the shining moon's crescent fills
> with her brother sun's flames,
> and together they conceal the lesser stars.

[53] metrum 5: Chaucer borrows frequently from this *metrum*, which deals with
the question of why God's providence does not seem as evident in human affairs
as it does in nature. See Jefferson, *Chaucer and the "Consolation"*, p. 155, who
cites several passages, including the following from *The Man of Law's Tale*:

> O myghty God, if that it be thy wille,
> Sith thou are rightful juge, how may it be
> That thou wolt suffren innocentz to spille,
> And wikked folk regne in prosperitee?
> (813–16)

Cf. also *The Franklin's Tale*:

> Eterne God, that thurgh thy purveiaunce
> Ledest the world by certein governaunce,
> In ydel, as men seyn, ye no thyng make.
> But, Lord, thise grisly feendly rokkes blake,
> That semen rather a foul confusion
> Of werk than any fair creacioun
> Of swich a parfit wys God and a stable,
> Why han ye wroght this work unresonable?
> (865–72)

Cf. also Milton's *Samson Agonistes* 667–73:

> God of our fathers, what is man!
> That thou towards him with hand so various,
> Or might I say contrarious,
> Temperest thy providence through his short course,
> Not evenly, as thou rulest
> The angelic orders and inferior creatures mute,
> Irrational and brute.

With her crescent emptied,
she loses her light.
At night's beginning,
Venus rises cold, the evening star,
and as Morning Star,
she pales with the rising sun.[54]
You shorten day's light,
and winter comes.
You quicken the night,
and summer comes.
The north wind whisks away
what the west wind returns as ripe leaves.
Sirius[55] burns the crops
Arcturus[56] guarded as seed.
Your law binds all but man.
How else could twisting Fortune bring ruin?
Crime squeezes the innocent.
Wicked men on earthly thrones
let fools tread upon sacred necks.
Virtue lies hidden in shadow,
so the just man bears the crime.
Fraud adorned in false colors
brings no harm to the evil ones.
Rejoicing in their power,
they subdue the mighty at whim.
O Fastener of earth's bonds—
look back on us!

---

[54] *At night's beginning . . . pales with the rising sun*: More literally: "The star that as Hesperus rises cold in the early night, at another time changes its accustomed reins and comes as Lucifer, which pales as the Sun rises." O'Donnell, *Consolatio philosophiae*, pp. 17–18, explains: "Hesperus (evening star) and Lucifer (morning star) are the names given to whatever planet (usually Venus or Jupiter) shines brightest at dawn and at dusk. Boethius's point is that the same planet can be evening star now, and morning star a few weeks from now."

[55] *Sirius*: Sirius, the Dog Star, appears before dawn during July, whence comes the term "dog days".

[56] *Arcturus*: Arcturus, the Bear Warden, a very bright star near Ursa Major, rises in early September, a time Virgil (*Georgics* 1.68) advises for planting.

Men battered by Fortune's seas
are no worthless part of Your effort.
Ruler, check the fierce waves!
Steady the earth, surround it
with Your law which rules the vast sky."

5. When I had barked out these complaints in my unending grief, Lady Philosophy looked at me serenely, untroubled by my lament: "When I saw you sad and full of tears, I knew at once that you were exiled and miserable. But had you not displayed it in your speech, I would not have known how far away your banishment had taken you. Indeed how far from your native land you are! And yet you haven't been expelled; you've simply strayed away. If you prefer to think of yourself as banished, then you should realize you've banished yourself. For in your case, such a banishment is something only you could do, not someone else. If you would just remember what country you are from, not one ruled like Athens by the power of the many, but one in which 'there is one ruler and one king'![57] He is one who delights in the company of his subjects, not in their expulsion. To be led by his reins and yield to his justice is perfect liberty.[58] Or don't you know the most ancient of the laws of that city, the one that prevents the exile of anyone who chooses to establish his home there? No man walled in by its fortress needs to fear that he will ever suffer exile. But anyone who no longer wishes to live there, by his own choice ceases to deserve the right to do so. And so it's not so much the appearance of this place that saddens me, but the vision of you yourself. I don't miss the walls of your library, decorated

[57] *there is one ruler and one king*: See Homer, *Iliad* 2.204–5: "Let there be one ruler, / one king" (trans. Lattimore), said by Odysseus to quell the beginning of a mutiny in the Greek camp. Boethius quotes directly in Greek here.

[58] *To be led . . . is perfect liberty*: The Stoics believed that only the wise man was truly free and that this freedom consisted of following the path of virtue. See Seneca, *Dialogues* 7.15.7: "We have been born in a kingdom; to obey God is liberty." See also Augustine, *De quantitate animae* 34.78: "Liberty is only to be found in pleasing him, in perfect service to him." (These and other references are cited by Gruber, *Kommentar zu Boethius*, p. 150.)

with their glass and ivory, so much as I miss my seat of honor in your mind, where I gathered together not books, but the things that give books their value.

"Now you have rightfully said much about the deeds you have done for the common good—you could have mentioned many more. Regarding the truthfulness of the charges against you—or rather the obvious falseness of them—you have given good account. Regarding the crimes and deceit of your accusers you have rightly spoken little, since the common crowd recognizes them well and makes them more widely known than you could. Indeed you have soundly railed against the unjust acts of the Senate. Regarding the charge leveled against us, you have grieved and wept, as you saw the assaults made to our reputation. Finally, your anger has grown hot at your bad fortune, and you have complained of rewards unequal to your merit. As you put an end to your raging Muse, you pleaded that the same peace that rules the heavens would also rule the earth. But since such a storm of passions has come upon you and you are pulled about by conflicting feelings of pain, anger, and sorrow, you can't, in such a mind, be given stronger remedies. And so I'll apply gentler ones for now, so that your wound, which has hardened and grown scarred by the constant pricks of your anxieties, may grow softer with gentle treatment and become ready to receive a more effective cure.

metrum 6

> When summer sky rages
> heavy with beams of the sun—
> man who plants seeds then,
> finds furrows refusing.
> Foiled—
> he must seek food beneath oaks.[59]

[59] *he must seek food beneath oaks*: According to tradition, acorns were originally man's primary food before he learned to grow grain. See Virgil, *Georgics* 1.147–50:

Never would you hunt
groves for violets
when fields have bristled
and creak with the north wind.
Nor would you prune spring branches
if you wish the grape,
for these are autumn-bestowed.
God gives the times their tasks.
These determined duties
cannot be mixed.
Whatever abandons this order
takes a dangerous journey—
with no good end.

6. "Now then," she said, "will you let me begin by asking a few questions to examine your state of mind, so I can see what cure is best for you?"

"Ask, and I will certainly answer whatever you think is fitting," I said.

"Do you suppose that this is a world ruled by random, chance events, or do you believe some reason guides it?"

"I could never think that such an ordered world is ruled by random accident," I replied. "I know quite well that God presides over the work he has created. And there will never come a time when I will abandon the truth of this assertion."

"Indeed, this is the very thing you proclaimed in verse a moment ago when you lamented that men only were separated from the care of God. But concerning other things, you had no doubt that reason provided energy and guidance. How strange! I really don't understand why you are sick when you

---

Ceres [goddess of grain] first taught men to till the earth with iron,
when the acorns and arbutes of the sacred wood
began to fail and Dodona [an oak grove sacred to Zeus]
refused to offer food.

If one does not obey the times for planting, one must revert to gleaning what one can. So, too, Philosophy must find the right "medicine" for Boethius at the right time.

have so healthy an opinion. But let us dig into this more deeply; there must be something missing.

"Now tell me, since you have no doubt that the world is governed by God, do you perceive what rudders are used to steer its course?"

"I can hardly understand what you are saying, much less answer your question," I replied.

"Wasn't I right to say that something was missing, that some sickness had created this unrest, slipping into your mind, as if it were passing through a crack in a wall?[60] But tell me, do you remember the end of all things or the goal to which all nature strives?"

"I've heard it," I said, "but sorrow has dulled my memory."

"Surely you know where all things have their origin?"

"I know," I said, and told her it was God.

"Then how can it be that you know the beginning of all things but are ignorant of their end? Indeed this is the nature of anxiety. It has the strength to make a man lose his footing, yet it can't overthrow him completely. Now I would like to ask you this, too: Do you remember that you are a man?"

"Remember it? Of course."

"Can you tell me, then, what a man is?"

"Are you asking if I know that I am a rational and mortal creature?[61] I know it and confess it."

She then replied, "Is there nothing more that you can add?"

"Nothing."

"Now I know the other, in fact the greatest, cause of your disease: you no longer know what you are. Now I understand why you're sick and how I can find a remedy to restore your health."[62] Since you're overwhelmed by forgetfulness of your

---

[60] *crack in a wall*: Gruber, *Kommentar zu Boethius*, p. 160, sees the image of the crack in the wall as a reference to Lady Philosophy's tower in 1 *prosa* 3. The philosophical bulwark that should protect Boethius has been breached.

[61] *rational and mortal creature*: This is a common definition among philosophers, as Gruber, *Kommentar zu Boethius*, p. 161, and O'Donnell, *Consolatio philosophiae*, p. 22, note. Lady Philosophy is, of course, looking for some acknowledgment from Boethius of the immortal soul.

[62] *health*: Gruber, *Kommentar zu Boethius*, p. 161, cites Cicero, *Tusculan Disputations* 3.23: "Just as [physicians] think they have found a cure when they find

nature, you grieve at being in exile and deprived of your goods. Indeed, since you are not aware of the end of all things, you think that base and wicked men are powerful and happy. And, since you have forgotten with what rudders the world is steered, you think the earth is tossed about by chance without a pilot. These things are great enough to cause not just illness, but even death. Yet I give thanks to the author of health that your true nature has not totally abandoned you. We have the best tinder for rekindling your health, a true opinion concerning the governance of the universe, a governance you believe to be dependent on divine reason rather than the whims of chance. Have no fear at all, then. Soon you will see this little spark give off light and life-giving warmth. But since it is not yet time for stronger remedies, and since it is the nature of the mind to put on false opinions when it has cast aside true ones, I will try to clear the mist a little with mild and gentle remedies. This way you will be able to recognize the brightness of the true light, as the shadows of deceptive desires have been pushed aside.[63]

metrum 7

> Stars, cloud-concealed,
> shed no light.
> If the south wind
> tangles the tide
> of a rolling sea,
> water once day-clear
> now muddied
> obscures sight.
> Every stream

---

the cause of a disease, so we will find a way of curing mental distress when we have found its cause."

[63] *This way you will . . . desires have been pushed aside*: Cf. the end of 1 *prosa* 2, when Lady Philosophy removes the clouds from Boethius' eyes. In *metrum* 7 the turbulence of nature obscures the perception of natural objects, just as the mind's turbulent passions obscure mental perception.

wandering
a mountain down
can be stopped
by rocks.
And you, to discern truth
with a clear light,
to seize the straight path—
banish joy,
banish hope,
banish fear.
Put them to flight!
The mind is shackled—
when these rule.

Book 2

1. After this, Lady Philosophy was quiet for a moment and then, when she had captured my attention with her modest silence, she spoke these words: "If I thoroughly understand the cause and nature of your sickness, you are wasting away with desire and longing for your previous state. You suppose it's the changes of Fortune[1] that have overthrown your soul. I know the many disguises of that monster and her endearing friendliness to those she tries to deceive—a kindness until she leaves them without warning and overwhelms them with unbearable pain. If you would recall her nature, her ways, and her worth, you would realize that she is not responsible for anything of beauty that you have ever had or lost. I don't suppose I'll have to work very hard to make you remember this. You used to attack her with courageous words when she approached you with her flattery, and you would chase her away with your wisdom drawn from our sanctuary. Yet every sudden change in circumstances seems to overcome a soul almost like a flood.[2] And so it happens that

[1] *Fortune*: The discussion of Fortuna and her wheel in book 2 is probably the most famous and most frequently alluded to passage in the entire *Consolation*. For a discussion of Boethius' influence, see especially Howard Rollin Patch, *The Goddess Fortuna in Medieval Literature* (Cambridge: Harvard University Press, 1927); Howard Rollin Patch, *The Tradition of Boethius: A Study of His Importance in Medieval Culture* (New York: Oxford University Press, 1935); and Pierre Courcelle, *"La consolation de philosophie" dans la tradition littéraire: Antécédents et postérité de Boèce* [Paris: Études augustiniennes, 1967], pp. 103–58. If Boethius is to begin his process of enlightenment and healing, he must learn that Fortuna cannot be looked to for beatitude or blessedness. He will learn the nature of blessedness in book 3.

[2] *Yet every sudden change . . . like a flood*: Cf. *Inferno* 7.88–89 (Virgil speaking): "Her permutations know no truce; necessity makes her swift" (*The "Divine Comedy" of Dante Alighieri*, vol. 1, *Inferno*, trans. Robert M. Durling and Robert L. Martinez [New York: Oxford University Press, 1996]). In these and subsequent lines, as Lynn Veach Sadler notes, Dante sees Fortuna in positive terms as God's

31

even you have lost your peace of mind for a little while. But now it's time for you to drink down some medicine that's pleasant and good, to make the way for stronger remedies. And let me apply the sweet persuasion of rhetoric, which only proceeds on the right path when it stands by our instructions and is in harmony with the homely music of our hearth. Let us sing out, first in a light measure, then in a heavier one.

"So what is it, mortal, that has plunged you into grief and mourning? I suppose you've seen something new and strange. You believe that Fortune has changed towards you: you are wrong. These have always been her ways and nature. She's retained her character in her very fickleness towards you. She was just the same when she fawned on you and tricked you with the promises of a counterfeit happiness.[3] You've learned of the fickleness of that blind spirit. Though she still hides herself from others, to you she has revealed herself completely. If you like her ways, make use of them and don't complain. If her treachery terrifies you, reject her and cast her off, as she plays her dangerous tricks. She is the one that causes you grief now, when she should have brought you peace of mind.[4] No one could ever count on her to be loyal, and now she has left you, too.

---

instrument (Lynn Veach Sadler, *Consolation in "Samson Agonistes": Regeneration and Typology*, Elizabethan and Renaissance Studies 82 [Salzburg: Institut für Anglistik und Amerikanistik, 1979]). Along the same lines, Durling and Martinez, *Inferno*, p. 123, cite Aquinas, *Summa theologica* I, q. 22, art. 2–3.

[3] *happiness*: Here we translate *felicitas* as "happiness"; we will translate *beatitudo* as "blessedness". Joachim Gruber notes that *felicitas* is a neutral term in Boethius and that it is often found with adjectives such as "true" and "false" that specify its nature (Joachim Gruber, *Kommentar zu Boethius, "De consolatione philosophiae"*, 2nd ed. [Berlin: Walter de Gruyter, 2006; originally published 1978], p. 235). It is useful to remember that the English word "happiness" literally refers to luck or "hap"—that is, Fortuna—while "beatitude" refers to the ultimate joy given by God. *Beatus* (blessed) in the Vulgate translates the Greek *makarios* in the Beatitudes (Matthew 5:3–12). Blessedness, *beatitudo*, Boethius sees as the result of seeking God, the highest Good (*summum bonum*).

[4] *You've learned of the fickleness . . . peace of mind*: Presumably Lady Philosophy means that Boethius should have learned long ago of Fortuna's inconstancy. This knowledge should have taught him that Fortuna is not the source of blessedness and that he should look to higher and more dependable things. Knowing that

"Do you really value a happiness that will pass away? Is present Fortune dear to you when she can't be trusted to stay and when she brings grief as she departs? But if she can't be retained through your own will, and if she brings ruin when she leaves, what else can she be but a sign of coming disaster? It's not enough, after all, to see what is placed before our eyes; wisdom takes thought for how things will turn out in the end. The temporary nature of any situation should keep a person from fearing Fortune's threats or hoping for her enticements. In short, as soon as you bow your neck to Fortune's yoke, you have to endure without complaint whatever happens under her terms. If you should try to impose rules upon her coming and going, when you've willingly chosen her as a mistress, won't your impatience worsen the bad luck that you can't change? If you entrusted your sails to the wind, you'd move forward in the direction it was blowing, not where you chose to go. If you entrusted seeds to the fields, you'd expect some good years and some bad ones. Now you've given yourself to the rule of Fortune; you must conform yourself to her ways. Would you try to hold back the force of a wheel in motion? O most foolish of men! If Fortune began to be permanent, she would cease to be Fortune.[5]

metrum 1

> Treacherous as the tide,
> twisting lives with
> the flick of her hand.[6]

---

the immutable God is the source of blessedness should have been a comfort to Boethius.

[5] *If Fortune began . . . to be Fortune*: Pandarus tells Troilus: "For if hire [Fortune's] whiel stynte any thyng to torne,/Than cessed she Fortune anon to be" (*Troilus and Criseyde*, 1.848–49).

[6] *twisting lives with the flick of her hand*: This is a reference to the famous wheel of Fortune. Similar ideas are seen earlier in antiquity; see Herodotus, *History*, 1.207.2; Cicero, *Against Piso*, 10.22; and Tibullus, *Elegy* 1.5.70. For other citations, see Courcelle, *Antécédents et postérité*, pp. 131–32. In medieval literature the image is often seen in Jean de Meun, *Romance of the Rose* (3990, 5842, 6414) and in Chaucer's work. See, e.g., *Troilus and Criseyde*, where Pandarus tells Troilus he

She tramples kings.
She encourages the destroyed,
laughing!
at the weeping and groaning
her harshness caused.[7]
This is her amusement,
proving her power—
she revels in her show.
The fortunate she prostrates—
in one hour."

2. The Lady continued, "But I would like to say a few things
to you in the words of Fortune herself; then you determine
whether or not she speaks fairly.[8] 'Mortal, why do you accuse

---

must give up Criseyde to ransom Antenor: "O mercy, God, who wolde have
trowed this?/Who wolde have wend that in so litel a throwe/Fortune our joie
wold han overthrowe" (4.383–85). For other examples, see *Troilus and Criseyde*
1.134–40, 837–54; 4.1–7, 323–26, 848–49; and *The Knight's Tale* 925–26 and
1238 (where Chaucer uses the image of Fortune's *dys* [dice]).

[7] *She encourages the destroyed . . . her harshness caused*: Cf. *Troilus and Criseyde*
4.6–7: "And whan a wight is from hire whiel ythrowe,/Than laugheth she and
maketh hym the mowe."
See also *The Monk's Tale* 2550.

[8] *But I would like to say . . . she speaks fairly*: The following speech of Fortuna
is an example of personification or *prosopopoeia*, the use of an imaginary person
or object to render an argument. For examples, see Cicero's *First Catilinarian
Oration*, in which Cicero depicts the fatherland chiding Catiline, and Plato's
Crito, where Socrates imagines what the laws of Athens would say to him if he
were to try to escape from jail before his forced suicide. Cf. also Lucretius on the
injustice of complaining about death:

> Then, too, if Nature suddenly should raise
> her voice, and take someone to task like this:
> "What troubles you, man, that you should thus indulge
> in bitter tears? Why weep and wail at death?
> For if your earlier years of life were happy
> and all your blessings haven't proved thankless—lost,
> drained off, as if poured into a punctured jar—
> why not, like one filled at life's table, leave
> in peace, you fool, and take your carefree rest?
> But if the joys you knew have all run out
> and life's a burden, why will you add still more,
> to see it again turn sour and all be lost?

me daily with your complaints? What injury have I done to
you? What goods of yours have I taken away? Find any judge
you like and take me to court over the possession of riches
and honors. If you can show that a single one of these things
belongs to any mortal, I'll willingly agree that what you seek
belongs to you.

"'When Nature brought you forth from your mother's womb,
when you were without resource or possessions of any kind, I
took you up. I supported you with my wealth, and now this
makes you unwilling to endure me.[9] I reared you most
indulgently with my generous favor. I surrounded you with a
conspicuous abundance of the things in my power. Now it
pleases me to pull back my hand. As one who borrowed the
possessions of another, you owe me thanks; you do not have
the right to complain as if you had completely lost the things
that belonged to you. Wealth, honors, and other things of that
sort are mine by right; they are slaves that belong to me and
come along with me, and so they depart with me. Let me tell
you plainly: if the things you are mourning over had been yours
in the first place, you would never have lost them.

"'Am I alone forbidden to exercise my rights? The heavens are allowed to bring forth brilliant days and then bury
them in shadowy nights; the year is allowed at one time to
crown the earth with flowers and at another to drown it in
cold and rain; the sea is allowed at one time to entice with a
smooth surface and at another to bristle with squalls and

(Lucretius, *The Nature of Things*, trans. Frank O. Copley [New York: Norton,
1977], 3.931–42.)

[9] *When Nature brought you forth . . . unwilling to endure me*: Cf. Chaucer, *Fortune* 41–46, in Fortune's reply to a "Pleintif":

> How many have I refused to sustene,
> Sin I thee fostred have in thy plesaunce.
> Wolthow than make a statut on thy quene
> That I shal been ay at thyn ordinaunce?
> Thou born art in my regne of variaunce,
> Aboute the wheel with other must thou dryve.

See also 57–60.

billows.[10] Does the insatiable desire of men bind us to a constancy alien to our ways? This is our power, this is the game
we always play. We turn our wheel on its flying course; we
delight in changing the low to the high and the high to the
low. Rise up, if you wish, but on this condition: don't consider yourself injured when you descend, as the rules of my
game demand.[11]

" 'Were you unaware of my ways? Didn't you know that Croesus, King of the Lydians and for a while the terror of Cyrus,
was soon pitifully handed over to the flames of a funeral pyre,
but then saved by a rain sent from heaven?[12] Surely you haven't

[10] *The heavens are allowed . . . squalls and billows*: Gerard O'Daly, *The Poetry of
Boethius* (Chapel Hill: University of North Carolina Press, 1991), p. 141, cites
Seneca, *Epistle* 107.8, where Seneca is speaking of how one must expect both
good and bad from life: "And Nature moderates this world-kingdom which you
see, by her changing seasons: clear weather follows cloudy; after a calm, comes
the storm; the winds blow by turns; day succeeds night; some of the heavenly
bodies rise, and some set. Eternity consists of opposites" (Seneca, *Ad Lucilium
Epistulae Morales*, trans. Richard M. Gummere, 3 vols., Loeb Classical Library,
75–77 [Cambridge: Harvard University Press, 1917–1925]).

[11] *This is our power . . . rules of my game demand*: Horace, *Ode* 2.1.3, speaks of
"obstinate Fortune playing her insolent game". In John Kennedy Toole's novel
A Confederacy of Dunces, the protagonist, a lover of Boethius, complains of Fortuna's tricks: " 'Oh, my God!' Ignatius mumbled to himself, watching the silhou-
ette of the streetcar forming a half-block away. 'What vicious trick is Fortuna
playing on me now?' " (John Kennedy Toole, *A Confederacy of Dunces* [New York:
Grove Press, 1980], pp. 296–97).

[12] *Croesus, King of the Lydians . . . rain sent from heaven*: Herodotus, *History*,
1.30–86, tells the story of Croesus. Solon, the great Athenian lawgiver, poet,
and philosopher, had once visited Croesus, who was the very wealthy and powerful king of the Lydians. When Croesus had asked Solon who was the happiest
man in the world, Solon had greatly annoyed Croesus by mentioning Athenians
who had died happily. After Croesus expressed his dissatisfaction with the answer,
Solon noted that one must not call a man happy until the day of his death.
Croesus eventually learned the wisdom of Solon's words when he lost his son in
a hunting accident and then was defeated by the Persian king Cyrus. Cyrus con-
signed Croesus to be burned alive but then relented, although the already-lit
pyre could not be extinguished until Apollo sent a shower.
    Chaucer speaks of "[t]he riche Cresus, kaytyf in servage" (*The Knight's Tale*
1946). In the *Romance of the Rose*, Reason states, "Croesus could in no way hold
back her [Fortuna's] wheel" (Guillaume de Lorris and Jean de Meun, *The Romance
of the Rose*, trans. Charles Dahlberg, 3rd ed. [Princeton: Princeton University
Press, 1995], 6489).

forgotten that Paulus spent honorable tears for the ruin of Perseus, whom he had captured.[13] What else do we weep for in tragedies but happy kingdoms overthrown by Fortune with her indiscriminate blows? Didn't you learn as a child that "twain jars, the one of evil, and other of good" rest on the threshold of Zeus' door?[14] Now suppose you've taken liberally from the one holding good. Suppose I haven't totally departed from you. Suppose this very fickleness is for you a source of hope for better things. Still you mustn't waste away in your heart desiring to live by your own law, though you reside in a kingdom inhabited by all men.

metrum 2

If Plenty should pour from her full horn[15]
wealth abundant as sea-stirred sand,
or countless as stars in the shining night sky,
nothing stopping her hand—
still man would complain of poverty.
Even if God answered prayers with gold,
heaped honors on those asking,
still this gain would seem nothing.[16]

[13] *Paulus spent honorable tears . . . he had captured*: Paulus (or Paullus) was a Roman consul in 182 and 168 B.C. who defeated the Macedonian king Perseus. See Livy's history of Rome, *ab urbe condita*, 45.8.6, where Paulus refers to Perseus as a "sign of the changeability of human affairs" and argues that one "must not trust in present fortune".

[14] *"twain jars . . ." rest on the threshold of Zeus' door*: See Homer, *Iliad* 24.527–28, where Achilles tries to console the mourning Priam. Boethius paraphrases the quotation somewhat. Courcelle, *Antécédents et postérité*, p. 167, and Luca Obertello, ed., trans., *La consolazione della filosofia; Gli opuscoli teologici* (Milan: Rusconi Libri, 1979), p. 166, suggest that Boethius takes the words from Neoplatonic sources of the *Iliad*, perhaps from Proclus.

[15] *If Plenty should pour from her full horn*: The goddess Plenty with her horn is a common classical motif in art and poetry. See especially Horace, *Carmen saeculare* 59–60: "Blessed Plenty appears with her horn full." See also Horace, *Epistle* 1.12.29.

[16] *Even if God answered prayers with gold . . . this gain would seem nothing*: In *Inferno* Virgil describes the avaricious and prodigal sinners in the fourth circle as

Their greed only opens new mouths.
What could curb such lust
when those with riches overflowing
thirst for more?
A man is never rich,
trembling and sighing,
believing himself in need.'

3. "So if Fortune were speaking these words to you in her own defense, you would be utterly unable to open your mouth in reply," Lady Philosophy continued. "Or if you do have any way of rightly justifying your complaints, you ought to speak out; I'll give you the chance to have your say."

Then I spoke: "Yes, these arguments sound good. Smeared as they are with the honey of sweet speech and poetry,[17] they bring some pleasure—but only while they are being heard. The pain of sorrow lies too deep when someone is miserable. As soon as the words stop sounding in the ears, the grief deep in a man's heart weighs him down."

And she replied, "Yes, of course, for this isn't yet the remedy for your disease but rather a sort of poultice for a pain that stubbornly resists a cure. I'll apply medicines that penetrate deeply when the time is right. But still, you shouldn't choose to think of yourself as wretched. Have you forgotten how many and how great are the sources of your happiness? I won't

follows: "[F]or all the gold that is under the moon and that ever was could not give rest to even one of these weary souls" (trans. Durling and Martinez, 7.64–66).

[17] *Smeared as they are . . . sweet speech and poetry*: Cf. Lucretius, *On the Nature of Things*, as he likens setting philosophy in poetic form to tricking children into taking their medicine:

> For just as doctors, who must give vile wormwood
> to children, start by painting the cup-lip round
> with sweet and golden honey . . .
> . . . .
> So now, since my philosophy often seems
> a little grim to beginners, and most men
> shrink back from it in fear, I wished to tell
> my tale in sweet Pierian song for you.
> (4.11–13, 18–22; trans. Copley)

mention how the very best men took you under their care when you lost your father, how you were chosen to belong to a family of leaders of the state, or how you were dear to them even before you married into their family.[18] Who didn't call you the happiest of all men because of the glory of your mother- and father-in-law, the modesty of your wife, and the gift of having your sons? I omit—for I prefer to pass over in silence the things we both know about—the offices you took up as a young man, honors often denied to much older men.[19] I wish to come to the height of your unparalleled happiness. If the enjoyment of mortal things brings some portion of blessedness, will any mountain of evils falling upon you be able to destroy the memory of that day when you saw your two sons together carried from your home as consuls, crowded by Senators and joyfully welcomed by the people?[20] When you spoke in honor of the King, as your sons were sitting on their thrones in the Senate House, you well deserved the glory granted to your talented eloquence. In the Circus Maximus, when you were placed between your two sons, the consuls, you satisfied the expectations of the multitude spread around you with a celebration worthy of a general's triumph. I would say you got the better of Fortune, when she was caressing you and cherishing you as her darling. You carried off a gift that she has never before bestowed on any private citizen. So do you want

[18] *you were dear to them . . . married into their family*: This refers to Boethius' adoption by Symmachus, whose daughter, Rusticiana, Boethius later married. On Symmachus' scholarship and interest in literature, see Henry Chadwick, *Boethius: The Consolations of Music, Logic, Theology, and Philosophy* (Oxford: Oxford University Press, 1981), pp. 6–16.

[19] *I omit . . . denied to much older men*: The rhetorical device Lady Philosophy uses of mentioning something by supposedly not mentioning it is called *praeteritio* (passing over). Boethius was consul in 510, at the age of about thirty.

[20] *your two sons together . . .welcomed by the people*: This occurred in 522. J. J. O'Donnell notes: "For two westerners to hold the consulship together was unusual at this time; two from the same family had not done so since 395 A.D. This is a sign that B. had friends in high places in Constantinople, where final decisions about the consulship were taken" (J. J. O'Donnell, ed., *Consolatio philosophiae*, vol. 2, Bryn Mawr Latin Commentaries [Bryn Mawr: Thomas Library, Bryn Mawr College, 1984], p. 30). Boethius' sons were named Boethius and Symmachus.

to make a reckoning with her? Now for the first time she has cast her glance of envy upon you. If you should consider the number and nature of your joys and sorrows, you still couldn't deny that you've been happy. But if you don't judge yourself fortunate, since you've lost what seemed to be your joys, you have no reason to consider yourself wretched, since what you think are sorrows are passing away. Or have you suddenly come now onto life's stage as if you were a first-time guest? Do you think there is any permanence inherent in human things, when the fleeting hour often dissolves a man himself? For even if there is little constancy in the ways of chance, still, a man's last day is also a kind of death to Fortune, as she lingers with him. What difference do you suppose it makes then whether you desert Fortune by dying or she deserts you by fleeing?

metrum 3[21]

> The sun scattering light on earth
> spreads flames over dimming stars
> and pales their white faces.
> The warming west wind's breath
> blushes groves with roses.
> Then the mad south wind rages, and
> glory vanishes from the thorned bushes.
> The sea unwavering in calm
> is stirred by the north wind's storms.
> Violent is the variable earth!
> Trust in tumbling fortunes—
> Believe in passing wealth!
> It is fixed by eternal law—
> nothing created remains."

[21] metrum 3: In this *metrum* Boethius again illustrates the theme that the created order of the natural world provides lessons for mankind. Just as nothing in nature abides forever, so too nothing of man's fortune is permanent. Regarding the theme, O'Daly, *Poetry of Boethius*, pp. 141–43, cites Seneca, *Epistle* 107; Horace, *Ode* 1.4 and 4.7; and Seneca, *Phaedra* 764–72.

4. Then I replied, "O nourisher of all virtues, the things you make me remember are true, and I can't deny that the course of my prosperity was very swift. But this is what burns more and more violently inside me as I recall it; for of all the adversities of Fortune the saddest is this: to have once been happy." [22]

"But you can't rightly blame anything else for the penalty you pay for your folly," she continued. "For if the empty notion of a chance happiness moves you, you can consider with me how many and how great are the gifts you've been given. If you retain anything that is most precious in judging your fortune, and if it is protected by the hand of Providence, safe and unharmed, can you with justice pretend that you are unfortunate, since you possess all the better things? Isn't your father-in-law, Symmachus, that greatest glory of the human race, still thriving in safety? With careless concern for himself, he groans for your affliction. He is a man molded completely of virtue and wisdom—gifts you would be quick to purchase with the price of your life. And your wife lives, modest in her nature, outstanding in her chastity and sense of honor, in short a daughter as worthy as her father. She lives, I say, and for you only she preserves the breath of a life she hates. In this one thing even I will admit your happiness is lessened: she wastes away with tears and longing for you. What should I say about your sons, consuls, who even in their youth show evidence of the nature of their father and grandfather? And so, though

---

[22] *the saddest is this: to have once been happy*: At *Inferno* 5.121–23 Francesca says, "There is no greater pain than to remember the happy time in wretchedness; and this your teacher knows" (trans. Durling and Martinez). It is possible that Boethius is thinking of Virgil's words that express the obverse of his own, as Aeneas rallies his men: "Perhaps someday it will bring joy to remember even these things" (*Aeneid* 1.203). Durling and Martinez, *Inferno*, p. 98, also compare Dante's words with Augustine, *Confessions* 10.14.

Chaucer borrows from Boethius in Troilus' words:

> For of fortunes sharpe adversitee
> The worste kynde of infortune is this,
> A man to han ben in prosperitee,
> And it remembren, whan it passed is.
> (*Troilus* 3.1625–28)

staying alive is a natural concern to man, you would be most fortunate if you knew the good things you possessed,[23] since even now you have those things that no one can deny are dearer than life.

"Dry your tears now; Fortune hasn't yet brought down her hatred upon everyone you love.[24] The storm that strikes you isn't so terrible that it doesn't allow a present solace or hope for the time to come; you still have anchors holding fast."

"May they hold fast, I pray. If they do, I will yet swim out of this flood, no matter what may happen," I said. "But you can see how much of my glory I have lost."

And she replied, "We've made some progress, if you no longer find your fate totally a source of grief. But I can't bear your childish self-indulgence! You're so worried and sorrowful because something is lacking from your bliss. Now whose happiness is so complete that he couldn't complain about some aspect of his life? Man's condition produces anxiety; it never proves wholly satisfactory; it never lasts forever. One man piles up wealth, but his low birth causes him embarrassment. Another man is famous for his ancestry, but his poverty makes him wish to be unknown. Another abounds in both these gifts, but weeps over being unmarried, while still another man, happily wed but bereft of children, builds his estate to be passed on to an outside heir. Yet another man has the joy of children, but sadly weeps over the sins of his son or daughter.[25] And so, no one is easily satisfied with the state of his fortune. In all aspects of life there

---

[23] *you would be most fortunate . . . good things you possessed*: Cf. Virgil, *Georgics* 2.458–59: "O farmers, how lucky you would be if you were aware of the good things you possessed."

[24] *Fortune . . . love*: Courcelle, *Antécédents et postérité*, p. 107, cites *Aeneid* 5.687–89, where a despairing Aeneas prays to Jupiter to save the Trojan fleet from fire: "Jupiter, omnipotent, if you have not brought your hand of hatred upon every one/of the Trojans, if your ancient faithfulness has any regard for human troubles,/ allow our fleet to escape the flames."

[25] *One man piles up wealth . . . sins of his son or daughter*: Gruber, *Kommentar zu Boethius*, p. 193, cites Aristotle's *Nichomachean Ethics* 1099b: "There are some things the lack of which takes the lustre from happiness, as good birth, goodly children, beauty; for the man who is very ugly in appearance or ill-born or solitary

are things that strike terror in a man who has experienced them, but they have no effect on someone who has not.

"Consider also that the most delicate emotions are those of happy men. Unless everything works according to their whim, they are overthrown by every little trouble, unaccustomed as they are to adversity. And so, things of the least importance can bring down the very lucky man from his 'great bliss.'[26]

"How many are there, do you think, who would consider themselves almost in heaven if they attained the smallest part of what remains of your fortune? This very place that you call exile is a fatherland to those residing here. You see, there is no situation that is miserable unless you think it so.[27] Likewise, every condition is blessed when a man endures it with an untroubled spirit. If he yielded to impatience, what man is so happy that he wouldn't want to change his state? How much bitterness is sprinkled on the sweetness of human happiness![28] But even this sweetness

and childless is not very likely to be happy" (*Introduction to Aristotle*, ed. Richard McKeon [New York: Random House, 1947]).

[26] *things of the least importance . . . 'great bliss'*: Boethius uses *beatitudo* here, probably ironically, since a man does not acquire blessedness through luck. Or perhaps Boethius suggests that it is possible for lucky men to acquire blessedness but that they are less sure in their hold upon it than those who have had difficulties.

[27] *there is no situation . . . unless you think it so*: Fortune, in Chaucer's poem *Fortune*, defends herself by saying, "No man is wrecched, but himself it wene" (25). Cf. also, of course, Hamlet's words: "[T]here is nothing either good or bad, but thinking makes it so" (William Shakespeare, *Hamlet*, ed. Joseph Pearce, Ignatius Critical Editions [San Francisco: Ignatius Press, 2008], 2.2.248–50).

[28] *How much bitterness . . . human happiness!* Courcelle, *Antécédents et postérité*, p. 107, compares Augustine, *Confessions* 1.14: "From the schoolmaster's cane to the ordeals of martyrdom, your law prescribes bitter medicine to retrieve us from the noxious pleasures which cause us to desert you" (Augustine, *Confessions*, trans. R. S. Pine-Coffin [New York: Penguin, 1961]).

Cf. also Lucretius, *On the Nature of Things*:

> We buy fine food, fine clothes and entertainment,
> garlands and perfume, wines for everyone;
> no use, since in the midst of bubbling joys,
> bitterness rises and turns bright bloom to pain.
> (4.1131–34; trans. Copley)

that seems blessed to a man enjoying it can't be prevented from fleeing when it wishes. Therefore it's clear how miserable this 'blessedness' of human things is. It won't endure for men who are contented, nor will it fully satisfy those who are anxious.

"O mortals, why do you seek outside yourselves for the happiness that has been placed within you? Ignorance and error seem to overwhelm you. I'll show you briefly the foundation of the greatest happiness. Is anything more precious to you than you are to yourself? 'Nothing,' you will say. And so, if you're in control of yourself, you will possess what you would never wish to lose and what Fortune can't take away from you. Now in order to recognize that blessedness does not rest in the things of Fortune, consider this. If blessedness is the highest Good for a being living by reason, and if the highest Good is something that can't be taken away in any manner—for what couldn't be taken away would be greater than it—clearly the instability brought by Fortune cannot hope for eternal blessedness. Consider, too, that the man lifted up by temporary happiness is either aware or unaware that this happiness is impermanent. If he doesn't know of Fortune's impermanence, how can he be blessed when he carries within him the blindness of ignorance? If he does know this, he can't avoid fearing that he will lose the things he knows can be lost. For this reason, unending fear won't allow him to be happy. Or if he does lose the goods of Fortune, does he suppose that the loss must be given little weight? In this case Fortune's goods must be very meager, if a man bears their loss with an untroubled spirit. And since, as I know well, you are the very same man who's been persuaded with many convincing arguments that human minds are in no way mortal, and since it's clear to you that the happiness of Fortune ends with the death of the body, you can't deny that, if Fortune is able to bring blessedness, then the whole race of mortals is slipping towards misery, since all men meet their end in death. But we know that many have looked for the reward of blessedness not just by their deaths but by sorrow

and suffering.[29] How, then, can present happiness make men
blessed, when it doesn't make them miserable if they lose it?

metrum 4[30]

> Shun the mountain top,
> the billowing sea—
> if an everlasting home you wish to build.
> For the breath of noisy wind
> will knock you low.
> If it's permanence you wish—
> avoid the quicksand.[31]
> Brash wind's power
> commands destruction.
> Foil evil fate!
> The cautious man,
> serene in a solid home, is confident.
> Then however the thundering wind
> confounds the sea,

[29] *many have looked . . . by sorrow and suffering*: Cf. 1 *prosa* 3. It is not necessary to assume the Christian martyrs here, although Boethius may have had them in mind too. C. S. Lewis claims that the Christian "martyrs are clearly referred to" here (C. S. Lewis, *The Discarded Image: An Introduction to Medieval and Renaissance Literature* [Cambridge: Cambridge University Press, 1964], p. 79); for an opposing view, see Gruber, *Kommentar zu Boethius*, p. 197.

[30] metrum 4: Gruber, *Kommentar zu Boethius*, p. 197, compares the opening of 1 *metrum* 4. Cf. also Horace, *Ode* 2.10.1–4: "Licinius, you will live better if you do not/seek the sea's depth, nor press too close to the hostile/shore in careful fear of ocean squalls." O'Daly, *Poetry of Boethius*, p. 143, notes that it is a "commonplace in Senecan tragedy" to see lofty places as "especially vulnerable to the blows of Fortune, to winds or lightning". The Stoic Seneca's writings had a great influence on Boethius.

[31] *Shun the mountain top . . . avoid the quicksand*: In other words, Boethius advises building one's house upon a rock. Adrian Fortescue compares Matthew 7:24–25 and Luke 6:48–49 (Adrian Fortescue, *Ancius Manlius Severinus Boethius De consolatione philosophiae libri quinque*, ed. G. D. Smith [Hildesheim: Georg Olms, 1976; originally published in London, 1925], p. 42). O'Daly, *Poetry of Boethius*, p. 144, also cites the passage in Matthew and suggests that it may provide the inspiration for Boethius here.

you, settled in your fortress,[32] may live—
and smile at the wrath of the sky.

5. "But since the medicines of my arguments have begun to
work on you, I think I'll use some cures that are a little
stronger.[33] Come then, if the gifts of Fortune were not momen-
tary and slipping away, what could you find in them that would
truly be your own? What wouldn't seem vile when considered and carefully examined? Can you truly own riches? Are
they precious by their very nature? If so, then what aspect of
them? The gold itself? The value of the heaping pile of money?
But money gleams more in the spending than in the piling
up, since avarice makes men hated, while generosity makes
them famous.[34] But if no one can keep what's given to someone else, money proves valuable only when one man passes
it to another in the practice of giving, and thus it ceases to
be possessed. For if all the world's money were piled together
for the use of one man, others would be in need of it. A
sound, when it fills the ears of many men, remains whole,
but your wealth can't be passed on to others unless you divide
it. Yet when this happens, those who lose their wealth become
poorer. O how limited and poor are riches! Many men can't
truly own them, and they come to no one without making
others poor.

[32] *fortress*: Again we see the image of wisdom's tower, as in 1 *prosa* 3.

[33] *medicines of my arguments . . . cures that are a little stronger*: The "medicines"
of Lady Philosophy's arguments refer to her showing that Fortuna's gifts are fleeting. But an awareness of this fact can bring only Stoic resignation. Lady Philosophy will have to "use cures that are a little stronger"; that is, she will have to
show that Boethius should not care if Fortuna's gifts are only temporary, since
they are essentially meaningless and have no relation to the true Good.

[34] *But money gleams . . . generosity makes them famous*: See Horace, *Ode* 2.2.1–4:
"Silver has no color, hidden in the greedy earth,/Money is no friend to you,
Crispus Sallust,/Unless you make it shine, by spending it wisely."

See similarly Horace, *Satire* 1.1.41–45, and Dante, *Convivium* 4.13.130–42.
In the *Purgatorio* Dante uses the same image but relates it to the concept of love.
Having been told that love increases as it is given, Dante asks how this can be:
"How can one good that's shared by many souls/make all those who possess it
wealthier/than if it were possessed by just a few?" (*Dante's "Purgatory"*, trans.
Mark Musa [Boomington: University of Indiana Press, 1981], 15.61–63).

"Perhaps the glitter of jewels attracts your eyes? If there's anything special in this splendor, it's the light belonging to the gems, not to the men that own them. What object lacking the movement or framework of a soul can rightly seem beautiful to a living being that has reason and a soul? Granted these jewels acquire some degree of true beauty through the work of the Creator and through their own special nature, but they don't in any way merit your admiration, since they have been placed beneath your excellence.

"Are you delighted, then, by the beauty of the fields? Why not? They're a beautiful part of a most beautiful work. So, too, at times, we take pleasure in the appearance of a calm sea; at other times we admire the sky, the stars, the moon, or the sun.[35] You don't have any part in their glory, do you? Do you dare take pride in the splendor that belongs to objects such as these? Are you the one who is decorated with flowers in the spring? Are you the one who swells richly with summer fruits?

"Why are you captivated by empty joys? Why do you embrace external goods as if they were your own? Fortune will never make them yours. They are alien to you by the course of nature. Indeed, there can't be any doubt that the fruits of the earth were made to serve as food for living things. But if you only wish to satisfy your needs, which is all that Nature requires, there's no reason you should seek an excess of Fortune's gifts. Nature is satisfied with few things and small ones at that.[36] If

[35] *Are you delighted . . . or the sun*: Cf. Augustine, *On the Trinity* 3.4: "For good is the earth with its high mountains and gentle hills, and level fields. . . . And good is a righteous man, and good are riches, because they make life easier, and good is the sky with sun, moon, and stars. . . . But why go on? This is good and that is good: take away this and that and look upon the Good itself if you can; then you will see God, who is good not by virtue of another good, but is the goodness of all good things" (quoted in Erich Auerbach, *Literary Language and Its Public in Late Latin Antiquity and in the Middle Ages*, trans. Ralph Manheim [New York: Random House, 1965], p. 55). Boethius is not quite ready for such medicine as this, but he will soon learn Augustine's lesson from Lady Philosophy in book 3.

[36] *Nature is satisfied . . . small ones at that*: See Cicero, *Tusculan Disputations* 5.35: "The situation is obvious, and every day Nature herself teaches us how few, how small, and how common her needs are." The *Tusculan Disputations* were written in 45 B.C., after Cicero had ended his second unsuccessful marriage and

48   *The Consolation of Philosophy*

you should wish to smother her plenty with excess, the things you pile on top of her bounty will be joyless or even harmful.

"So, then, do you consider it a fine thing to parade in all sorts of clothing?[37] If the clothing is pleasing to gaze on, I will choose to admire the nature of its material or the ingenuity of its maker. Or perhaps a long train of attendants makes you happy? But if these attendants are corrupt, they become a deadly burden to the household and a terrible enemy to their master. And if these servants are honest, how can their worthiness be counted among your riches? Not a single one of the things you count among your goods can be clearly shown to be a good that belongs to you. And if there is no beauty in them that you should seek, how can you grieve if you lose them or rejoice if you keep them? But if these are beautiful by their nature, how does that affect you? They would have been pleasing all by themselves, even if they weren't part of your possessions. For they are certainly not precious because they are part of your wealth. It's because they seem precious that you have chosen to consider them riches.

"Now what do you men want from Fortune as you rail against her? You're looking for a way to ward off poverty, I suppose. But just the opposite happens to you—you have to obtain extra resources to protect your household wealth. In reality, men who possess very many things need very many things, while men who measure their abundance by the necessities of Nature and not by the excesses of desire need very little.

---

after his beloved daughter had died. Not unlike Boethius, Cicero tries to show the consolations inherent in philosophy and seeks to render the best of the Greek philosophers to a Roman audience.

Cf. also Horace, *Satire* 1.1.49–51: "But tell me, what difference does it make,/ to one living within the bounds of Nature/ whether he plant a hundred acres or a thousand?"

[37] *So, then, do you consider . . . all sorts of clothing?* Cf. Plato, *Phaedo* 64D, where Socrates is discussing what the philosopher seeks in life: "Well, do you think such a man would think much of the other cares of the body—I mean such as the possession of fine clothes and shoes and the other personal adornments?" (Plato, *Euthyphro; Apology; Crito; Phaedo; Phaedrus*, trans. Harold North Fowler, Loeb Classical Library 36 [Cambridge: Harvard University Press, 1914]).

"Are you so impoverished that you have no innate good that belongs to you? Must you seek your good in things that are external and not your own? Is your condition such that you, an animal made godlike by your reason,[38] think you can gain glory only through the possession of lifeless objects? Other things are content with their own nature, but you, like God in having an intellect, want to adorn your superior nature with the beauty of inferior things, and you do not understand what a great injury you do to your Creator.[39] For God willed that the human race surpass all other earthly creatures, but you have thrust your dignity beneath the lowest of things. For if every good belonging to every man is agreed to be more precious than the one who possesses it, and if you judge the vilest of things as your goods, you place yourself beneath those very things by your own judgment—and a fair judgment it would be. Indeed, human nature is such that a man surpasses other things only when he is aware that he does so. But that same human nature is reduced to being lower than the beasts if it ceases to know itself.[40] Although it is the nature of other animals not to know themselves, such ignorance proves to be a vice in man.

"How far off your path you wander when you think you can find adornment with things that are not your own! And yet this can't be; for if anything gains luster from objects placed beside it, those objects are the ones that earn praise. The other thing, covered and concealed by those objects, retains its baseness anyway.

---

[38] *animal made godlike by your reason*: Lady Philosophy, unlike Boethius in 1 *prosa* 6, defines man in terms of divinity.

[39] *Creator*: Gruber, *Kommentar zu Boethius*, p. 203, notes that "here the Platonic World-creator, earlier designated as *conditor* (compare to 1 m. 5, 1), is quite strongly adapted to the Christian creator-god, to whom men must be accountable" (our translation from the original German). In the following sentence we also see, perhaps, Christian thought. See Fortescue, *Boethius De consolatione*, p. 45, who cites Genesis 1:27 and Psalm 8.

[40] *to know itself*: Tradition says that the famous saying "Know thyself" was inscribed on Apollo's temple at Delphi. This saying became a commonplace in Greek and Roman philosophy. See Plato, *Protagoras* 343B (cited by Fortescue, *Boethius De consolatione*, p. 45). See also Seneca, *Dialogue* 6.11.3.

50   *The Consolation of Philosophy*

"But I, at least, deny that anything is good if it causes harm to the one that has it," she continued. "Am I wrong? 'Certainly not,' you'll say. But very often riches do harm to those that own them; for wicked men are naturally eager to have whatever gold and silver belong to another, and so they think that they alone are worthy of these things. The man who lived in fear of swords and staves would sing out loud in the face of the thief, if he only set out on the path of life as a penniless traveler.[41] O wonderful bliss[42] of mortal wealth! When you attain it, you cease to be secure!

metrum 5

> Fortunate, that first age[43]—
> satisfied men with faith in the land,
> not ruined by excess—
> accustomed to easy hunger
> soothed by acorns.
> No honey was yet mixed
> with Bacchus' gift.[44]

[41] *The man who lived in fear . . . penniless traveler*: Cf. Juvenal, *Satire* 10.21–24:

> If you are on the road at night, and carrying with you
> Only an item or two of your less elaborate silver,
> You fear a sword or a club or a reed that stirs in the moonlight,
> But your poor man sings a song in the face of the robber.

(*The "Satires" of Juvenal*, trans. Rolfe Humphries [Bloomington: Indiana University Press, 1958].)

[42] *bliss*: *Beatitudo* is used ironically here.

[43] *Fortunate, that first age*: Boethius is employing a familiar motif in antiquity, a golden age when men were innocent and happy. The tradition goes back to Hesiod's *Works and Days* (110–20), c. 725. Among the many passages containing the motif are Ovid, *Metamorphoses* 1.89–112; Virgil, *Georgics* 1.125–46; Horace, *Epode* 16; and Seneca, *Phaedra* 329–34, 525–39. D. W. Robertson compares the end of the golden age with the Fall of Man in the Christian tradition (D. W. Robertson, *A Preface to Chaucer: Studies in Medieval Perspectives* [Princeton: Princeton University Press, 1962], p. 27). For later treatments, see, e.g., Chaucer, *The Former Age*; Jean de Meun, *Romance of the Rose* 8355–9664; and Shakespeare, *Twelfth Night* 2.4.46.

[44] *Bacchus' gift*: Bacchus (Dionysus) was the god of wine. Adding honey to wine (Bacchus' gift) could be seen as luxurious.

Bright Tyrian dye[45] hadn't yet
joined with eastern fleece.[46]
Herbs granted sleep;
the fleet river gave drink;
the pine offered shade.
No strangers cut the sea
seeking trade in faraway places,
observing foreign shores.[47]
Battle cries weren't yet sounded;
no blood from bitter hate soaked rough[48] fields.
Now the fury is to strike first—
men can see cruel wounds,
and no prize for bloodshed.
To return to those ancient ways!
Fiercer than Etna's[49] fires boiling
burns the desire to possess.
Ah, who was that first man?
Who first dug those secret burdens?
Gold and jewels gladly hidden—
precious dangers![50]

[45] *Tyrian dye*: The Tyrian dye Boethius refers to was highly prized and suggested royalty or noble birth; in the golden age, however, classes did not exist. In Virgil's *Eclogue* 4, often called the "Messianic eclogue", a future golden age is conceived of, in which sheep produce wools of various colors all by themselves.

[46] *eastern fleece*: Boethius refers to silk as "eastern fleece". O'Donnell, *Consolatio philosophiae*, p. 37, notes that Justinian (emperor at Constantinople from 527 to 565) wanted to import silkworms because the demand for silk was so great.

[47] *No strangers cut the sea . . . observing foreign shores*: Sailing is often considered as inappropriate to the golden age, since it is typically viewed as a form of hubris (arrogance) caused by greed. See also Horace, *Ode* 1.3, a farewell to Virgil as he prepares for a voyage about which Horace expresses misgivings.

[48] *rough*: The word translated here as "rough" is *horrida* in Latin, which literally means bristling. Boethius may mean bristling with fear, on the part of the soldiers, or bristling with weapons, or likely both.

[49] *Etna*: Mount Etna is an active volcano in Sicily. In Greek mythology, the rebellious monster Typhon was trapped beneath this mountain by Zeus.

[50] *Who first dug . . . precious dangers!* The digging of the earth to find jewels or minerals was often seen as a sign of greed for unnecessary wealth in defiance of the natural order. Cf. Ovid, *Metamorphoses* 1.136–42. See also Dante, *Convivium* 4.12.35–39 (cited by Fortescue, *Boethius De consolatione*, p. 48).

6. "What should I say, on the other hand, about offices and might, which in your ignorance of true worth and power you equate with heaven?[51] But if power and high office fall to a wretched man, what belching flames of Etna, what flood could cause such destruction? I'm sure you'll remember how your ancestors once thought it necessary to abolish the powers of the consuls—which used to be the source of freedom—because of the consuls' arrogance.[52] It was this same sort of haughtiness that caused even the name of King to be removed from the state.[53] But when power is handed over to just men—a rare case indeed—what else do we praise them for but their just use of that power? So it isn't the office that brings honor to virtue, but virtue that brings honor to the office.

"And what is that excellent and desirable power of yours? O earthly creatures, do you consider what ruling means, you who seem to rule? If you saw a mouse lording it over his fellows, you would be moved to laughter. But consider the human body: what could you find weaker than a man?[54] He can be killed by a tiny fly that bites him or crawls deep within his organs. And how can anyone exert power upon anything else besides his own body or his circumstances, which are even less important? Can you command someone whose soul is free? Can

[51] *What should I say . . . you equate with heaven?* "Might" is the translation of *potentia*, which is contrasted with *potestas* (here translated as "power"). *Potentia* suggests raw strength, while *potestas* suggests legitimate authority. See Gruber, *Kommentar zu Boethius*, p. 209.

[52] *your ancestors once thought . . . consuls' arrogance*: O'Donnell, *Consolatio philosophiae*, p. 38, notes: "The allusion is to the rise of the tribunes of the people as a balance to oligarchic power, itself a revolt against the kings." The Romans, under the leadership of Brutus, expelled their last king, Tarquinius Superbus (Tarquin the Proud), in 510 B.C. The office of the tribunes of the people was created around the early fifth century B.C. to protect the rights of the plebeians.

[53] *It was this same sort . . . removed from the state*: Gruber, *Kommentar zu Boethius*, p. 210, cites Cicero, *Republic* 2.52: "The Roman people had such a hatred of the name implying royalty . . . that after Tarquin was expelled they could not endure hearing the name of king."

[54] *what could you find weaker than a man*: Gruber, *Kommentar zu Boethius*, p. 211, compares Seneca, *Dialogue* 6.11.3: "What is man? A weak and fragile body." Seneca wrote this work as a consolation to a woman named Marcia on the loss of her son.

you take a man whose mind is whole and firmly fixed with reason and steal away the peace that belongs to him? Once a tyrant thought that he would punish a certain free man and force him to betray those aware of a conspiracy against him; the man bit into his tongue, tore it off, and threw it in the face of the raging tyrant.[55] Thus the tortures that the tyrant considered a means of cruelty were turned by the wise man into a means of virtue. For what can one man do to another that someone else can't do to him? It is said that Busiris, who used to kill his guests, was slain by his guest Hercules.[56] Though Regulus chained many Carthaginians captured in war, he soon offered his hands to fetters.[57] So would you suppose that a man has any power, when he can't keep someone from doing to him what he can do to others?

"Furthermore, if there were any natural and inherent good in power and offices themselves, they would never come to evil men. For things of opposite natures don't join together; nature revolts against such a thing. And so, since there's no doubt that evil men commonly hold offices, offices can't be inherently good, for they let themselves be attached to evil men. Indeed, we can make this judgment about all the gifts of Fortune that rain down on the most wicked of men. Furthermore, I think we should also consider this: no one doubts a

[55] *Once a tyrant thought . . . face of the raging tyrant*: The identity of the "free man" is unknown but is probably Anaxarchus or Zeno. See Gruber, *Kommentar zu Boethius*, p. 211. On Zeno, see Plutarch, *Moralia* 505D, Diogenes Laertius 9.5.27, and Boethius, *Consolatio* 1 *prosa* 3. On Anaxarchus, see Diogenes Laertius, *Lives of the Philosophers*, 9.5.59 and Valerius Maximus, *Memorable Deeds and Sayings*, 3.3. Both Zeno and Anaxarchus were famous for their strength in the face of torture. See, e.g., Cicero, *Tusculan Disputations* 2.52.

[56] *It is said that Busiris . . . was slain by his guest Hercules*: Busiris was a wicked king of Egypt who customarily sacrificed one stranger each year to Zeus. Unfortunately for Busiris, he chose Hercules one year as his victim and was killed by the hero. See Apollodorus, *Library*, 2.5.11.

[57] *Though Regulus chained . . . his hands to fetters*: Regulus fought successfully against the Carthaginians in the First Punic War but was captured in 255 B.C. After giving his pledge to return to Carthage, he was sent to the Roman Senate with instructions to ask first for a truce or at least for a trading of prisoners. He successfully persuaded the Senate to reject both options. True to his promise, Regulus returned to Carthage and was executed. See Livy, *Epitome* 18.

man is brave if bravery is found within him, and whoever has swiftness is obviously swift. In the same way music makes musicians, healing makes healers, and oratory makes orators.[58] For the nature of each thing causes whatever is proper to it, and this nature does not mix with what is caused by things unlike itself; in fact, it drives away things that are opposed to it. So wealth cannot quench insatiable greed, nor does power grant anyone the possession of himself, if corrupting desires hold him in unbreakable chains. Honor conferred upon evil men not only fails to make them honorable, but it actually gives away and highlights their lack of honor. For you men enjoy giving false names to things that are not what they seem to be, when these names are easily contradicted by the effects of the things themselves. Thus these things are not rightly to be called riches, and that one called power, and this one called honor. Finally, one can come to the same conclusion about Fortune as a whole. In her there is nothing worthy of seeking, nothing with innate goodness; for Fortune does not always join herself to those who are good, and she does not make good those to whom she is joined.

metrum 6

> Mark the ruin he caused!
> Rome burned, senators slain.
> He murdered his brother,
> then, with cold vision,
> gazed upon his mother,
> pouring forth blood—
> a critic of her extinct beauty.
> Yet beneath his scepter
> were those seen by the sun
> as its beams sink below the sea,
> and those seen as it rises from the east.

[58] *music makes musicians . . . oratory makes orators*: Gruber, *Kommentar zu Boethius*, p. 213, cites Seneca, *Epistle* 87.12: "What is good makes men good; for in the art of music, what is good makes a musician; the things of chance do not make men good, so those things are not goods."

Those guarded by Ursa Major's[59] seven stars
he ruled, and those scorched
by the raging south wind, baking desert sands.
Even this power couldn't transform
twisted Nero![60]
With savage poison the sword
adds to harsh destiny."

7. Then I spoke: "You yourself know that ambition for earthly things hasn't held any power over me, but I've looked for the opportunity to do the things that would keep my virtue from growing old and stale."

And she replied, "Minds that are excellent in their nature but haven't yet reached the perfection of their virtue can still be enticed by this one thing: the love of glory and the fame of

---

[59] *Ursa Major's*: Ursa Major is a constellation in the northern sky that contains the Big Dipper, a highly visible group of seven starts. Boethius poetically notes that Nero's reign stretched far in all directions.

[60] *Nero*: Nero (Roman emperor from A.D. 54 to 68) was the classic example of the tyrant and is implicitly compared with Theodoric in the *Consolation*. See, e.g., J. Magee, who also makes pertinent comments on the implied connections between Boethius and the Stoic Seneca (J. Magee, "Boethius' *Consolatio* and the Theme of Roman Liberty", *Phoenix* 59 [2005]: 348–64).

In the Middle Ages, Chaucer used Nero as a negative example in *The Monk's Tale*:

> Although that Nero were as vicius
> As any feend that lith ful lowe adoun,
> Yet he, as telleth us Swetonius,
> This wyde world hadde in sujeccioun
> Both est and west, [south], and septemtrioun.
>
> . . . .
>
> His mooder made he in pitous array,
> For he hire wombe slitte to biholde
> Where he conceyved was; so weilaway!
> That he so litel of his mooder tolde.
>
> No teere out of his eyen for that sighte
> Ne cam, but seyde, "A faire womman was she!"
> Greet wonder is how that he koude or myghte
> Be domesman of hire dede beautee.
>   (2463–67, 2483–90)

See similarly Jean de Meun, *Romance of the Rose* 6185–250. For the classical sources, see Suetonius, *Nero* 34; and Tacitus, *Annals* 14.9.

great services done for the state.[61] Now consider how lacking
in substance and empty of weight this fame is. It is established, as you have learned from astronomical proofs, that the
entire circle of the earth is comparable to the space of a point
when measured against the heavens.[62] The earth is such that
we would judge it had no space at all if it were set beside the
magnitude of the heavenly sphere. And of this very little part
of the universe, only about one fourth is inhabited by living
things that we know of, as you have learned from the proofs
of Ptolemy. Of this fourth, if you remove from consideration
the parts covered by seas and swamps and the vast regions of
desert, scarcely the narrowest portion is left to be inhabited
by men. And so, when you're enclosed and hedged within this
sort of point within a point, do you consider trying to spread
your name around and make your fame known to all? Do you
think that glory confined within such narrow bounds would
have any magnitude or grandeur? And remember, too, that

[61] *the love of glory . . . done for the state*: In the Greek and especially the Roman
world, fame and glory were often considered the only certain way to gain immortality and therefore were the highest goal to be obtained. See, e.g., Cicero, *Manil-
ius* 7, and Sallust, *Catiline* 7.3. O'Donnell, *Consolatio philosophiae*, p. 41, compares
Boethius' words with Milton, *Lycidas* 70–71: "Fame . . . that last infirmity of the
noble mind."

[62] *It is established . . . .*: The rest of prosa 7 follows Cicero's *Dream of Scipio* and
Macrobius' long Neoplatonic commentary on it. Macrobius' *Commentary* heavily influenced Boethius, whose father, Symmachus, had edited it. For a discussion, see Courcelle, *Antécédents et postérité*, p. 121. Macrobius also strongly
influenced Chaucer.

The *Dream of Scipio*, which originally formed part of Cicero's *Republic*, a work
now only partially extant, tells of an imaginary dream that Scipio Africanus Minor
had of his adoptive grandfather, Scipio Africanus Major. In the dream, the elder
Scipio takes his grandson to the heavens to predict the future for him and to tell
him the nature of the afterlife, fame, the universe, and so forth. See conve-
niently Lewis, *Discarded Image*, pp. 23–28. For a translation of the *Dream* and
the *Commentary*, see Macrobius, *Commentary on the "Dream of Scipio"*, trans.
William Harris Stahl (New York: Columbia University Press, 1952).

For the idea that the earth is only as small as a point, see, e.g., Cicero, *Tusculan Disputations* 1.17.40. See also Martianus Capella, *On the Marriage of Mercury and Philology* 6.584.7–8. For an elaborate discussion of the regions of the
earth, see *Dream of Scipio* 6 and Macrobius' *Commentary* 2.5–9.

Dante describes the world as comparable to a "threshing floor" at *Paradiso*
22.151 and 27.85. Chaucer, *House of Fame* 907, refers to the earth as a "prikke";
see also *Troilus* 5.1814–20.

this very narrow portion of habitable land is the home for nations that differ in language, customs, and way of life. Difficulties in traveling, diverse languages, and infrequent trade prevent these nations from hearing not just about one man's fame but about the fame of whole cities.

"In the time of Cicero, for instance, as he himself writes in a certain place, the fame of the Roman Republic, which then was thriving and most formidable to the Parthians and surrounding nations of that region, had not yet gone beyond the Caucasus.[63] Don't you see how narrow and confined is the glory that you work to spread out and extend? Will the glory of a man of Rome reach out to where the knowledge of the name of Rome itself hasn't reached? And remember that the customs and institutions of various nations differ from each other, so that what some consider worthy of fame is judged by others to be worthy of punishment. So it happens that if someone enjoys having his fame spread around, it does no good to have his name carried to every land. Therefore every man must be content simply to have his name spread amongst his own people. His distinguished and immortal fame will be confined within the boundaries of one nation!

"How many famous men of your own era have been lost to memory because of forgetfulness and the absence of written records! And what good would these records do, when Time has obscured both the men and their chroniclers? Truly you think you produce immortality for yourself, when you take thought for your future. But if you should ponder the infinite stretches of eternity, what reason would you have for delighting in the longevity of your name?[64] Although it's only a

---

[63] *In the time of Cicero . . . beyond the Caucasus:* The Parthians lived in the area of ancient Persia, while the Caucasus was a range of mountains between the Black Sea and the Caspian Sea. Cf. Cicero, *Dream of Scipio* 6.4 (= *Republic* 6.22): "Has your name or the name of any of you been able to cross the Caucasus, which you can see, or the Ganges?", and Macrobius, *Commentary* 2.10.3.

[64] *But if you should ponder . . . longevity of your name?* Fortescue, *Boethius De consolatione*, p. 54, cites Dante, *Purgatorio* 11.103–8, where a painter, Oderisi, is telling Dante about the uselessness of human fame:

> Were you to reach the ripe old age of death,
> instead of dying prattling in your crib,
> would you have more fame in a thousand years?

fragment of time, even a moment can be compared with ten thousand years, since there is a certain likeness in things that are finite. But there can never be a similarity between the finite and the infinite. For that reason a fame that lasts however long you wish, if it should be compared with inexhaustible eternity, would seem not simply small but nonexistent.

"But you don't know how to act rightly except when you're courting the winds of popularity[65] and empty rumors," she continued. "Leaving aside the superiority of your conscience and virtue, you demand rewards in the words of other men. Listen to how cleverly one man made light of this sort of arrogance. Once a certain man insulted another who had falsely assumed for himself the title of philosopher—not for the sake of seeking true virtue but to gain pride and glory. The man further added that he would know if the title philosopher were justified by seeing how patiently and gently the other man would endure these insults. For a while the 'sage' summoned up his patience and bore the insult, but finally he retorted, 'Now then, do you judge me a philosopher?' The reply came with biting sarcasm, 'I would have done so, if you had remained silent.'[66] I ask you, when death releases the soul from the body, what good does fame do for these distinguished men who seek glory from virtue, these who are the butt of this joke? For if men really perish—although Reason refuses to let us believe this—there is no glory left, since

---

What are ten centuries to eternity?
Less than the blinking of an eye compared
to the turning of the slowest of the spheres.
(trans. Musa)

[65] *winds of popularity*: See *Aeneid* 6.816, where Ancus, the fourth king of Rome, is said to have enjoyed too much "the winds of popularity". Following Ancus' description is that of Brutus, with whom Virgil finds fault for killing his children, after they had plotted to betray the newly formed Republic. Brutus' actions are attributed to his "huge love of praise" (6.823). In these vignettes Anchises is telling his son Aeneas about the souls of future Roman heroes who are yet to be born. Aeneas is visiting his father in the underworld.

[66] *Once a certain man . . . if you had remained silent*: The source for this story is unknown. Gruber, *Kommentar zu Boethius*, p. 222, compares Macrobius, *Saturnalia* 7.1.11: "The orator is proved by his orations. The philosopher is sometimes proved philosophical by his being quiet as by his speaking."

the one to whom the glory was attributed no longer exists. But if the mind, conscious of itself and freed from its earthly prison,[67] seeks heaven, won't it spurn earthly concerns and enjoy that heaven, freed from the things of this world?

metrum 7

> Let glory-seeking man perceive
> the tight build of earth,
> the immense breadth of heaven.
> He'll bow his head!
> For even earth's small space
> can't be filled by his name.
> Men try eagerly to ease
> the burden of a mortal yoke.
> It is in vain.
> A household may shine with honor,
> with fame known through the world,
> yet death spurns this glory.
> Death tumbles and tangles both lofty and humble.
> Where wait Fabricius'[68] bones?
> What of Brutus or stiff Cato?[69]

[67] *the mind . . . freed from its earthly prison*: Gruber, *Kommentar zu Boethius*, pp. 222–23, cites several instances of Epicurean and especially Stoic philosophers who speak of "the mind at peace with itself". See, e.g., Seneca, *Epistle* 4.1. Cf. also *Aeneid* 1.603–5, where Aeneas is speaking to Dido: "If the divinities care for men, if there is justice anywhere, may the gods and a mind at peace with its righteousness bring you worthy rewards."

The idea that the body limits and wars against the spirit is a commonplace in Platonic, Neoplatonic, and Christian (especially Pauline) thought. See, e.g., Romans 8:4–13. On the body as a prison, see, e.g., Plato, *Phaedrus* 250C, *Phaedo* 62B, and *Cratylus* 400.

[68] *Fabricius'*: Fabricius was a great hero in the Roman war against Pyrrhus (c. 280 B.C.). Alfred the Great, in his translation of the *Consolation*, renders the line on Fabricius as "What now are the bones of Weland, of the wise and illustrious goldsmith?" (Anne F. Payne, *King Alfred and Boethius* [Madison: University of Wisconsin Press, 1969], p. 66).

[69] *What of Brutus or stiff Cato?* The elder Brutus helped depose the evil Etruscan king Tarquin in 510 B.C.; Brutus' younger namesake, of course, helped assassinate Julius Caesar in 44 B.C. The elder Cato (consul in 195 B.C.) is probably

Empty names marked in old books.
Do we know the dead by their noble words?
They lie unknown.
If you suppose the breath of a name
might lengthen life,
the day comes that snatches fame as well.
It persists—that second death.

8. "But so you won't think I'm waging an inexorable war against Fortune," she continued, "there is a time when she treats man well, not deceiving him at all. It's when she shows herself, uncovers her face, and confesses her ways. Perhaps you don't yet understand what I say: what I'm trying to express is strange, and so I can hardly explain it. Indeed, I think Fortune is of more benefit when she is adverse than when she brings prosperity, for in the latter case she approaches under the guise of happiness. When she seems kind, she lies; but when she shows herself fickle and unstable, she is truthful. In the first case she deceives; in the latter she instructs. In the first instance she uses the appearance of false goods to bind the minds of men that enjoy them; in the second she frees these minds by the knowledge of the fragility of happiness. And so, in her first role you see that Fortune is without substance, impermanent, and always uncertain of herself; in her second role she is sober, well girded, and made wise by the experiences of adversity.[70] In short, happy Fortune uses her allure-

---

most famous for advocating the destruction of Rome's longtime rival and foe, Carthage. The younger Cato lived during the time of Julius Caesar and, like his ancestor, was famous for his austerity. As O'Donnell, *Consolatio philosophiae*, p. 44, notes, it is impossible and unnecessary to know whether Boethius was speaking of the younger or elder Catos and Brutuses. All were known for their strong moral character and their eagerness for gaining honor. Such desires, however, gained them no true immortality.

On the theme that even famous men die and are no more, see, e.g., Lucretius, *On the Nature of Things* 3.1025–44, and Horace, *Ode* 1.28. Gruber, *Kommentar zu Boethius*, p. 228, also cites Claudian (fl. A.D. 400) 17.163–65 and 22.380–85, who links together Fabricius, Brutus, and Cato.

[70] *And so, in her first role . . . experiences of adversity*: In his translation of the *Consolation*, Chaucer renders the passage: "The amyable Fortune maystow seen alwey wyndy and flowynge, and evere mysknowynge of hirself; the contrarie Fortune is atempre and restreyned and wys thurw exercise of hir adversitie."

ments to draw men astray from the true Good, but adverse Fortune, for the most part, uses her claw to drag men back to the things that are good. Or do you think it should be considered a small thing, that this bitter and horrible Fortune has uncovered for you the hearts of your friends who are faithful,[71] that she has shown you which of your companions have sincere countenances and which have changeable ones, taking her own men as she departs and leaving yours behind? How much you would have paid for this gift when you were whole and, as you thought, fortunate! Now wail over lost wealth! You have discovered your friends—the most precious form of riches.

metrum 8[72]

> The world unwavering, changes—
> cycling in progression of harmony.
> An eternal charter checks
> Nature, treaty-bound.
> The sun rules the day;
> the moon guided by Hesperus

---

[71] *Fortune has uncovered . . . friends who are faithful*: Gruber, *Kommentar zu Boethius*, p. 225, and Fortescue, *Boethius De consolatione*, p. 67, compare Ovid, *Tristia* 1.9.5–7, on the theme of how most friends fail to remain loyal during adversity: "As long as you are fortunate you will/number many among your friends, but if/times become dark, you will be alone."

[72] metrum 8: O'Daly, *Poetry of Boethius*, p. 146, notes that this poem echoes 1 *metrum* 5, with its "concluding wish for stability and order in human affairs". He also sees the poem as pointing forward to 3 *metrum* 9 and "the other *amor* [love] poem, 4 m. 6".

In *metrum* 8, Boethius has Lady Philosophy demonstrate the stability of divine order by using several motifs of Neoplatonism and Pythagoreanism that show the harmony of the universe. D. S. Chamberlain shows that Boethius is alluding to the notion of "world music", which appears in three forms: "the motion of the spheres, the binding of the elements, and the variation of the seasons" (D. S. Chamberlain, "Philosophy of Music in the *Consolation* of Boethius", *Speculum* 45 [1970]: 81–88). It will be remembered that Boethius wrote an influential treatise on music, *De institutione musica*. There are also elements of Epicurean terminology in the *semina pugnantia* (warring elements; line 3 in original Latin), reminiscent of Lucretius' *On the Nature of Things*. See also Ovid, *Metamorphoses* 1.9, and Martianus Capella, *On the Marriage of Mercury and Philology* 1.1 (quoted in the following footnote).

rules the night.
The sea's hungry waves
would devour the land—
if not for Love's bonds.
Love, from the sky commanding,
binds both earth and sea.
If these reins are loosed,
loving falls to war—
this perfect engine running
would be wrecked.
Love weaves people, too,
knotting with sacred law.
Love's worthiness dictates justice.
O happy race of men!
If that Love which rules the heavens
might also rule your hearts!"[73]

[73] *Love, from the sky commanding . . . rule your hearts!* Cf. Chaucer, *Troilus* 3.1744–50, where Troilus is speaking:

> Love, that of erthe and se hath governaunce,
> Love, that his hestes hath in hevenes hye,
> Love, that with an holsam alliaunce
> Halt peples joyned, as hym lest hym gye,
> Love, that knetteth lawe of campaignie,
> And couples doth in vertu for to dwelle,
> Bynd this acord, that I have told and telle.

Cf. also the opening of Martianus Capella, *On the Marriage of Mercury and Philology* 1.1: "You who play the strings in marriage chambers, who, they say, was born from a Muse, a sacred coupler of the gods, who draw together warring elements with secret embrace (for you join the elements through their transformations, impregnate the universe, and associate the breath of the mind with bodies in that pleasing bond by which Nature is yoked, reconciling the sexes in loving loyalty), O fair Hymenaeus [god of marriage]" (Danuta Shanzer, *A Philosophical and Literary Commentary on Martianus Capella's "De nuptiis Philologiae et Mercurii", Book 1* [Berkeley: University of California Press, 1986]).

Book 3

1. Now she had finished her song, and its sweetness struck me with joy and amazement as I listened with ears still eager. After a while, I spoke: "What a great comfort you are for weary minds! How you have restored me by the weight of your judgments and the delight of your singing! Now I think I'm equal to the blows of Fortune![1] I've not only lost my fear of the remedies you were calling too strong a little while ago, but I'm burning to hear them."

She then replied, "I sensed this as you seized upon my words quietly and earnestly, and I was waiting for this disposition of your mind—or, rather, I should say that I caused it. Indeed the remedies that await you are bitter when tasted but become all the more sweet when they are swallowed down deep. And how you would burn to hear what you say you are eager for, if only you knew where you were being led!"

"To where?" I said.

"To true happiness,"[2] she replied, "the happiness your soul dreams of, but which it can't now see, since you are occupied with the mere shadows of things."[3]

---

[1] *Now I think I'm equal to the blows of Fortune!* Boethius has progressed to the point that he is no longer dependent on Fortuna. Now that he has learned something about the falsity of what had earlier seemed good to him, he must continue his process of healing by seeing the nature of the true Good.

[2] *true happiness*: Boethius qualifies the word "happiness" (*felicitas*) with the adjective "true" (*verus*), implying that many things considered happiness are not ultimate. Boethius will generally use *beatitudo* for the ultimate and proper goal of man, while *felicitas* much of the time represents a false joy, desire, or goal. As noted in book 2, in this translation *felicitas* is generally translated as "happiness", and *beatitudo* as "blessedness" (see p. 32, footnote 3).

[3] *shadows of things*: Speaking of the prisoners in his "Allegory of the Cave" in *Republic* 515A, Socrates asks, "[D]o you think that these men would have seen anything of themselves or of one another except the shadows cast from the fire on the wall of the cave that fronted them?" (Plato, *Republic*, trans. Paul

"Do this, I beg you," I replied. "Show me now what that true happiness is."

"I will gladly do it for you," she said. "But first I'll try to point out and put into words a type of happiness that is more familiar to you, so that when you have looked at it, you may turn your eyes in the opposite direction and be able to recognize the appearance of true blessedness.

metrum 1

> Man must first free fields of brush,
> must sickle fern and bramble,
> if he wishes to plant virgin land.
> Then Ceres arrives, laden with young grain.[4]
> Sweeter the labor of a bee,[5]
> if first a bitter taste bites the tongue.
> Brighter seem the stars
> when the south wind ceases its rainy noise.
> Morning Star expels the darkness—
> then fair Day drives her magenta steeds.
> And you, gazing after empty blessings,
> withdraw your neck from the yoke!
> Then truth may slip into your mind."

2. Afterwards, she looked down for a moment, as if withdrawing into the noble sanctuary of her mind, and she began to speak: "Every concern of man, which he pursues in his many efforts and seeks by various paths, aims nevertheless at the single

---

Shorey, 2 vols., Loeb Classical Library 237, 276 [Cambridge: Harvard University Press, 1935, 1937]). The prisoners in the cave see only shadows of images dimly cast by the light of a fire. Their perception of reality is accordingly greatly flawed.

[4] *Man must first . . . laden with young grain*: Lady Philosophy suggests that the mind must first have its misconceptions of happiness removed before it can understand true beatitude. This theme continues throughout *metrum* 1. Ceres is the goddess of grain.

[5] *labor of a bee*: The "labor of a bee" is periphrasis for honey.

goal of blessedness.[6] For when a man acquires that good, there is nothing left that he can desire. This is truly the highest of all goods, containing all good things within it, since there is nothing beyond it which anyone could wish to obtain. And so it is obvious that blessedness is a state made perfect by the coming together of all good things. This state, as we said, is the one that all men strive for by their different paths. Indeed, the desire for the true Good has been planted naturally in the minds of all men, but deceitful error leads men astray to things that are false. Some believe that the highest Good is to lack nothing, and so they struggle to abound in riches. Others believe that whatever is most worthy of esteem is the highest Good, and so they strive to gain honors and to be revered by their fellow citizens. Then, there are those who think that the highest Good lies in the greatest power; these men either want to rule or to attach themselves to those who do. To some, fame seems something very fine, and so they rush to earn glory for their name through skills in war or peace. Even more men measure the fruits of goodness by their joy or gladness; these men think the greatest happiness is to drown themselves in pleasure.[7] There are also those who confuse ends with means,

[6] *Every concern of man . . . single goal of blessedness*: Adrian Fortescue cites Dante, *Purgatorio* 27.115–17 (Virgil speaking): "That precious fruit which all men eagerly / go searching for on many different boughs / will give, today, peace to your hungry soul" (Adrian Fortescue, *Ancius Manlius Severinus Boethius De consolatione philosophiae libri quinque*, ed. G. D. Smith [Hildesheim: Georg Olms, 1976; originally published in London, 1925]), p. 61; *Dante's "Purgatory"*, trans. Mark Musa [Bloomington: University of Indiana Press, 1981]). Fortescue, *Boethius De Consolatione*, p. 62, also cites Aquinas, *Summa theologica* I, q. 26, art. 1 ad 1, on the definition of *beatitudo*. Joachim Gruber cites the beginning of Aristotle's *Nichomachean Ethics*: "Every art and every inquiry, and similarly every action and pursuit, is thought to aim at some good, and for this reason the good has rightly been declared to be that at which all things aim" (1094a; Joachim Gruber, *Kommentar zu Boethius, "De consolatione philosophiae"*, 2nd ed. [Berlin: Walter de Gruyter, 2006; originally published 1978], p. 239; *Introduction to Aristotle*, ed. Richard McKeon [New York: Random House, 1947]).

[7] *these men think . . . drown themselves in pleasure*: Although the idea of drowning in pleasures is sometimes seen as Epicurean, the practice is actually hedonism (the pursuit of physical pleasure for its own sake), since the Epicureans realized that unrestrained pleasures actually brought pain, which was to be avoided. (See footnote 9 below.)

so that some want wealth for the sake of power and pleasure, while others seek power for the sake of money or to spread their fame.

"And so the aim of human actions and prayers is directed towards these goals or others like them—such as nobility and popular favor, which seem to bring a certain renown, or having a wife and children, which are sought for the sake of the joy they will bring. Indeed, friendship is the most sacred good,[8] since it results from virtue, not chance, while other goods are culti-vated for the sake of power or delight. Surely the good of bodily health can also be compared with those already mentioned; for strength and size seem to offer might, good looks and speed pro-duce glory, and good health brings pleasure. In all these goods blessedness alone is sought, since whatever each man seeks beyond all else he judges the highest Good. But we have already defined blessedness as the highest Good, and so each man believes that state is blessed which he desires above the others.

"Thus you have the basic model of human happiness placed before your eyes: wealth, honors, power, glory, pleasures. Con-sidering only these, Epicurus believed the highest Good was pleasure, because everything else seemed to bring joy to the mind.[9] But I return to the study of men, who, although their memory remains clouded, still seek the highest Good, but seek it as if they were drunk and didn't know the path that led to their home.[10] Do these men really seem mistaken in trying to

---

[8] *friendship is the most sacred good*: True friendship, in antiquity, was consid-ered one of the greatest goods. See, e.g., Aristotle, *Nichomachean Ethics*, book 8, and Cicero, *De amicitia*.

[9] *Epicurus believed . . . joy to the mind*: Epicurus (fl. 310 B.C.) posited that the chief good was to seek pleasure, which to him was the avoidance of pain and anxiety. Presumably Boethius is here presenting the more stereotypical view of Epicurus, which saw him more as a hedonist concerned with bodily pleasures.

[10] *But I return to the study of men . . . path that led to their home*: See Chaucer, *The Knight's Tale*:

> We witen nat what thing we preyen heere;
> We faren as he that dronke is as a mous.
> A dronke man woot wel he hath an hous,
> But he noot which the righte way is thider,

supply all their needs? There is nothing that truly brings blessedness other than a state that has an abundance of all good
things and that needs nothing belonging to anyone else but
rather is sufficient in itself. Can men be deceived in thinking
that what is best is also worthy of respect? Not at all, for one
can't despise as worthless the goal that almost all men strive
to attain. Or is power not to be included among the things
that are good? Well, we can't consider as weak or without power
something that is agreed to be more excellent than the others. Or is renown of no value? But it can't be denied that whatever seems to surpass other things is the most renowned. Why
do we need to add that blessedness is not anxious or sad, or
subject to pain or harm, since even in small matters men seek
what is pleasing to have and enjoy? And these are the things
men want to acquire; they desire riches, honors, rule, glory,
and pleasures, because they think that through them they will
acquire sufficiency, respect, power, fame, and joy. And so, it is
the Good that men seek in their various pursuits. In this we
can see how great is the power of nature, since men agree in
choosing the end of the Good, though they differ in their various opinions about how to achieve it.

metrum 2[11]

> Now I sing of Nature's faith—
> the music of loyalty, a song of power.
> Her grip curves and binds,
> uniting with firm law.

> And certes, in this world so faren we;
> We seken faste after felicitee,
> But we goon wrong ful often, trewely.
> (1260–67)

[11] metrum 2: In this poem Boethius speaks of how created things return to
their natural state. For man, this means a return to God. J.J. O'Donnell notes
that the poem follows up on 1 *prosa* 6, where Lady Philosophy has to remind
Boethius that, since God is man's beginning, he must also be man's end (J.J.

A lion in Carthage wearing beautiful chains,
eating food from a hand, still fears—
he fears flogging from his fierce master.[12]
But, if blood touches his lips,
a long-settled spirit revives—
with roars, he remembers![13]
Bursting the knots from his neck—
the first to sate his fury
is the tamer, mangled by his teeth.
A tree-loving bird from a high branch
is closed in a cage like a cave.
Her care is man's sport—
he feeds her a bounty, offering
honeyed drink, pleasing himself.
While hopping in her small cage
if the shade of the grove she spies,
she scatters her food beneath her feet.
Then murmuring with sweet voice,
she longs for her forest.[14]

O'Donnell, ed., *Consolatio philosophiae*, vol. 2, Bryn Mawr Latin Commentaries [Bryn Mawr: Thomas Library, Bryn Mawr College, 1984], p. 49). Gerard O'Daly compares the poem to 2 *metrum* 8, in which love, like nature in this poem, controls the world (Gerard O'Daly, *The Poetry of Boethius* [Chapel Hill: University of North Carolina Press, 1991], p. 157).

[12] *A lion in Carthage . . . his fierce master*: Boethius refers to lions obtained for the gladiatorial games. Fortescue, *Boethius De consolatione*, p. 64, compares Martial, *Epigram* 2.75.1: "The lion is accustomed to endure the blows of the master he can't harm", and Statius, *Achilleid* 1.858–63.

[13] *But, if blood touches . . . he remembers!* O'Daly, *Poetry of Boethius*, p. 158, sees in the example of the lion (and of the caged bird below) "a kind of recollection" akin to Platonic anamnesis (see footnote 14 below). (See further ibid., pp. 158–61.)

[14] *A tree-loving bird . . . longs for her forest*: C. S. Lewis notes Chaucer's borrowing in *The Squire's Tale* (C. S. Lewis, *The Discarded Image: An Introduction to Medieval and Renaissance Literature* [Cambridge: Cambridge University Press, 1964], p. 84):

> I trowe he hadde thilke text in mynde,
> That 'alle thyng, repeirynge to his kynde,
> Gladeth hymself': thus seyn men, as I gesse.
> Men loven of proper kynde newefangelnesse.
> As briddes doon that men in cages fede.
> For though thou nyght and day take of hem hede,

If a sapling is bent down
and by the same hand released—
straight skyward it springs again.
The sun sets in Hesperus' waves
and backward comes by secret path—
turning his chariot east.[15]
Each thing finds its return and rejoices!
Nothing continues its way
unless the end is yoked to the source—
making the circle eternal.

3. "You too, earthly creatures, dream of your origin, although only in faint images.[16] And you envision that true goal of blessedness, although you do so with the reason you possess, one that is very short-sighted. For this reason your natural inclination leads you to the true Good, while numerous errors lead you away from it. Now consider whether men are able to reach their desired goal by obtaining the things they think will bring happiness.

And strawe hir cage faire and softe as silk,
And yeve hem sugre, hony, breed and milk,
Yet right anon as that his dore is uppe,
He with his feet wol spurne adoun his cuppe,
And to the wode he wole and wormes ete.

(607–17)

Cf. also *The Manciple's Tale* 162–74 (cited by Bernard L. Jefferson, *Chaucer and the "Consolation of Philosophy" of Boethius* [Princeton: Princeton University Press, 1917], p. 148). As Jefferson notes, Chaucer in both places reverses Boethius' idea that man seeks good. Instead, Chaucer tries "to prove that men, by instinct, follow their 'likerous appetyt'" (*The Manciple's Tale* 189). See also Jean de Meun, *Romance of the Rose* 13941–58.

[15] *The sun sets in Hesperus' waves . . . turning his chariot east*: Helios the Titan sun god and Apollo the Olympian god of light, or the sun, were often conflated. Both were imagined as driving a chariot holding the sun across the sky each day circling Oceanius, hence the reference to Hesperus, the evening star.

[16] *You too, earthly creatures . . . faint images*: Lady Philosophy also uses the phrase "earthly creatures" in 2 *prosa* 6, paragraph 2. Cf. the words of the Eagle in Dante, *Paradiso* 19.85: "O earthbound creatures! O thick-headed men" (*Dante's "Paradise"*, trans. Mark Musa [Bloomington: University of Indiana Press, 1984]). The reference to "faint images" again reminds one of Plato's cave. Boethius understands man's problems in searching for the Good as the result of flawed perception. Lady Philosophy will show that men try to seek after particular attributes of the Good rather than after the Good itself.

For if money or honors or the rest brought such a state that seemed to lack nothing good, then I, too, would confess that some men can become happy by acquiring them. But if these goods can't bring about what they promise and prove lacking in many good things, don't we find in them a false image of blessedness? So let me ask you first, since you were overflowing with wealth not long ago: when you possessed your tremendous wealth, was there ever a time when your spirit was shaken by anxiety, as the result of some sort of harm you received?"

"Well, I can't ever recall having such freedom of mind that I was not distressed by something," I said.

"Either what you wanted wasn't present, or what you didn't want was?"

"Exactly," I said.

"And so you wanted the presence of this thing or the absence of that one."

"Yes, I admit it," I said.

"Now a man is lacking in that which he desires," she said.

"Yes, he is."

"Then the one who is lacking in something is not entirely self-sufficient."

"No, indeed," I replied.

"Did you suffer this insufficiency even though you had plenty of wealth?"

"Of course," I said.

"And so riches can't make a man self-sufficient and lacking nothing, which was the very thing wealth seemed to offer. And I also think this should be considered carefully: that money possesses nothing by its own nature which prevents it from being taken against the will of those who possess it."

"I admit it," I said.

"Of course you do, since every day some stronger man snatches it from someone against his will. For where do legal quarrels come from, except through the efforts of victims to retrieve money taken by force or fraud?"

"Exactly."

"And so each man will need some outside source of protection for guarding his money?"

"Who could deny it?" I replied.

"But he would not need this, if he didn't have the money which he was capable of losing."

"Without a doubt," I replied.

"Then the situation has reversed itself, for the riches that were thought to make man self-sufficient instead cause him to need some outside protection. So how is it that wealth removes need? Can't rich men get hungry? Can't they be thirsty? Can't the limbs of the wealthy feel the cold of winter? But you will say, 'The rich man has means to satisfy his hunger or drive away his thirst or cold.' Yes, in this way need can be assuaged with wealth, but it can't be entirely removed. For if this need, always grasping and demanding something, is satisfied through riches, the need itself must still exist, since it can be satisfied. I won't mention the fact that nature is satisfied with very little, while nothing is enough for avarice. And so, if wealth can't eliminate need and even creates its own kind of need, in what way can it offer sufficiency?[17]

metrum 3

A man rich with rivers of gold
to gather in piles,

[17] *Then the situation has reversed itself . . . can it offer sufficiency?* Boethius' point in this paragraph seems to be threefold. The rich man causes himself extra needs because he must protect his wealth. Furthermore, although wealth can temporarily satisfy some needs, it cannot be the highest Good (*summum bonum*), since it does not eliminate all needs. Finally, Boethius argues that the gaining of wealth can be a smokescreen for greed. Cf. Horace, *Satire* 1.1:

> You sleep gaping over piled-up money bags,
> and force yourself not to touch them as if they were sacred
> or to enjoy looking at them as if they were painted pictures.
> Don't you know the value of money or what its use is?
> To buy bread, greens, or a little wine and those other
> things that human nature would sorrow at not having.
> What good does it do to stay awake lifeless with fear,
> day and night to be in terror of wicked thieves, fire, and your slaves,
> who might rob you and run away?

(70–78)

Red Sea jewels[18]
to weight his neck,
hundreds of oxen[19]
to plow his fields,
remains dissatisfied.
His companion in life is gnawing care;
and wealth deserts him in death.

4. "Now high offices do bring honor and respect to those who obtain them. Yet is there really any power in offices that enables one possessing them to implant virtue in his mind or to cast out vices? On the contrary, offices tend to bring wickedness to the surface rather than remove it, and so it happens that we often become angry when they come to worthless men. Thus Catullus called Nonius a 'tumor,' although he sat in a magistrate's chair.[20]

"Don't you see how much shame high office brings to evil men? But their lack of worth will be less obvious if they aren't made famous by honors. Would any amount of danger have led you to hold office with Decoratus,[21] when you saw he was a worthless buffoon and an informer? We, at least, can't believe that honors make a man worthy of renown, if we think the men themselves are unworthy of those very honors. But if you saw a man endowed with wisdom, you couldn't consider him unworthy of respect or of that wisdom with which he was endowed, could you? Not at all. For there is a worthiness inherent in virtue that flows into those who possess that virtue.

---

[18] *Red Sea jewels*: Red Sea jewels are pearls. As O'Donnell, *Consolatio philosophiae*, p. 52, notes, the Red Sea can mean the Persian Gulf or the Indian Ocean, as well as what we call the Red Sea.

[19] *hundreds of oxen*: On the man with hundreds of oxen, cf. again Horace, *Satire* 1.1.45–46: "Suppose your threshing floor offers a hundred thousand measures of grain; will your belly hold more than mine?"

[20] *Thus Catullus called Nonius . . . in a magistrate's chair*: See Catullus, *Carmen* 52.2: "Nonius sits as a tumor on the magistrate's chair."

[21] *Decoratus*: Decoratus served as quaestor for Theodoric around 520. At this time the questor, originally a Roman official in charge of finances or public works, served as "legal advisor, and drafter of state documents for kings and emperors" (S. J. B. Barnish, trans. and ed., *Variae*, by Cassiodorus [Liverpool: University of Liverpool Press, 1992], p. 186). We do not know specifically why Boethius did not like Decoratus.

Since this can't be said of public honors, they obviously don't possess the beauty inherent in worthiness. Along the same lines, we should consider this: if a person becomes more and more dishonored when many people despise him, then high office makes a wicked man more despised, since it can't make him honorable and it puts him on display to more people. And, indeed, the offices pay a price, for the wicked men do equal harm to their offices, and infect them with their own disease.

"So you can recognize that true respect cannot come through these shadows of worthy pursuits[22]—suppose a man who had been consul many times were to travel among foreign nations. Would his office make him respected by the foreigners? But if the office itself had this inherent gift, it would hardly change its nature among any people, just as fire continues giving off heat wherever in the world it happens to be. But since honor is not inherent in an office but is only an attribute assumed through human error, that honor vanishes immediately when it appears before men who don't consider it honor.[23] Now this is the case in foreign lands; but do these honors last forever even among men in the place where the honors were given? The power of the praetor, for instance, was once great, but now praetor is just an empty name. So, too, the rank of senator is only a heavy burden.[24] Once, if a man had charge over the grain supply, he was considered great;[25] now what office is

[22] *shadows of worthy pursuits*: On Boethius' "shadows of worthy pursuits" (*umbratiles dignitates*), see Gruber, *Kommentar zu Boethius*, p. 252, who compares Cicero, *Tusculan Disputations* 3.3: "Searching for true honor, a natural pursuit, they find themselves among empty things and strive to win not virtue but a shadowy image [*adumbratum imaginem*] of glory." O'Donnell, *Consolatio philosophiae*, p. 53, aptly notes that "to a philosophic observer even public life is a petty matter of parochial concern."

[23] *men who don't consider it honor*: Boethius suggests that humans are wrong to assume that a person with an office is automatically a worthy person.

[24] *The power of the praetor . . . a heavy burden*: O'Donnell, *Consolatio philosophiae*, p. 53, notes that the "praetorship (*praetura*) had been an important judicial office in classical Rome, but in the late empire it had become an onerous glory and was regarded as a virtual tax." The role of senator had also lost much of its earlier desirability.

[25] *great*: On the word "great" (*magnus*), see O'Donnell, *Consolatio philosophiae*, p. 53, who suggests "wordplay, alluding to Pompey (106–48 B.C.), who was called

considered lower than this one? For, as we said a little earlier, a thing that possesses no inherent beauty sometimes receives splendor from those who are associated with it, but at other times it loses that splendor. Therefore, if honors can't make men worthy of reverence, if honors grow foul from the disease of wicked men and cease to shine because of the vicissitudes of time, if they become vile in the judgment of other nations, what beauty do these honors have within themselves, let alone offer to other men?

metrum 4

> In Tyrian purple with snow-white jewels,[26]
> so pridefully was he adorned,
> cruel Nero, hated by all.[27]
> Without shame
> nominating tainted consuls
> for election by Senators—
> granted by such miserable men—
> is this honor?

5. "Then can kingdoms or friendships with rulers create true power? Why not, since they bring happiness that lasts forever! But antiquity is full of examples—and so is the present time—of kings whose happiness turned into calamity. O wonderful power that can't even preserve itself! If this power from kingship is the source of blessedness, wouldn't it diminish happiness and bring on misery if it were weak in some aspect? Yet

---

Magnus and who had distinguished himself in looking after the grain supply (*annona*); in later times the prefect of the *annona* had a thankless task, trying to keep an adequate supply coming from Africa and Sicily and performing related chores; in times of short supply, the office could be a dangerous one if the mob rioted."

[26] *snow-white jewels*: With the phrase "snow-white jewels", Boethius again refers to pearls.

[27] *cruel Nero, hated by all*: The reference to Nero is intended to make the reader think of Theodoric.

however widely human kingdoms extend, there must be many
people left who aren't ruled by these kings. Wherever the power
of these rulers is unable to make them blessed, weakness creeps
in and makes them wretched, and so in this way a greater portion of misery must be found in kings. Once there was a tyrant
who knew the dangers of his position, and he likened the fears
of kingship to the terror of a sword hanging over a man's head.[28]

"So what is this power that cannot drive away gnawing
anxieties or repel stinging fears? These kings would like to
live their lives in security, but they can't. And so they glory
in their power! Do you judge powerful a man wanting to
accomplish what he cannot? Do you judge powerful a man
who surrounds himself with guards, who is himself more afraid
than those he terrifies, who in order to look powerful has placed
himself into the hands of his servants? And what should I
say about those who are the friends of kings, when I have
shown that kingship itself is full of weakness? Royal power
often destroys the friends of kings, both when this power is
strong and when it has fallen away itself. Nero compelled his
friend and teacher Seneca to take his own life.[29] Papinian,
a man who had long been powerful at court, was put to
the sword by Antoninus.[30] What is more, both Seneca and

[28] *Once there was a tyrant ... sword hanging over a man's head*: Boethius is
referring to the story of Damocles and King Dionysius of Syracuse (reigned 405–
367 B.C.). When Dionysius grew tired of the flattery of Damocles, who constantly praised the king's good fortune, Dionysus asked Damocles if he wished to
see what it was like to be king. Damocles foolishly agreed, and Dionysus had a
great feast set out for him. But despite the richness of the surroundings and the
obsequious service he received, Damocles lost his zest for the royal life when he
saw that Dionysius had caused a sword to be suspended on a string and hung
over Damocles' head. For versions of the story, see Cicero, *Tusculan Disputations*
5.61–62, and Macrobius, *Commentary* 1.10.16. See also Horace, *Ode* 3.1.17–19:
"When the bared sword hangs over the neck of the wicked man, the savor of
the Sicilian banquet loses its sweet taste."

[29] *Nero compelled his friend ... to take his own life*: When Seneca sensed that
Nero's corruption was irretrievable, he tried to retire from court life and to give
Nero most of his wealth. The emperor took this as an affront, which seemed to
precipitate Seneca's downfall. See Tacitus, *Annals* 14.53–54.

[30] *Papinian ... was put to the sword by Antoninus*: Aemilianus Papinianus was
a famous jurist in Rome. Septimius Severus (emperor from A.D. 193 to 211) asked

Papinian wanted to renounce their power; Seneca even tried to give his wealth to Nero and retire into seclusion. But when these men were dragged down to destruction, carried by their own weight, neither of them could accomplish what he had desired.

"What is that power, then, which makes men fear so greatly when they possess it? When you want to have it, you are not safe, and if you want to abandon it, you can't do so. Are friends a defense when you are united by fortune and not by virtue? A man that is your friend in happiness will be your enemy in misfortune. Indeed what more harmful source of ruin is there than an enemy who is close to you?

metrum 5

> The man desiring power
> must tame his fierce spirit,
> must not submit his neck
> to disgraceful reins, conquered by lust.
> Even though far away Indian land
> shakes beneath your law
> and remote Thule serves you,[31]
> still you cannot dispel dark worry
> nor banish wretched complaint—
> this isn't power!

6. "And glory—how foul and deceitful it often proves! That is why the tragic poet rightly proclaimed:

Papinianus to be the tutor of his sons, one of whom, Antonius Carcalla, later became emperor and eventually had Papinianus executed.

[31] *Even though far away Indian land . . . remote Thule serves you:* Thule perhaps refers to Iceland and is taken as representing the northernmost part of the world, while India represents the easternmost part of the world known to the ancients (Virgil, *Georgics*, ed. Richard F. Thomas, vol. 1, *Books 1 and 2* [Cambridge: Cambridge University Press, 1988], p. 74). Boethius is probably referring to two Virgilian passages in which Augustus is referred to as ruling over "remote Thule" (*Georgics* 1.30) and the lands past India (*Aeneid* 6.794).

O glory, glory! You have raised up high
thousands of men born base.[32]

For haven't many men stolen a glorious name through the
false opinion of the crowd? Can you think of anything more
shameful than this? Men who are extolled without reason
should blush at hearing themselves praised. But even if these
praises are deserved, how do they add to the wise man's knowledge of himself, if he measures the highest Good by the truthfulness of his self-knowledge and not by the words of men?
Now if it seems a fine thing to have one's name spread around,
does it not follow that it is disgraceful not to have done so?
But since, as I showed earlier, there must be many nations
that one man's fame can't reach, it follows that a man you
think glorious may be considered inglorious in a land border-
ing yours.

"Along the same lines—I don't think public favor is even
worthy of mention, since it does not arise from wisdom and
never lasts forever. Now truly, who can't see how empty and
worthless a noble name is![33] If it comes from fame, it is clearly
the fame that belongs to someone else; for nobility seems to
be a certain kind of honor that comes from the merits of one's
parents. But if praise from men brings renown, it must be the
men who are praised that become renowned.[34] So the renown
of others doesn't make you great, if you do not possess your
own renown. The only good there is in nobility, I think, is
this: noble men seem obliged to live up to the virtue of their
ancestors.

[32] *O glory, glory! . . . thousands of men born base*: Boethius quotes directly in
Greek from Euripides, *Andromache* 319–20.

[33] *Now truly, who can't see . . . noble name is!* Chaucer, in his translation of
the *Consolation*, renders the passage: "But now of this name of gentilesse, what
man is it that ne may wele seen how veyn and how flyttynge a thyng it es?"

[34] *But if praise from men . . . become renowned*: Boethius suggests that the glory
of our ancestors truly belongs to them, not to us. Lewis, *Discarded Image*, p. 84,
notes, "This doctrine had a flourishing progeny in the Middle Ages and became
a popular subject for school debates." He cites the opening of book 4 of Dante's
Convivio and Dante's *De monarchia* 2.3, as well as Gower, *Confessio amantis*
4.2261ff., and Jean de Meun, *Romance of the Rose* 18607–34.

metrum 6

> All mankind springs from a single source.
> One is the Father, one tends to all.[35]
> He grants
> beams to the sun,
> horns to the crescent moon,
> men to the earth,
> and stars to the heavens.
> He limits
> souls with bodies.[36]
> This Noble Seed discharges all.
> Why boast of birth and ancestors?
> Contemplate your origin, your Maker.
> All are worthy except—
> the man who, cherishing his failings,
> abandons the true Source.

7. "And what should I say about the pleasures of the body, when the appetite for them is full of anxiety and their fulfillment brings regret? How many diseases, how many grievous pains they bring upon the body, creating, so to speak, fruits of the prodigality of those enjoying them. I do not know what joy is brought by pursuing them. Certainly anyone wishing to recall his own desires knows that the end result of these pleasures is sorrow. If bodily pleasures could make men become blessed, there is no reason why we shouldn't call cattle blessed, since the aims of these beasts are entirely directed to fulfilling

[35] *One is the Father, one tends to all*: Boethius seems to be thinking of the Father in the Judeo-Christian sense, although the idea of Zeus as "father of gods and men" goes back to Homer (e.g., *Iliad* 1.544).

[36] *He limits / souls with bodies*: The idea that souls are in Heaven before being confined in bodies and leaving their "lofty citadel" is found in Plato, *Phaedrus* 246E: "Now the great leader in heaven, Zeus, driving a winged chariot, goes first, arranging all things and caring for all things" (Plato, *Euthyphro; Apology; Crito; Phaedo; Phaedrus*, trans. Harold North Fowler, Loeb Classical Library 36 [Cambridge: Harvard University Press, 1914]). The souls to be born in humans, however, lose their wings for failing to keep sight of the truth (248C) and must be born on earth and strive to regain their wings through contemplation of the truth.

their bodily wants.[37] Indeed, there would be a very proper joy
in having a spouse and children, but it has been said naturally
enough that one man found his sons to be his tormentors.[38] I
don't need to tell you how painful this situation is. You have
experienced it very well, and still experience it now in your
anxiety. In this matter I call as witness my own Euripides, who
said that a childless man was happy in his misfortune.[39]

metrum 7

> All pleasure has this thing,
> pricking those enjoying it
> like the swarming bees
> after shedding sweet honey—
> pleasure flees, and with tenacious grip
> hurts hearts, stricken by the sting.

8. "There's no doubt, then, that these paths to blessedness stray
somewhat from the path, and they are not really able to lead
anyone to the place they promise to bring him. Indeed I will
show very quickly with what troubles they are intertwined.

"Suppose you will try to acquire wealth? But you will seize
it from someone who possesses it. Do you want the splendor
of honors? You will pay the price to the one who gives them.
If you desire to surpass others in these honors, you will become
base through the humiliation of asking for them. Do you want
power? You will be subject to danger and open to the plots of

[37] *If bodily pleasures . . . fulfilling their bodily wants*: Cf. Seneca, *Epistle* 74.15:
"Animals enjoy pleasures more frequently and more easily [than humans], and
without any fear of shame or regret."

[38] *one man found his sons to be his tormentors*: We are following the manuscript
reading of *tortures* (tormentors). There is strong support for reading *torturem* (tormentor), in which case the translation would run: "some tormentor invented
children." See Gruber, *Kommentar zu Boethius*, p. 264. The original source of the
saying is uncertain. Cf. Sophocles, *Antigone* 645–47, where Creon says, "Whoever produces sons that are no use to him, what can you say but that he produces sorrows for himself and laughter for his enemies."

[39] *I call as witness . . . happy in his misfortune*: Boethius refers to Euripides, *Andromache* 418–20.

those you rule. Would you seek glory? Then you will cease to be secure, as you are dragged down difficult paths. Would you live a life of pleasure? But who wouldn't despise a slave of the body, which is the vilest and most fragile of all things? What a meager and fragile possession you rely upon when you boast of the body's goods! Can you surpass elephants in mass or bulls in strength? Can you outrun the tiger with your speed? Look at the size, the speed, the stability of the heavens; then cease to marvel at worthless things.[40] And indeed, it is not so much these qualities of the heavens that should excite your wonder as the intelligence that governs them. How the body's beauty slips away; how swiftly it passes; how it speeds by, faster than the successions of flowers in the springtime![41] As Aristotle said, if men could use the eyes of Lynceus, so their sight pierced through everything in its way, wouldn't the body even of Alcibiades, with all its surface beauty, seem very base as the internal organs became visible?[42] And so it is not your own nature that makes you handsome but the limitations of the eyes of those that see you. Go ahead and value the goods of the body as much as you wish—just remember that whatever you admire can be destroyed by a three-day fever.

"From all these arguments we can conclude briefly that these things aren't able to offer what they promise or to become perfect by the acquisition of all good things, and they neither lead to beauty along their various paths, so to speak, nor do they themselves make men blessed.

---

[40] *Look at the size . . . worthless things*: Cf. Dante, *Purgatorio* 14.148–50: "The heavens wheeling round you call to you, / revealing their eternal beauties—yet, / you keep your eyes fixed on the ground alone" (trans. Musa). See also *Paradiso* 10.7–24. (Both passages are cited by Fortescue, *Boethius De consolatione*, p. 76.) Cf. also Augustine, *On the Trinity* 1.4.

[41] *How the body's beauty . . . in the springtime!* Cf. Seneca, *Phaedra* 761–63: "O beauty of the body, what an ambiguous good to mortal men! A brief gift for a very short time, how swiftly you leave, slipping away with swift foot." Cf. also Ovid, *The Art of Love* 2.113–15.

[42] *As Aristotle said . . . internal organs became visible?* Alcibiades (c. 450–404 B.C.) was famed for his handsomeness. (See Plato, *Symposium* 33 [216D].) Lynceus was one of Jason's Argonauts famed for his keen eyesight. (See Apollonius, *Argonautica* 1.153–54.) The reference to Aristotle is from a work only surviving in fragments, *Protreptius* (see frag. B 105D).

metrum 8

What ignorance seduces senseless men!
You do not glean gold from green trees
nor do you pluck gems from vines.[43]
You do not set the snare on a mountain
to enrich a feast with fish.
Nor if you hunt the she-goat
do you search Etruscan shoals.[44]
Man knows the sea's secret depths
hidden beneath the waves—
which waters hold snowy jewels
and which the scarlet dye;
which coasts contain tender fish
and which store spiny urchins.
But the good he desires is obscured—
he blindly holds back his sight.[45]
Men seek what is buried in the earth
and ignore what soars the starry pole.
What curse is worthy of such dull minds?
Let him pursue power and honor!
When heavy toil gains these lies—
may he recognize the true Good.

[43] *You do not glean gold . . . gems from vines*: The literary trope that some attempts are useless is referred to as the *adunaton* (meaning "impossible" in Greek) motif. See Ernst Robert Curtius, *European Literature and the Late Middle Ages*, trans. Willard R. Trask (New York: Pantheon, 1953; originally published 1948), pp. 95–98.

[44] *Etruscan shoals*: The reference to the Etruscan shoals is an erudite allusion to the waters of the Tyrrhenian Sea between Italy and Corsica and Sardinia. The Etruscans were an early Roman people who invented the toga and the arch. The modern name Tuscany ultimately derives from the word "Etruscan".

[45] *But the good he desires . . . holds back his sight*: The idea is that man uses common sense to know where to find the earthly objects he desires, but he does not know where to find the true Good. At the end of the poem, Boethius seems to suggest that there is hope for man when he has acquired the false goods and has seen how hard he has worked to obtain what isn't really good at all.

9. "So far it has been enough to show the form of deceptive happiness," she continued. "If you see this clearly, we can next point out what the true happiness is."[46]

"Yes," I said, "I do see that sufficiency does not result from wealth, or power from kingdoms, or reverence from offices, or renown from glory, or joy from pleasures."

"But have you also grasped the reasons why this is so?"

"I think I perceive them, but only as if I were looking through a little crack in the wall, and I would like to learn them more clearly from you."

"Well, the explanation is close at hand. For what is simple and indivisible by its nature is broken apart by human error and transferred from the true and perfect to the false and imperfect. Now do you suppose a thing that needs nothing could be lacking in power?"

"Of course not," I said.

"Quite correct. For if something is weak in any aspect, it must be in need of some assistance in that aspect."

"Exactly," I said.

"So the nature of power and the nature of sufficiency are one and the same."

"So it seems."

"And should whatever has this nature be spurned, or is it instead the worthiest of all things to be revered?"

"Why, the latter," I said, "without a doubt."

"Then let us add reverence to sufficiency and power, so we can consider these three things to be one."

"We should add reverence, if we want to admit the truth."

"So then," she said, "do you think this thing we are talking about is unknown and ignoble, or is it most renowned in every aspect of fame? Be careful, now, and make sure that what we

---

[46] *If you see this clearly . . . what the true happiness is:* Gruber, *Kommentar zu Boethius,* p. 271, notes that the following sections serve as a second part of book 3, in which true happiness (*beatitudo*) can be demonstrated now that the other types of happiness have been proven false. Whereas the first part of the book consisted of both diatribe and Socratic discourse, this portion, which will reveal truth, is more completely Socratic discourse.

have judged to be lacking in nothing, most powerful, and most worthy of honor doesn't lack renown and prove unable to secure it, and therefore in some manner prove despised."

"I can't avoid admitting that this thing, such as it is, is also most renowned."

"So it follows that we confess renown to be no different from these previous three things."

"Yes, it follows," I said.

"And whatever needs nothing outside of itself, and is renowned and revered—wouldn't we agree that it is most full of joy, too?"

"Well, I can't imagine how any sorrow could attack such a thing. So we must confess it is full of joy, if our previous arguments still hold."

"And by the same reasoning it must be true that the names of sufficiency, power, renown, reverence, and joy are different, though they are in no way different in substance."[47]

"It must be true," I said.

"So this thing that is by nature one and the same has been divided by human perversity. And this perversity tries to obtain parts of a thing that has no parts, but it obtains neither a portion of it, since there aren't any, nor the thing itself, since the thing itself is not being sought."

"How can that be?" I said.

"A man who seeks wealth out of his fear of poverty makes no attempt to acquire power and prefers to be unknown and common, and he even robs himself of many natural joys lest

[47] *names of sufficiency . . . different in substance*: Here, as in several other passages in this section, Boethius uses an argument similar to that found in Plato's *Protagoras*. See 329C–D, where Socrates is addressing Protagoras: "[I]t was frequently stated in your discourse that justice, temperance, holiness and the rest were all but one single thing, virtue: pray, now proceed to deal with these things in more precise exposition, stating whether virtue is a single thing, of which justice and temperance and holiness are parts, or whether the qualities I have just mentioned are all names of the same thing. This is what I am still hankering after" (Plato, *Laches; Protagoras; Meno; Euthydemus*, trans. W. R. M. Lamb, Loeb Classical Library 165 [Cambridge: Harvard University Press, 1924]).

he lose the wealth he has gained. But in this way not even sufficiency comes to him, since he is deserted by health, plagued by troubles, and buried in obscurity.

"The man who only wants power squanders wealth, scorns pleasure, and despises any glory and honor that bring no might. But you see how many things he lacks, for it happens that he is sometimes in need of necessities and that he is eaten up with worries, and so he loses the power he sought when he can't rid himself of his anxieties. We come to the same conclusion when we consider honors, glory, and pleasures. For since each of these is the same as the others, whoever seeks one of them without the other ones doesn't even acquire the thing he desires."

"Then what if someone wanted to acquire all of them at the same time?" I said. "He would be seeking the totality of blessedness."

"But he won't find it in these things that can't produce what they promise, will he?"

"Not at all," I said.

"So a man must not in any way seek blessedness from things that he believes will offer only one of the things he seeks."

"I confess it," I said. "Nothing truer than this can be said."

"You have, then, both the form and the causes of false happiness. Now turn your mind's gaze in the other direction, for there you will see immediately the true happiness that I promised you."

"But the conclusion is obvious even to a blind man," I said, "and you pointed it out a little while ago, when you were trying to lay open the causes of the false happiness. Unless I'm mistaken, the true and complete happiness is the one that makes a man perfectly sufficient, powerful, revered, renowned, and joyful. And so that you'll know that I've considered these things deeply within, I will admit without a doubt that the complete blessedness is that which can truly offer any of these things, since they are all the same."

"O my child,[48] how happy you would be in having this opinion, if you would add one thing!"

"What?" I said.

"Do you think there is anything in these mortal, transitory affairs that can bring about such a condition?"

"Not at all, I think. You have demonstrated this well enough that no further arguments are needed."

"Then these things seem to give men images of true good, or some sort of imperfect goods, but they can't confer the true and perfect Good."

"I agree," I said.

"So, since you recognize the blessedness that is true and the ones that are falsely called blessedness, you must now learn where you can seek the true one."

"This is the very thing I've been wanting for a long time now!" I said.

"But since we ought to pray for divine aid even in the least things, as our Plato says in the *Timaeus*,[49] what do you think we should do when we are looking for the foundation of the highest Good?"

"We should call upon the Father of all things. If we leave this out, we can't make a proper beginning for our work."

"Correct," she said, and immediately she began to sing:

[48] *my child*: Gruber, *Kommentar zu Boethius*, p. 276, notes the similarity to 1 *prosa* 3, where Lady Philosophy addresses Boethius as her child (*alumnus*) and promises that she will not abandon him. Lady Philosophy, of course, is true to her word, for she is very close to teaching Boethius the true source of happiness.

[49] *But since we ought to pray . . . in the* Timaeus: In Plato's work *Timaeus*, when Timaeus is about to explain how God made the universe, he notes the need to implore divine aid (27C): "[A]ll men who possess even a small share of good sense call upon God always at the outset of every undertaking, be it small or great: we therefore who are purposing to deliver a discourse concerning the Universe, how it was created or haply is uncreate, must needs invoke Gods and Godesses" (Plato, *Timaeus; Critias; Cleitophan; Menexenus; Epistles*, trans. R. G. Bury, Loeb Classical Library 234 [Cambridge: Harvard University Press, 1929]). The *Timaeus*, which forms the basis for the following poem, "was well known in Boethius' time in partial Latin translation and had been commented on in Greek by the Neoplatonic Proclus (5th century A.D.)" (O'Donnell, *Consolatio philosophiae*, p. 61). On the dialogue itself, see Bury's introduction to the Loeb Classical Library edition, pp. 5–15.

metrum 9[50]

"O Governor of the universe,
Ruler with perpetual reason,[51]
Father[52] of earth and of heaven,
You propel time towards eternity—
Unmoved, you cause all to be moved.[53]
Nothing external bid you make
Your work of flowing matter,
but rather this form, the highest Good innate.[54]

---

[50] *metrum* 9: Gruber, *Kommentar zu Boethius*, p. 275, notes that this poem is found in the middle of the *Consolation* and forms the "pivot and core of the entire work" (our translation of the original German).

On Platonic and Neoplatonic elements in *metrum* 9, see Friedrich Klingner, *De Boethii Consolatione philosophiae*, 2nd ed. (Zurich: Weidmann, 1966; originally published 1921), pp. 38–67, and the long footnote in the Penguin translation (V. E. Watts, *The Consolation of Philosophy* [New York: Penguin, 1969], p. 98).

[51] *O Governor . . . with perpetual reason*: As seen in 1 *metrum* 5 and 1 *prosa* 6, God is the helmsman (here translated as "governor"). Boethius' phrase *perpetua ratione* is rendered here as "with perpetual reason". Some translations use "eternal" instead of "perpetual". Gruber, *Kommentar zu Boethius*, p. 277, suggests that *perpetua* (continuous) is used here instead of *aeterna* (eternal) because of the Platonist view that the world was perpetual rather than eternal. As we will see below, eternal, in the strictest sense, connotes a being that is uncreated and that sees all time at once. See 5 *prosa* 6. See also the references in Fortescue, *Boethius De consolatione*, p. 81.

[52] *Father*: "Father" translates the original Latin *sator* (sower), which perhaps recalls *Aeneid* 1.254 (= 11.725), where Jupiter is spoken of as "sower of gods and men".

[53] *unmoved, you cause all to be moved*: The unmoved mover is defined as follows by Aristotle (*Metaphysics* 1072a24–25): "[T]here is something which moves without being moved, being eternal, substance, and actuality" (trans. W. D. Ross in McKeon, *Introduction to Aristotle*). Gruber, *Kommentar zu Boethius*, p. 278, also cites Augustine's famous description of God in which he describes him as "unchangeable, yet changing all things" (*Confessions* 1.4.4).

[54] *Nothing external bid you make . . . highest Good innate*: S. J. Tester notes that "the only reason for God's creation is the outpouring of good, since the Form of the Good is in him. . . . God creates on the pattern of the eternal Forms, which for the Neo-platonists and their Christian followers were in the mind of God" (H. F. Stewart, E. K. Rand, and S. J. Tester, trans., *The Theological Tractates and the "Consolation of Philosophy"*, Loeb Classical Library 74 [Harvard: Harvard University Press, 1973; originally published 1918], p. 272). Tester's reference to "the Form of the Good" is understood in terms of Plato's theory of forms or ideas. Plato suggested that there were eternal truths, like Justice and Beauty, that the

From heaven's pattern You, in generosity,
derive all, Yourself the most beautiful,[55]
bearing in Your mind a beautiful world,
forming it in like image, ordering
perfect parts to become a perfect world;
all You have completed, bound with numbers.[56]
You join the cold with flame,
the arid with wet,
lest the fire, too light, spin out,
or the earth, by weight overburdened, should sink.
You connect the Soul, triple nature's middle part.[57]

---

soul encountered in a heavenly world it inhabited before it was joined with the body. The body corrupted the soul, causing it to lose memory of these truths. Through anamnesis, a recollection that occurs through the contemplation of the forms, the soul regains knowledge of them, although the knowledge remains incomplete in the earthly world. See Andrew Louth, *The Origins of the Christian Mystical Tradition* (Oxford: Clarendon Press, 1981), pp. 1–7.

[55] *beautiful*: Since the time of Homer, beauty, which was not limited to physical appearance, was the quintessential virtue to the Greeks. In the *Timaeus* (30A–B), Plato refers to the "most good" God as doing nothing except "what is most fair" (*kalliston*); in the *Symposium* (210D–211B), Plato refers to the love of the form of the Beautiful. See Louth, *Origins of the Christian Mystical Tradition*, p. 11, where he refers to "the Form of the Beautiful as transcending the realm of the Forms".

[56] *all You have completed, bound with numbers*: Boethius was a lover of mathematics and saw numbers as expressing divine order. In the *Timaeus* (e.g., 31C) and elsewhere, Plato had made the same connection.

[57] *You connect the Soul, triple nature's middle part*: This line begins a very difficult section. Boethius is again dependent on the *Timaeus*. Fortescue, *Boethius De consolatione*, p. 83, elucidates the Platonic theory as follows (our translation of the original Latin):

> Matter was originally rude, unformed, brutish. To this matter God gave Soul, by which it is given form, is ordered, and lives.... Further, in order that the universe correspond more accurately to the archetype (namely, to divine perfection itself), he confers on it mind or intelligence. The World's Soul not only gives form to and enlivens matter, but it is the chain by which material is connected to the mind; for the mind is not able to connect directly to matter.... Thus we have a triple nature: mind, soul, and matter.... The soul is the middle, able to apprehend both mind and material sensation.... From these three God made one; and in the same way man, a *mikrokosmos*, is one from three: mind, soul, and body.

Fortescue also compares Virgil, *Aeneid* 6.724–32. See also footnote 58 below.

Dispersed through harmonious members,
this Soul, which moves all things,
divided into two orbits,
gathers motion, making a return, and passes
into itself, encircling the vast Mind,
turning the heavens in the same manner.[58]
From like causes You bring forth souls and lesser lives,
equipped with fleet chariots;[59] You plant them aloft
into the heavens and on the earth;
and by Your kind law order them home—
back to You in a journey of fire.
Father! Flash forth in splendor
and scatter the mists of earth!
Permit my spirit to rise—
and grant light to my mind
that I might fix clear sight on You,
Source of all good.
To the blessed, You are quiet calm.
To see You is both purpose and end;
You are the Leader and the Way—
The First and the Last.[60]

10. "So, since you have seen the form of the imperfect good as
well as that of the perfect one, I think we should show where
this perfection of happiness is to be found. In this matter
we must first ask whether any good of the type you defined a

---

[58] *Dispersed through harmonious members . . . in the same manner*: O'Donnell,
Consolatio philosophiae, p. 63, notes that the World Soul "is divided in two parts,
whose motions take the form of twin circles", each of which returns to its origin.
The World Soul also encircles the Mind "at the inner heart of being, and sets
heavens moving in a similar circle". (See also Gruber, *Kommentar zu Boethius*,
p. 282.)

[59] *fleet chariots*: On the winged soul, see Plato, *Phaedrus* 246–47.

[60] *You are . . . the Last*: Watts, *Consolation of Philosophy*, p. 98, and Gruber,
Kommentar Zu Boethius, p. 288, compare John 14:5 where Jesus says "I am the
way, the truth, and the life." See also Rocco Murari, *Dante e Boezio* (Bologna:
Ditta Nicola Zanichelli, 1905), p. 135, regarding the Christian flavor of the
prayer.

little earlier[61] can exist in the world of objects so that we won't be deceived by an ill-conceived image, in contradiction to the truth of the matter at hand. But it can't be denied that this perfect Good exists and is a sort of fountain of all good things; for each thing that is said to be imperfect is given this name because perfection is lessened in it. And so it is that if any sort of thing seems to be imperfect, another thing of the same sort must be perfect; in fact, when the perfection has been removed, one can't even imagine what is the source for the thing that is called imperfect. For the world of objects has not taken her origin from lesser, incomplete things but proceeds from whole and complete objects and slips down into these weak and very lowly ones. But if, as we showed a little while ago, there is a certain imperfect happiness coming from a fragile good, it can't be doubted that there is some steadfast and perfect happiness too."[62]

"Absolutely true, without a doubt," I said.

---

[61] *any good . . . a little earlier*: In 3 *prosa* 9 above, Lady Philosophy had argued that blessedness, equivalent to the highest Good, is indivisible and cannot be acquired piecemeal, by securing individual, finite, temporal things, such as wealth, prestige, or power.

[62] *But it can't be denied . . . perfect happiness too*: Gruber, *Kommentar zu Boethius*, p. 289, compares Aristotle's *De philosophia*, frag. 16: "If there is something better among things, there must be something among them that is best. . . . Accordingly what is best would be God." Fortescue, *Boethius De consolatione*, p. 86, notes that Aquinas' fourth proof for the existence of God reflects the thought of Aristotle and Boethius. Étienne Gilson explains Aquinas' proof as follows:

> [W]e notice that there are things more or less good, more or less noble, more or less true and so on for all kinds of perfection. But the 'more or less' can only be applied to things according as they approximate in different degrees to that which is the particular kind of thing in its supreme degree. Something, for instance, is hotter as it approximates to the highest degree of heat. . . . Consequently there must exist some other thing which is the cause of being and of goodness and of all the perfections of whatever kind which are found in all things, and this is precisely what we call God.

(Étienne Gilson, *The Philosophy of Thomas Aquinas*, translated by Edward Bullough from the 3rd rev. and enlarged ed. of *Le Thomisme* [New York: Barnes and Noble, 1993], p. 87.) Fortescue, *Boethius De consolatione*, p. 86, and Gilson, *Philosophy of Thomas Aquinas*, p. 96, cite *Summa theologica* I, q. 2, art. 3.

"So then, consider where this happiness resides," she said. "The common opinion of human minds concludes that God, the ruler of all things, is good. Since nothing greater than God is able to be imagined, who can doubt that the thing that is surpassed by nothing is good?[63] Truly reason shows that the Good is God, so that He is completely filled with the perfect Good. If it were not so, He would not be able to be the ruler of all things, because there would be something more excellent than He, which would possess perfect Good and would seem to be before Him and more ancient. Things that are perfect are clearly older than things that are less complete.[64] And so, in order not to draw out this argument into eternity, we must confess that God, who is the most high, is completely full of the highest and most perfect Good. But we have concluded that the perfect Good is true blessedness, and thus true blessedness must reside in the most high God."

"I agree," I said. "There's no way anyone could utter a word against this."

"But I ask you," she said, "look at how reverently and without question you approved of our assertion that God, the most high, is completely filled with the highest Good."

"What do you mean?" I said.

"You must not think that this Father of all things either received from outside this highest Good with which He is filled or that He possesses it through nature in such a way that there could be a difference between the substance of the blessedness possessed and the God who possessed it. If you think it has been received from outside, you could judge that the thing which gave it is more excellent than the thing that received it, yet we most rightly confess that He is the most excellent of all things. Now if the Good is present by nature but conceptually

---

[63] *Since nothing greater than God . . . thing that is surpassed by nothing is good*: Fortescue, *Boethius De consolatione*, p. 86, cites Anselm, *Proslogion* 3: "Now we believe that you [God] are something than which nothing greater can be thought" (*Anselm of Canterbury: The Major Works*, trans. Brian Davies and G.R. Evans [Oxford: Oxford University Press, 1998]).

[64] *complete*: The word we have translated as "complete" is *integer*, which implies a wholeness and self-sufficiency.

different from the one whom we are speaking of as God, the ruler of all things, can anyone imagine who joined together these different things? Finally, whatever is different in any way from anything else is not that thing which it differs from. So, whatever is different from the highest Good by its own nature can't be the highest Good, and it would be unspeakable to say this about the one whom we agreed to be surpassed by nothing. In no way can the nature of a thing be better than its origin. So, the thing that is the origin of all things, I would conclude most truly, is the highest Good by its very nature." [65]

"Quite correct," I said.

"But we have admitted that the greatest Good is blessedness."

"So it is," I said.

"And so we must conclude that God is blessedness itself."

"I can't argue against your earlier arguments, and I see clearly that this conclusion follows from them."

"Consider," she said, "whether we can then draw from this argument the same inference with even more certainty: that two highest goods which differ from each other cannot exist. For when goods differ from each other, it is obvious that they can't be the same as each other. So neither can be perfect, since one does not possess the other. What is not perfect is clearly not the highest, so in no way can the goods that are highest differ from each other. But we have concluded that both blessedness and God are the highest Good, and therefore whatever is the highest divinity is also the highest blessedness."

"No conclusion is more true in actuality, more certain in reasoning, or more worthy of God," I said.

"In addition to these arguments, I will provide you with a little corollary, just as geometricians take established premises

[65] *So, the thing that is the origin . . . highest Good by its very nature*: Lady Philosophy argues that God *is* the highest Good, blessedness, not that he simply *contains* it. If the latter were the case, this highest Good would have to come from a source outside God, which would necessarily be greater than God. Fortescue, *Boethius De consolatione*, p. 86, cites Augustine, *On the Trinity* 5.1.2 and 5.2.5, and Aquinas, *Summa theologica* I, q. 3, art. 6–7, and q. 26, art. 2.

and draw conclusions—or *porismata* as they call them.[66] Since
men become blessed from the acquisition of blessedness, and
blessedness is indeed divinity, it is clear that men become
blessed through the acquisition of divinity. But as men become
just by the acquisition of justice, and wise by the acquisition
of wisdom, so it is necessary by the same reasoning that men
who have acquired divinity become gods. Each blessed man is
therefore a god, but indeed in nature God is one; by participation there is nothing to prevent there being as many gods
as you like."[67]

"This is beautiful and priceless, whether you want to call it
a *porisma* or a corollary."

"And nothing can be more beautiful than this conclusion,
which reason would tell us is connected with the former one."

"What?" I said.

"Since blessedness would seem to contain many things, do
these many things all join together like a 'body of blessedness'
with a certain variety of parts, or is there a certain one of them
that brings about the substance of blessedness so that the others are bound up with it?"[68]

---

[66] *In addition to these arguments . . .* porismata *as they call them*: Fortescue,
Boethius De consolatione, p. 88, cites two Dantean parallels, *Purgatorio* 28.134–36
and *Paradiso* 8.137–38. On the word "corollary", see note of O'Donnell, *Consolatio philosophiae*, p. 65: "originally 'a trifling gift' (usually a crown of flowers,
hence a diminutive of *corona*); Boethius uses it to capture the serendipitous quality of this conclusion; something unlooked for but welcome." *Porisma* (*porismata*
in the plural) is the Greek word.

[67] *by participation . . . as many gods as you like*: Luca Obertello notes that the
idea of man's becoming divine by participation has Platonic, Neoplatonic, and
Christian antecedents (Luca Obertello, trans. *La consolazione della filosofia*, Gli
opuscoli teologici [Milan: Rusoni Libri, 1979], p. 224; see Proclus, *In Platonis theo-
logiam* 3.7; John 10:34–35; and 2 Peter 1:4. Fortescue, *Boethius De consolatione*,
p. 88, cites other Christian sources. See especially Aquinas, *Summa theologica*:
"Now men are blessed, as Boethius says, through participation, and thus are called
gods by participation" (I–II, q. 3, art. 1 ad 1). In the Eastern Church, *theosis*, or
divinization, is a fundamental concept. See, e.g., Norman Russell, *The Doctrine
of Deification in the Greek Patristic Tradition* (New York: Oxford, 2006).

[68] *Since blessedness would seem . . . bound up with it?* See *Protagoras* 329B, where
Socrates questions Protagoras' assertion that justice, holiness, and so forth, are
"parts" of virtue: "Do you mean parts, I [Socrates] asked, in the sense of the parts

"Would you clarify this by reminding me of the things them-selves?" I asked.

"Don't we believe that blessedness is a good?" she said.

"And the highest one, too," I said.

"And you can come to the same conclusion about all of these goods. For sufficiency is also the highest blessedness, and power is the highest, and so, too, are respect, and fame and pleasure. What then? Are all these things—goodness, sufficiency, power, and the rest—certain 'limbs' of blessedness, so to speak, or are they all bound to the Good as if it were the 'head'"?

"I understand what you propose to consider, but I want to hear your opinion."

"Then listen to how we'll sort out this question. If these things were 'parts' of beauty, they would, in turn, differ from each other. For it is the nature of parts that, being different, they make up one body. But all of these qualities have proven to be the same thing, and so they are in no way parts; other-wise, blessedness will seem to be something combined from one part, which cannot be."

"That can't be doubted, but I'm waiting for what is yet to come."

"It is clear that the other things are bound up with the Good," she continued. "For that reason, then, sufficiency is sought, since it is considered a good; so, too, with power, since it also is believed to be a good. We can come to the same conclusion concerning respect, fame, and joy. And so the great-est reason for seeking these is the Good. Now something can't in any way be sought unless it contains good in actuality or seems to contain it. Yet, on the other hand, if things are not good by nature, but nevertheless *seem* to be good, they are sought as if they were truly good. And so it happens that the cause and principal reason for seeking all things is rightly thought to be goodness. The *purpose* for which something is

---

of the face, as mouth, nose, eyes, and ears; or, as in the parts of gold, is there no difference among the pieces ... ?" (trans. Lamb). In the subsequent sections, Socrates argues that the latter comparison, with gold, is more apt.

sought seems to be the thing that a person most desires; for
example, if, for the sake of his health, a man wanted to ride a
horse, he would not so much desire the motion of riding as
the result of good health. Therefore, since everything is sought
for the sake of the Good, it is not the things, but the Good
itself, that all desire. And we have concluded that the purpose for which all things are sought is blessedness; therefore,
in this way, too, blessedness alone is sought. From this conclusion, it is obvious that the substance of the Good and of
blessedness are one and the same."

"How could anyone disagree?" I said.

"But we have shown that God and true blessedness are one
and the same."

"Yes," I said.

"So surely we can conclude that the substance of God is
also located in the Good itself and not anywhere else.

metrum 10

> Come here and be freed,
> chained captives of earth
> caught in desire-bound minds.
> Relief, gentle quiet, an asylum—
> a refuge awaits.[69]
> Neither Tagus nor Hermus[70]
> offering ripe golden sands,
> nor hot-flowing Indus,
> brewing its jewels,
> sparkling, gleaming, clear and green[71]—

[69] *Come here and be freed . . . a refuge awaits*: One thinks again of Plato's "Allegory of the Cave" (*Republic* 514A–518B). See also 1 *metrum* 2.24–27. Gruber,
Kommentar zu Boethius, p. 296, and Fortescue, *Boethius De consolatione*, p. 90,
cite Matthew 11:28–29: "Come to me, all you who labor and are heavy laden,
and I will refresh you . . . and you will find rest for your souls" (our translation of
the Vulgate).

[70] *Tagus nor Hermus*: The Tagus is a river in Spain known in antiquity for its
gold. The Hermus, a river in Asia Minor, was similarly known for gold. (See
Virgil, *Georgics* 2.137.)

[71] *hot-flowing Indus . . . clear and green*: The Indus, one of the world's longest
rivers, has its source in Tibet and runs the entire length of Pakistan. The region

can illuminate the vision
of man's darkened mind.
All that charms
has already been nourished
in earth's lowest caverns.
The vast shining Splendor[72]
abhors souls' collapse.[73]
Whoever sees *this* Light,
will say that even the sun—
is not bright." [74]

11. "I agree," I said, "for all of these things are bound together
and are based on the soundest reasoning."

Then she replied, "How much do you think it would be
worth to learn what the Good itself is?"

"It would be beyond price," I said, "if indeed I will come to
recognize God, too, who is the Good."

"I will reveal this with the soundest of reasoning," she said,
"provided we abide by the conclusions we drew a while ago."

"We will."

"Didn't we show," she said, "that those things sought by the
many are not on that account true and perfect goods, since
these objects differ from each other in turn, and since, when
one object lacks the other it can't bring full and absolute good?
And, on the other hand, we agreed that they become the true
Good when they are collected together as one in form and
effect, so to speak, so that what is sufficiency is also power,
reverence, renown, and joy; truly, unless all of them are one
and the same, they do not possess in themselves the things
worth seeking."

---

was famous for its gems, especially pearls and emeralds. See Horace, *Satire* 1.2.80–
82: "Not among white and green jewels is the leg more pretty and tender" (cited
by Gruber, *Kommentar zu Boethius*, p. 297).

[72] *vast shining Splendor*: O'Donnell, *Consolatio philosophiae*, p. 67, compares 2
metrum 8 and 1 *metrum* 5.

[73] *souls' collapse*: O'Daly, *Poetry of Boethius*, p. 167, notes that the soul's collapse "is undoubtedly reflecting the Platonic notion of the soul's fall" in the *Phaedrus*.

[74] *bright*: Boethius uses *candidus* (bright, sparkling white), the same adjective
used to describe the pearls above.

"This has been shown," I said, "and can't in any way be doubted."

"And so these things aren't goods at all when they differ from each other, but when they become one, on the other hand, they become goods. So does it not happen that they become good by the acquisition of unity?"

"So it seems," I said.

"But everything that is good—would you grant that it is good through participation in the Good?"[75]

"Yes, it is."

"So we must admit that oneness and the Good are the same, by a similar reasoning, since they have the same substance, when, by their natures, their effects are not different."

"I can't deny it," I said.

"Do you know, therefore," she said, "that everything which exists remains and continues for as long as it is one, but it perishes and dissolves as soon as it ceases to have unity?"

"How so?"

"Just as in living things, when body and spirit come together into one, it is called a living thing;[76] but when this unity is dissolved by the separation of the two, one can say that the living thing has died and no longer exists. When the body itself continues in one form, by the union of its parts, a human appearance is seen. But if the parts of the body, divided and separated, dissolve, the unity of the thing that had once existed ceases to be. In the same way, if one examines other things, it will be obvious without a doubt that everything continues while it is one, but perishes when it ceases to be one."

"I can think of many other examples, and they all lead to the same conclusion," I replied.

---

[75] *it is good through participation in the Good*: In one of the theological tractates, "How Substances Are Good in Their Existence without Being Substantial Good" (*Quomodo substantiae . . .*), Boethius explains how objects are good by participation, thus owing their goodness to God. See Stewart, Rand, and Tester, *Theological Tractates*, pp. 38–51.

[76] *when body and spirit . . . a living thing*: Cf. Augustine, *City of God* 9.9: "For a living thing, that is, an animal, consists of spirit and body."

"Then is there anything, while acting according to its nature, that leaves behind its desire to exist and wishes to arrive at death and destruction?"

"If I consider living creatures that have some capacity to want something or not to want it, I find nothing that casts away its desire to exist and willingly hurries to its own destruction without being compelled by an outside force. For every living thing strives to preserve its safety and indeed to avoid death and ruin. But I have no idea what to think about plants and trees and about things that don't contain life."

"But you shouldn't have any doubt about them either, since you see plants and trees growing in places suitable to them, where, insofar as nature allows, they can't dry up and die. For some spring up in fields and others in mountains; swamps bear others, and others cling to rocks; still others are nourished by the sterile sands and would shrivel up if someone tried to transplant them anywhere else. But to each being nature gives what is needed and strives to keep it from dying, as long as it is able to exist. Consider how all these plants draw nourishment through their roots, as if their mouths were plunged down into the ground, so to speak, and how they distribute their nourishment through their bark and fibers. Consider how anything soft, like the pith, is always hidden in the interior recesses, with a somewhat tougher part of the wood outside it. Then the bark is placed on the outside against the intemperance of the heavens, as an enduring defense against harm. How much diligence nature has in propagating everything through the multiplication of seed! Who wouldn't know that all of these things are a sort of 'mechanism,' not just for a time but everlasting into eternity. These things that are believed to be inanimate desire in similar ways what accords with their nature. Why does lightness lift up flames, while weight presses down the earth, unless it is because these places and motions are suitable for each object?[77] Moreover, every object seeks what

[77] *Why does lightness . . . suitable for each object?* Cf. Virgil's words in Dante's *Purgatorio* (cited by Fortescue, *Boethius De consolatione*, p. 93):

is fitting for itself; similarly, each one destroys what is hostile. For instance, things that are hard, like stones, cling tenaciously to their parts and resist being easily dissolved. Those that are fluid, like air and water, easily yield to things dividing them, but quickly flow back to what they were separated from; fire, however, resists all separation.

"We are not dealing with the voluntary impulses of a conscious mind, but with natural impulses, such as when we digest without thinking about the food we receive or draw breath unaware in our sleep. For the desire to exist, even in living things, doesn't come from the wishes of the mind, but rather from the laws of nature.[78] Often, when circumstances bring death, which nature abhors, the will embraces it; on the other hand, the task of reproducing, by which alone mortal creatures continue to exist, is always sought by nature but restrained by the will. And so this love for oneself proceeds not from the promptings of the living thing, but from natural impulse. Providence gave to things created by themselves this greatest concern for existing, so that they naturally seek to exist insofar as they are able. And so there is no reason to doubt that all living things naturally seek permanent existence and avoid destruction."

> "Just as a fire's flames always rise up,
> inspired by its own nature to ascend,
> seeking to be in its own element,
>
> just so, the captive soul begins its quest,
> the spiritual movement of its love,
> not resting till the thing loved is enjoyed."
> (18.28–33; trans. Musa)

Virgil goes on to suggest that the goodness of love is to be determined by the object of the love.

[78] *For the desire to exist . . . laws of nature*: Boethius argues that by nature all things seek to exist as intact entity. As Henry Chadwick notes, "The will to subsist is the desire not to fall apart but to remain one. . . . Accordingly we look for an infinite first cause which is a simple undivided whole, free of the limitation resulting from division" (Henry Chadwick, *Boethius: The Consolations of Music, Logic, Theology, and Philosophy* [Oxford: Oxford University Press, 1981], p. 236). In theological terms one could argue that the creature, by natural law, seeks its Creator.

"I agree," I said, "and I perceive now without a doubt those things that seemed uncertain before."

"And a thing that seeks to subsist and endure desires to be one, for if this unity is taken away, nothing can continue to exist," she said.

"It is true," I replied.

"So everything desires oneness," she said.

"I agree."

"But we have shown that this very oneness is the Good."

"Yes, indeed."

"So everything seeks the Good, and indeed you may describe this Good as that which is desired by all."

"Nothing can be more true," I said, "for either all things are bound up with no oneness and, being deprived of oneness, they flow without a guide, or if there is anything to which all things universally hurry, it will be the highest of all goods."[79]

And she replied, "I am delighted that you have planted in your mind this very cornerstone of truth. And in this assertion, the thing you were unaware of a little while ago[80] becomes obvious."

"What?" I said.

"The end of all things. For it is surely that which is desired by all, and since we were calling this the Good, we must confess that the end of all things is the Good.

[79] *either all things are bound up . . . highest of all goods*: Fortescue, *Boethius De consolatione*, p. 94, again cites *Purgatorio*:

> Now, since it is a fact that love cannot
> ignore the welfare of the loving self,
> there's nothing in the world can hate itself;
>
> and since no being can be conceived as being
> all in itself, severed from the First Being,
> no creature has the power to hate his God.
> (17.106–11; trans. Musa)

Musa, *Dante's "Purgatory"*, p. 185, notes that this important discourse on love is found at the very center of the *Divine Comedy*.

[80] *thing you were unaware of a little while ago*: In 1 *prosa* 6 Boethius had expressed uncertainty regarding the end to which all things strive.

metrum 11

> He who would track the truth,
> and resist false paths,
> must turn back the light of innermost sight.
> Guiding reflection into a circle curved round,
> Reason finds that what is labored for without
> can be discovered—from a treasury within.[81]
> This image once buried in darkness
> dawns forth! Shining brighter than Phoebus[82] himself—
> for not all mind's light is captured
> by man's matter and mass.
> Inside clings truth's seed, submerged in the soul.
> Learning summons—like breath blown
> on the kindling of right judgment.
> If Plato's Muse sings the truth,
> what man learns is but memory forgotten."[83]

12. Then I replied, "I strongly agree with Plato, for you are reminding me of these things now for the second time. The first time was after I lost my memory from the contamination of the body, and then I lost it when I was pressed down by the heavy weight of my sorrow."

Then she said, "If you should look at the conclusions drawn earlier, you will not be far from remembering what you said a while ago you didn't know."

[81] *Reason finds that what is labored . . . treasury within*: Gruber, *Kommentar zu Boethius*, p. 303, compares Augustine, *Confessions* 7.10: "Under your [God's] guidance I entered into the depths of my soul, and this I was able to do because *your aid befriended me*. I entered and with the eyes of my soul, such as it was, I saw the light that never changes casting its rays over the same eye of my soul, over my mind" (Augustine, *Confessions*, trans. R. S. Pine-Coffin [New York: Penguin, 1961]; emphasis in original).

[82] *Phoebus*: Phoebus Apollo was considered the god of the sun.

[83] *If Plato's Muse sings . . . memory forgotten*: Plato considered learning to be anamnesis (remembering), when the soul in this life recalls what it had known before it was born into a body. See *Meno* 81C–86C and *Phaedrus* 72E–77E and 249C. See also Cicero, *Tusculan Disputations* 1.58 (cited by Gruber, *Kommentar zu Boethius*, p. 305): "So learning is nothing other than remembering." Fortescue, *Boethius De consolatione*, p. 96, notes that the Platonic concept of souls existing before birth was supported by Origen and others in the Church but was condemned in 1215 by the Second Lateran Council.

"What?" I said.

"With what rudders the world is steered," [84] she said.

"I remember," I said, "that I confessed my ignorance. But I still want you to tell me plainly what you are coming to, although now I can see it at a distance."

"You were thinking a little while ago that one could hardly doubt that the world was ruled by God," she said.[85]

"I don't think it can be doubted now either, nor will I ever think so. And I will briefly give my reasons for coming to this conclusion. The world would not have come together from so many diverse, contrary parts, unless there were one who had joined together such diverse things.[86] The diversity of natures joined together, discordant from each other in turn, would divide and break apart, without someone to hold together what he had joined. Such an established order of nature would not proceed, nor would things order themselves into motions determined as they are in location, time, efficiency, space, and properties,[87] unless there were one who, while remaining the same, ordered these various alterations. Whatever this thing is through which created things exist and are set in motion, I will call by a name that all men use, God."

Then she spoke, "Since you have this opinion, I think I only need to do a little more work to enable you to return to

[84] *With what rudders the world is steered:* See 1 *prosa* 6, where Boethius professed not to know the answer to this question.

[85] *You were thinking . . . world was ruled by God:* See again 1 *prosa* 6, where Boethius states that he never doubted that there was a God but that he was unable to understand the apparent unfairness of God's actions. Essentially he was doubting God's goodness and concern for mankind. In the following paragraph, Boethius begins to take charge of the direction of the dialogue—a sign of his progress.

[86] *The world would not have come together . . . such diverse things:* Fortescue, *Boethius De consolatione*, p. 97, notes that this argument is the basis for Aquinas' fifth proof for the existence of God. See *Summa theologica* I, q. 2, art. 3, and Gilson, *Philosophy of Thomas Aquinas*, pp. 92–93. Fortescue also notes that a similar argument had been made by Cicero in *Tusculan Disputations* 1.28–29.

[87] *location, time, efficiency, space, and properties:* O'Donnell, *Consolatio philosophiae*, p. 71, notes that "these five terms are a virtual inventory of the ancient philosophical terms for all possible forms of motion."

your fatherland[88] safe and possessed of happiness. But let's look at the conclusions we have proposed. Didn't we count sufficiency as a part of blessedness, and haven't we concluded that God is blessedness itself?"

"Yes, indeed."

"And so," she said, "He will be in no need of outside support to help Him govern the universe; otherwise, if He should need anything, He will not have full sufficiency."

"That must be the case," I said.

"And He orders all things through Himself alone?"

"It cannot be denied," I said.

"Now God has been shown to be the Good itself."

"I remember," I said.

"So He orders all things in accordance with the Good, if, in fact, He rules everything through Himself, whom we have concluded to be good. And He is, so to speak, a kind of helm and rudder[89] with which the mechanism of the universe is preserved stable and incorrupt."

"I couldn't agree more, and that was what I expected you to say, although I was a little uncertain."

"I believe you," she said, "for I now think you are directing your gaze more carefully in discerning the truth. But what I am getting ready to say is no less obvious."

"What?" I said.

"Since God," she said, "is rightly believed to steer all things with the helm of goodness, and all these very things, as I taught you, hurry towards the Good by natural inclination, surely it can't be doubted that things possessing a will freely direct themselves towards the will of the one ordering them, as if they were agreeable and accommodating to their ruler?"

"This would be necessary," I said. "The governance would not seem to be blessed if it were a yoke for those refusing it, rather than a source of protection for those compliant to it."

[88] *return to your fatherland*: Lady Philosophy again uses the metaphor of the return from exile to describe Boethius' spiritual crisis, as we saw often in book 1 (e.g., *prosa* 5).

[89] *a kind of helm and rudder*: Gruber, *Kommentar zu Boethius*, p. 307, refers the reader to 1 *prosa* 6 and 3 *metrum* 9.

"So is there nothing that tries to act contrary to God, while still following nature?"

"Nothing," I said.

"But if it should try, surely in the end it would have no success in opposing the one we have rightly judged most powerful because of His blessedness."

"No success at all," I said.

"So there is not anything that would either want or be able to resist this highest Good?"

"Nothing, I think."

"So it is the highest Good that rules all things boldly, and pleasantly arranges them,"[90] she said.

Then I replied, "How delightful your conclusion is, and the words you use bring even more delight. They are enough to make Folly itself feel ashamed as she tears down things that are great."

---

[90] *So it is the highest Good . . . pleasantly arranges them*: There is great dispute as to whether or not Lady Philosophy is supposed to be referring to the book of Wisdom (8:1). Here is the Latin of both passages: "'Est igitur summum,' inquit, 'bonum quod regit cuncta fortiter suaviterque disponit'" (*Consolation*); "[Sapientia] attingit ergo a fine usque ad finem fortiter et disponit omnia suaviter" ([Wisdom] reaches boldly from end to end, and arranges all things pleasantly). Edward Kennedy Rand sees the similarity as accidental (Edward Kennard Rand, "On the Composition of Boethius' *Consolatio philosophiae*", *Harvard Studies in Classical Philology* 15 [1904]: 26), while Fortescue, *Boethius De consolatione*, p. 98, considers it *certissima* (most certain) and also compares Wisdom 12:15. Lewis, *Discarded Image*, p. 79, and O'Donnell, *Consolatio philosophiae*, p. 72, also seem to accept the words as a scriptural allusion. For further discussion, see Gruber, *Kommentar zu Boethius*, p. 308; P. G. Walsh, trans., *"The Consolation of Philosophy"*, *Translated with Introduction and Explanatory Notes* (Oxford: Clarendon Press, 1999), p. 143; and Margaret Gibson, ed., *Boethius, His Life, Thought and Influence* (Oxford: Basil Blackwell, 1981), p. 102.

It seems likely that the book of Wisdom is being referred to for the following reasons: (1) the great similarity of the wording; (2) Boethius' approval of Lady Philosophy's wording; (3) the likelihood that Boethius would be attracted to a passage on Sapientia (Wisdom); and (4) the great popularity of the book of Wisdom among the Church Fathers and in the liturgy. Sapientia is personified in the book of Wisdom and was often identified by the Fathers as referring to Christ the incarnate Word (Latin *verbum* or Greek *logos*).

Jean de Meun has Reason approvingly cite the Boethian passage at *Romance of the Rose* 6291–99.

"You have heard in stories about the Giants who provoked the heavens, she said, but kindly strength dealt appropriately with them."[91]

"Now do you want us to bring our ideas together into conflict?" she continued. "Perhaps from such a collision some beautiful spark of truth might fly forth."

"As you think best," I said.

"No one doubts that God holds power over everything," she said.

"No one of sound mind would have any doubt."

"But if a person has power over everything, there is nothing he can't do."

"Nothing," I said.

"Surely, then, God can do evil."

"Not at all," I said.

"So evil is nothing," she said, "since the one who can do everything is unable to do it."[92]

"Are you toying with me and turning me around in an impossible maze of logic? For now you enter by the way you left, and then you leave by the way you entered. Or are you weaving some wonderful web of divine simplicity?[93] A little while

---

[91] *Giants who provoked . . . dealt appropriately with them*: The story of the Giants attacking Zeus goes back to Hesiod, although Boethius is probably thinking of Horace, *Ode* 2.11.21–22, or Ovid, *Metamorphoses* 1.152, or both. The attack was seen as a vain act of hubris and as such was depicted on the east pediment of the Parthenon. Cf. the image Lady Philosophy uses in 1 *prosa* 3 of the unsuccessful attack on the tower of wisdom.

[92] *So evil is nothing . . . unable to do it*: As Boethius will note below, Lady Philosophy's proposition is initially hard to accept but is logical. Evil, as such, does not exist but is only the absence of good. Gruber, *Kommentar zu Boethius*, p. 309, cites Augustine, *Confessions* 7.12: "Therefore, whatever is, is good; and evil, the origin of which I was trying to find, is not a substance, because if it were a substance, it would be good" (trans. Pine-Coffin), and *Soliloquies* 1.2.71: "God, who . . . showest evil to be nothing" (Augustine, *Basic Writings of Augustine*, ed. Whitney J. Oates, vol. 1 [New York: Random House, 1948]). Fortescue, *Boethius De consolatione*, p. 99, cites Aquinas, *Summa theologica* I, q. 14, art. 10. One thinks also of the goodness ascribed to creation in Genesis 1.

[93] *Or are you weaving . . . divine simplicity?* On weaving (*complicare*) a web of simplicity (*simplicitas*), see O'Donnell, *Consolatio philosophiae*, p. 73, who notes, "[T]he two words [*simplicitas* and *complicare*] from the same root but with opposed

earlier, you started with blessedness and showed that it was the highest Good, which you were saying was located in God, who is highest. And you were also saying that God was the greatest Good and the fullness of blessedness, and you added as a little bonus that no one was blessed unless he was united with God. And, likewise, you were saying that the form of the Good was of the same substance as that of God and blessedness, and you taught me that oneness was also goodness itself, since all things sought it by their nature. And you argued that God ruled the universe with the rudders of goodness, that everything willingly obeyed Him, and that nothing had a nature that was evil. Moreover, you explicated these not by premises taken from elsewhere,[94] but rather by inherent and natural proofs drawing their support from each other."

Then she replied, "No, I am not toying with you, and we worked out this, the greatest matter of all, through the gift of the God whom we prayed to a while ago. For the form of divine substance is such that it does not slip away into external things, nor does it assume external things into itself; rather, as Parmenides speaks of it: 'like a sphere in body, well-rounded on all sides,'[95] it turns the moving orb of the universe, while it keeps itself unmoved.[96] But, if we have used arguments not

<hr/>

meanings emphasize the paradox of divine order: innately simple but complex from the point of view of human understanding. Boethius will continue to play with words containing the root—*plic* [wind, coil]—throughout the rest of the *Consolatio*."

[94] *you explicated these not by premises taken from elsewhere*: O'Donnell, *Consolatio philosophiae*, p. 73, notes that this phrase is "taken by some to be a way of saying that no reference is made here to Christian revelation."

[95] *as Parmenides speaks of it: 'like a sphere . . . on all sides'*: See Parmenides in Hermann Diels, *Die Fragmente der Vorsokratiker* (Berlin: Weidmann, 1954), 28B.8.43, also quoted by Plato, *Sophist* 244E, and by many Neoplatonic philosophers. See Pierre Courcelle, *"La consolation de philosophie" dans la tradition littéraire: Antécédents et postérité de Boèce* (Paris: Études augustiniennes, 1967), p. 166.

[96] *it turns the moving orb . . . it keeps itself unmoved*: It is a commonplace since Aristotle (*Metaphysics* 1072a) that God is the Prime Mover, always causing motion but not itself being moved: "[T]here is something which moves without being moved, being eternal, substance, and achievability" (trans. W. D. Ross in McKeon, *Introduction to Aristotle*). See also Augustine, *Confessions* 1.4: "You [God] are

sought from outside but those within the borders of the subject, you shouldn't at all be surprised, since you have learned
under Plato's blessing that conversations are supposed to be
related to the things they are discussing.[97]

metrum 12[98]

> Happy is he who can see,
> who perceives the clear source of the Good,
> Happy is he who loosens the bonds,
> who slips the prison of earth.[99]
> Consider the Thracian bard,[100]

---

unchangeable and yet you change all things, you are ever new, ever old, and yet
all things have new life from you.... You are ever active, yet always at rest"
(trans. Pine-Coffin).

[97] *conversations are supposed to be . . . things they are discussing*: See O'Donnell,
Consolatio philosophiae, p. 73: "a reference to *Timaeus* 29 B (the same part of the
work which provided the content for [3 *metrum* 9])".

[98] *metrum 12*: This is one of the most discussed of Boethius' poems. See
O'Daly, *Poetry of Boethius*, pp. 189–207; Seth Lerer, *Boethius and Dialogue: Literary Method in the "Consolation of Philosophy"* [Princeton, N.J.: Princeton University Press, 1985], pp. 154–65; Anna M. Crabbe, "Literary Design in the *De
consolatione philosophiae*", in *Boethius: His Life, Thought and Influence*, ed. Margaret Gibson (Oxford: Basil Blackwell, 1981), pp. 313–18; Gruber, *Kommentar zu
Boethius*, pp. 311–15; and Helga Scheible, *Die Gedichte in der "Consolatio
philosophiae" des Boethius* (Heidelberg: Carl Winter, 1972), pp. 118–25.

[99] *Happy is he who loosens . . . prison of earth*: On the soul as bound or in
prison, see 2 *prosa* 7 and Plato, *Republic*, "Allegory of the Cave"; *Phaedrus* 250C;
Phaedo 62B; and *Cratylus* 400.

[100] *Thracian bard*: The Thracian bard is Orpheus, a famous singer in antiquity
whose music was so beautiful that it had the power to soothe beasts or move inanimate objects. His story is often told, the most famous versions being found in
Virgil, *Georgics* 4.453–558; Ovid, *Metamorphoses* 10.1–122 and 11.1–117ff.; Seneca,
Hercules furens 569–89; and Seneca, *Hercules Oetaeus* 1031–99. The general version of the story is that on the day that Orpheus was to marry his beloved Eurydice,
she was bitten by a snake and died. Orpheus went to the underworld to retrieve
her, and with his music he charmed the denizens of the underworld, including
Hades himself. The latter agreed to let Orpheus bring Eurydice back to the world
above, provided that he not look back at her until they reached the realm of the
living. Of course, Orpheus, at the last minute, looks at Eurydice and loses her.

Boethius uses the Orpheus motif throughout the *metrum*. Although a purely
allegorical reading of the poem fails, we could probably liken Orpheus to Boethius or anyone else who is attempting to ascend, in a Platonic manner, to the

who, with sad song,
mourned the death of his wife.
He, who compelled still forests to run
and swift waters to stand,
yoked mild deer to savage lion.
And the hound, made placid by his song,
is no longer feared by the hare.
He, whose songs subdued all—
when his own passion burned hot,
these songs their own master couldn't soothe.
Bewailing the harshness of the gods,
he traveled to their home below.
Blending soothing songs with lyre strings,
skills learned from his goddess mother,[101]
he laments all, all which his mourning gave—
and he rues the love that doubled his grief.
He moved Taenarus,[102] and with sweet prayer—
he begs pardon from the lords of the shades.
The threefold doorkeeper[103] stands still,
captured by his strange song;
the avenging goddesses, who drive by fear
the guilty wicked ones, now become sad,
and drench themselves with tears.
Ixion's swift-turning wheel halts,
no longer hastening his head in circles;

---

light but fails through looking (downward) at earthly, temporal things. Orpheus'
love for Eurydice is noble and admirable but in the end earthly, as Crabbe, "Literary Design", pp. 314 and 317, notes.

[101] *his goddess mother*: Orpheus' mother is the Muse Calliope.

[102] *Taenarus*: Taenarus, in the Greek Peloponnese, was fabled to be an entrance
to the underworld.

[103] *threefold doorkeeper*: Cerberus is the three-headed dog that guards the underworld. Boethius will go on to include the usual cast of characters in the underworld: "the avenging goddesses" (the Furies), Ixion, Tantalus, and Tityus. Ixion,
who had attempted to rape Juno, was tied to a wheel that spun eternally. Tantalus, who had tried to feed his son to the gods, was "tantalized" by having food
and water placed just out of his reach. Tityus, who had tried to rape Leto, the
mother of Apollo and Diana, was condemned to have an eagle eat his liver
(which continued to regrow, only to be eaten again). The "arbiter of the shades"
is Hades.

desperate Tantalus with eternal thirst
spurns the river's water;
and the vulture, tearing Tityus' liver, stops.
Finally, 'We are conquered,'
declared the merciful arbiter of the shades:
'We grant him his companion,
his spouse bought with song.
But let this law bind the gift:
Until he leaves Tartarus' [104] darkness—
he mustn't turn back his gaze!'
Who can give rules to lovers?
Love itself is a greater law.
Alas, near the end of his night,
Orpheus his own Eurydice
saw, lost, and killed.
This story is for you,
for those who wish to lead
the mind into the upper day.
Since, whoever, having been weakened,
turns back a gaze to Tartarus' chasm—
whatever excellence he has gained,
looking back, he loses."

---

[104] *Tartarus*': Tartarus is another name for the underworld, although it usually
denotes specifically the place of punishment.

Book 4[1]

1. Lady Philosophy had finished her sweet, soothing song, all the while keeping a look of dignity and a serious expression, and she intended to say something more, when I broke in, still remembering the grief deep within. "You who lead the way for the true light,"[2] I said, "the words you've said so far are clearly divine in and of themselves, and they seem compelling, too, when I consider your arguments. The recent pain of my mistreatment made me forget, though earlier I had the knowledge of them. But this one thing is the cause of my sorrow: if the ruler of the universe is in fact good, how can evil exist or go unpunished? Surely you've thought about how strange this is. And I'll add one thing more: while wickedness thrives and rules the day, virtue lacks reward and is even overthrown and trampled underfoot by wicked men.[3] Virtue, not vice, is punished. A man can't find words to express his confusion and anger that all these things occur in the kingdom of One who has all knowledge, all power, and who wants only good."

Then she replied, "It would be infinitely strange and more frightening than any horrors if, as you suppose, in this

[1] *Book 4*: So far Boethius has learned the futility of passing goods (books 1 and 2) and the nature of the highest Good (book 3), which alone brings true happiness, or blessedness. Boethius still must deal with two troubling questions. In book 4, Boethius will examine the nature of evil and God's apparent indifference to it. In book 5, he will come to grips with the question of divine foreknowledge, which Boethius initially sees as a challenge to man's free will and hence to the possibility of appropriate reward or punishment for human actions.

[2] *true light*: Joachim Gruber notes, "Das *verum lumen* ist Gott" (the true light is God) and cites 3 *metrum* 9 and 5 *prosa* 6, paragraph 5 (Joachim Gruber, *Kommentar zu Boethius, "De consolatione philosophiae"*, 2nd ed. [Berlin: Walter de Gruyter, 2006; originally published 1978], p. 317).

[3] *But this one thing . . . trampled underfoot by wicked men*: These were Boethius' complaints in book 1.

best-ordered house of such a Father, the cheap household stuff[4]
were cherished, so to speak, and the precious things were left
uncared for. But it is not so. If those conclusions we reached a
while ago aren't overturned, the very God whose rule you were
speaking of will make you see that the good are always powerful and the wicked always abject and helpless, that vices are
never without punishment or virtues without reward, and that
happiness always falls to good men and misfortune to evil ones.[5]
And there are arguments of this sort that will lay your complaints to rest and strengthen you with certain confidence. Since
a while ago you saw the form of the true blessedness I showed
you, and since you recognized where it was placed, I'll show
you the way back home, after we've been though the arguments we must consider. I'll give you wings that will lift you
up on high,[6] so your fear can be cast aside, and you can return
unhurt to your fatherland. I will guide you, lead you, and even
carry you on your way.

metrum 1

> With swift wings your mind
> will soar the heaven-heights,

---

[4] *household stuff*: Boethius uses the word *vasa* (pots, vessels). Adrian Fortescue
compares the use of the word in the Vulgate in Romans 9:21–23 and 2 Timothy
2:20 (Adrian Fortescue, *Ancius Manlius Severinus Boethius De consolatione
philosophiae libri quinque*, ed. G. D. Smith [Hildesheim: Georg Olms, 1976; originally published in London, 1925], p. 102).

[5] *the good are always powerful . . . misfortune to evil ones*: Cf. Plato, *Republic*
354A: "The just soul and the just man then will live well and the unjust ill."
See other citations by Fortescue, *Boethius De consolatione*, p. 103. Like Boethius,
Plato argues that justice is intrinsically linked with true happiness.

[6] *I'll give you wings that will lift you up on high*: Again, the idea of the winged
mind is reminiscent of Plato's *Phaedrus*. The motif of the soul's exile was prominent in book 1. For Lady Philosophy as both a guide and a path, cf. Augustine,
De doctrina christiana 1.11, where Augustine speaks of wisdom personified: "So
since she herself is our home, she also made herself for us into the way home"
(Augustine, *Teaching Christianity: De doctrina christiana*, trans. with notes by
Edmund Hill [New York: New City Press, 1996], p. 111). In 1.9–10, Augustine,
like Boethius, uses the metaphor of exile to illustrate a mind lacking in perception.

above the sky,[7]
leaving clouds behind,
will look and scorn the earth.
Climbing beyond the fire point,[8]
it will reach the house of stars
and join Phoebus on his path.
It will ride with cold Saturn,
companion of the flashing sphere,[9]
a soldier of his shining rays.
Turning with the starry circles,
watching the night be made,
higher and higher it will climb
reaching the farthest pole—
then share the holy light.
Here the Lord of kings,
the shining Master of all,
holds the reins, though unmoving,
and guides the swift chariot.[10]
If then the path turns you back

[7] *With swift wings your mind . . . above the sky*: Fortescue, *Boethius De conso-latione*, p. 103, cites Dante, *Paradiso* 15.53–54, where a soul in heaven refers to Beatrice's aid of Dante: "[T]hanks be to her/who gave you wings to make this lofty flight" (*Dante's "Paradise"*, trans. Mark Musa [Bloomington: University of Indiana Press, 1984]).
[8] *fire point*: The "fire point" refers to the ether, which was conceived of as the lightest of the four elements: water, earth, air, and fire (ether). See, e.g., Ovid, *Metamorphoses* 1.34–40, where the creation of the earth is being described:

> The fiery and weightless aether leapt
> to heaven's vault and claimed its citadel;
> the next in lightness to be placed was air;
> the denser earth drew down gross elements
> and was compressed by its own gravity;
> encircling water last found its place,
> encompassing the solid earth entire.

(Ovid, *Metamorphoses*, trans. Charles Martin [New York: W. W. Norton and Co., 2004].)
[9] *cold Saturn,/companion of the flashing sphere*: Saturn was considered a cold planet, while the "flashing sphere" refers to Mars, the god of war.
[10] *swift chariot*: See *Phaedrus* 246E: "Now the great leader in heaven, Zeus, driving a winged chariot, goes first, arranging all things and caring for all things"

to this forgotten place you seek,
you will cry out, 'I remember![11]
This is my home, my source, my end.'
Should you choose to gaze on the night
of the earth left behind,
you will see tyrant exiles,[12]
whom the wretched fear."

2. "Wonderful! What great things you promise! And I have no doubt you can follow through with them," I replied. "But don't keep me waiting when you've raised my hopes like this."

"First, then," she said, "you can see that good men always have power and that evil ones lose all their strength; and we can prove one of these assertions from the other.[13] For since good and evil are opposite, if goodness is agreed to be powerful, then the weakness of evil is obvious, and if the fragility of evil is manifest, the strength of good is manifest. But so you can have more faith in my conclusions, I'll go down both paths and demonstrate our proposition first in one direction and then in the other.

"Human actions are accomplished through two means: will and power. If either of them is absent, nothing can be done. If the will is lacking, no one even begins anything, since he doesn't want to do it. But if power is lacking, the will to act would be in vain. So it is, that if you should see someone wanting to obtain something that he wasn't obtaining, you would have to assume that he didn't have the strength to obtain it."

(Plato, *Euthyphro*; *Apology*; *Crito*; *Phaedo*; *Phaedrus*, trans. Harold North Fowler, Loeb Classical Library 36 [Cambridge: Harvard University Press, 1914]).

[11] *I remember!* Through Platonic anamnesis the soul regains the knowledge of where it originated, the divine world of the forms.

[12] *tyrant exiles*: Despite tyrants' formidable appearance in the world, which one sees when one's eyes are focused on the earth, such rulers are exiled and unconnected with the homeland; they therefore have no real power. Cf. 1 *metrum* 4: "Why do miserable men wonder at raging tyrants with no true strength?"

[13] *you can see that good men . . . these assertions from the other*: In sections 2 and 3, Boethius will follow closely the arguments of Socrates in Plato, *Gorgias* 466–527, where Socrates argues that good men are more fortunate than bad ones and that those who do evil and go unpunished are the most miserable of all. These men, as Boethius will later conclude, do not receive the healing of soul that is brought about by just punishment.

"That's obvious," I said. "There's no way to deny it."

"But if you saw that someone had accomplished what he wanted, you wouldn't doubt that he had the power to do it, would you?"

"No," I said.

"Now in whatever area a man has ability, he is strong, but in whatever area he doesn't have ability, he is weak."

"I agree," I said.

"So then," she said, "do you remember from our earlier arguments that all efforts of the human will work together to pursue blessedness, although it is pursued by different paths?"

"Yes, we've shown this; I remember," I said.

"And so you recall that blessedness is the Good itself, and therefore all men desire the Good when they seek blessedness?"

"I don't just recall it; I have it fixed firmly in my mind."

"So all men, both good and bad alike, with the same intent, strive to reach the Good." [14]

"Yes," I said, "that follows."

"But certainly men become good by attaining the Good."

"Certainly."

"So good men acquire what they seek?"

"Yes, it seems that way," I replied.

"But if evil men acquired what they wanted, which is the Good, then they couldn't be evil."

"Yes, that's true."

"Now since both seek the Good, but good men acquire it and evil men don't, we can hardly doubt that good men are powerful and evil ones are weak." [15]

"Anyone who doubts it can't be thinking of the way things work or of the conclusions we reached," I said.

---

[14] *So all men, both good and bad alike, . . . strive to reach the Good*: Fortescue, *Boethius De consolatione*, p. 106, cites Aquinas, *Summa contra gentiles* 3.3, and Dante, *Purgatorio* 17.127–29. In the passage from the *Purgatorio*, Virgil is discussing the nature of love and how humans pervert it: "All of you, vaguely, apprehend and crave/a good with which your heart can be at rest;/and so, each of you strives to reach that goal" (*Dante's "Purgatory"*, trans. Mark Musa [Bloomington: University of Indiana Press, 1981).

[15] *Now since both seek the Good . . . evil ones are weak*: See *Gorgias* 463E, 469B, and 469E (cited by Fortescue, *Boethius De consolatione*, p. 106).

"Now again, if there were two men, and they were given the same natural action to do, and one of them performed the action in a natural way and accomplished it, but the other man couldn't carry out the natural task, but failed to accomplish it in a natural manner, instead imitating the one who accomplished it, which of the two would you consider the stronger?"

"I can guess what you're aiming at," I said, "but I would still like to hear it expressed more plainly."

"You wouldn't deny that the motion of walking is natural to humans, would you?"

"No, indeed," I said.

"And so if one man moved about by walking on his feet, and another one couldn't walk naturally with his feet but tried to walk by using his hands, which of the two would you consider more able?"

"Construct the rest of your argument," I said. "For there's no doubt that the one who could perform the natural function would be more able than the one who couldn't."

"But indeed good men seek through the natural function of their virtues the highest Good, which is set before good men and evil ones alike, while evil men seek to attain the very same thing through their changeable desires, which is not the natural function for obtaining the Good. Or do you have a different opinion?"

"No," I said, "and what follows is also obvious. From these arguments I've granted, we have to conclude that good men are truly powerful and evil men weak."

"Right!" she said. "You're getting ahead of me. This is the sort of thing physicians hope for, a sign of an alert and resilient nature. But since I see you're so quick to understand, I'll pile up a lot of arguments.

"Look at how obvious the weakness of flawed men is, since they can't even reach the goal to which their natural inclination leads and in fact almost drives them. And what if they were deserted by the great and nearly invincible aid of their nature, which guides them along the way? Consider, too, what great weakness possesses wicked men. For it's not 'small and

trifling prizes'[16] they pursue but cannot reach or obtain. They
fall short of the highest summit of all things, and in their misery they have no success in the thing they strive for day and
night. But this is where the strength of good men stands out.
It's like this: If a man were traveling on foot and came all the
way to a place where there was nowhere left for him to go,
you would consider him the most powerful in walking. In the
same way, if a man reached the goal of things worthy to seek,
so there was nothing else he could strive for, you would judge
him most powerful.

"On the other hand, the wicked seem to be lacking any
strength. Otherwise, why would they abandon virtue and pursue vice? Is it because they don't know what is good? But what's
weaker than the blindness of ignorance? Or does desire overwhelm them and turn them off their course, even when they
know the things they should pursue? In that case they are also
weak in self-control, since they can't struggle against vice. Or
do they knowingly and willingly desert the Good to turn to
vice? In this case they not only cease to be powerful but cease
to be at all, for a man who abandons the common goal of all
things at the same time ceases to exist.

"Now it might seem strange to say that evil men, who make
up the majority of mankind, don't exist, but this is the way
the situation is. I won't deny that evil men are evil, but I do
deny that they exist in a real and essential way.[17] For just as
you could call a corpse a dead man but not simply a man, so I
would say that wicked men are evil but not concede that they
really exist. For a thing exists when it retains its role and preserves its nature, but what falls short of this truly ceases to be,

[16] *small and trifling prizes*: Boethius quotes directly from *Aeneid* 12.764: "For
it's not small and trifling prizes". The quotation comes at the climax of the *Aeneid*,
when Aeneas is fighting Turnus.

[17] *I do deny that they exist in a real and essential way*: As Luca Obertello notes,
"being" (*esse*) consists of "the unity granted through adherence to the cosmic
order and hence to the divine will that gave it birth" (Luca Obertello, trans. *La
consolazione della filosofia; Gli opuscoli teologici* [Milan: Ruscone Libri, 1979], p. 249;
our translation of the original Italian). On "being" in Boethius, see Ralph McInerny, *Boethius and Aquinas* (Washington, D.C.: Catholic University of America
Press, 1990), pp. 163–98.

since its being is contained in its nature. But you'll say evil
men can do things. I won't deny it, but their power comes not
from strength but from weakness. For they can do evil, which
they couldn't do if they had been able to continue pursuing
good. This ability[18] to do evil shows even more clearly that
they can do nothing; for if evil is nothing, as we concluded a
little while ago, it is certain that the wicked can do nothing,
since evil is all they can do."

"This is obvious," I said.

"And to help you understand what kind of strength their
power has, we determined a little earlier that nothing is more
powerful than the highest Good."

"Yes, indeed," I said.

"But the highest Good can't do evil."[19]

"Not at all."

"Well, is there anyone who believes that men can do everything?" she said.

"No one who's sane."

"But these men can do evil."

"I only wish they couldn't," I said.

"Then since the One who can do only good can do everything, but men who can do evil can't do everything, then those
who can do evil are clearly less powerful than those who can't.
Furthermore, we've shown that all power should be considered among the things to be sought and that all things to be
sought are related to the Good, as if it were the summit of
their natures. Now the ability to do wickedness can't be related
to the Good; therefore, it's not a thing to be sought. But all

[18] *ability*: When discussing the ability to accomplish things (see the third paragraph of this *prosa*), Boethius had used the words "will" (*voluntas*) and "power"
(*potestas*). Here, in referring to the capacity for action on the part of evil men,
Boethius uses "ability" (*potentia*), a word that does not convey the same notion
of proper and inherent strength that "power" (*potestas*) does.

[19] *But the highest Good can't do evil*: According to Boethius' logic, God cannot
do evil, since evil is truly nothing and is only the absence of good. Augustine
addresses God as "creator and arbiter of all natural things, but arbiter only, not
creator, of sin" (Augustine, *Confessions*, trans. R.S. Pine-Coffin [New York: Penguin, 1961], 1.10).

power is to be sought, so it's therefore obvious that the ability
to do evil is not power. From all these arguments we see the
power of goodness and the manifest weakness of evil. And Plato's statement is clearly true that only the wise can do what
they desire, but the wicked strive for what pleases them and
can't accomplish what they desire.[20] For they do the things
that are pleasing, while they think they will gain the Good
itself, which they desire, through the things that delight them.
Yet they don't attain it, since wickedness doesn't arrive at
blessedness.

metrum 2

> See those lofty kings, sitting
> atop their high thrones, distinguished
> in their shining purple finery, protected
> by sullen troops, threatening
> with grim faces, panting
> in their rabid hearts.
> If someone would snatch their false cloaks,
> immediately would be seen: men
> strangled with inner chains; desire[21] within

[20] *And Plato's statement . . . what they desire*: For sources of this idea, see Plato,
Gorgias 466D–E and 507C and *Alcibiades* 1.124Eff. See Friedrich Klingner, *De
Boethii Consolatione philosophiae*, 2nd ed. (Zurich: Weidmann, 1966; originally
published 1921), p. 85. At *Gorgias* 466D–E, Plato says to Polus, a student of the
Sophists and a young man convinced of the great power of orators: "For I say,
Polus, that the orators and despots alike have the least power in their cities, as
I stated just now; since they do nothing that they wish to do, practically speak-
ing, though they do whatever they think to be best" (Plato, *Lysis; Symposium;
Gorgias*, trans. W. R. M. Lamb, Loeb Classical Library 166 [Cambridge: Harvard
University Press, 1925]).

[21] *desire*: Boethius mentions four passions—*libido, ira, maeror,* and *spes* (desire,
anger, sorrow, and hope)—that are closely linked to the life of the tyrant (the
other three are mentioned in the following lines). See Helga Scheible, *Die Gedichte
in der "Consolatio philosophiae" des Boethius* (Heidelberg: Carl Winter, 1972),
pp. 133–45, and Gerard O'Daly, *The Poetry of Boethius* (Chapel Hill: University
of North Carolina Press, 1991), pp. 94–96. O'Daly's thorough treatment of the
poem is excellent, discussing the numerous Platonic and Stoic antecedents as

disturbs hearts poisoned with greed.
There, anger as destructive wave lashes
the mind; either sorrow exhausts, or
hope, fleeting, torments the captive.[22]
And so, when you see this one head,
which all tyrants bear—he,
pressured by these masters of malcontent,
does not do what he himself wishes.[23]

3. "So, do you see in what wickedness filth wallows, and in what light goodness shines? From this it is clear that goodness always produces rewards and that wickedness always brings its own punishment. For we can see with certainty that the purpose behind every deed is the reward for that deed, just as the garland that runners seek is the prize for running. But we have shown that blessedness is the very good itself for which everything else is done; therefore, the Good itself has been set forth as a sort of common prize. For this Good cannot be separated from good men—for a man will no longer rightly be called good if he lacks goodness—and so, right actions have their own rewards. Therefore, however much evil men may rage, the wise man will not lose his crown, nor will it wither away,[24]

---

well as the resonances from elsewhere in the *Consolation*, such as Boethius' frequent use of the "chain" metaphor (pp. 94–103).

[22] *hope, fleeting, torments the captive*: Martianus Capella, in *On the Marriage of Mercury and Philology* 1.21, writes, "Uncertain hope exhausts" (Danuta Shanzer, *A Philosophical and Literary Commentary on Martianus Capella's "De nuptiis Philologiae et Mercurii"*, Book 1 [Berkeley: University of California Press, 1986]).

[23] *he, / pressured . . . does not do what he himself wishes*: As O'Daly, *Poetry of Boethius*, p. 96, comments: "Now from a Platonic point of view, and especially from one that has been modified Stoically, as Boethius has been observed to do, all non-philosophical politicians fail to do 'whatever they want' when they perform actions which result in harm of them, for they, like all human agents, aim at a presumed good."

[24] *the wise man will not lose his crown, nor will it wither away*: The crown of laurel or other leaves was a popular prize for victory in antiquity. On the symbolism of the wise man's crown, Gruber, *Kommentar zu Boethius*, p. 329, compares Proverbs 14:24: "The crown of the wise is their riches" (Douay-Rheims translation of the Vulgate). See also Saint Paul, 1 Corinthians 9:24–25: "Know you not that they that run in the race, all run indeed, but one receiveth the

nor will the wickedness of another man take away the glory due to upright souls.

"Now if a man rejoiced in receiving glory from an outside source, then some other person or the man who conferred the glory would be able to take it away. But since every virtuous man receives his glory from his own virtue, then he will lose his reward only when he ceases to be virtuous. Finally, since every reward is sought because it is believed to be good, who will think that the man possessing goodness is without his reward? And what is this reward? The greatest and most beautiful thing of all! Just remember that wonderful corollary that I gave you a while ago, and consider this: since the Good itself is blessedness, it is obvious that all good men become blessed through the very fact of their goodness, and those who are blessed are rightly called gods.[25] This, then, is the reward of good men that the future will never erase, that no man's power can diminish, that no man's wickedness can darken—to become gods.

"Since this is so, no wise man can doubt that the wicked are not without their punishment. For since good and evil are diametrically opposed, just as reward and punishment are, the things we see coming to a good man as a reward must have their counterpart in punishment for the evil man. So virtue itself becomes the reward of the virtuous man, and wickedness the punishment of the evil one.[26] Now, truly, whoever experiences punishment has no doubt that he is suffering

---

prize? So run that you may obtain. And everyone that striveth for the mastery, refraineth himself from all things: and they indeed that they may receive a corruptible crown; but we an incorruptible one" (Douay-Rheims).

[25] *those who are blessed are rightly called gods*: Lady Philosophy at 3 *prosa* 10 had told Boethius that becoming blessed also entails participating in God's divinity. On goodness by participation in the divine, see Étienne Gilson, *The Philosophy of Thomas Aquinas*, translated by Edward Bullough from the 3rd rev. and enlarged ed. of *Le Thomisme* (New York: Barnes and Noble, 1993), p. 112.

[26] *So virtue itself . . . punishment of the evil one*: Fortescue, *Boetius De consolatione*, p. 111, notes that this is an extremely popular maxim among classical philosophers and the doctors of the Church. He cites the Diogenes Laertes, *Lives of the Philosophers*, 6.11; the Stoic Marcus Aurelius, *Meditations* 7.73 and 11.4; Cicero, *Pro Milone* 13.61; and Ambrose, *De officiis* 1.12.46.

evil. And so, if they should wish to reflect upon themselves,
can they consider themselves without punishment, when
wickedness—the greatest of all evils—not only affects them
but infects them? And look at the punishment that follows
evil men, compared with the reward of good men. For you
learned a little earlier that everything that exists is one, and
that oneness itself is good, so it follows that everything that
exists would also seem to be good.[27] In this way, therefore,
whatever falls short of the Good ceases to be. Thus it happens that evil men cease to be what they had been—though
the remaining appearance of the human body shows that these
men had once been humans. And so, since they turned to
evil, they have also lost their human nature. And since virtue alone is able to make a person surpass his fellow men, it
must be the case that those whom wickedness brings down
from their human state are sunk so low that they don't deserve
to be called human. Thus it happens that if you saw a man
transformed by vices, you couldn't consider him human.[28]

"Suppose a violent robber burns with desire for another man's
riches—you would say he's like a wolf. A wild and restless man,
who busies his tongue with lawsuits—you would compare him
to a dog. A man who sneaks and lurks about hoping to trip up
others by deceit—he's just like a little fox. A man who can't
control his rage seems to bear the spirit of a lion. A timid,
frightened man who flees from things he shouldn't fear is like
a deer. A sluggish, dull, lazy man lives the life of an ass.[29]

[27] *everything that exists is one . . . seem to be good*: It was a commonplace among
the Scholastic philosophers that "whatever has being is one, true, and good or
perfect" (*quodlibet ens est unum, verum, bonum seu perfectum*).
[28] *if you saw a man transformed . . . couldn't consider him human*: Gruber, *Kommentar zu Boethius*, p. 331, cites several parallels, including the following two
from Cicero: "What difference does it make whether someone turns from being
human into being a beast or whether a human form carries the brutality of a
beast?" (*De officiis* 3.82) and "Although [the tyrant] has a human shape, he exceeds
huge beasts in the brutality of his ways" (*Republic* 2.48). Plato earlier suggested
that wicked souls after death can be reborn as beasts having characteristics of
their inhuman traits (*Timaeus* 42C and *Republic* 620 A–C ["The Myth of Er"]).
[29] *Suppose a violent robber . . . life of an ass*: See also Dante, *Purgatorio* 14.40–54
and *Convivio* 2.8.26–27 (cited by Fortescue, *Boethius De consolatione*, p. 112).

Suppose a fickle, inconstant man keeps changing his pursuits—
he's no different from a bird. A man who drowns in foul and
impure lusts—he's held by the pleasures of a dirty sow. And so
it happens that a man who abandons virtue, since he can't
become godlike, turns into a beast.

metrum 3

The sails of Neritian[30] Ulysses
on his boats wandering the sea
caught the southeast wind and were blown
to the island of beautiful Circe.[31]
She, born from the seed of the Sun,[32]
mixes for each new guest
a potion touched by her song.
With hands skilled in herb craft,
her guests she changes into various shapes.
A boar's appearance covers this one,
and that one, an African lion,
increasing in tooth and claw.

[30] *Neritian*: Neritus was the name of a mountain on the island of Ithaca, the home of Ulysses (Odysseus in Greek). Neritus was also the name of an island near Ithaca.

[31] *Circe*: In book 10 of the *Odyssey*, some of Odysseus' men are turned into animals by the magic potion of the witch Circe. When Odysseus tries to rescue them, he is helped by Hermes (Mercury in Latin), who gives him a magic root called moly, which enables him to withstand Circe's spell. Odysseus eventually persuades Circe to turn his men back to their proper forms.

Odysseus/Ulysses becomes a prominent example for philosophers, especially in the Stoic tradition and the Platonic and Neoplatonic tradition. He is considered a paradigm of the soul that successfully resists passions and temptations on its journey to find its true home. O'Daly, *Poetry of Boethius*, p. 210, cites Horace, *Epistle* 1.2.17–26, where the Latin poet refers to Ulysses as a man of virtue (*virtus*) and wisdom (*sapientia*) who will not drink Circe's cup as a stupid (*stultus*) and greedy (*avidus*) man would do. O'Daly, pp. 209–20, offers extensive discussion of the passage, especially in terms of its Neoplatonism. See also Ann Astell, *Job, Boethius, and Epic Truth* (Ithaca: Cornell University Press, 1994), passim, esp. pp. 9–10 and 60–64).

[32] *She, born from the seed of the Sun*: Circe was the daughter of the sun god, Helios, as well as the sister of the witch Medea.

Here, one, just now a wolf,
attempts to cry, but can only howl.
Another one, who seems an Indian tiger,
prowls softly about the house.
All around helpless Ulysses
these plenteous evils abound.
But through Mercury's will, the winged Arcadian,[33]
from this host's destruction, Ulysses is permitted release.
Too late for the unfortunate oarsmen,
who already downed tainted drinks.
They eat now as hogs, lost,
trading Ceres' bread for acorns.
Nothing, neither body nor voice, appears intact—
nothing but their minds remain steadfast,
able to mourn their monstrous forms.
Oh! Hand too weak!
Your powerful herbs change human limbs,
but potions cannot change hearts.
Within is man's strength: concealed in a hidden fortress.
Those poisons which draw man from himself,
these are the potent ones—dire potions—
which pass deep inside, harmless to the body,
but ravaging with wounds to the mind."

4. Then I replied, "I agree, and I see that we can rightly say
that corrupt men, though they keep the appearances of a human
body, are turned into beasts through the state of their souls.
But their wicked, cruel minds rage against good men and cause
them harm; this is what I wish were not allowed."

"It is not allowed," she said, "as I'll show you at the proper
time. But still, if what you believe they can do were taken
away, the punishment of wicked men would be greatly lightened. Although some may find this incredible, evil men are

[33] *Arcadian*: Mercury was said to have been born in Arcadia, part of the Greek
Peloponnese. The name comes from Arcas, son of Callisto and Jupiter; Arcas
eventually transformed into the constellation Ursa Minor. Arcadia was also the
home of Pan, who was half man/half goat and played panpipes.

necessarily more unfortunate when they accomplish their desires than when they fail to achieve what they want.[34] For if it is miserable to want to do evil, it is more miserable to be able to do it, since without the accomplishment of evil, the miserable will has no effect. Because each of these conditions has its own degree of misery, those who want to do evil and can do it and carry through with it must be oppressed by a triple misfortune."

"Yes, I admit this," I said. "But how I wish they would quickly lose their misfortune and lose the ability to commit their crimes."

"They will lose it sooner, perhaps, than you might wish or than you might think they will. For there is nothing in the span of a life, short as it is, that the immortal soul should consider long. The great hopes and towering siege engines of crime[35] that these men create are often destroyed with a sudden and unanticipated ending, and this, in fact, sets a limit to their misery. For if wickedness makes men miserable, then men who are wicked longer than others must be more miserable. And I would judge them more unfortunate if death did not finally put an end to their evil. For if we concluded rightly concerning the misfortunes of evil, then misery that has no end must be infinite."

Then I replied, "Your conclusion is strange and hard to admit, but I realize that I well agree with what we've already determined."

"You're quite correct," she said, "and anyone who has trouble agreeing with a conclusion is bound to show either that

---

[34] *evil men are necessarily . . . achieve what they want*: That the person who is "successful" in accomplishing evil is more wretched than the one unsuccessful in accomplishing evil is a philosophical commonplace. See Plato, *Gorgias* 525E. Augustine (*On the Trinity* 13.5.8) quotes from the *Hortensius* of Cicero, a work now extant only in fragments: "For to want what is not fitting; this is most wretched; it is not so wretched to fail to obtain what you want as to want to obtain what isn't fitting" (fragment 39). The *Hortensius* was the work that initiated Augustine's process of converting from Manichaeism to Christianity. See *Confessions* 3.4.

[35] *towering siege engines of crime*: Cf. Boethius' complaint, at the end of 1 *prosa* 4, of the "workshops of unspeakable crimes".

some false premise has preceded it or that the sequence of arguments doesn't inevitably lead to that conclusion. Otherwise, if the previous propositions are granted, there's no excuse for finding fault with the conclusion. And what I am about to say may seem just as strange, but it follows with equal necessity from the assumptions we've made."

"What?" I said.

"That the wicked are happier when they suffer punishment than when they are not restrained by the punishment that is their due," [36] she replied. "I'm not just speaking of what everyone knows, that retribution corrects wicked behavior and that the fear of punishment steers a man to goodness, and that these men serve as an example to others to avoid blameworthy deeds. Everyone realizes these things. But in a certain way, I think the wicked are unhappier when they are unpunished even if we ignore the need for correction and set aside their role as examples."

"How do you mean, aside from these things?" I said.

She replied, "Haven't we agreed that the good are happy and the evil truly miserable?"

"We have," I replied.

"So if something good is added to the misery of someone," she said, "isn't he happier than the man who has pure and complete misery, without any good added to it?"

"So it would seem," I said.

"What if something else bad were added to this miserable man who had nothing good but only things that made him miserable? Wouldn't he be considered much unhappier than the man whose misfortune was lightened by some contact [37] with the Good?"

---

[36] *That the wicked are happier . . . punishment that is their due*: At *Gorgias* 472E, Socrates tells Polus: "[T]he wrongdoer or the unjust is wretched anyhow, more wretched, however, if he does not pay the penalty and gets no punishment for his wrongdoing, but less wretched if he pays the penalty and meets with requital from gods and men" (trans. Lamb).

[37] *contact*: Boethius uses *participatio* here, the same word that had been used earlier (e.g., 3 *prosa* 10) to illustrate the righteous man's participation in divinity.

"I suppose," I said.

"And it is just that the wicked are punished and unfair that they escape punishment?"

"Who would deny it?" I replied.

"And no one will deny that everything that is just is good, and what is unjust is bad," she said. "So the wicked have some contact with the Good, when they are punished, namely the punishment, which is good because it is just.[38] When these same men lack punishment, they have a further evil, their very lack of punishment, which you rightly confessed was an evil."

"I can't deny it," I said.

"Then the wicked are more unfortunate when they are granted unjust impunity than when they are punished with just retribution."

I replied that it was certain. Then I said, "Those ideas follow the ones we agreed on a little while ago. But tell me, do you allow for no punishments for souls after the death of the body?"[39]

"Yes, and great ones. Some, I think, are applied as bitter punishments and some as purifying kindness, but it isn't my intention to speak of these now.

"So far," she continued, "we've made you understand that the power of evil men, which you considered most unfair, is nothing. And we've also made you see that the men you complained of as being unpunished are never without a punishment for their wickedness. And you've learned that their license,

---

[38] *So the wicked have some contact . . . because it is just*: Fortescue, *Boethius De consolatione*, p. 115, cites Aquinas, *Summa theologica* I, q. 48, art. 6, and Dante, *Inferno* 3.124–26. The latter reads: "[A]nd they [the damned] are ready to cross over the river [Acheron], for God's justice so spurs them that fear turns to desire" (*The "Divine Comedy" of Dante Alighieri*, vol. 1, *Inferno*, trans. Robert M. Durling and Robert L. Martinez [New York: Oxford University Press, 1996]).

[39] *But tell me . . . death of the body*: Here and in the following lines, Boethius' words have a Christian tone that could reflect a belief in Hell and Purgatory. Boethius' main source, however, may be Plato. See *Gorgias* 523–27, *Phaedo* 113D, and *Republic* 614–16 ["The Myth of Er"]. See also Seneca, *Dialogues* 6.25.1 ("Letter to Marcia"), where Seneca speaks of life on earth as a purgation: "For a little while he [Marcia's son] spent time above with us while he was being purified [*expurgatur*] and cast off the vices inherent in him and all of his mortal nature; then he was lifted up on high and raced away to the joyous spirits."

which you prayed would end soon, isn't long, and that the longer it is, the more unfortunate it will be—indeed, most unfortunate if it will be forever. And, finally, you've learned that the wicked are more miserable when they escape their just punishment than when they are punished with just retribution. It follows from this conclusion that exactly when they seem to escape justice, they're being pressed by heavier punishments."

Then I responded, "When I consider your arguments, I think that nothing more true could be said, but if I turn back to the opinions of men, who would consider these ideas worthy to listen to, let alone be believed?"

"That's true," she said, "for men cannot lift their eyes, which are accustomed to darkness, to look at the bright light of truth.[40] They're like birds that see clearly at night but are blind during the day; for, while they look at their passions rather than at the order of things, they think that license and unpunished wickedness bring happiness.

"But look at what eternal law has decreed," she continued. "If you've conformed your mind to better things, you won't need a judge to offer you a reward; you yourself will have reached things that are higher. But if you've turned your desire to worse things, you won't need to seek someone to punish you; you'll be the one who has cast yourself down to baser things. It's as if you should take turns looking back and forth from the dirty earth to the heavens, with everything else being blocked out. On the basis of your vision, you would seem to be in the dirt one moment and in the stars the next. But the crowd doesn't understand this. Should we imitate these men, then, when they seem to be like beasts? Suppose someone were completely blind and even forgot that he had ever possessed sight, and thought that nothing was lacking in his human

---

[40] *men cannot lift their eyes . . . bright light of truth*: Again Boethius refers to the "Allegory of the Cave" (*Republic* 514–17B).

In the *Parliament of Fowls* by Chaucer, the tercelet (young male eagle) chides the "doke" and "goos" for their lack of understanding of the nature of love: "Thow canst nat seen which thyng is wel beset! / Thow farst by love as oules don by lyght; / The day hem blent, ful wel they se by nyght" (598–600).

perfection. We who see surely wouldn't agree with the blind man, would we? But men won't even agree that those who commit injuries are more unfortunate than those who suffer them, though the conclusion rests on equally sound arguments."

"I'd like to hear those arguments," I said.

"You don't deny, do you, that every man who is wicked deserves punishment?" she replied.

"No."

"And it's clear in many ways that the wicked are pitiable?"

"Yes," I replied.

"Then you don't doubt that those who deserve punishment are pitiable?"

"Certainly not," I said.

"Then if you were sitting as judge, whom would you consider worthy of punishment, the one who committed a crime or the one who suffered it?"

"I'm quite sure I would satisfy the one who suffered the injury in giving pain to the one who committed it," I said.

"So the one who committed the crime would seem to you more pitiable than the one who suffered it."

"That follows," I said.

Then she continued, "So for this and other reasons based on the same principle, that wickedness by its very nature makes men pitiable, it's obvious that an injury done to someone creates misery for the doer of the deed and not for the sufferer of it. But nowadays prosecutors take the opposite approach. They try to stir up sympathy from the judges towards those who have suffered some serious and bitter injury, when pity is more rightly owed to those who committed the crime, who should be brought to judgment not by angry accusers, but by well-disposed and merciful ones, who would lead them to a judge as if they were leading sick men to a doctor,[41] so the disease

[41] *who would lead them ... sick men to a doctor*: Here again Boethius is closely following Plato's *Gorgias*. See 480A–B, where Socrates is speaking of how a wrongdoer must willingly accept punishment, since it is just and will hence make him better: "But if he is guilty of wrongdoing ... he must go of his own freewill where he may soonest pay the penalty, to the judge as if to his doctor, with the

of their faults could be cut away through punishment. In this way, advocates of the guilty would no longer be needed, or if they wanted to help people they would adopt the role of prosecutors. And the wicked themselves, if they could peek out and catch some glimmer[42] of the virtue they had abandoned, would see that they were going to put away the foulness of their wickedness by enduring their punishment. In exchange for acquiring virtue, they wouldn't consider their punishment torment, and so they would reject the use of defense advocates and would yield themselves completely to their judges and accusers.

"So it is, that to the wise men there is absolutely no place for hatred.[43] Who except the most stupid would hate good men? And it is most unreasonable to hate evil men. If wickedness is a sort of disease of the soul, just as weakness is a disease of the body, when we consider those sick in body as not at all worthy of hatred but rather pity, we should all the more pity and not attack those whose minds are oppressed by a wickedness more cruel than any physical weakness.

metrum 4

Why would a man delight in rousing such a cause
and with his very own hand tempt fate?
If you seek death, she won't delay.
Of her own accord, she hastens her horses.[44]
The serpent, lion, tiger, bear, and boar with teeth
seek those who themselves seek each other with swords.

---

earnest intent that the disease of his injustice shall not become chronic and cause a deep, incurable ulcer in his soul" (trans. Lamb). The image of sin as disease is common in Christianity, especially in the East.

[42] *glimmer*: See the same image at 3 *prosa* 9, paragraph 4.

[43] *to the wise men ... no place for hatred*: This is a common thought in classical philosophy. Gruber, *Kommentar zu Boethius*, p. 341, cites Epictetus, *Dissertations* 1.18.9; Seneca, *Dialogues* 3.16.6; and Marcus Aurelius, *Meditations* 7.26.1.

[44] *she hastens her horses*: O'Daly, *Poetry of Boethius*, p. 170, notes that there is no exact parallel in antiquity to the idea of the chariot of death. He does compare Andrew Marvell's phrase "Time's winged chariot" ("To His Coy Mistress").

Surely these men don't quarrel, provoking unjust battles
in uncivilized wars because of differing customs.
Surely they don't wish to die, one after another,
    by weapons?
Never is there right reason for savagery.
You wish suitable recompense for merit mattered:
then, in justice, cherish the good; pity the evil."

5. Then I replied, "I see both the happiness attached to the
deeds of the just and the misery of the deeds of the unjust.
But in what people call fortune, I think both good and bad
are present. No one who's wise would want to be an exile,
poor and disgraced, instead of always living well in his own
city, being mighty in his resources, respected for his honors,
and strong in his power.[45] For in this way the use of wisdom
is displayed in a more distinguished and open manner, when
in some way the blessedness of rulers is transferred to their
subjects, especially when the law requires death, prison, or
other painful punishments for those who are dangerous, since
it's for them that the penalties are established. But I can't
understand at all why things are turned around, so that the
punishments due to the wicked are inflicted on the good,
and evil men snatch the rewards of virtue. I would like you
to tell me what the reason is for such unfairness and disorder.
You see, I would wonder less if I thought that everything
was mixed up through random chance, but the belief that
God governs everything increases my amazement. One who
often gives blessings to the good and harsh things to the
bad, and then on the other hand offers difficulties to
good men and fulfills the hopes of evil men—how would his
actions differ from random chance, unless some explanation
is found?"

[45] *No one who's wise . . . strong in his power*: This comparison of the ill-fated
man in exile versus the one who is able to do good by exercising authority in
government is of course most applicable to Boethius, as we saw in book 1, when
he expressed his love of displaying virtue in governmental activities. As in book
1, Boethius still does not understand why good seems to be punished and evil
rewarded when God is in control. Boethius' confidence in God has increased,
but he still retains this fundamental uncertainty.

"It isn't strange," she said, "for a person to consider something random and confused if he doesn't know the order behind it. But just because you don't know the reasons for such arrangements, you shouldn't doubt that everything is done rightly, since a good ruler governs the world.

metrum 5

The man who can neither grasp the gliding
of Arcturus' star near heaven's highest pole,
nor understand why Boötes slowly tracks
his wagon, is late to dip his flames into the sea,
even though his rising soon unfolds—
the laws of heaven will stun his mind![46]
Let the full moon's horns pale,
covered by night's dark,
and let Phoebe dimmed, reveal the stars[47]
once hidden by her shining face,
and man's confusion shakes the nations,
as gongs tire with constant blows.[48]
Northwest wind's blasts
hammering shores with waves
and snow's hard mass, freed by Phoebus' heat
frightens no one, for the causes are easy to see.

[46] *The man who can neither . . . stun his mind!* Arcturus, the Bear Warden, shines in the north near the Big Dipper, also called the Wain (Wagon). Arcturus belonged to the constellation Boötes, which was considered the driver of the wagon. J.J. O'Donnell notes: "Boötes seems slow because his apparent motion (rotation around the pole star) in twelve hours of the night covers a smaller arc of the visible sky than that of stars further from the pole" (J.J. O'Donnell, ed., *Consolatio philosophiae*, vol. 2, Bryn Mawr Latin Commentaries [Bryn Mawr: Thomas Library, Bryn Mawr College, 1984], p. 89). Boethius' point is that if one does not know simple (to him) matters of astronomy, one cannot understand divine reason.

[47] *Let the full moon's horns . . . reveal the stars:* Phoebe is the moon, and Boethius is describing an eclipse.

[48] *gongs tire with constant blows:* The ancient Romans considered a lunar eclipse to be a bad omen, so the banging of gongs would be employed to bring the moon back.

Hidden things trouble men's hearts:
things rare and sudden strike fear.
But even these will cease to astound
when the clouds of unknowing melt away."

6. "So it is," I said, "but since it's your role to disclose the reasons behind things that are hidden and to uncover explanations clouded in mists,[49] I beg you to tell me fully the reasons you find for this marvel, since it disturbs me greatly."

Then she gave a little smile and said, "You're asking me to deal with the greatest question of all, one that can hardly be exhausted fully. It's the kind of subject where countless uncertainties arise like the heads of a hydra[50] when one question is laid to rest. And there's no way to deal with them unless someone sears them back with the most lively fire of the mind. Here we deal with the simplicity of Providence,[51] with Fate's course of events, with unexpected occurrences, with divine thought and foreknowledge, and with the freedom of the will. You yourself know how weighty these questions are. Yet since it's also part of your medicine to know these things, though we're limited to a short amount of time, we'll try to consider them somewhat. But if you enjoy the delights of music and

[49] *mists*: The mists are again reminiscent of book 1 (*prosa* 2). In book 1, Boethius learned the instability of Fortuna, the goddess of earthly things. In books 4 and 5, he will learn in greater depth the nature of God. As Lady Philosophy will soon note, the first dose of medicine was gentle and easy to understand, while the second is much more powerful and intellectually demanding.

[50] *heads of a hydra*: One of Hercules' labors was to slay the hydra, a poisonous monster with nine heads. As he cut off each head, the neck split into two and produced new heads. Eventually Hercules had his nephew use a torch to cauterize each neck as it was cut, and he was thus able to kill the monster. The story probably accounts for the reference to the "fire of the mind" in Boethius' next sentence.

[51] *simplicity of Providence*: God possesses the attribute of simplicity (*simplicitas*) in that he is "pure being" and not a composition of other things. See Gilson, *Philosophy of Thomas Aquinas*, p. 101, and Aquinas, *Summa contra gentiles* 1.16–18. Robert Barron notes: "What God's simplicity entails, in a word, is that the divine is not any *sort* of being, any *particular instance* of being, but is rather the sheer act of existing itself. God is not this or that; God simply is" (Robert Barron, *Thomas Aquinas: Spiritual Master* [New York: Crossroad, 1996], p. 76; emphasis in original).

song, you must set aside that pleasure for a moment, while I weave a web of arguments for you."

"As you please," I said.

Then as if setting out on a new beginning, she explained in this way: "The origin of all things, and all growth of beings with changing natures, and all things that are moved in any way obtain their causes, their order, and their form from the stability of the Divine Mind.[52] The Mind, settled in the citadel of its own simplicity,[53] has determined many means for accomplishing its purposes. The means that is viewed in terms of the purity of Divine Intelligence itself is called Providence. When we speak of things that are set in motion and arranged, the means has been called Fate in the past. And anyone can see easily that these terms are different if he looks at the nature of each of them. Providence, which arranges everything, is the divine power of Reason itself, established in the highest ruler of all things. But Fate is the arrangement inherent in whatever is set in motion, and it allows Providence to connect everything with its proper order.[54] For Providence encompasses all things equally, no matter how different they are, but Fate sets in motion individual objects that are distributed according to space, form, and time. This unfolding of the temporal order, which is unified through the foresight of the Divine Mind, is

[52] *Divine Mind*: The Divine Mind is a central concept in Neoplatonic thought. See, e.g., Andrew Louth, *The Origins of the Christian Mystical Tradition* (Oxford: Clarendon Press, 1981), pp. 37–39.

[53] *The Mind, settled in the citadel of its own simplicity*: For a similar view of the divine gaze, see Milton, *Paradise Lost* 3.77–78: "Him [Satan] God beholding from his prospect high/Wherein past, present, future he beholds." Cf. also Dante, *Paradiso* 8.97–103 (cited by Fortescue, *Boethius De consolatione*, p. 123).

[54] *Providence, which arranges . . . its proper order*: Henry Chadwick notes, "The Neoplatonists from Plotinus onwards (*Enn.* iii, 3, 5, 14) distinguish between providence, which concerns the higher realm, and fate which is another name for the unalterable chain of cause and effect in this inferior and determined world" (Henry Chadwick, *Boethius: The Consolations of Music, Logic, Theology, and Philosophy* [Oxford: Oxford University Press, 1981], p. 242). Cf. Chaucer, *The Knight's Tale*: "The destinee, ministre general,/That executeth in the world over al/The purveiaunce that hath seyn biforn" (1663–65). Cf. also *Troilus and Criseyde* 3.617–23.

Providence, but the same union, arranged and set in order in time, is called Fate.

"Although these two concepts are separate, one depends on the other; for the order of Fate proceeds out of the simplicity of Providence. Just as the craftsman has in mind a model[55] for the thing he is going to make, when he executes the work and leads through its stages of progression the object that he has preconceived simply and in a moment, so God with His Providence permanently and at one time disposes the things to be done. By Fate, He tends to those very same things individually throughout time. Therefore, whether Fate is carried out by some divine spirits as its servants, or by the World's Soul,[56] or through the service of all of nature, or by the heavenly movement of the stars, or by the power of angels,[57] or by the various skills of spirits, it is certain that Providence is the immovable and simple plan for divine things, and Fate is the movable interlacing and temporal outline for those things that divine simplicity has determined are to be done.[58]

"And so it comes about that all things subject to Fate are also subject to Providence, to which even Fate itself is subject. But some things that are placed under Providence lie above the course of Fate. These things, fixed firmly and closely to

[55] *model*: We have translated Boethius' *forma* as "model". Boethius' analogy has its roots in Platonism but probably comes most immediately from Aristotle, *Metaphysics* 1032a.

[56] *World's Soul*: The concept of the World Soul has Platonic and Neoplatonic roots. Fortescue, *Boethius De consolatione*, p. 124, cites Plato, *Philebus* 30A, *Laws* 10.897C, and *Timaeus* 30D and 34B. Gruber, *Kommentar zu Boethius*, p. 350, also cites Plotinus, *Enneads*, 3.1.4.

[57] *angels*: Despite the pagan echoes in Boethius' explanation of how fate is carried out, Fortescue argues that the idea of angels arranging God's providence is a sign of Christian influence. For an opposing view, which links the angels to Platonic thought, see Pierre Courcelle, *"La consolation de philosophie" dans la tradition littéraire: Antécédents et postérité de Boèce* (Paris: Études augustiniennes, 1967), p. 205. See also R. W. Sharples, ed. and trans., *Cicero: "On Fate"; Boethius: "The Consolation of Philosophy" IV. 5–7, V.* (Warminster: Aris and Phillips, 1991), pp. 30–31, 204–5.

[58] *Providence is the immovable . . . are to be done*: Fate, being set in motion by God, is moved (set into action) and works in time. By contrast, God himself is not set into motion and so is unmovable (*immobilis*) and simple (*simplex*).

134 The Consolation of Philosophy

the Supreme Divinity, move outside the ordering of Fate's motions. It's as if circles were spinning around the same axis.[59] The innermost circle moves towards the simplicity of the center, and serves as a sort of axis for the others located beyond it, around which they will turn in a larger orbit. The further away the circles are from the unity of the center, the more they extend into a larger space. But if anything is joined with the middle and has a share in it, it is forced into simplicity and ceases to be spread out and dispersed. In a similar way, what departs further from the Supreme Mind is wound up in greater links of Fate, and the more a thing seeks the center of things, the freer it is from this Fate the more nearly it seeks the center of things. And if it clings to the stability of the Celestial Mind, it does not move, and it also surpasses the necessity of Fate. Therefore, as reasoning differs from understanding, as that which is produced differs from that which is, as time differs from eternity, and likewise a circle differs from its center, so the moving course of Fate differs from the unchanging simplicity of Providence. This course moves the sky and stars, and orders the mixing together of the elements, and transforms them in their successive changes, and it renews these very things as they arise and die through similar progressions of seeds and offspring.

"This course also binds the actions and fortunes of men by an unbreakable chain of causes,[60] and since this chain has its origin in immovable Providence, it is necessary that these causes themselves be unchangeable. And this succession restrains with its own changelessness the things that are changeable and would otherwise flow forth without restraint.

"So it happens that the limits imposed on each thing dispose it and direct it towards the Good, although to you humans

[59] *It's as if circles were spinning around the same axis*: Chadwick, *Boethius*, p. 242, notes that Augustine, *On the Trinity* 3.9.16, speaks of the "highest axis of causes". Fortescue, *Boethius De consolatione*, p. 125, cites Dante, *Paradiso* 28:64–66 (Beatrice speaking): "The course of the material spheres is wide/or narrow in accord with more or less/of virtue that infuses each throughout" (trans. Musa).
[60] *unbreakable chain of causes*: Gruber, *Kommentar zu Boethius*, p. 352, compares Augustine, *City of God* 5.8: "They call by the name of fate that connection and series of causes by which what comes about comes about."

who aren't able to understand this order everything seems confused and disturbed. There is nothing that is done for the sake
of evil—not even by wicked men themselves—for as we've
shown conclusively, perverted error leads them astray as they
seek the Good, and the order proceeding from the divine center does not at all turn them aside from their origin.

"Now you will say, 'Can anything be more confused and
disordered than for good men to have things turn out well at
one time and badly at another, while bad men obtain both
the things they want and the things they hate?' But do you
really think men have such integrity of mind that the ones
they judge good or wicked must necessarily be the sort of men
they are believed to be?[61] It is in this very thing that men's
judgments are in conflict; those that some consider worthy of
reward, others consider worthy of punishment. But let's suppose someone were able to discern between good and bad men.
Would that make him able to look into men's souls and see
the inner temper of their being, as we speak of the soul in
union with the body?[62] A man who doesn't understand finds
it strange and wonderful that sweet things agree with some
men who are healthy while bitter things agree with others, or
why one sick man is helped by gentle remedies and another
by harsh ones.[63] But a physician, who understands the ways
and natures of health and sickness, isn't amazed at all. And
what else is the preserver of good and the averter of evil, but
God, the guide and physician of souls? He is the one who looks

[61] *But do you really think . . . believed to be?* Fortescue, *Boethius De consolatione*,
p. 126, cites Dante, *Paradiso* 13.139–41: "No Mr. or Miss Know-It-All should
think,/when they see one man steal and one give alms/that they are seeing
them through God's own eyes" (trans. Musa).

[62] *inner temper of their being . . . in union with the body:* Gruber, *Kommentar zu
Boethius*, p. 353, notes the ancient belief that well-being is a matter of the proper
blending of qualities producing the right temperament. He cites Plato, *Phaedo*
86B. For the application of this view in the Middle Ages and the Renaissance,
see E. M. W. Tillyard, *The Elizabethan World Picture* (New York: Random House,
1967), pp. 68–71.

[63] *sweet things agree . . . another by harsh ones:* See Augustine, *De doctrina christiana* 1.14.

out from the lofty watchtower[64] of His Providence and sees what is best for all and works out what He knows is suitable for them. Here occurs the greatest wonder of the ordering of Fate, when a knowing God works out the things that the ignorant wonder at.

"Now to touch on a few examples of divine profundity that the human mind can comprehend, look at a person you consider most just and devoted to righteousness;[65] Providence that knows all sees things differently. Our friend Lucan noted that the winning side was pleasing to the gods but the losing side to Cato.[66] So here, when you see something happen that isn't what you expected, it seems to you to be twisted confusion, but it's part of the proper order of things. Now suppose there were a man so good in his morals that both divine and human judgment agreed about him, yet he has little strength of soul. If any trouble should come to him, he might stop practicing his virtue, since it failed to secure his good fortune. The wise

[64] *lofty watchtower*: Boethius' reference to the "lofty watchtower" (*alta . . . specula*) probably borrows from Virgil's words at *Aeneid* 3.239–40. (From his lofty watchtower, Misenus gives the signal with his hollow trumpet.) There are Platonic antecedents: Gruber, *Kommentar zu Boethius*, p. 353, cites *Republic* 445C, as well as the Virgilian passage; P. G. Walsh cites *Statesman* 272E (P. G. Walsh, trans., *"The Consolation of Philosophy"*, *Translated with Introduction and Explanatory Notes* [Oxford: Clarendon Press, 1999], p. 153).

[65] *most just and devoted to righteousness*: Boethius follows closely Virgil's description of the hero Rhipeus, whose undeserved death Aeneas laments as Troy is being destroyed; see *Aeneid* 2.426–27: "and Rhipeus fell most just among the Teucrians (Trojans) and most devoted to righteousness".

[66] *Our friend Lucan . . . losing side to Cato*: In the *Civil War* (or *Pharsalia*) 1.128, Lucan notes that "the victorious cause was pleasing to the gods, but the losing side to Cato." Cato was a famous Stoic who, in support of the Republic, conspired against Julius Caesar and subsequently sided against Mark Antony. As O'Donnell, *Consolatio philosophiae*, p. 92, notes, Lucan uses the line ironically, in the sense that the gods seem not to care about justice. Boethius uses the line straightforwardly, suggesting simply that man see things differently from God. There is dispute over whether Boethius misses Lucan's irony or whether he simply alters the line for his own purposes. See Sharples, *"On Fate"*; *"Consolation"*, pp. 206–7.

Boethius refers to Lucan as "our friend" (*familiaris noster*), no doubt because of his Stoicism. Lucan is included in the *Inferno* as one of the five great poets of antiquity (Virgil, Homer, Horace, Ovid, and Lucan), who reside among the virtuous pagans (4.85–90).

judgment of God spares him from suffering if adversity would harm him, since he is not suited for it. Suppose there is another man, perfect in virtue,[67] and holy and close to God; Providence judges it unthinkable for him to be touched by any adversity, even bodily illness. For as one man more excellent than I said:

The heavens didst build the body of the holy man.[68]

"But it often happens that supreme authority is given to good men, so growing wickedness can be checked. To some men, Providence distributes a mixture of good and bad fortune according to the nature of their soul. Some Providence troubles, so they won't be spoiled by a long period of happiness. Others Providence vexes with hardships, so they can strengthen the virtues of their souls by the use and practice of patience. Some fear too much the things they can endure, while others do not take enough thought for what they can't endure; Providence uses sorrows to teach these men to understand themselves. Some men have paid the price of death and bought a name of honor in this world. Some men, undefeated by torments, have offered to others an example that virtue is not conquered by evil. And there can be no doubt how rightly and carefully ordered and how beneficially these things turn out to men.

"And the fact that both desirable and undesirable things happen to evil men occurs for the same reasons. About the sorrowful things, no one is surprised, since everyone thinks that wicked men deserve evil—and indeed their punishments deter others from crime and then also improve the ones who suffer them. The joys of evil men, on the other hand, provide

---

[67] *perfect in virtue*: As Gruber, *Kommentar zu Boethius*, p. 354, notes, the man "perfect in virtue" would have been a reference to the wise man in Stoic literature.

[68] *The heavens didst build the body of the holy man*: The source of this quotation is not certain. Chadwick argues for the Chaldean Oracles, which were important writings for the Neoplatonists (Chadwick, *Boethius*, p. 243). See also Gruber, *Kommentar zu Boethius*, pp. 354–55, and Sharples, *"On Fate"*; *"Consolation"*, p. 207, for various possible sources.

a good example to virtuous men of how they should judge the kind of happiness they often see falling to the wicked. And along these lines, I think something similar happens if some-one has such a headstrong and violent nature that poverty might drive him to crime—Providence offers a cure for his disease by providing him with money.

"Another man," she continued, "looking at his conscience stained with wickedness, might become frightened as he com-pares his conduct with his fortunes, fearing that he will suffer the sad loss of what he has been happy to possess. Therefore he will change his ways and abandon his wickedness, fearing the loss of his good fortune. A happiness that is enjoyed unworthily has hurled others to a ruin they deserve. Some men are given authority to punish others, so the good can be tested and the evil punished. For just as there is no partnership between good men and evil ones, so even the wicked them-selves cannot agree with each other. How could they, when each one even disagrees within himself? Their very wicked-ness rips apart their conscience, and they often do things that they later realize they should not have done.

"And so it happens that highest Providence often provides a great wonder in having bad men make bad men good. For some men, when they think they suffer injustice from those who are worse than they, burn with hatred at the harm they receive, and they return to the fruits of virtue, since they are trying to be unlike the men they hate. For only divine power, to which bad things too are good, can use these bad things and bring about some good effect. For a certain order embraces all things, so that what departs from the order assigned by Rea-son can still fall back into another order. Nothing can happen by accident in the realm of Providence.

But 'tis grievous to speak of all these things as if I were a god.[69]

It isn't right for a mortal to try to understand in his mind or express with his words all the tools of divine workmanship.

[69] *But 'tis grievous . . . as if I were a god*: This is a slight variation from Homer, *Iliad* 12.176.

Let this be enough to consider, that the same God who is the origin of all nature disposes all things and directs them to the Good,[70] while He moves quickly to keep all things that He produces in the likeness of Himself, and He eliminates from the boundaries of His kingdom all evil by the course of the necessity of Fate. And so it is with all the evils that men think are abundant on earth. If you look at how Providence disposes them, you wouldn't consider them evils at all. But I see that you have been burdened for a long time now by the weight of this topic and worn down by the length of this explanation, and that you are looking for some sweetness of song. Take this drink, then, so you can be refreshed and strengthened for the rest of your journey.

metrum 6[71]

> If you, clever, want to understand God's[72] law,
> to discern with a pure mind,
> then look to the heavens' heights.
> There, in a just treaty with the universe
> the stars keep their ancient peace.
> There, the sun ignited in red flames
> impedes not the moon's cold rotation.
> Nor does Ursa, who bends her rapid course

[70] *the same God . . . directs them to the Good*: Walsh, *Consolation*, p. 154, cites *Timaeus* 29E: "He [God] was good, and in him that is good no envy ariseth ever concerning anything; and being devoid of envy He desired that all should be, so far as possible, like unto Himself. . . . For God desired that, so far as possible, all things should be good and nothing evil." It is hard also not to think of Romans 8:28: "And we know that to them that love God, all things work together unto good" (Douay-Rheims).

[71] *metrum* 6: This poem is in the same meter and discusses the same theme as 1 *metrum* 5, in which a sorrowing Boethius asks the God who governs the physical universe to show equal concern for man. Here Lady Philosophy is singing and argues that God does indeed do this and that the order in the physical universe mirrors the order in God's interactions with man. Note also the similarities with 2 *metrum* 8, which focuses on the love that rules the universe.

[72] *God's*: The original Latin gives *Tonantis*, the Thunderer, an epithet of Jupiter. Boethius, of course, is simply referring to the idea of a monotheistic deity here, not the Roman god in particular.

about the highest pole of the earth,
desire to sink her flames into the ocean.[73]
She observes the stars submerged
as they fall into the depths of the sea.
Always with time's measured succession,
Vesper announces the dark of the evening,
and Lucifer returns the kind day.[74]
Thus, in turn, Love renews the eternal course.[75]
From the star-filled shores of the sky
the discord of war is banished.
Here concord tempers in fair measure
the beginnings, so that the struggle
of the wet yields in turn to the dry.[76]
And winter cold joins faith with the sun,
its hanging fire rises on high,
while the earth settles with ponderous weight.
In warm spring comes the flowering time;
from this same cause breathes forth fragrance.
Hot summer dries the grain,
autumn returns heavy with fruit,
and falling rain waters the winter ground.
These measured portions nourish and provide
all that breathes life on earth.
He creates, who seizes and takes away the same.
In the final setting rises the first beginning—
all the while sits the Creator on high
guiding the universe, directing the reins.
King and Lord, Beginning and Source,
Law and Wisdom, Arbiter with justice.

---

[73] *Nor does Ursa . . . her flames into the ocean*: Ursa (Major), the Great Bear, as O'Donnell, *Consolatio philosophiae*, p. 95, observes, "never goes below the horizon for observers in the northern temperate climate".

[74] *Vesper announces . . . Lucifer returns the kind day*: Vesper and Lucifer (Light Bearer) are the evening and morning stars.

[75] *Thus, in turn, Love renews the eternal course*: Cf. 2 *metrum* 8, lines 11–12: "Love, from the sky commanding,/binds both earth and sea."

[76] *the struggle/of the wet yields in turn to the dry*: Ovid, *Metamorphoses* 1.19, likewise speaks of the struggle between cold and warm, and wet and dry, elements.

That which He impels, goes into motion.
He steadies and prevents from wandering;
for unless He summons their paths with direction,
compelling their winding paths back onto course,
that which is contained by stable order—
would split, separated from its source.
Here is Love, common to all things.
And they seek to hold their end, the Good;
for in no other way are they able to endure,
unless the Cause which gave them being
fetches them back again in love.

7. "So now," she continued, "do you see what conclusion follows from all these things we've said?"

"What?"

"That every kind of fortune is completely good," she said.

"And how can that be?" I replied.

"Listen," she said. "Since all fortune, either pleasant or bitter, is given to reward or test the good or to punish or correct the bad, it is entirely good, since it is either just or useful."

"Yes, indeed," I said, "your conclusion is true, as I consider what you taught me a little while ago concerning Providence and Fate, an opinion based on solid arguments. But might we not also consider this among the conclusions you set forth a while ago as impossible to believe?"

"How so?" she said.

"Because men commonly claim, indeed very often, that the fortune of some men is bad."

"And so, do you want to agree with what men commonly say for a while," she said, "so we don't seem to depart from the general consensus, so to speak?"

"As you wish," I replied.

"Now don't you consider whatever is useful to be good?"

"Yes," I replied.

"And a fortune that tests or corrects someone is useful?"

"I agree," I said.

"Then good?"

"Of course."

"But this is the fate of those who are firmly positioned in virtue and wage war against difficulties or turn from their vices to seize the path of virtue."

"I can't deny it," I said.

"What about a pleasant fortune that is given to the good as a reward? Surely the crowd wouldn't consider that bad, would they?"

"Not at all. They would consider it good, and so it is."

"What about the other kind of fortune, the one that's harsh but restrains bad men through just punishments? People would not call it good, would they?"

"No indeed," I said. "They consider it the worst fortune they can imagine."

"But make sure we don't do something completely illogical by following the opinion of the people."

"What?" I said.

"From these things that we have concluded," she said, "it is clear that the fortune of those who either possess virtue or pursue it or are acquiring it is entirely good, whatever it is, and that it is all bad to those who remain in wickedness."

"This is true," I said, "although no one would dare to admit it."

"So, then," she said, "a wise man shouldn't be upset when he has to battle with fortune, just as a brave man mustn't complain when the cry of war breaks out. For to one of them, difficulty is the means of increasing his glory, and to the other the means of shaping his wisdom. And so we call it virtue, because a virile man fights and wins against adversity;[77] for you who are progressing in virtue have not come to wallow in pleasure. In your soul you're engaged in a bitter battle with every kind of fortune to make certain it won't weigh you down

[77] *And so we call it virtue . . . wins against adversity*: Boethius makes a pun on *virtus* (manliness; related to *vir*, "man") and *vires* (strength). (The words are not actually related.) See similarly Cicero, *Tusculan Disputations* 2.43: "For the word 'virtue' [*virtus*] comes from the word 'man' [*vir*], for truly fortitude is appropriate for man [*vir*]."

when it's bitter, or corrupt you when it's pleasing. With unyielding strength take the middle road; whatever remains below or passes beyond thinks little of happiness and does not have a reward for its toil. You have in your hands the ability to create the kind of fortune you want;[78] for every fortune that seems harsh, unless it tests or corrects a man, punishes him.[79]

metrum 7

Atreus' son[80] after warring ten years
atoned for his brother's emptied bed.
He bought wind with blood
to sail the Greek ships,
put his fatherhood aside, and as priest,
made a pact with his daughter's throat.
The Ithacan[81] mourned comrades lost

[78] *You have in your hands . . . kind of fortune you want*: C. S. Lewis cites Spenser, *Fairie Queene* 6.9.30: "Each unto himself his life may fortunize" (C. S. Lewis, *The Discarded Image: An Introduction to Medieval and Renaissance Literature* [Cambridge: Cambridge University Press, 1964], p. 87).

[79] *for every fortune that seems harsh . . . punishes him*: This closing sentence does not seem initially comforting, but as Gruber, *Kommentar zu Boethius*, p. 364, notes, it corresponds to sentence 6 of this section, in which Lady Philosophy states that all fortune has a purpose, whether it be the reward of good fortune or the testing, correction, or punishment of adverse fortune.

[80] *Atreus' son*: Atreus' son is Agamemnon, who fought against the Trojans for ten years, seeking revenge for the theft of Helen, the wife of his brother Menelaus. As he prepared to set sail for Troy, the goddess Artemis (Diana in Latin), who was angry with Agamemnon (for various reasons in various versions), demanded that he sacrifice his daughter Iphigenia in order to obtain suitable winds for the voyage. Eventually Agamemnon's desire to please his troops overcame his fatherly instinct, and Iphigenia was sacrificed. Needless to say, not all versions depict Agamemnon as worthy hero. Boethius, however, will focus on Agamemnon's Stoic devotion to duty.

[81] *Ithacan*: The Ithacan is Odysseus, or Ulysses in Latin. In book 9 of the *Odyssey*, the Greek hero is captured by the Cyclops Polyphemus, who eats several of Odysseus' men before Odysseus blinds him and escapes. Odysseus, like Hercules, in the myths following, is a favorite hero of the Stoics. See Astell, *Job, Boethius, and Epic Truth*, pp. 8–9. Astell (p. 8) and O'Daly aptly quote Seneca, *De constantia sapientis* (*On the Constancy of the Wise Man*) 2.1: "For these men [Ulysses and Hercules] our Stoics declared to be sages, unconquered in their toils,

to the belly of cruel Polyphemus.
Savage Cyclops lying in his cave
shrieked in rage, his one eye blinded,
his earlier joy repaid with tears.
Harsh labors glorified Hercules:[82]
he tamed the proud centaurs,
skinned the fierce lion,
with sure arrows pierced the birds,
from the gaze of the dragon snatched fruit,
his hands now heavy with gold.
With triple chain he dragged Cerberus
and as victor served savage horses severe food:
their very own master.
The hydra perished, its venom he burned.
The River Achelous in shame buried his face,
within his own banks, disfigured in brow.
Across Libyan sand he stretched Antaeus;

---

despisers of pleasure, and victors over all the earth" (trans. O'Daly, *Poetry of Boethius*, p. 227).

[82] *Harsh labors glorified Hercules*: Among Hercules' many feats are (1) the taming of the centaurs (creatures that were half man and half horse); (2) the killing and skinning of the Nemean lion; (3) the killing of the Stymphalian birds; (4) the fetching of the golden apples (guarded by a dragon) of the Hesperides; (5) the capture of Cerberus from the underworld; (6) the capture of the man-eating horses of Diomedes; (7) the killing of the Lernean hydra, whose multiple poisonous heads had to be cut off and the necks cauterized to stop the heads from reduplicating; (8) the defeat of the river god Achelous, whose horns he broke off; (9) the killing of the monster Antaeus, who gained strength whenever his feet were in contact with the earth (his mother); (10) the killing of the fire-breathing giant Cacus, who terrorized the land of King Evander (see *Aeneid*, book 8); (11) the capture of the Erymanthian boar; and (12) holding the heavens for Atlas. This list of twelve is not the usual one given by mythographers. See Scheible, *Gedichte*, p. 154. In some versions, as here, the labors were seen as a prerequisite for Hercules' eventual divinity.

In the following passage, Boethius is heavily dependent on Seneca's tragedies *Agamemnon* (808ff.), *Hercules Oetaeus,* and *Hercules furens*. For citations, see Gruber, *Kommentar zu Boethius*, pp. 364–68, and O'Daly, *Poetry of Boethius*, pp. 226–34. There are also several evocations of the *Aeneid*, in which Aeneas is often connected with the Stoic Hercules. Like Hercules, Aeneas is a man of toil (*labor* in Latin, a word used twice in the Hercules section of this poem).

Cacus' death sated Evander's wrath.
Those shoulders upon which heaven would rest,
the bristling boar flecked with foam.
And his last labor—to hold the weight of the sky
brought heaven!—borne on his unbending neck.
Go then, brave men, don't look back!
By these ways find example—
Follow the high path!
Earth overcome grants the stars."

Book 5[1]

1. She had finished her speech and now was turning to other matters she would discuss and explain. But then I spoke, "Your words of encouragement are true indeed and worthy of your great authority. I know firsthand what you said a while ago, that the question of Providence is bound up with many other questions. And I am wondering what you think chance is, if it is anything at all."

Then she replied, "I'm hurrying to pay the debt I promised and to open up for you a return to your homeland.[2] Now these

[1] *Book 5*: Book 4 dealt with the concept of justice, which had troubled Boethius throughout the work, since he has seen evil men prospering, or at least seeming to. In book 4, Lady Philosophy showed that pursuing the Good brought its own inherent reward, without regard to how things seemed. In book 5, however, Boethius is troubled by the idea of free will. If there is true reward for doing good and punishment for doing evil, justice requires that men be free to choose what they will do. Lady Philosophy notes that, although men's evil actions and thoughts sometimes cloud their freedom, men are essentially free to choose their actions.

In examining this topic, Boethius raises several questions that Lady Philosophy answers. Boethius first asks if there is chance or pure luck, which Lady Philosophy denies can exist. All things must have a cause. This makes Boethius ask if man can then have free will, since God foreknows all things. Either God's knowledge causes the event, or the event causes God's knowledge. In either case there is necessity. Lady Philosophy answers Boethius' argument by noting that he misunderstands God's way of knowing. God does not see into the future as we do, but he sees all things from all times during the ever-present moment. Thus man's decisions can be free, even though they are seen by God, just as a man who sees someone walk doesn't cause him to walk.

Thus, Lady Philosophy argues, there can be no doubt that man is free and that God rewards or punishes him in a way that is fair. Thus it is possible and indeed necessary to look to God and to pray to him as an all-knowing judge. Boethius has found that he does indeed have a homeland and a divine, omnipotent Father.

[2] *homeland*: The reminder of Boethius' homeland brings us back to the original goal in book 1. See 1 *prosa* 5.

topics, though very useful to understand, carry us a little off the path of the journey we've begun. I'm afraid that you'll grow tired from the side trips and not have the strength to finish your proper course."

"Don't be afraid of that!" I said. "To learn about the things that delight me most will be like finding a place to rest. And, at the same time, since every part of your argument would then stand on sure footing, there wouldn't be any doubt about the arguments that followed."[3]

Then she replied, "I'll humor you," and she immediately began to speak these words: "If anyone should define chance as a happening produced at random and without causal relationships, I would say that accidents don't occur at all, and I believe chance is an utterly empty word, without any real reference to an underlying reality; for since God directs things into their order, is there any place left at all for random events? It's a true statement that nothing can come from nothing,[4] and none of the ancients argues against it, although they applied it not to the First Mover but to matter subject to Him, as a sort of fundamental notion of all reasoning concerning nature. But if something should arise without causes, it would seem to arise from nothing. And if

[3] *since every part of your argument . . . arguments that followed*: Boethius seems to consider the idea of free will as an essential element of his argument. Although the topic at first glance seems to have little of the element of *consolatio*, Boethius' central question throughout the whole work has been "Does the world make sense?" If there is no free will, there is no justice, and then the world would not make sense.

Many of the arguments in this section are difficult to follow. The explanations in R. W. Sharples, ed. and trans., *Cicero: "On Fate"; Boethius: "The Consolation of Philosophy" IV. 5–7, V.* (Warminster: Aris and Phillips, 1991), which we cite frequently, are very helpful.

[4] *nothing can come from nothing*: This is a common observation in antiquity, found, e.g., in Plato (*Philebus* 26E and *Timaeus* 28A) and in Lucretius, *On the Nature of Things* 1.150. (These and other citations are found in Joachim Gruber, *Kommentar zu Boethius, "De consolatione philosophiae"*, 2nd ed. [Berlin: Walter de Gruyter, 2006; originally published 1978], p. 371.) Lady Philosophy will note that the First Mover, God, does not have an origin or cause of himself. Boethius borrows the idea of the Prime Mover from Aristotle, who applies the term to the one who initiates all activity.

this can't happen, chance of the sort that we described can't even exist."

"Well, then," I asked, "is there nothing that can properly be called chance or fortune? Or is there something that escapes common notice to which we can apply these words?"

"My friend Aristotle in the *Physics* briefly and rather accurately defined it." [5]

"In what way?" I said.

"When something is done for a specific purpose," she said, "but for various reasons something else happens that is different from what was intended, that is called chance—such as if a man were digging in the ground in order to till his field and found a mass of gold. This is believed to have happened by a stroke of luck, but it does not happen out of thin air; it has its causes. But these causes come together unexpectedly and without being hoped for, and so they seem to have produced an accident. Yet if the farmer hadn't been digging, and unless a man had dug a hole in that place and planted his money there, the gold wouldn't have been found. These causes, then, are the source of chance profit, which occurred by causes that came together and met each other, not through the intention of the one performing the action of digging. For neither the one who buried the gold nor the one who worked the ground intended that the money be discovered, but, as I said, it happened and came about that this man dug where the other man buried the money. Therefore, we can define chance as an unexpected outcome that happened through the coming together of causes in situations where things were done for other purposes. But truly, that order which proceeds with its inevitable connections and which flows down from the fountain of Providence makes these causes flow together and unite, and it directs all things in their time and places.

[5] *My friend Aristotle . . . accurately defined it*: See Aristotle, *Physics* 2.4 and 5. Gruber, *Kommentar zu Boethius*, p. 372, notes that Boethius recalls from memory and would more accurately cite *Metaphysics* 1025a.

metrum 1

> The Tigris and Euphrates together spring forth[6]
> and rise from Achaemenian[7] rocks.
> The land where arrows shot by Parthians turn,[8]
> these rivers flow and are cleft.
> What if these streams once more would combine?
> Ship would meet ship,
> tree trunks torn from the banks
> would mingle, twist, and entwine,
> weaving random paths down the land.
> These wanderings, seeming chance,
> are not: they are controlled by the slope.
> Even chance wears a bridle, heeds the law."

2. "I see this," I said, "and I agree with what you're saying. But in this series of causes bound together, is there any room for freedom of the will, or does the chain of Fate bind every movement of human souls?"

"There is," she said, "for rational natures could not exist if there were no freedom of the will.[9] Anything that by its nature uses reason also possesses judgment, which allows it to make decisions about things. By its own power it determines what it should seek and what it should avoid. Indeed, everyone strives after what he thinks is desirable, and he avoids what should be avoided. Therefore, everything that has reason possesses the freedom to want something or

---

[6] *The Tigris and Euphrates together spring forth*: The ancients believed that the Tigris and Euphrates had a common source.

[7] *Achaemenian*: "Achaemenian" refers to Achaemenes, the first Persian king; the word simply means "Persian" here.

[8] *arrows shot by Parthians turn*: The Parthians were famous opponents of the Romans. Part of their success lay in their ability to shoot arrows while seeming to ride in retreat, a technique referred to in the original Latin of this poem.

[9] *rational natures could not . . . freedom of the will*: Adrian Fortescue compares Dante, *Paradiso* 5:22–24 (Adrian Fortescue, *Ancius Manlius Severinus Boethius De consolatione philosophiae libri quinque*, ed. G. D. Smith [Hildesheim: Georg Olms, 1976; originally published in London, 1925], p. 140).

not to want it, although I don't think this freedom is equal in all beings. Heavenly, divine beings have keen judgment and uncorrupted will, and they have within them the power to achieve what they want. Human souls are necessarily more free when they continue to contemplate the Divine Mind, but they are less free when they fall down to human bodies.[10] Their ultimate slavery comes when they are given over to vices and fall away from the possession of their reason.[11] For when they have cast their eyes from the light of supreme truth to lower, darker things, they are soon blinded in a cloud of ignorance and disturbed by destructive passions. Assenting and yielding to these passions, they increase the servitude they've brought upon themselves, and in a certain way they're made captive by their own freedom. Still, that gaze of Providence, looking forth from eternity, sees all things and, in accordance with men's merits, arranges everything as it has been predetermined ahead of time.[12]

---

[10] *Human souls are necessarily more free . . . fall down to human bodies*: See Plato, *Phaedrus* 247D. As we have seen, Plato posits that the soul originally lived in contemplation (*theoria*) of the divine. When the soul receives a body, it becomes forgetful and falls to earth, where, it is to be hoped, it attempts to regain its knowledge of the divine through philosophy.

[11] *Their ultimate slavery . . . possession of their reason*: As Henry Chadwick notes, "Both the Neoplatonists and the Christian Augustinian tradition treat freedom as a moral quality. No one is less free than the person dominated by vice. Freedom is attained by continual contemplation of the divine mind, lost when one slips down into the corporeal. The upward look is full of light, the downward of darkness" (Henry Chadwick, *Boethius: The Consolations of Music, Logic, Theology, and Philosophy* [Oxford: Oxford University Press, 1981], p. 245). See also Andrew Louth, *The Origins of the Christian Mystical Tradition* (Oxford: Clarendon Press, 1981), pp. 1–17.

[12] *arranges everything . . . ahead of time*: Lady Philosophy's claim that God "works out" what has been "predetermined" is seen by Boethius (the character) as a contradiction of human free will. "Predetermined" (*praedestinata*) is perhaps an unfortunate choice of words by Boethius the author, since he will show in the rest of Book 5 that God sees things in advance but does not cause them. Lady Philosophy's main point here seems to be that the all-seeing God administers the rewards or (corrective) justice that each man has merited by his proper or improper use of human freedom.

metrum 2

> The sun, clear with pure light,
> 'All things sees and hears,' [13]
> sang Homer with honeyed voice.
> But the sun prevails not in the earth's womb,
> the light of its rays too weak
> to burst even the sea's depths.
> Not so the Builder of the universe.
> No mass of earth nor dead of night can stop
> His gaze from the heights.
> What is, what has been, what is to come—
> He discerns. He surveys all.
> He alone is the true Sun." [14]

3. Then I replied, "But wait, I'm disturbed again by an even greater difficulty." [15]

---

[13] *The sun, clear . . . "All things sees and hears"*: The first line of this poem is in Greek in the original and is an adaptation from Homer, *Iliad* 3.277 and *Odyssey* 11.109 and 12.323. The following line is a translation of *Iliad* 1.605.

[14] *He alone is the true Sun*: In the original Latin, there is a play on the words *solus* (alone) and *sol* (sun): "quem, quia respicit omnis solus, / verum possis dicere solem" (13–14). There is no connection between the words, but it was a common false etymology. See Varro, *Lingua latina* 5.68 (cited by Gruber, *Kommentar zu Boethius*, p. 378), and Cicero, *On the Nature of the Gods* 2.68. Gruber notes the reference in the New Testament to Christ as the "true light" (John 1:9). Cf. also Milton, "On the Morning of Christ's Nativity":

> The sun himself withheld his wonted speed,
> And hid his head for shame,
> As his inferior flame,
> The new enlightened world no more should need;
> He saw a greater sun appear
> Than his bright throne, or burning axletree could bear.
> (79–84)

[15] *even greater difficulty*: In the following section, which covers the question of the supposed conflict between divine foreknowledge and human free will, Boethius is followed closely by Chaucer, in book 4 of *Troilus and Criseyde*, and by Jean de Meun in the *Romance of the Rose*. Chaucer probably wrote *Troilus and Criseyde* while he was translating the *Consolation* around 1380. In the poem, the Trojan Troilus has learned that his beloved Criseyde will be handed over to the Greeks. He considers suicide and ponders whether man's life is completely

"What is it?" she asked. "Though I can already guess what's troubling you."

"It would seem contradictory and conflicting," I answered, "for God to know everything and for there to be free will. If God sees all things ahead of time and can't be deceived, it must be true that what He foresees by His foresight will come about. So, if He has foreknowledge from eternity not only of the deeds of men but of their plans and wishes, there will be no freedom of the will, since no deed or wish will be able to exist, except what He has foreseen by a divine Providence that can't be deceived.[16] Otherwise, if desires can turn away from the manner in which they have been foreknown, then

---

controlled by destiny. The *Romance of the Rose* was a long French dream allegory written by two authors, Guillaume de Lorris and Jean de Meun, during the thirteenth century. Jean de Meun, *Romance of the Rose* 17101–526, examines the supposed conflict between predestination and free will, particularly with regard to the fairness of divine punishment for human evil. Nature is speaking, arguing against the idea that man's destinies are determined. Instead, she argues that men should make their decisions by listening to Reason.

[16] *So, if He has foreknowledge . . . can't be deceived*: Although Boethius will be shown wrong, he sees a potential conflict with free will in God's knowledge of future events. Similarly, in *Troilus and Criseyde*, Troilus ponders whether his loss of Criseyde was predestined:

> For some men syn, if God seth al biform,
> Ne God may nat deceived ben, parde,
> Than moot it fallen, theigh men hadde it sworn,
> That purveiance hath seyn before to be.
> Wherefor I sey, that from eterne if he
> Hath wist byforn oure thought ek as oure dede,
> We han no fre chois, as thise clerkes rede.
>
> (4.974–80)

Cf. also Jean de Meun, *Romance of the Rose* (17127–45):

> But He knows when they [human deeds] will happen, how, and what result they will work toward, for if it could be otherwise than that God knew beforehand, He would not be all-powerful, all-good, or all-knowing, nor would He be sovereign, the fair, sweet, the first of everything. He would not know what we do, or, along with men, who live in doubtful belief, He would believe without the certainty of knowledge. To attribute such an error to God would be to commit the devil's work; no man who wanted to enjoy Reason should hear it.

(Guillaume de Lorris and Jean de Meun, *The Romance of the Rose*, trans. Charles Dahlberg, 3rd ed. [Princeton: Princeton University Press, 1995].)

foreknowledge of the future will not be secure but will instead
be an uncertain opinion—which I consider unthinkable when
speaking of God.[17]

"I don't agree with that argument which some think can
untie the knot of this question. They say that something will
come about not because Providence has seen that it will happen, but rather on the contrary that, since it will happen, it
can't escape the notice of divine Providence, and so the necessity falls on the other side. And they say that it is not necessary that the things that are foreseen happen but that it is
necessary that what will happen be foreseen. It is as if it were
a matter of finding what is the cause of what—that the foreknowledge is the cause of the necessity of the future or that
the necessity is the cause of the foreknowledge of the future—
rather than trying to show that, however the ordering of causes
works, the outcome of things foreseen is necessary, even if the
foreknowledge does not seem to bring about for the future
events the necessity of their occurrence.[18]

"For if someone were sitting, the opinion that he was sitting would have to be true, and then on the other hand, if the
opinion that someone is sitting is true, he must be sitting.[19]
In any case, then, there is necessity: in the latter case it is
necessary that he be sitting; in the former it is necessary that
the opinion be true. But the person is not sitting because the
opinion is true, but the opinion is true because it happened

[17] *Otherwise, if . . . speaking of God:* Here see Chaucer, *Troilus and Criseyde*
4.981–94.
[18] *I don't agree with that argument . . . necessity of their occurrence:* This paragraph is adapted in Chaucer, *Troilus and Criseyde* 995–1022, and Jean de Meun,
Romance of the Rose 17267–90. De Meun even uses Boethius' image of untying
the knot.
[19] *For if someone were sitting . . . he must be sitting:* In *Troilus and Criseyde*, Chaucer uses this image:

> For if ther sitte a man yond on a see,
> Than by necessite bihoveth it
> That, certes, thyn opynyoun sooth be,
> That wenest or conjectest that he sit.
> (4.1023–26)

See further lines 1027–43.

first that the person sat down. So, although the cause of the truth does not come from the opinion, there is still necessity present on both sides.

"We can certainly reason along the same lines concerning Providence and things in the future. For indeed, if things are foreseen because they will happen, they don't really happen because they are foreseen, but it is still necessary that either what will come about is foreseen by God or that the things foreseen will come about as they are foreseen. This alone is enough to do away with freedom of the will. Besides, it's preposterous for the occurrence of temporal things to be the cause of eternal foreknowledge. But if we suppose that God foresees future events because they are going to come about, what else are we doing but thinking that once they happen they are the cause of His most high Providence? Furthermore, just as it is necessary that something exist if we know it exists, so, if we know something will happen, it must happen. Thus it comes about that the occurrence of the thing that's foreseen can't be avoided.[20] Finally, if someone perceives something other than the way it is, not only is that perception not knowledge, but it's a false belief and not at all like the truth of knowledge. So, if something will happen in such a way that its occurrence is not certain or necessary, how can that occurrence be foreknown? For just as knowledge isn't mingled with falsehood, so that which is conceived through knowledge can't be any other than the way it is conceived to be. And this is the reason why knowledge is lacking in falsehood, since the thing must be just the same as knowledge understands it to be.

"Tell me then, how can God know that these uncertain things will be? If He has judged that things will eventually happen, when it is possible for them not to happen, He is deceived—something we can't even consider, let alone say out loud. But if He determines that things will simply occur the way they will occur, so that He knows that they can just as well happen as not happen, what kind of foreknowledge is that, when it doesn't grasp anything with certainty or sureness? How does this differ from the foolish prophecy of Tiresias:

What should I say? It either will be or it won't.[21]

Then how is Divine Providence better than human opinion, if He, just like humans, judges without certainty the things whose outcome is uncertain? But if in the case of Providence, the most certain fountain of all things, there can be no uncertainty, then there is a certain outcome for the things He foreknows will surely be.

"And so, there is no freedom for human plans and actions, since the Divine Mind that sees all without error binds and constrains them to one outcome. As soon as we accept this idea, we can see how much damage is done to the sphere of human actions. In vain we offer to good men and to bad ones rewards and punishments that are not merited by the voluntary actions of the soul. This would seem to be the greatest injustice of all, though it's now considered very just, that wicked men be punished or good ones rewarded, since these men would have no free will urging them to either course but would instead be compelled by the fixed necessity of the future. And so there would be neither vices nor virtues, but rather a mixed-up and indistinguishable confusion of merits. We can conceive of nothing more wicked than this, since the order of all things would be carried out through Providence, and nothing would be allowed to human intentions; it would happen that our faults proceed from the Author of all things. And so there is no reason for hoping for something to happen or for praying that something won't happen; for why should a person hope or pray to avoid something when all things are tied up in unchangeable bonds?

"And so, we will lose that single interaction between God and man[22] that happens when we hope for something or pray

---

[21] *What should I say? It either will be or it won't*: See Horace, *Satire* 2.5.59. Boethius seems to be saying that there must be a necessity in God's foreknowledge. It would be absurd, he reasons, to say that God simply sees something as equally possible and not possible.

[22] *single interaction between God and man*: C. S. Lewis sees Boethius' portrayal of the interaction (*commercium*) between God and man as Christian, "in

for help, and we gain the priceless reward of divine grace[23] in exchange for our proper humility. This alone is the means by which men seem to be able to speak with God and become united through prayer with that inaccessible light[24] before they enter into it. But if we accept the necessity of future events, these prayers will seem to have no force. Then what will there be that will let us connect with the highest Lord of all things and become united with Him? Thus the human race will have to grow weak, being separated and severed from its source.

metrum 3[25]

What discordant cause dissolves the world's laws?
What god establishes a war between two truths,
so that each which singly stands, if mixed

---

contradiction to the Platonic view that the Divine and the human cannot meet except through a *tertium quid* [third party]" (C. S. Lewis, *The Discarded Image: An Introduction to Medieval and Renaissance Literature* [Cambridge: Cambridge University Press, 1964], p. 79). See also C. J. de Vogel, "*Amor quo caelum regitur*", *Vivarium* 1 (1963): 4–5, and Christine Mohrmann, "Some Remarks on the Language of Boethius, *Consolatio philosophiae*", in *Latin Script and Letters*, A.D. 400–900, ed. John J. O'Meara and Bern Naumann (Cambridge: Cambridge University Press, 1976), p. 56; the latter considers the passage "of undeniable Christian influence" on theological grounds and on the basis of apparent liturgical influences. The strong emotion that Boethius seems to be showing regarding the importance of a personal connection with God does seem to suggest Christian influence rather than Neoplatonism.

[23] *grace*: The use of "grace" (*gratia*) has been considered by many as a nod to Christianity. See the references in Gruber, *Kommentar zu Boethius*, p. 383; see especially Vogel, "*Amor quo caelum regitur*", p. 4, and Mohrmann, "Language of Boethius", p. 58.

[24] *inaccessible light*: The "inaccessible light" (*inaccessae luci*) brings to mind 1 Timothy 6:16: "Who only hath immortality, and inhabiteth light inaccessible, whom no man hath seen, nor can see: to whom be honour and empire everlasting. Amen" (Douay-Rheims).

[25] *metrum 3*: Gerard O'Daly notes that this poem is one of *aporia* (Greek for uncertainty, confusion) and is the only one spoken by Boethius since 1 *metrum* 5, a poem that uses the same meter as this one (Gerard O'Daly, *The Poetry of Boethius* [Chapel Hill: University of North Carolina Press, 1991], p. 175). Both poems express the sorrow of a theist who questions whether the world really

wishes not to be joined?[26]
Or is there no discord between truths,
and each to the other surely adheres,
while the mind buried in the darkness of the flesh,
its light's fire suppressed,
can't know the finely fastened world?
Why does the mind burn with such love
to discover hidden signs of truth?
Does it know what it desires in anxiety to know?
But who labors to know things already known?
And if he doesn't know, why seek in blindness?
For who chooses or is able to follow the unknown
or how to discover the same?
May ignorance devise to learn a form?
Or when it perceives the Divine Mind,
does it know the sum and the parts?
Now hidden in the clouds of the body,
it is not totally oblivious to self.
Losing the single things, it holds on to the whole.[27]
Therefore whoever seeks the truth
is in neither condition:
for within neither does he know nor not know all things.
But retaining the sum he remembers;
and pulling them forth—
considers the things seen on high,
so that to those things saved,
he may add parts forgotten."

---

does make sense after all. Here Boethius fears that if we are to assume that everything in life is foreordained, then there is no need to have a personal relationship with God.

    [26] *What god establishes . . . wishes not to be joined?* Boethius here wonders if
God has caused two truths to be somehow irreconcilable. In the following question, he posits the idea that man may simply not understand. This, of course, is
the option to which he holds, since, as he will argue in the next several lines,
man's (Platonic) remembrance of the truth is severely limited.

    [27] *Losing the single things, it holds on to the whole*: Sharples, "On Fate"; "Con-
solation", p. 222, suggests the interpretation that "we are aware in general terms
of the truth we are seeking, but have forgotten the particular truths that go to
make it up."

4. Then she replied, "This is an old complaint concerning Providence, one that Tully,[28] when he classified the nature of prophecy, gave great attention to. And it is something that you yourself have looked into thoroughly and at length, but it hasn't been disentangled carefully or thoroughly enough by any of you. The reason for this cloud of confusion is that the movements of human reason are not able to approach the simplicity of divine foreknowledge. If they could understand it in any way, no uncertainty would remain. I will eventually try to untangle the question and solve it, after I have worked through the things that are disturbing you.

"Now I wonder why you consider as ineffective the argument of those who say that foreknowledge is not the cause of the necessity of the things that will be, and that the freedom of the will is not impeded by foreknowledge. Surely you don't have any other opinion regarding the necessity of future events except that those things that are foreknown cannot fail to come about? Therefore, if knowledge in advance is not tied up with the future events, which you yourself said a little earlier, how is it that the outcome of things dependent on the will are forced into a fixed outcome?[29]

"Now for the sake of argument, so you can consider what would follow, let's suppose there were no foreknowledge. Surely the things that come about through the will wouldn't be forced by necessity, would they?"

"Not at all," I replied.

"Well, on the other hand, let's suppose there is foreknowledge, but that this foreknowledge confers with it no necessity

[28] *Tully*: Tully is Marcus Tullius Cicero, who writes of the topic of providence in his *De divinatione* 2.7.18, although there is some discrepancy between Boethius' comments and those of Cicero. See P. G. Walsh, trans., *"The Consolation of Philosophy", Translated with Introduction and Explanatory Notes* (Oxford: Clarendon Press, 1999), p. 105. Boethius discusses the topic in his *De interpretatione* 225.9ff.

[29] *Therefore, if knowledge in advance . . . forced into a fixed outcome?* Lady Philosophy will show that it is not the knowledge that causes the necessity of the future events. In some causes the necessity will be simple (e.g., the sun must rise), and in others the necessity will be conditional or logical (if a man is walking, it is necessary that he walk). In neither event does the knowledge of the event cause it to happen. Knowledge of the event on God's part will be shown to be more like a person viewing something happening at the present moment.

upon things. The same freedom of the will would remain absolute and intact, in my opinion. But foreknowledge, you will say,
may not entail the necessity of outcome for future events, but it
is still a sign that they are necessarily going to happen. In this
way, then, even if there had not been foreknowledge, it would
stand to reason that the outcome of future things would be
necessary. For indeed every sign shows what exists; it doesn't
bring about what it points to.[30] So it must be demonstrated first
that nothing happens without necessity, if it is to be evident
that this preawareness is a sign of necessity. Otherwise, if there
is no necessity, then the preawareness could not be a sign of a
thing that doesn't exist. Now, truly, it is certain that a proof
relying on firm reason ought to proceed not from signs and arguments sought from outside but from inherent and necessary causes.

"But how can it be that future events which are foreseen
should not come about? It would be as if we believed that the
things Providence foreknows will happen won't happen, instead
of thinking only that they might happen, and that no necessity in their nature would make them happen.[31] And you can
easily consider this argument from the following. We see many
things subject to our vision as they are happening, such as
what we see charioteers doing as they guide and steer their
teams, and other things of this sort. Does any necessity cause
any of these things to come about?"

"Not at all," I replied. "For then the use of skill would be in
vain, if everything were moved by compulsion."

"And so, in the case of the things that are freed from any
necessity of being the way they are, if we were to see them
before they occurred, we would see that they will happen

[30] *every sign shows what exists . . . what it points to*: Lady Philosophy argues that
a sign does not cause something to happen. Similarly, divine foreknowledge is
an indication of something that will happen, but it doesn't cause it to happen.
Necessity is not inherent in the foreknowledge.

[31] *no necessity in their nature would make them happen*: Sharples, "On Fate";
"*Consolation*", p. 223, explains: "The issue is not whether what is foreknown
comes about or not; of course it does. The question is rather whether it must,
not just come about, but come about through necessity; and this Boethius [the
author] denies, using *present*-tense examples to prove the point" (emphasis in
original).

without any necessity. So there are certain events whose outcome is freed from all necessity. For I don't think anyone will
say this: the things we are seeing now weren't going to happen before they occurred. And so the occurrence of these things,
even though they are foreknown, is free. For just as knowledge of things in the present conveys no necessity on them as
they happen, so the foreknowledge of future things places no
necessity on them to make them come about. But you will say
that this very question is in doubt, whether there can be any
foreknowledge of the things that have no necessary occurrence.[32] For these ideas seem to you to be in conflict, and you
think that if things are foreseen ahead of time that necessity
must result, and that, if necessity isn't present, things can't be
foreknown and that nothing can be perceived by knowledge
unless the thing is certain. But if things of uncertain outcome
are seen as if they were certain, this view is clouded error, not
the truth of knowledge. For you believe that to think things
are different from the way they are is opposed to the integrity
of knowledge. The cause of this error is that everything that
any person knows, he thinks is known only from an object's
nature and ability to be known. But the truth is the exact opposite, for everything that's known is known not according to its
ability to be known but rather according to the ability of the
knower.[33] To show this with a brief example—sight recognizes the roundness of an object in one way, while touch recognizes the same roundness in another. By sending out its rays,
sight at a distance sees simultaneously the whole object, but

[32] *whether there can be . . . no necessary occurrence*: As Sharples, *"On Fate"*;
"Consolation", p. 223, notes, here the issue is whether future events not caused
by necessity, i.e., contingent events, can be known. (How can something be
known if it isn't necessary for it to happen?) In this instance, Lady Philosophy
explains that the nature of divine reason offers the answer. It knows things in a
manner superior to human understanding.
[33] *everything that's known is known . . . ability of the knower*: Friedrich Klingner
notes that this idea goes back to Iamblichus, according to Ammonius (Friedrich
Klingner, *De Boethii Consolatione philosophiae*, 2nd ed. [Zurich: Weidmann, 1966;
originally published 1921], pp. 107–8). See also Sharples, *"On Fate"*; *"Consolation"*, pp. 26–27, and Gruber, *Kommentar zu Boethius*, pp. 388–89. The Scholastic formation is "Everything is received according to the measure of the receiver."
See references in Fortescue, *Boethius De consolatione*, p. 150.

touch takes hold of the round object, joins together with it, and by moving around the whole circumference understands its roundness part by part.

"In the same human being the senses perceive in one way, the imagination in another, reason in another, and intelligence in another.[34] For the senses understand a figure as it is bound up in the matter subject to it, but the imagination understands the figure alone without its matter. And reason also goes beyond the figure and examines with a universal outlook the form of the thing itself as it appears in individual objects. But the eye of intelligence is loftier still; going beyond the bounds of the sphere, it gazes with the pure vision of the mind upon the simple form itself. And we must consider this carefully, since the higher power of understanding embraces the lower, but the lower does not in any way rise up to the higher. Indeed the senses are of no value apart from the material, nor does the imagination see the universal forms, nor the reason grasp the simple form.[35] But intelligence, as if looking down from above and grasping the form, distinguishes everything subject to the form, although it does so in the manner in which it comprehends the form itself, which cannot be known to anything else. For it understands the reason's view of the whole, and the imagination's view of the figure, and also the matter

[34] *In the same human being . . . intelligence in another*: Boethius borrows the idea of these four ways of knowing—sense, imagination, reason, and intelligence— from Aristotle, *De anima* 427b6–24. Sense refers to the perceptions of the senses, imagination is the ability to form mental images of things not seen, reason is abstract thinking, and intelligence is the "understanding of the unity that underlies the multiplicity of forms" (J. J. O'Donnell, ed., *Consolatio philosophiae*, vol. 2, Bryn Mawr Latin Commentaries [Bryn Mawr: Thomas Library, Bryn Mawr College, 1984], p. 107).

[35] *Indeed the senses . . . reason grasp the simple form*: In the following discussion, Boethius combines Aristotelian and Platonic thought. Aristotle believed that there were universals, types of objects that showed similar characteristics (e.g., dogs, stones). These universals are objectively real but do not have an existence separate from the earth. Plato's view of forms, on the other hand, suggests that there are models in a reality outside the earth after which earthly objects or concepts are patterned. For the distinction between reason and intelligence, see Lewis, *Discarded Image*, pp. 156–57, where he cites Aquinas, *Summa theologica* I, q. 79, art. 8. Intelligence perceives the truth without actively working to figure things out, which is the task of reason.

that is perceived by senses, but not by using reason, imagination, or the senses, but by one stroke of the mind, looking
forth at all things according to form, so to speak. And reason,
too, when it considers something universal, using neither imagination nor the senses, understands what is subject to both
the imagination and the senses. For reason is that which defines
the universal nature of things it has conceived in such a way
as this: 'Man is a rational animal with two legs.' And though
this is a universal idea, no one is unaware that it is a thing
perceivable by sense and the imagination, but that reason considers it not by these means but in a rational conception. The
imagination also, although it takes from the senses the origin
of its seeing and forming of figures, still, without the senses,
surveys all sensible things in a way that is not characteristic of
the senses, but of the imagination's means of judging things.

"Do you see, then, that in understanding, everything uses its
own ability rather than the ability of the things to be known?
This is as it should be; since every judgment is the act of someone judging, it must be the case that everyone accomplishes this
work not from a power outside him but through his own power.

metrum 4

> The Porch[36] once brought obscure old men
> who believed that from outside the body
> senses and ideas were impressed on the mind—
> just as when with a quick stylus
> we fix letters on a smooth, unmarked page.
> But if the mind flourishing with its own activity
> explicates nothing but patiently lies waiting,

[36] *Porch:* "The Porch" refers to the Stoa poikile (painted porch) in Athens,
where the Stoics were accustomed to meet and which was the origin of the name
Stoic. As Walsh notes, "The Stoics . . . followed Aristotle in maintaining that all
knowledge comes through the senses; objects imprint themselves on the soul like
a seal on wax. The Neoplatonists rebut this notion of the mind/soul as a *tabula
rasa*, as a mere recipient of sensations. Such an empirical outlook was opposed to
the traditional Platonist view that the mind has its own dynamic, recalling its
earlier experiences from the world of the Forms" (Walsh, *Consolation*, p. 162).

imprinted with marks of others,
so that just as a mirror, it returns empty images,
how does the concept thrive,
discerning all things with mind?[37]
What power perceives single things—or
what power divides things known?
What collects again things divided,
and taking one path or another;
what now introduces the head to highest things,
now falls to things of earth;
then returning to itself,
contradicts falsehoods with truth?
This is the efficient cause more powerful
than that which passively waits
for marks impressed from outside.[38]
Yet senses affected first in the living body
move and excite the power of the mind
as when light strikes the eyes or
when a voice rattles in the ear.
Then the excited mind's vigor
summons ideas held within,
calls them to similar motions,
and applies them to marks from without;
outward images to inner forms are mingled.

[37] *But if the mind flourishing . . . discerning all things with mind?* Boethius contradicts the Stoics' claim that knowledge comes simply from experience. He argues that concepts or ideas must come from above rather than through the accumulation and assessment of sensory data. Instead of believing that the mind is the target of sensory data that eventually cause perception based on experience, Boethius argues that sensory data stimulate the mind to connect them to a form that they resemble. Augustine had argued for the Neoplatonic over the Stoic view of epistemology in *City of God* 8.7 (cited by Gruber, *Kommentar zu Boethius*, p. 391). For a thorough discussion of the epistemology found in this difficult poem, see Sharples, "On Fate"; "Consolation", pp. 225–26.

[38] *This is the efficient cause . . . marks impressed from outside*: Boethius argues that the mind, using its previous knowledge, is the efficient cause of understanding. The term "efficient cause" goes back to Aristotle, who argued that for everything there must be a cause that brings it into being. The second of Aquinas' proofs for the existence of God is based on the idea of the efficient cause. See Étienne Gilson, *The Philosophy of Thomas Aquinas*, translated by Edward Bullough from the 3rd rev. and enlarged ed. of *Le Thomisme* (New York: Barnes and Noble, 1993), p. 81.

5. "But when we perceive objects, even though characteristics from these objects affect the instruments of the senses when they encounter them, and although the effect upon the body precedes the strength of the mind as it does its work and calls forth upon itself the mind's action, meanwhile stirring up the forms resting within, still, I tell you the mind within the body is not engraved upon by the object perceived through sense, but by its own strength makes judgment about the effect occurring to the body.[39] By all the more do all those beings freed from bodily limitations not follow external objects in making determinations, but rather they set free the act of their mind. And so, on the same principle, many different ways of knowing belong to different kinds of beings. Sense alone, which lacks all other ways of knowing, belongs to beings that lack motion, such as sea mollusks and things that are nourished by clinging to rocks; imagination belongs to beasts that move, in which there seems to be some desire to seek or avoid things. But reason belongs to the human species alone, while intelligence belongs alone to the divine; and so it happens that knowledge, knowing not only its own sphere but what pertains to others, surpasses those others.

"So then, what if sense and imagination oppose the concept of reasoning, saying that the universal, which reason thinks it sees, is nothing? For what can be sensed or imagined cannot be universal, they would argue. And they would argue that either the judgment of reason is true and nothing can be perceived by the senses, or that since it is known that many things are subject to the senses and the imagination, reason's view is groundless, for reason considers what is individual and subject to sense as if it were something universal.

---

[39] *mind within the body . . . effect occurring to the body*: Boethius seems to be suggesting that sense perceptions have no actual physical effect on the mind but rather that the mind begins its proper work after it perceives sensory stimulation. In contrast, in the case of touch, the skin is affected by the object. The mind is thus superior in not being affected by the object perceived. Fortescue, *Boethius De consolatione*, p. 153, cites Dante, *Purgatorio* 18.22–24: "For what is real your apprehensive power / extracts an image it displays within you, / forcing your mind to be attentive to it" (*Dante's "Purgatory"*, trans. Mark Musa [Bloomington: University of Indiana Press, 1981).

"Now suppose reason should reply to these arguments, saying that it perceived what was subject to the senses or to the imagination by consideration of the universal, and that the senses and the imagination were not able to aspire to the understanding of the universal, since their knowledge can't go beyond physical objects, and that, concerning the understanding of things, we must believe in the stronger and more perfect judgment. In a debate of this sort, should we who have the power of reasoning, imagining, and sensing set aside reason's claims? In the same way it is true that human reason doesn't think divine intelligence can see the future, except as it itself does.[40] For this is the way you argue: 'If in any way future events don't seem to be fixed, necessary outcomes, it can't be known with certainty that those events will come about. Therefore, there is no foreknowledge of these things, and if, on the other hand, we should believe there is such foreknowledge concerning them, there won't be anything that doesn't result from necessity.' Now suppose we could have the judgment of the Divine Mind, just as we are users of reason. In that case, since we have judged that imagination and sense should yield to reason, we would consider it most just that human reason should yield to the Divine Mind.

"Now let's climb up to the peak of that intelligence; from there reason will see what it cannot contemplate by itself, namely how things that have no determined outcome are still seen by a certain and definite foreknowledge, and how this knowledge will not be opinion, but the simplicity of the highest knowledge, limited by no boundaries.

metrum 5

What singular shapes travel the earth!
Some with bodies stretched scour the fields,
drawing unbroken tracks with powerful breasts.
Some whip the wind lightly with wandering wing,

[40] *human reason doesn't think . . . except as it itself does:* Boethius tends to view intelligence as belonging to God alone.

floating to heaven's space in fluid flight.
Others delight to press footprints on land
and with steps cross green fields, beneath forests.
Consider these, each in their forms—
their faces bent down, senses dulled.
Only the race of man lifts his head
and, standing upright, looks down upon earth.
Shouldn't this show (unless you are wrong!)[41]
that men with upturned faces seek the heavens?[42]
Thrust your countenance forward!
Don't let thoughts weight your mind;
bear your soul aloft!

6. "Therefore, since everything that's known is understood according to the nature of the one understanding, rather than according to the nature of the thing itself, as we showed a little earlier, let's contemplate—at least as far as we're allowed to—the state of the Divine Being, so that we can recognize what sort of knowledge it possesses. Now it's the common view of all living creatures endowed with reason that God is eternal. Let's consider what eternity is, for this will shed some light for us on both the divine nature and divine knowledge.

---

[41] *unless you are wrong*: The original Latin reads "nisi terrenus male desipis" (unless, earthly, you are terribly foolish). In Boethius' Platonic thinking, *terrenus* (earthly), when applied to man, suggests a terrible perversion of man's purpose and goal.

[42] *men with upturned faces seek the heavens*: The idea that man alone lifts his head to look into the heavens is a common motif in classical literature. Probably the most famous example comes from Ovid's *Metamorphoses*:

> And even though all other animals
> lean forward and look down toward the ground,
> he gave to man a face that is uplifted,
> and ordered him to stand erect and look
> directly up into the vaulted heavens,
> and turn his countenance to meet the stars.
> (1.83–86)

(Ovid, *Metamorphoses*, trans. Charles Martin [New York: W. W. Norton, 2004].)
See also Plato, *Timaeus* 47B–C.

"Eternity is total and perfect possession at one time of unlimited life—which is made clear by comparing it with temporal things.[43] Whatever lives within the present time goes forward from past events to future ones; and nothing has been created within time in such a way that it can embrace at once the whole course of its life. It doesn't yet grasp tomorrow, but it has already lost yesterday; and in daily life you also live no more than in the moment that changes and passes by. And so, whatever experiences time in this way, even if it does not ever begin to be or cease to be—just as Aristotle thought was the case with the world[44]—and though its life might extend to an infinity of time, it is still not something that can rightly be considered eternal. For it doesn't comprehend and embrace the entire space of the time it lives, even if it is infinite, and it doesn't yet possess the future, and it no longer has a past. Now whatever comprehends and possesses all at once the complete fullness of unlimited time and also possesses all of the future and has lost none of the past, this is rightly claimed to be eternal. It is necessary that this thing be in possession of itself, be always present for itself, and have at hand the infinity of passing time.

[43] *Eternity is total and perfect possession . . . temporal things*: As Fortescue, *Boethius De consolatione*, p. 157, notes, Boethius' formulation of eternity was very popular in the Middle Ages, being cited approvingly by Albertus Magnus and Thomas Aquinas, among others. Boethius' formulation is similar to that of the Neoplatonic Plotinus, *Ennead* 3.7.3. The point is that eternity is more than unending time; rather, it is the capturing of all time within the moment. The mind of God is not bound by time. Albertus Magnus notes: "It is the property of God alone, as Boethius says in book 5 of *The Consolation of Philosophy*, to exist always and totally in one simple and ever-present eternity" (*Summa theologica* II, tract 1, q. 4; cited by Fortescue, p. 158). Lewis, *Discarded Image*, p. 89, notes: "Eternity is quite distinct from perpetuity, from mere endless continuance in time. Perpetuity is only the attainment of an endless series of moments, each lost as soon as it is attained. Eternity is the actual and timeless fruition of illimitable life. Time, even endless time, is only an image, almost a parody, of that plenitude. . . . That is why Shakespeare's Lucrece calls it 'thou ceaseless lackey of eternity'" (*Rape*, 967)."

[44] *whatever experiences time in this way . . . case with the world*: See Aristotle, *De caelo* 283b26–284b5. Aristotle believed that the world had always existed and presumably always would. Continued existence, however, falls short of true eternity.

"And so, some men wrongly think that the created world is coeternal with its Creator, when they hear that this world seemed to Plato not to have a beginning and not to have an end. For it is one thing to live an unlimited life, which Plato attributed to the world,[45] but another to embrace all at once the complete presence of unlimited life, which characterizes the Divine Mind alone. For God should not be seen as greater than created things in quantity of time, but rather in His property of having a simple nature.

"Now the infinite movement of temporal things imitates the present state of a life that does not move, since it cannot copy it or equal it, and since it falls short of motionless into movement, and passes down from the simplicity of the present into an infinite quantity of the future and past.[46] And this infinite movement can't possess all at once the complete fullness of its life, and, by, in a certain way, never ceasing to exist, it only seems to emulate somewhat the thing that it cannot fulfill and express, and it binds itself to a kind of presence of the brief and swiftly passing moment; and this presence bears a kind of image of that permanent presence, and it makes whatever things it contacts seem to have true being. Since this presence couldn't really be permanent, it took the path of infinite time, and in this way it was able to continue a life whose fullness it could not fully embrace by being permanent. And so, if we should choose to give suitable names

---

[45] *unlimited life, which Plato attributed to the world*: See Plato, *Timaeus* 37D–38C.

[46] *Now the infinite movement . . . infinite quantity of the future and past*: Boethius means here that something that perpetually exists, but which is not divine, is not eternal but only perpetual, imitating God only in a limited sense. God grasps all at one moment rather than living moment after moment. Fortescue, *Boethius De consolatione*, p. 158, notes that Aquinas frequently cites the following saying, which he attributes to Boethius (*Summa theologica* I, q. 10, art. 2, obj. 1): "The present passing makes for time, the present standing makes for eternity" (*nunc fluens facit tempus, nunc stans facit aeternitatem*). As Fortescue notes, the saying is not found in Boethius, although the idea is present here. Fortescue also cites Boethius' *De Trinitate* 4: "To us 'now' suggests flowing and unending time, but to God it suggests abiding, unmoving, immovable, and eternal time."

for such things, we would follow Plato and say that God is eternal but the world is only perpetual.[47]

"Therefore, since every human judgment understands the things subject to it according to its own nature, and since the condition of God is eternal and abiding, then His knowledge also surpasses all movement of time and remains in the simplicity of its presence. Embracing the limitless spaces of the past and future, it understands all things simply and considers them as if they were being done now. If you want to examine God's foreknowledge carefully, you'll consider that it's not so much foreknowledge of the future but rather never-failing knowledge of the present moment. And so we might do better to call it forth-sight rather than fore-sight,[48] because set far away from the lowest things as if from the lofty summit of the world it looks forth on all things. Why, then, do you think that what's revealed by the divine light becomes necessary when not even humans make what they see become necessary? When you see something happening in the present, your gaze doesn't convey any necessity upon the object, does it? No.[49]

"But if there is any just comparison between divine and human present, just as you men see something in this temporary present of yours, so He discerns all things in His eternal present. Therefore, this divine foreknowledge does not change the nature or integrity of things. It sees the things that will happen in the future as being present to itself. And it does not confuse the judgment of things, but with one glance of its mind distinguishes both the things that will necessarily come about and those that will come about without necessity, just

[47] *we would follow Plato . . . world is only perpetual*: See *Timaeus* 37D–38B.

[48] *forth-sight . . . fore-sight*: In the original, there is a play on the words *praevidentia* (foresight) and *providentia*, which we have translated as "forth-sight". Lewis, *Discarded Image*, p. 89, again offers a good commentary: "Strictly speaking, He [God] never *foresees*; He simply sees. Your 'future' is only an area, and only for us a special area, of His infinite Now. He sees (not remembers) your yesterday's acts because yesterday is still 'there' for Him; He sees (not foresees) your tomorrow's acts because He is already in tomorrow."

[49] *When you see something . . . No*: On this topic, see Aquinas, *Summa theologica* I, q. 14, art. 13.

as when you humans see at the same time a man walking on the earth and the sun rising.[50] Although you perceive them both at the same time when you are looking at them, you determine that the one act is voluntary and the other necessary. In this way, therefore, the divine gaze, seeing all things clearly, does not at all misunderstand the nature of different things that are present to it but that are future events with regard to time. And so it is that this is not opinion but rather knowledge based on reality, when it knows what will happen, although it knows that the things themselves lack all necessity of happening.

"Here, if you should say that what God sees will happen cannot help coming about, and that what cannot keep from coming about occurs through necessity, and if you should bind me to this word 'necessity,' I will confess that it is a thing of most certain proof, but that only a person who contemplated divine matters could arrive at understanding it. And I will reply that the same future event seems necessary in terms of divine knowledge, but truly when considered according to its own nature, it seems totally free and absolute. You see, there are two necessities: one simple, such as 'It is necessary that all men be mortals' and another conditional, like 'If you know someone is walking, it is necessary that he be walking.'[51] For what any person knows cannot be any different from the way

[50] *a man walking on the earth and the sun rising*: The man, of course, walks by choice and so his walking is only a contingent necessity when seen by God. The sun, on the other hand, must necessarily rise; it has no choice. Boethius uses the same idea in his *De interpretatione* 241.4. See the discussion in Sharples, "On Fate"; "Consolation", p. 230.

[51] *there are two necessities . . . 'If you know . . . he be walking'*: This distinction makes its way into *The Nun's Priest's Tale* in the *Canterbury Tales*:

> "Nedely," clepe I symple necessitee;
> Or elles, if free choys be graunted me
> To do that same thyng, or do it noght,
> Though God forwoot it er that it was wroght;
> Or if his wityng streyneth never a deel
> But by necessitee condicioneel.
> (4435–40)

Fortescue cites Aquinas, *Summa theologica* I, q. 14, art. 13 ad 2 (Fortescue, *Boethius De consolatione*, p. 161). As Fortescue notes, the simple necessity could also be considered "physical" and the conditional necessity "logical".

it is known to be, but this condition does not bring with it that simple necessity.

"This necessity is not caused by something's own nature but by the adding of a condition, for no necessity forces man walking of his own accord to go forward, although when he is walking, it is necessary that he be going forward. In the same way, then, if Providence, being present, sees something, it is necessary for that to be, although it has no such necessity in its nature. But God sees as present those future things that occur through the freedom of the will; therefore, these things, when considered according to the divine gaze, become necessary through the condition of divine knowledge, but when considered in and of themselves, they don't lose the absolute freedom of their nature. So, without a doubt, all things that God foreknows will happen will come about, but some of them proceed from freedom of the will. These things, although they will happen, don't through their occurrence lose their own nature, which would have allowed them not to happen before they occurred. And what does it matter that these things have no necessity, when the appearance of necessity comes about in every way because of the nature of divine knowledge? For this reason, consider those examples I suggested a little earlier, the rising sun and the walking man. When they are happening they cannot avoid happening, but one of them, before it happened, was necessarily going to happen, while the other wasn't necessarily going to happen. And so, the things that God possesses in the present will happen without a doubt, but some of these happen through the necessity of things, while others occur through the power of the things that do them. And so, we were not wrong when we said that those things are necessary when seen in terms of divine knowledge, but if considered in and of themselves, they are freed from the bonds of necessity, just as anything that is manifest to the senses, if seen in terms of reason, is universal, but if you look at the thing itself, it is individual.[52]

---

[52] *And so, we were not wrong . . . it is individual*: From the point of view of the divine, future events are necessary, either simply or conditionally. From the point of view of a person preparing to do or not do an action, the event is free. The

"But you will say, 'If I have within me the power to change my intention, I will cancel out Providence, if I should happen to change the things that it foreknew.'[53] I will reply that you alter your intentions, but since the present truth of Providence sees that you can do it, whether you will do it, and in what way you will change things, you can't avoid divine foreknowledge, just as you can't avoid the gaze of an eye that is present, although you turn from one action to another by your free will. 'So then,' you'll say, 'will divine knowledge be changed by my choice of action, so that when I choose now one thing and now another, this knowledge seems in turn to change what it knows?' Not at all. For the divine gaze runs in advance of everything in the future, calls it, and turns it back to the presence of its own knowledge, without, as you suppose, changing and foreknowing now one thing and now another. Instead, with one stroke of the mind, staying still, it anticipates and comprehends your changes. And God obtains this presence by comprehending and seeing all things not through the outcome of future events but through His own simplicity. And on this basis we can resolve the question you put forward a little earlier, that it is not right for our future actions to be said to provide the cause for God's knowledge. For this power of knowledge, embracing all things with a present awareness, itself determines boundaries for all things, but owes nothing to events that will happen later.

"Since these things are so, freedom of the will remains unviolated for mortals, and the laws are not unfair when they propose rewards and punishments, since the will is free from all

difference is in the way of knowing of the divine and the human. Similarly, from the point of view of the senses, a dog can be perceived by the senses, although the senses cannot figure out that it is a dog. The senses just perceive the four legs, hair, barking, and so forth. Reason must take what the senses give it and then figure out the universal concept of the dog.

[53] *But you will say, 'If I have . . . things that it foreknew'*: For this argument, see Aquinas, *Summa theologica* I, q. 14, art. 15. Man cannot change God's foreknowledge by changing his own mind, since God really exercises not foreknowledge but simply knowledge.

necessity. And God still remains a watchman on high, foreknowing all things, and the ever-present eternity of His vision moves together with the future nature of our actions and dispenses rewards to the good and punishments to the bad. And not in vain are hopes and prayers placed before God, since when they are just, they cannot be without effect. So let us shun vices and cultivate virtues, lifting our minds to proper hopes and offering humble prayers on high.[54] For, if you wish to speak the truth, a great necessity[55] has been placed upon you men to do good, since you live in front of a judge who sees all things."

---

[54] *So let us shun vices . . . humble prayers on high*: Perhaps Chaucer was think-ing of this Boethian passage as he wrote the authorial charge to the reader at the end of *Troilus and Criseyde*:

> Repeyreth hom fro worldly vanyte,
> And of youre herte up casteth the visage
> To thilke God that after his ymage
> Yow made, and thynketh al nys but a faire
> This world, that passeth soone as floures faire.
>   (5.1837–41)

[55] *necessity*: Boethius is making a play on the word "necessity" here, using it in a more straightforward way rather than as a technical philosophical term, as he had earlier.

Contemporary Criticism

The Ladder of Knowledge and the Ascent to Wisdom in Boethius' *The Consolation of Philosophy*

Mitchell Kalpakgian
Wyoming Catholic College

Evil assumes the appearance of injustice in *The Consolation of Philosophy* as Boethius undergoes, in the manner of classical tragedy, a sudden fall from high to low. A distinguished Roman consul respected for his vast learning and honored by Theodoric and the emperor of Constantinople for his public service, a member of an ancient aristocratic family who married into another patrician family, and a father who witnessed the singular honor of his two sons' appointments to the consulship, Boethius finds himself without titles, wealth, honor, or happiness as he awaits his death sentence in prison. His mind in a state of shock, stupor, and despair, Boethius sees no purpose or value to his suffering—a blow caused by the power of blind Fortune, whose very nature predicates irrationality, whim, arbitrariness, injustice. In the light of this tragedy, Boethius feels that, as the ancient atomists thought, "Whirl is king": the forces of chance and chaos rule supreme over law and divine providence. Boethius' confrontation with evil brings physical pain (prison), emotional anguish ("for of all the adversities of Fortune the saddest is this: to have once been happy" [2.pr.4]),[1] and intellectual confusion ("if the ruler of the universe is in fact good, how can evil exist or go unpunished?" [4.pr.1]).

In the midst of this grief, Lady Philosophy appears as a physician to heal Boethius' suffering and compose his passions, and she comes as a teacher to illuminate his mind and lead him to wisdom. While fickle Fortune suddenly topples Boethius

---

[1] Boethius, *The Consolation of Philosophy*, trans. and ed. Scott Goins and Barbara Wyman, Ignatius Critical Editions (San Francisco: Ignatius Press, 2012). All quotations from the *Consolation* are from this edition.

from high to low, Lady Philosophy calmly lifts him from the pain of tragedy to the equanimity of wisdom. Boethius' ascent from ignorance to knowledge has its precedent in the prisoner's escape from the darkness of the cave to the splendor of sunlight in Plato's "Allegory of the Cave". Boethius' journey follows the course that Saint Bonaventure describes in *The Soul's Journey to God*: "In relation to our position in creation, the universe itself is a ladder by which we can ascend into God. Some created things are vestiges, others images; some are material, others spiritual; some are temporal, others are everlasting; some are outside us, others within us."[2] Boethius' progression from sensory reactions to contemplative knowledge likewise compares to Dante's travel from the dark forest of his middle age and from the lower realms of the Inferno to the glorious radiance of Paradise in the *Divine Comedy*. Just as Virgil and Beatrice guide Dante from the state of darkness and ignorance to the fullness of light and truth, Lady Philosophy leads Boethius through the steps of the ladder of knowledge from memory to reason, and finally, via philosophy, to God.

Philosophy's first lesson involves awakening Boethius' memory and leading him to self-knowledge. She criticizes her pupil's exaggeration of Fortune's malice and his neglect of Fortune's blessings. Philosophy calls to memory Fortune's great gifts. After his father died, Boethius was raised in the household of Symmachus, a Roman consul who provided him with an outstanding liberal education. Fortune further blessed Boethius in his marriage to Rusticiana, Symmachus' daughter, a woman constantly praised for her virtue in the *Consolation*. Fortune favored Boethius again by the many honors he received in his lifetime, "honors often denied to much older men". Boethius' good fortune climaxed when both of his sons were elevated to the consulship on the same day: "[W]ill any mountain of evils falling upon you be able to destroy the memory of that day?" As Boethius remembers Fortune's blessings along with her curses,

[2] Bonaventure, *The Soul's Journey to God*, trans. Ewert Cousins (Mawhawk, N.J.: Paulist Press, 1978), 1.2.

he admits the sobering truth that Philosophy exposes: "Now for the first time she has cast her glance of envy upon you." She adds, "[Y]ou still couldn't deny that you've been happy" (2.pr.3). Philosophy teaches her student that Fortune is not a malevolent deity that has singled out Boethius for punishment but is a neutral power that is neither loving nor hateful. Fortune simply follows the law of her nature, her essential mutability. As Boethius regains his memory and recovers a portion of his composure, his view of Fortune changes. Instead of resentfully blaming her as his personal enemy, he comes to view Fortune in the broader sense of a universal power that circumscribes all people in all places at all times rather than as a wicked goddess seeking revenge against her enemies.

Philosophy continues the liberal education of her student, correcting other errors in the hope that he will see his suffering in a new light. Accusing Boethius of wandering, of losing that "natural inclination" (3.pr.3) that leads to the "true good", Philosophy explains that "adverse Fortune, for the most part, uses her claw to drag men back to the things that are good" (2.pr.8). Philosophy finds fault with Boethius, who as a dignitary had false ideas of happiness in terms of power, fame, and honor and tells him (regarding offices and might), "[I]n your ignorance of true worth and power you equate [these honors] with heaven" and "[Y]ou don't know how to act rightly except when you're courting the winds of popularity" (2.pr.6; 2.pr.7). Failing to distinguish between the temporal and the eternal, between false goods and the true Good, Boethius has deceived himself about the lasting sources of human happiness: riches, power, and fame do not deliver what they promise. Subject always to the mutability of fortune, time, and death, the temporal blessings of the world, according to Philosophy, are deceptive: "Indeed, I think Fortune is of more benefit when she is adverse than when she brings prosperity, for in the latter case she approaches under the guise of happiness. When she seems kind, she lies; but when she shows herself fickle and unstable, she is truthful. In the first case she deceives; in the latter she instructs" (2.pr.8).

Philosophy's second important lesson is that bad fortune enlightens (2.pr.8). She explains that often a larger plan or deeper design underlies the apparent madness of Fortune's methods—the curative, edifying aspects of suffering as discipline or correction that lead to self-knowledge and awareness of God. Philosophy clarifies an idea never fully grasped by Boethius, the mystery of a divine providence that proportions tribulations according to the specific circumstances of each person:

> To some men, Providence distributes a mixture of good and bad fortune according to the nature of their soul. Some Providence troubles, so they won't be spoiled by a long period of happiness. Others it vexes with hardships, so they can strengthen the virtues of their souls by the use and practice of patience. Some fear too much the things they can endure, while others do not take enough thought for what they can't endure; Providence uses sorrows to teach these men to understand themselves. (4.pr.6)

Thus Philosophy's instruction not only points to the self-evident truths about man's rational nature, Fortune's eternal fickleness, and bad fortune's truthfulness but also opens Boethius' mind to the subtle notion of Fortune as the handmaiden of Providence. The capriciousness of human events is not simply chance. The seemingly arbitrary dispensations of happiness and misery proceed from intelligent foresight, not unjust lawlessness. Grasping this third valuable lesson about Fortune—her subservience to Divine Providence—Boethius goes beyond remembering self-evident truths to wondering at the paradoxes that Philosophy now presents to him: all luck is good luck; there is no such thing as chance; evil is nothing.

Continuing her pupil's liberal education as she leads him from blindness to self-knowledge and from knowledge to wisdom, Philosophy now prepares Boethius' mind for a grasp of some startling propositions: there is no evil, no fortune, and no time. She introduces the notion that knowledge is received according to the mode of the knower and the idea of the four levels of knowledge: sense, imagination, reason, and intellect:

Indeed the senses are of no value apart from the material, nor does the imagination see the universal forms, nor the reason grasp the simple form. But intelligence, as if looking down from above and grasping the form, distinguishes everything subject to the form, although it does so in the manner in which it comprehends the form itself, which cannot be known to anything else. For it understands the reason's view of the whole, and the imagination's view of the figure, and also the matter that is perceived by senses, but not by using reason, imagination, or the senses, but by one stroke of the mind, looking forth at all things according to form, so to speak. (5.pr.4)

In short, only God, under the aspect of eternity (*sub specie aeternitatis*), sees all—past, present, and future—in one glance through the mode of intellect: the vantage point of the Eternal Now that, "[e]mbracing the limitless spaces of the past and future . . . understands all things simply and considers them as if they were being done now" (5.pr.6). God's all-knowing intellect, in its capacity to behold "the knowledge of the present moment", sees not only the immediate evil or tragedy of fortune but also foresees the ultimate providential good that can proceed from evil—an omniscience that Boethius' limited human reason obviously lacks. The apparent power, independence, and randomness of Fortune are also deception, for, as Philosophy explains, all that moves or changes has a hidden, intelligent first cause that ultimately governs it and orders it to a good end: an unmoved mover or still point that originates motion from afar and controls it through many secondary causes and intermediate agents: "Therefore, as reasoning differs from understanding, as that which is produced differs from that which is, as time differs from eternity, and likewise a circle differs from its center, so the moving course of Fate [Fortune] differs from the unchanging simplicity of Providence" (4.pr.6).

All motion has a cause. Fortune in her wheel is always moving and changing, but she does not have absolute control of all her actions because she owes obedience to the higher law of God's divine providence. Following Philosophy's logic,

Boethius concedes that what temporarily appears evil to human eyes or to sense, such as his own tragedy, is not ultimately evil in the comprehensive vision or intellect of God. He comes to see that his own misfortune led him to Lady Philosophy, that is, to Wisdom herself, who shows him the mystery of God's ways: "And so it is with all the evils that men think are abundant on earth. If you look at how Providence disposes them, you wouldn't consider them evils at all" (4.pr.6). The teacher has led the pupil from the laws of cause and effect to a contemplation of God's eternal divine nature.

Boethius now completes his liberal education, having progressed in his own perception of reality from the level of sense (his immediate physical and emotional suffering in prison) to the level of imagination (the remembrance of past blessings and the recollection of his rational nature) to the level of reason (the knowledge of Fortune's universal law of mutability and the perennial truth about the mixed nature of human happiness) and to the level of intellect (the recognition of the limits of human knowledge and the unfathomability of the Divine Mind). Boethius has risen above the simplistic explanations of evil that self-deceptively blame Fortune for temporal suffering. His mind has reached the transcendent heights of human wisdom where logical, discursive reason leads to contemplative, loving wonder. Enlightened and inspired, Boethius no longer feels passive in suffering. He recalls the twelve labors of Hercules and rediscovers the meaning of equanimity, the power to be strong in the face of adversity (4.pr.7). From the darkness of prison and ignorance Boethius ascends to the illumination of philosophy and truth.

As Boethius once learned, forgot, and then rediscovered, wisdom means an understanding of the given, fixed, unchangeable nature of things that forms the structure of reality in classical philosophy. Everything has a nature—the planets and stars; the four elements of earth, air, fire, and water; animals; plants; man; Fortune; and God. This endowed nature that all created things possess directs the course of their motion and informs them of their purpose or natural end. Just as planets travel in

orbits, fire moves upward, and dogs chase rabbits, so man and
Fortune likewise possess a direction and design to their movement. It is as natural for man to wonder, philosophize, and
contemplate as it is for the sun and moon to follow their natural course. Just as Dante learns from his teacher Beatrice that
God's divine order disposes all created things toward their end
and directs their motion according to his purpose and design—
both "irrational creatures" and "those endowed with loves and
reasonings"[3]—Boethius also hears a similar explanation from
Lady Philosophy as he ascends the ladder of knowledge from
sense to reason and acquires a knowledge of the whole and
the relationship of the parts to the whole.

Man's nature is rational. As a rational animal, man by nature
possesses the power of self-control, the ability to regulate the
passions, and the willpower to resist temptations. In succumb-
ing to immoderate grief, anger, and despair, Boethius had abdi-
cated the throne of reason and let passions overrule his reason.
As a rational being, Boethius in his emotional outbursts has
failed to reflect on the first principles and final causes of things,
the knowledge of the beginnings and ends that leads the mind
to the apprehension of the truth. In short, Philosophy criticizes her pupil's failure to remember "the end of all things . . .
the goal to which all nature strives" and urges him to recall
"what rudders are used to steer [the world's] course" (1.pr.6).
Likewise, Boethius has not exercised his reason to grasp the
nature of Fortune as he elevates her to a supreme power or
views her as a malicious deity rather than acknowledging her
true nature. Correcting her student, Philosophy once again
defines Fortune's unchanging nature: "She was just the same
when she fawned on you and tricked you with the promises of
a counterfeit happiness" (2.pr.1). Philosophy, then, gradually
leads her student to wisdom, an apprehension of the nature of
things, of the eternal laws that govern the movements and
that explain the purposes of an intelligible world ordered by

[3] Dante, *The Divine Comedy, Cantica III: Paradise*, trans. Dorothy Sayers and
Barbara Reynolds (Baltimore, Md.: Penguin Books, 1973), canto I, 118–19.

the mind of God. The ascent up the ladder of knowledge cul-
minates in God, the source of truth, goodness, and happiness
and the natural end of man's desire for truth.

Boethius not only allowed anger and grief to darken his reason, obscure his own rational nature, and cause him to mis-
judge the erratic nature of fickle Fortune's wheel, but he also
erred in his knowledge of God's nature when he doubted the
role of divine providence in human affairs. God's providence
is both general and particular, governing both the order of
nature and the lives of individual men. The order of human
affairs—the lives of persons in history—illustrates God's particular providence in each person's life as he leads individuals
by the wheel of fortune to truth and wisdom, to self-discovery
(4.pr.4), as Boethius' own example testifies. Once Philosophy
leads Boethius to this superior level of understanding, he
acquires the virtue of a wise man educated by Philosophy: "So,
then, ... a wise man shouldn't be upset when he has to battle
with Fortune, just as a brave man mustn't complain when the
cry of war breaks out.... And so we call it virtue, because a
virile man fights and wins against adversity" (4.pr.7). Philosophy not only illuminates the mind; it fortifies the will.

Once Boethius grasps again the nature of things—man's
moral and rational nature, Fortune's fickle nature, and God's
eternal nature—his state of mind acquires the mastery of self-
possession and equanimity that provide the consolation of philosophy that derives from the knowledge of the truth. Whereas
Boethius at the height of his career as consul equated happiness with pleasure, wealth, fame, and power—all appearances
of the true Good—he learns from his tragic fall from high to
low the lesson Philosophy illuminates: good fortune deceives;
bad fortune teaches. Only the truth consoles, only the truth
strengthens, only the truth leads to lasting happiness.

The truth that Philosophy leads Boethius to discover and
contemplate with wonder gives purpose, meaning, and hope
to human life. God rules the world like a helmsman (4.pr.1),
and he rules the world by the "rudder" of goodness and wisdom. Whirl is not king, the forces of chaos do not govern the

universe, and Fortune is not a tyrannical goddess. Created in goodness and inclined toward goodness by God, who is goodness itself, all things achieve their end or happiness by following the order of their God-given natures. Man, whose rational nature is created for truth, goodness, and the contemplation of God, finds this happiness by ascending the ladder of knowledge from sense to imagination to reason to an understanding of God's intellect until he reaches his "fatherland" (3.pr.12). True happiness does not depend on the shifting favors of Fortune but on the stability and equanimity of a mind that rests in the knowledge that God, "a judge who sees all things" (5.pr.6), governs the universe and the affairs of men with an all-seeing wisdom and an infinite love that epitomize his eternal nature: "He is the one who looks out from the lofty watchtower of His Providence and sees what is best for all and works out what He knows is suitable for them. Here occurs the greatest wonder of the ordering of Fate, when a knowing God works out the things that the ignorant wonder at" (4.pr.6). Lady Philosophy, like a true teacher and an intelligent physician, leads her pupil and patient from darkness to light and from weakness to strength by awakening the light of his own mind and by exercising his natural strength and capacity for virtue.

Lady Philosophy as Physician

Jeffrey S. Lehman
Thomas Aquinas College

Now my eyes drank in the bright light of heaven, and I could recognize the face of the one who was healing me. When I cast my eyes upon her and fixed my gaze, I saw it was the one whose home I had visited since my youth—the Lady Philosophy, my nurse. (1.pr.3)[1]

The image of Lady Philosophy as physician of Boethius is fundamental to the dramatic dialogue that unfolds in *The Consolation of Philosophy*. In the first book, we are introduced to the characters, Boethius the patient and Philosophy the physician, and are made aware of the patient's desperate condition. In the four books that follow, Philosophy undertakes a gradual curative regimen in an attempt to heal Boethius of his malady. Reflecting upon this therapeutic image and how the author employs it yields crucial insight into the nature, purpose, unity, and structure of this crowning achievement of Boethius, the "last of the Romans, the first of the Scholastics".[2] To guide our inquiry, we begin by posing a question: How does Lady Philosophy exercise her therapeutic arts in the *Consolation*? To answer this question, we must consider three elements of the work: the characters in the dialogue, the initial condition of Boethius, and the cure proposed and carried out by Philosophy in the course of their conversation.

---

[1] Boethius, *The Consolation of Philosophy*, trans. and ed. Scott Goins and Barbara Wyman, Ignatius Critical Editions (San Francisco: Ignatius Press, 2012). All quotations from the *Consolation* are from this edition.
[2] Howard Rollin Patch traces the origin of this description in *The Tradition of Boethius: A Study of His Importance in Medieval Culture* (New York: Oxford University Press, 1935), p. 127.

188 Jeffrey S. Lehman

The Characters: Patient and Physician

Boethius

We begin with the characters. First we meet Boethius, who is composing elegiac verses of self-pity as the work opens (1.met.1). For the sake of clarity, we must distinguish between two Boethiuses—one, the author of *The Consolation of Philosophy*, and the other, the patient who comes under the care of the physician, Lady Philosophy, within the dramatic context of the written work. We do well also to keep in mind the time of the dialogue as it relates to these two Boethiuses. The dialogue recounts the conversation of the patient Boethius with Philosophy; as the dialogue unfolds, Philosophy instructs him and leads him gradually toward health. Boethius the author, on the other hand, has already undergone the therapeutic regimen of Philosophy and recalls and reconstructs their conversation in written form.[3]

Significantly, Boethius the soon-to-be patient begins in a state of total passivity: "Torn Muses bid me write—/elegies drench my face" (1.met.1). In other words, he has completely abandoned himself to despair, passively receiving the communications of the Muses and composing self-absorbed verses of lamentation.[4] Indeed, he longs for death: "Death, ... [who] shuns my wretched cries,/refuses to close my weeping eyes." Boethius begins so enmeshed in self-pity that he is literally unable to see anything else; he is wallowing in the depths of despair yet incapable of judging his own condition, blinded by his tears. Within the dialogue, there is one element of Boethius' passivity that is particularly telling—namely, his

[3] Robert McMahon, *Understanding the Medieval Meditative Ascent: Augustine, Anselm, Boethius, and Dante* (Washington, D.C.: Catholic University Press, 2006), p. 211.

[4] For a similar reading, see Krista Sue-Lo Twu, "This Is Comforting? Boethius's *Consolation of Philosophy*, Rhetoric, Dialectic, and 'Unicum Illud Inter Homines Deumque Commercium'", in *New Directions in Boethian Studies*, ed. Noel Harold Kaylor Jr. and Philip Edward Phillips, Studies in Medieval Culture 45 (Kalamazoo, Mich.: Western Michigan University Press, 2007), p. 34.

silence.[5] On one hand, silence can be a virtue. The studious pupil who attends carefully to the teachings of a master is often silent. But this silence typically follows much active conversation, questioning the principles of the master to see that they are sound, raising reasonable objections to arguments along the way. This is a silence that is born of prior, often vigorous, dialectical exchange. On the other hand, there is the silence of one who passively receives the opinions and sentiments of others, never minding to weigh their relative merit or concordance with the truth. The silence of Boethius in these opening lines is of the latter sort. He passively receives poetic "inspiration" from the Muses, allowing his passions to get the better of him and blinding himself with his own tears.

Boethius the author brings a host of other "characters" into the discussion—although they are not, strictly speaking, interlocutors in the dialogue—by means of literary allusions or mention of their names. Many of the figures have biographies that are strikingly similar to that of Boethius himself. Of course, the dramatic setting for the dialogue has Boethius imprisoned in Pavia, awaiting his execution; from the opening lines, Boethius the author incorporates references and allusions to various literary and philosophical figures who found themselves in similar predicaments. Among these are Ovid, Seneca, Cicero, and Socrates, all of whom left public witness of how they responded to their respective adversities.[6] One task of the reader of the *Consolation* is to reflect upon these responses and consider how Boethius' response measures up. The responses amount to a kind of "hierarchy of reactions to adversity"[7] that

[5] Seth Lerer makes much of this in his reading of the *Consolation*, contrasting "the listlessness of the prisoner's laments with the power of Philosophy's eloquence" (Lerer, *Boethius and Dialogue: Literary Method in the "Consolation of Philosophy"* [Princeton, N.J.: Princeton University Press, 1985], p. 102).

[6] In my account of these figures, I rely upon the masterful treatment of Anna Crabbe, "Literary Design in the *De consolatione philosophiae*", in *Boethius: His Life, Thought and Influence*, ed. Margaret T. Gibson (Oxford: Basil Blackwell, 1981), pp. 242ff.

[7] The phrase is Crabbe's ("Literary Design", p. 245).

can and should be compared with the response of Boethius the patient throughout the dialogue.

For example, there is a clear allusion to Ovid in the opening poem of book 1. Elegy and exile are two central themes in the life of Ovid, "the last and the youngest of the Augustan elegiac poets".[8] In ancient times, elegiac verse was typically associated with two things: lament and love. Ovid was banished by Augustus, ostensibly for the eroticism of his love poetry, and ended his life in exile at Tomi on the Black Sea, where he composed his *Tristia* and *Ex ponto*, both lamentations on his predicament. So the excesses of Ovid's elegiac love poetry led to his exile, which in turn led to his composition of elegiac lament poetry. In the opening poem of the *Consolation*, Boethius is like Ovid, a man in exile whose passions have overcome him and who bathes himself in tears while composing poetry of self-pity. The allusion to Ovid is to show us just how far Boethius has fallen.

In the "hierarchy" mentioned above, the poet Ovid is clearly at the bottom. At the top is Socrates, the philosopher who chose death by hemlock rather than exile from his native city, Athens. The contrast between Ovid's and Socrates' responses to adversity is illuminating and worthy of meditation, particularly for understanding where Boethius the patient begins and where he hopes to end. The poet Ovid lacks self-mastery (a theme we will come to shortly) and composes erotic poetry that leads him into exile, where he laments his situation and remains subdued by his passions. The philosopher Socrates, conversely, is the ancient model of self-mastery and retains his composure to the end, preferring death to self-imposed exile. Thus, one way to think about the progress of Boethius the patient would be to see it as a move from poet to philosopher.[9] While this may generally be true, it requires careful qualification, as we will see below.

---

[8] Ibid., p. 244.

[9] See Seth Lerer, introduction to *The Consolation of Philosophy*, by Anicius Manlius Severinus Boethius, trans. David R. Slavitt (Cambridge, Mass.: Harvard University Press, 2008), p. xvii.

For all the similarities between the lives of Boethius and Socrates, there is one key difference, a difference that comes to light in Boethius the patient's "political apologia"[10] in book 1. Whereas Socrates spent his days largely outside the realm of public service (save for obligatory military duty), Boethius lived a life of ongoing and exemplary statesmanship. In the fourth prose section of book 1, Boethius the patient recounts his distinguished career in Roman politics. Spurred on by the ideal of Plato's philosopher-king in the *Republic* (473d, 487e), Boethius held a number of influential political positions.[11] Yet, as Boethius the patient discloses, it is his political service that led to his downfall. Defending truth and justice in an environment of widespread political corruption, Boethius fell prey to trumped-up charges of treason.

Allowing for this notable difference, it is still the case that Socrates is "the worthiest example in the *Consolatio*"[12] and that we are intended to see Boethius the patient's progress in terms of a return to the philosophical principles that had guided him earlier in his life. Moreover, it is with Boethius the patient that the reader is meant to identify, "learning from the method of dialectical argument, moving from the avowal of opinion to the recognition of truth".[13] In a sense, Boethius the patient is "partly everyman".[14] To one degree or another, we all find ourselves in his situation. And as he is reminded to keep first things first and live the examined life, the reader is invited to probing self-examination as well.

[10] Henry Chadwick, *The Consolations of Music, Logic, Theology, and Philosophy* (Oxford: Clarendon Press, 1981), p. 227.

[11] Boethius served as a consul in 510 and was serving as master of the king's offices—one of the highest offices in the Western Empire—at the time of his downfall in 523.

[12] Crabbe, "Literary Design", p. 243.

[13] Lerer, introduction to the *Consolation* (Harvard University Press ed.), p. xv.

[14] Richard Green, introduction to *The Consolation of Philosophy*, by Boethius, trans. and ed. Richard Green (New York: Macmillan Publishing Company, 1962), p. xxii.

Lady Philosophy

Lady Philosophy comes on the scene in the first prose section of book 1. She appears standing above Boethius, a woman who had "a holy look" and whose "eyes showed fire [*oculis ardentibus*] and pierced with a more-than-human penetration" (1.pr.1). Unlike Boethius the patient, she can *see things clearly*. Significantly, "[h]er height was hard to tell; at one moment it was that of an ordinary human, but at another she seemed to strike the clouds with the crown of her head." Lady Philosophy's varying height is certainly symbolic, most likely to be interpreted in connection with the Greek letters on her robe: "On its bottom hem was woven the Greek letter *pi* [Π], with a series of steps ascending to a *theta* [Θ] that rose above it." The Π and Θ stand for the two species of philosophy: the practical and the theoretical, respectively. She is able to lead men to action in this world through practical philosophy (e.g., ethics, politics, and economics); she is also able to lead them to contemplation through theoretical philosophy (e.g., natural science, mathematics, and metaphysics). And as the stairs would imply, she can guide them gradually from one to the other. More important, the varying height of Philosophy makes clear that she can direct her students in a philosophical ascent to the highest things, culminating in an approach to God. This ability is crucial to the healing of Boethius. Among other things, the cure proposed in books 2–4 can be understood as a stepwise ascent whose ultimate goal is to bring Boethius back to God.[15]

While the Muses of poetry make only a cameo appearance in the *Consolation*, we are surely meant to contrast them with Lady Philosophy, who no sooner comes on the scene than she orders them to leave immediately, calling them "whorish stage girls" (*scenicas meretriculas*) and "Sirens" (1.pr.1).[16] Tellingly,

---

[15] Crabbe argues in a similar manner ("Literary Design", pp. 243–44). See also McMahon, *Understanding the Medieval Meditative Ascent*, pp. 214–26.

[16] On which, see Helen M. Barrett, *Boethius: Some Aspects of His Times and Work* (New York: Russell and Russell, 1965), pp. 77–78, and Crabbe, "Literary Design", p. 249.

Philosophy reveals the Muses as false physicians: "It's more pain they bring than remedies. No, they make things worse with their sweet-tasting poison. These are the kind of women who choke off a mind's rich fruit, wrapping it up in sterile thorns of passion. They make a mind more used to disease, instead of setting it free from pain." Philosophy, on the other hand, offers true medicine for her patient's sorrow; she aims to reinvigorate his reason, thereby enabling him to subdue his passions, and she seeks to liberate his mind, restoring him to the dignity he once knew.

All of the above sounds well and good, and we might naturally expect Philosophy to take such a stance toward poetry. In Boethius' time, there was already a long-standing tension, if not outright opposition, between poetry and philosophy. And Philosophy's peremptory dismissal of the Muses is undoubtedly a literary echo of Socrates' banishment of the poets from the ideal city in Plato's *Republic*. Even so, in both Plato and Boethius, the relation between philosophy and poetry is far more nuanced than may appear at first. For while Plato's Socrates banishes the poets, Socrates nevertheless engages in poetry himself, creating a host of poetic images as the dialogue unfolds. Indeed, he even speaks of making an "apology in images" (488A) and ends the conversation with the remarkable "Myth of Er" in book 10 (614Bff.). In like manner, Philosophy sends the Muses of poetry away; but no sooner are they dismissed than she announces: "[L]eave him to *my Muses* to be cured and made whole" (1.pr.1; emphasis added). From this point on, the literary form of the *Consolation* alternates between poetry and prose.

Furthermore, the poems of the *Consolation* are not mere window dressing for the philosophy of the prosaic sections. To begin with, many of the poems are quite excellent on their own terms.[17] And although they frequently revisit the themes of the immediately preceding prose sections, providing relief from the rigor of the philosophic discourse, they often do so in ways

[17] The crowning achievement is no doubt the ninth poem in book 3 (see Chadwick, *Consolations of Music, Logic, Theology, and Philosophy*, pp. 234–35).

that clarify or even carry forward the overall argument.[18] Thus, there is a "dialogue" of sorts between the prose and poetry of the *Consolation*, a dialogue that underscores certain points, refines others, and brings about a further level of dialectical exchange that transcends the scope of the prosaic argument. Moreover, we know from Boethius himself that he probably *did not* include the poems simply as an amusing diversion from the serious matter of the dialogue.[19] For Boethius, as for many ancient and medieval authors, "poetry was made to please and to teach, or, more precisely, to please *in order* to teach."[20] A careful reading of the poetry of the *Consolation* reveals that it is integral to the overall argument. There is a delicate interplay between the poetry and prose, creating a dialogical whole that is greater than either of its parts.

Even though the poetry is integral to Philosophy's therapeutic plan, it would be a mistake to infer from this that the prose and poetry are on a par. As one reader has put it, "It is not by accident that the *Consolation* begins with verse and ends with prose."[21] Philosophy's purged poetry is consciously subordinated to her philosophic ends.[22] Its aim is to help restore

[18] This view is defended in different ways by Barrett, *Boethius*, p. 77; Green, introduction to the *Consolation* (Macmillan ed.), p. xxi; V.E. Watts, introduction to *The Consolation of Philosophy*, by Boethius, trans. V.E. Watts (New York: Penguin Books, 1969), p. 20; and Elaine Scarry, "The Well-Rounded Sphere: The Metaphysical Structure of the *Consolation of Philosophy*", in *Essays in the Numerical Criticism of Medieval Literature*, ed. Caroline D. Eckhardt (Lewisburg, Pa.: Bucknell University Press, 1980), pp. 99–103.

[19] In his *Quomodo substantia*, Boethius remarks: "[I] would rather bury my speculations in my own memory than share them with any of those pert and frivolous persons who will not tolerate an argument unless it is made amusing" (as quoted in Scarry, "Well-Rounded Sphere", pp. 92–93).

[20] Green, introduction to the *Consolation* (Macmillan ed.), p. xxi; emphasis in original. This account echoes that of Horace in the *Ars poetica*, who says, "Poetry wants to instruct or else to delight;/Or, better still, to delight and instruct at once" (*The Epistles of Horace*, bilingual ed., trans. David Ferry [New York: Farrar, Straus, and Giroux, 2001], p. 175).

[21] Watts, introduction to the *Consolation* (Penguin ed.), p. 20.

[22] We have already seen Philosophy's reference to "my Muses" in 1 *prosa* 1. In the first prose section of book 2, she says, "[L]et me apply the sweet persuasion of rhetoric, *which only proceeds on the right path when it stands by our instructions and is in harmony with the homely music of our hearth*" (emphasis added). In this context, rhetoric and music are part of the poetry of the *Consolation*.

the order that has been lost in the soul of her patient. As we will discuss in detail later on, over the course of the remaining four books Philosophy seeks to restore the powers of Boethius' soul to their rightful order and proper function. One of these powers is the imagination, a faculty that mediates between sensation (whose object is material and particular) and reason (whose object is immaterial [or formal] and universal).[23] The imagination shares the formality of its object with reason; it shares the particularity of its object with sensation. At least one purpose of the poetry in the *Consolation* is to restore the faculty of imagination to its rightful place in the hierarchy of the soul's faculties. As the imagination mediates between sensation and reason, so too the poems with their images mediate between the prosaic sections.[24] Furthermore, the final poem of each book includes an admonition to look up (toward reason) rather than down (toward sensation). Philosophy is determined that the poetry point beyond itself to higher things.[25]

There is, of course, another lady in Boethius the patient's life: Fortune. Philosophy has a harder time separating Boethius from his attachment to her, and Philosophy's doing so takes us well into the physician's cure. So for now, we will set Fortune aside and turn our attention to the patient's condition and Philosophy's diagnosis.

The Patient's Condition

We have already made some headway in determining Boethius the patient's condition in our treatment of him as a character. Let's resume our discussion where we left off with Lady Philosophy. After ejecting the Muses of poetry and installing her own Muses in their stead, the focus turns once again to Boethius, whose eyes are "so bathed with tears" that he cannot

[23] For a similar line of reasoning based upon the imagination as a mediating faculty, see Scarry, "Well-Rounded Sphere", pp. 99ff.

[24] This insight is Scarry's (ibid., p. 102).

[25] This, of course, is also why the *Consolation* ends in prose, not poetry. For an excellent account of poetry in the *Consolation*, see Gerard O'Daly, *The Poetry of Boethius* (Chapel Hill: University of North Carolina Press, 1991).

recognize Philosophy: "I cast my gaze upon the ground [*in terram*] and quietly waited to see what she would do next" (1.pr.1). In the "song" that follows, Philosophy reproves Boethius for his anxiety, reminding him that he was once a man "free to walk/under open heavens" who "understood many causes"; now, however, he lies, "his mind light-forsaken,/neck pressed with chains,/face cast down,/forced to discern nothing/but the ground" (1.met.2).

At least three details from these passages shed light on Boethius the patient's condition at this point in the dialogue: his silent passivity, his earthbound gaze, and his literal and figurative bondage. Earlier we drew attention to Boethius' initial silent passivity; here too he waits in silence for his unknown deliverer to take action. Boethius is truly a *patient* in the basic sense of the word's Latin root *patior*—one who "suffers" or undergoes action rather than carrying it out himself. Second, there is his earthbound gaze. Philosophy's reference to the "ground" (*terram*) recalls Boethius' own comment about staring at the earth. He looks only downward; he cannot redirect his eyes upward to higher things. Third, and closely connected with the first two, is his bondage. He was once a free man; now he is bound by chains. We have mentioned his literal, physical imprisonment above. This is only external. Even when the body is bound with physical chains, the mind can still be free. But as Philosophy tells us, his mind is "light-forsaken". This internal bondage is far worse than any physical chains. In essence, Boethius the patient has relinquished his freedom; he has snuffed out the light of his mind by allowing his passions to overcome his reason. Enlightened freedom and its recovery is one of the recurring themes throughout the *Consolation*. It becomes explicit in the discussion of providence and free will in book 5, a discussion that "hinges on the question of '*libertas*' [freedom]".[26] So in one sense, the

[26] Crabbe, "Literary Design", p. 242. The themes of freedom and its recovery is crucial; she elaborates: "It is not just the material world in general, but actual imprisonment and exile, perhaps even physical chains and certainly physical death towards which [Boethius] must learn indifference in order to return to his former philosophical state. The paradox involved in the apparently identical nature

movement of the *Consolation* is a movement from the darkness of bondage to the light of freedom.

Philosophy's Initial Impression and Examination

But what is the exact nature of this bondage? We get our
first glimpse in the second prose section, where Philosophy
rebukes Boethius: "Did I not give you all the weapons you
needed, ones that would have kept your mind safe from harm?
At least they would have, if you hadn't thrown them away"
(1.pr.2; see also 1.met.4). After the rebuke, she offers him
some words of comfort: "There's no danger here. He's simply
dazed, as one would expect of a man suffering under delusion. He's *forgotten who he is* for a moment. He'll easily remember again soon—that is, if indeed he ever knew me. But first
we'll have to wipe away the cloud of mortal cares that darkens his eyes" (emphasis added). Philosophy's initial diagnosis—
that Boethius has "forgotten who he is"—appears to have some
merit. After Philosophy wipes away "the cloud of mortal cares
that darkens his eyes", Boethius is able to recognize her. This
is just a beginning, though. Shortly thereafter, she encourages him to "uncover [his] wound" (1.pr.4), which he does at
length in the fourth prose section.[27] Boethius the patient
recounts how, inspired by the example of Plato's philosopher-
king, he embarked upon a life of public service. In his determined efforts to safeguard justice, Boethius made many powerful
enemies who eventually used their power (and the rampant
political corruption in the regime) to entrap him. The whole
of the fourth prose section is a "long protestation of innocence"[28] that calls into question God's providential justice
in governing human affairs. Similar themes are underscored
in the embittered prayer that follows:

---

of his physical and spiritual situation and the long struggle to establish the unreality of the physical prison and escape the reality of mental chains provides the
work's impetus" (ibid.).

[27] *Prosa* 4 is by far the longest prose section in book 1.

[28] Chadwick, *Consolations of Music, Logic, Theology, and Philosophy*, p. 227.

You are the commander.

. . . .

Your law binds all but man.
How else could twisting Fortune bring ruin?

. . . .

Ruler, check the fierce waves!
Steady the earth, surround it
with Your law which rules the vast sky
[*firma stabiles . . . terras*].

(1.met.5)

This response makes clear to Philosophy that Boethius' condition is far worse than she initially supposed: "When I saw you sad and full of tears, I knew at once that you were exiled and miserable. But had you not displayed it in your speech, I would not have known how far away your banishment had taken you. Indeed how far from your native land you are! And yet you haven't been expelled; you've simply strayed away" (1.pr.5). As with Boethius' imprisonment, so with his exile: the outward, physical exile is far less devastating then the inward, spiritual one. He is dissociated from himself, estranged from himself, exiled from himself. Furthermore, his exile is self-imposed. The severity of the problem is evident in his response to Philosophy's request to uncover his wound. "She asks what is wrong with *him*, but he responds by telling her what is wrong with *the world*."[29] He interprets his plight in an entirely earthbound, physical way; and as his prayer indicates, he asks for an external, physical solution—*firma stabiles terras*—"Steady the earth!"[30] Given the severity of the case, Philosophy decides upon a treatment plan that is carefully proportioned to his condition: "But since such a storm of passions has come upon you and you are pulled about by conflicting feelings of pain, anger, and sorrow, you can't, in such a mind, be given stronger remedies. And so I'll apply gentler ones for now, so that your wound, which has hardened and

[29] Twu, "This Is Comforting?", pp. 35–36; emphasis in original.
[30] Ibid., p. 36.

grown scarred by the constant pricks of your anxieties, may grow softer with gentle treatment and become ready to receive a more effective cure" (1.pr.5).

The Final Diagnosis

In the next prose section (1.pr.6), Philosophy decides to ask Boethius a series of questions to test his state of mind (*statum mentis*). First, she asks him a number of questions leading up to one about how the world is governed. He is perplexed by the question and doesn't know how to respond. She next asks what the end or goal (*finis*) of all things is. He says that he has heard it once, but grief has dulled his memory; he does know, however, that all things come from God. Finally, she comes to the question "Can you tell me ... what a man is [*quid homo sit*]?" Boethius replies, "I am a rational and mortal creature [*rationale animal atque mortale*]." Philosophy encourages him to say more, asking whether he knows anything else about what he is. He says no, "Nothing" (*Nihil*). "Now", she says, "I know the other, in fact the greatest [*maximam*], cause of your disease: you no longer know what you are."

This exchange between patient and physician is crucial to understanding Boethius' condition.[31] Recall Philosophy's initial, provisional diagnosis—"He's forgotten who he is for a moment" (1.pr.2). Since that initial diagnosis, she has been tirelessly laboring to help her patient remember himself. The more Boethius says, the more he reveals just how grave his condition is. When Philosophy finally asks him what man is, she is not looking for the common textbook answer; rather, she is trying to get him to remember who he is in relation to God—that is, he has an immortal soul with a destiny beyond the death of his mortal body. This is precisely what he is most deeply confused about in his own account of his situation and the prayer that follows it. With head downcast and eyes focused

---

[31] In the analysis that follows, I am indebted to the insightful reading of this passage proposed by Twu, ibid., p. 37.

on the ground, he has no hope either of knowing himself or of understanding his place in the providential plan of God.

With her patient's telling admissions of ignorance in mind, Philosophy gives her full and final diagnosis:

> Since you're overwhelmed by forgetfulness of your nature, you grieve at being in exile and deprived of your goods. Indeed, since you are not aware of the end of all things, you think that base and wicked men are powerful and happy. And, since you have forgotten with what rudders the world is steered, you think the earth is tossed about by chance without a pilot. These things are great enough to cause not just illness, but even death. (1.pr.6)

Philosophy's diagnosis lays out the three fundamental causes of her patient's sickness. In the order of her dialectical examination, they go from least to most grave; in the diagnosis, the order is reversed. Beginning with the least grave, Boethius acknowledges that the world is governed by God, but he does not know how. Ignorance of how the world is governed leads Boethius to believe that his reversal of fortune occurred with no purpose. Second, while he believes God to be the source or origin (*principium*) of all things, he is ignorant of the end or purpose (*finis*) of all things. Lacking this knowledge, he has come to believe that wicked men are powerful and happy. Finally, the greatest (*maximam*) cause of his illness is that he has forgotten what he is. This lack of self-knowledge gave rise to his willingness to surrender himself to grief, self-pity, and even despair at the loss of his position and possessions.

In typical Socratic fashion, Philosophy begins by revealing to her patient the knowledge of his own ignorance—Boethius comes to know what he does not know. With this threefold diagnosis in place, we are poised to see how Philosophy's plan of treatment unfolds. The first book has introduced us to the characters and informed us of the patient's condition. The remaining books take up the cure—that is, the "consolation" of Philosophy, strictly speaking.

The Physician's Cure

Books 2–5 all contribute to Philosophy's "discursive therapy" of Boethius.[32] Her program is fundamentally Platonic in inspiration, incorporating different types of anamnesis or "recollection" throughout the dialogue. First, there is recollection in the simple sense of reminding. Recall that the change Boethius undergoes in the *Consolation* is not a conversion but a reconversion. It is not simply a turning but a returning to Philosophy, "the one whose home [he] had visited since [his] youth . . . [his] nurse" (1.pr.3). So much of what Philosophy has to say is simply intended to remind Boethius the patient of what he has learned before. A second, more overtly Platonic, sense of recollection is also present. Turning away from the external world and toward oneself enables a person to "remember" himself, unimpeded by the "distractions and confusions of a material world".[33] The need for this kind of recollection is primarily what Philosophy has in mind when she tells Boethius that he has "forgotten who he is for a moment". A further distinction within recollection as anamnesis needs to be made, given Philosophy's diagnosis. Boethius' disease is both moral and intellectual. Thus her therapeutic program is meant to lead him toward moral and intellectual recollection. Moral recollection is essentially ethical self-mastery.[34] To be morally recollected is to have an undivided will, guided by reason and willing only what is good.[35] Intellectual recollection involves remembering that the soul is immortal and recognizing what follows from this fundamental truth.[36]

---

[32] McMahon, *Understanding the Medieval Meditative Ascent*, p. 211.

[33] For a fuller discussion of this theme, see Crabbe, "Literary Design", p. 258.

[34] In the fourth poem of book 1, Philosophy says, "The anxious man dreads and desires;/he cannot be firm,/under his own authority [*sui iuris*]." Self-mastery (*sui iuris*) and self-possession (*sui compos*) are two complementary ways of speaking about moral recollection. See the discussion of book 2 below. See also Chadwick, *Consolations of Music, Logic, Theology, and Philosophy*, p. 230.

[35] McMahon, *Understanding the Medieval Meditative Ascent*, p. 243.

[36] Ibid., p. 237.

202 *Jeffrey S. Lehman*

Within the context of this general program aimed at recollection, what gives order and structure to the dialogue of
books 2–5? Many readers of the *Consolation* have noticed a
progressive ascent from one mode of knowing to another,
beginning with sensation, passing through imagination and
reason, and culminating in understanding.[37] The most per-
suasive reading, in my view, sees each of the four remaining
books as primarily dedicated to the restoration of one of these
powers, moving from lowest to highest. In other words, book
2 primarily concerns the rehabilitation of sensation, book 3
focuses on imagination, book 4 treats of reason, and book 5
concerns understanding. While this scheme is not likely to
come to the mind of a first-time reader of the *Consolation*, it
can nevertheless prove very helpful when reflecting upon the
work. Given that Boethius the author does not explicitly
address these modes of knowing until book 5, it seems more
than likely that he intends for us to read this structure back
into the *Consolation* as a way of "recollecting" the work as a
whole, drawing it together in retrospect and seeing an order
and structure that is mostly implicit along the way. Rather
than rehearse the evidence for this structure, which has already
been described in detail,[38] I will assume the basic structure
and focus instead on other aspects of Philosophy's therapeutic program in the remaining books. Since the lion's share of
passages that refer explicitly to Philosophy as physician and
her therapeutic program occur in the first book, most of what
we can say has already been covered. Even so, the basic image
of Philosophy as physician and her progressive treatment plan

---

[37] Their inspiration comes from the account of the four acts of knowing found
in book 5 of the *Consolation* (5 *prosa* 4). Among others, the following readers
represent three distinct ways of seeing this progressive ascent manifest in books
2–5: Thomas F. Curley, "How to Read the *Consolation of Philosophy*", *Interpretation* 14 (1986): 211–63; Scarry, "Well-Rounded Sphere", pp. 91–140; and McMahon, *Understanding the Medieval Meditative Ascent*, pp. 214–26. Of these
alternatives, McMahon's accounts for all the virtues of the other accounts and
makes the best sense of the text; in what follows, then, I will lay out the four
books along the lines established by McMahon.

[38] I refer to McMahon's masterful treatment mentioned in the previous note.

informs books 2–5. So in what follows we will give an over-
view of how these elements are present in the rest of the
Consolation.

Book 2

Philosophy begins her treatment plan by reminding Boethius
of the nature and the habits of the goddess Fortune. Philosophy wants him to come to see Fortune for what she really is.
This is the beginning of her "medicine that's pleasant and good"
that is meant to prepare Boethius for "stronger remedies" later
(2.pr.1). This gentle and pleasant remedy incorporates rhetoric, "the sweet persuasion . . . which only proceeds on the right
path when it stands by our instructions and is in harmony with
the homely music of our hearth", whose songs are sometimes
"light" and sometimes "heavier".[39] Philosophy clarifies her purpose a little later in book 2: "[This discourse] isn't yet the remedy for your disease but rather a sort of poultice for a pain that
stubbornly resists a cure. I'll apply medicines that penetrate
deeply when the time is right" (2.pr.3). So the cure, properly
speaking, does not occur early on in these books, where gentler medicine is administered.

    It takes Philosophy some time to wean Boethius away from
his attachment to Lady Fortune; in particular, he is captivated
by the idea that happiness is dependent upon good fortune. In
terms of overall strategy, Philosophy labors to help Boethius
take a longer view of things: "It's not enough, after all, to see
what is placed before our eyes; wisdom takes thought for how
things will turn out in the end. The temporary nature of any
situation should keep a person from fearing Fortune's threats
or hoping for her enticements" (2.pr.1). As they discuss the
nature of happiness, Philosophy proposes that true and perfect
happiness consists in self-possession: "And so, if you're in control of yourself [*tui compos*], you will possess what you would

---

[39] For more detailed accounts of Philosophy's use of rhetoric and music, see
Barrett, *Boethius*, p. 83, and Twu, "This Is Comforting?", p. 38.

never wish to lose and what Fortune can't take away from you" (2.pr.4). Significantly, this same term (*sui compos*, "self-possessed") is used of God in book 5 (pr.6).

Convincing Boethius of the virtue of self-possession is foundational to Philosophy's plan. Soon after introducing this account of happiness, she is ready to "use some cures that are a little stronger" (2.pr.5). Neither riches, nor honor and power, nor fame is adequate for true happiness. "Finally," Philosophy argues, "one can come to the same conclusion about Fortune as a whole. In her there is nothing worthy of seeking, nothing with innate goodness [*natiuae bonitatis*]; for Fortune does not always join herself to those who are good, and she does not make good those to whom she is joined" (2.pr.6). She concludes her argument in book 2 by contending—somewhat paradoxically at first glance—that bad fortune is to be preferred to good fortune. "In short, happy Fortune uses her allurements to draw men astray from the true Good, but adverse Fortune, for the most part, uses her claw to drag men back to the things that are good" (2.pr.8).

Book 3

Book 3 dramatizes the "conversion" of Boethius; he turns away from the multiplicity of false goods and toward the unified simplicity of true happiness. Philosophy spoke of this true happiness in the previous book; now she intends to lead him there (3.pr.1). Before she can, though, she needs to convince him fully that all other false goods are insufficient. She begins by defining the supreme good ("For when a man acquires that good, there is nothing left that he can desire") and perfect happiness ("a state made perfect by the coming together of all good things" [3.pr.2]). Next, she revisits the false goods—riches, honor, power, fame, and bodily pleasure—showing how each is a limited, transitory good that, in and of itself, cannot bring true happiness. Indeed, at times each can be positively harmful.

At this point in the dialogue, we see the beginning of a change in Boethius as an interlocutor. Whereas up to now he

has been fairly passive, receiving the teachings of Philosophy
but not contributing in any substantial way to the discussion,
here he starts to take a more active role. He begins by saying
that he sees as through a little crack in the wall, but he wants
to learn more clearly[40] why the false goods are insufficient
(3.pr.9). From this modest beginning, Boethius' active engage-
ment in the dialogue gradually builds for the remainder of the
Consolation.[41] As his knowledge of true happiness, which is
self-sufficient, grows, so does his own self-sufficiency as an interlocutor. Book 3 ends with a significant poem. Like the final
poem in book 2, the central theme is love; this time, the subject is the myth of Orpheus descending to the underworld out
of love for his dead wife. The tale as a whole and the closing
lines in particular are a pointed warning to Boethius:

> This story is for you,
> for those who wish to lead
> the mind into the upper day.
> Since, whoever, having been weakened,
> turns back a gaze to Tartarus' chasm—
> whatever excellence he has gained,
> looking back, he loses.
>
> (3.met.12)

As we have seen before, the *Consolation* is a tale of reconversion. Boethius, like Orpheus, has turned back to look into the
pit of Hell. By the end of book 3, Boethius has made significant progress; but he is by no means out of danger.[42]

Book 4

After hearing Philosophy tell the myth of Orpheus, Boethius
breaks in on her, "still remembering the grief deep within"

---

[40] "Tenui quidem ueluti rimula mihi uideor intueri, sed ex te apertius cog-
noscere malim."
[41] For a detailed treatment, see Twu, "This Is Comforting?", pp. 40–41.
[42] For a similar analysis, see Crabbe, "Literary Design", p. 259.

(4.pr.1). He identifies the greatest cause (*maxima causa*) of his grief: "[I]f the ruler of the universe is in fact good, how can evil exist or go unpunished?" Boethius' response gives reasons for both concern and hope. On the one hand, it is troubling that after all his progress, Boethius is still in the grip of grief. On the other hand, this "very respectful protest"[43] gives at least two signs of progress. First, it is a sign that Boethius is becoming even more active in the dialogue. In this book, there is an increasing willingness on his part to initiate dialogue and even disagree with his physician. When reasonable and respectful, dialectical opposition can be a sign of philosophical maturity. It is just this healthy sort of dialectical opposition that we see developing in the remarks of Boethius in book 4. Second, the content of his protest reveals that Boethius is beginning to see beyond his self-pity. Whereas at the beginning of the dialogue, Boethius was preoccupied with his own pain and suffering, he now shows signs of taking a larger view of things. Rather than focusing on personal injustices received, he is showing an ever-greater concern for the human condition and the problem of evil as these relate to all human beings. And in asking and seeking answers to these larger questions, Boethius is directed increasingly toward God.

It is not surprising, then, that much is accomplished in this book in terms of Boethius' cure.[44] Recall Philosophy's final diagnosis, where she identifies three causes of his disease and their respective effects:

> Since you're overwhelmed by forgetfulness of your nature, you grieve at being in exile and deprived of your goods. Indeed, since you are not aware of the end of all things, you think that base and wicked men are powerful and happy. And, since you have forgotten with what rudders the world is steered, you think the earth is tossed about by chance without a pilot. (1.pr.6)

[43] Chadwick, *Consolations of Music, Logic, Theology, and Philosophy*, p. 240.

[44] In the account of the causes of Boethius' illness and their respective resolutions, I follow McMahon's analysis (*Understanding the Medieval Meditative Ascent*, pp. 241–42), not Barrett's (*Boethius*, p. 81).

In the third prose section of book 4, Philosophy argues that good men are always rewarded and wicked men are always punished. Only good men achieve the blessedness that all men by nature desire: "[S]ince the Good itself is blessedness, it is obvious that all good men become blessed through the very fact of their goodness, and those who are blessed are rightly called gods. This, then, is the reward of good men that the future will never erase, that no man's power can diminish, that no man's wickedness can darken—to become gods" (4.pr.3). By coming to know what man is, Boethius has come to see man's immortal end, an end that cannot be taken away (unlike his physical freedom and possessions). This answers Boethius' first cause of sickness and its effects. As for the second cause and its effects, it is already resolved by identifying man's immortal end or purpose (*finis*). Wicked men cannot be happy because they are not good. The pursuit of happiness, and thus goodness, is bound up in what it means to be a man. "And so, since they turned to evil, they have also lost their human nature" (4.pr.3). Wicked men, then, cannot be happy.

The third cause and its effects are addressed in the latter part of book 4. Boethius still has grave doubts about whether good men are always rewarded and wicked men always punished: "But I can't understand at all why things are turned around, so that the punishments due to the wicked are inflicted on the good, and evil men snatch the rewards of virtue. I would like you to tell me what the reason is for such unfairness and disorder" (4.pr.5). Philosophy responds at length by making a "new beginning" in the sixth prose section (4.pr.6).[45] What ensues is a detailed examination of the relationship between providence and fate. In essence, the relation is as follows: "Providence, which arranges everything, is the divine power of Reason itself, established in the highest ruler of all things. But Fate is the arrangement inherent in whatever is set in motion, and it allows Providence to connect everything with its proper order" (4.pr.6). Fate derives from and thus is dependent upon

---

[45] The longest prose section in the entire work, in fact.

providence. In the seventh and final prose section of the fourth book, Philosophy draws out the implication of her teaching regarding fate and providence, namely, that "all fortune . . . is entirely good" (4.pr.7). The implications for the third cause and its effects are clear: the world is governed by providence; and all fortune is good, including the change in Boethius' fortune.

The final poem of book 4 reveals the progress Boethius has made and how close he is to his cure. Citing the heroic struggles of Agamemnon, Ulysses, and Hercules, Philosophy exhorts Boethius to endure to the end: "Go then, brave men, don't look back! / By these ways find example— / Follow the high path! / Earth overcome grants the stars" (4.met.7). Boethius began with head downcast, his gaze fixed upon the ground. Now there is hope of overcoming the earth with his eyes fixed upon the stars.

Book 5

One might wonder whether book 5 is necessary. After all, Philosophy has addressed all three causes of Boethius' sickness. And the book itself begins with a detour into the question of chance (5.pr.1). It might appear, then, that the topics treated in book 5 are superfluous and that the real dramatic action of the work has already been completed. Much remains unresolved, however. Although Philosophy has addressed each of the causes of Boethius' disease, it is not at all clear that Boethius has fully internalized these truths and attained the moral and intellectual recollection that doing so would imply. There are still serious unresolved questions in his mind; he has made remarkable progress, but more needs to be done.

The discussion on chance in the first prose section leads to a discussion of freedom in the second, where the interlocutors agree that rational natures must be endowed with free will. Boethius is then confused by an even greater difficulty: "It would seem contradictory and conflicting . . . for God to know everything and for there to be free will" (5.pr.3). If the conflict is irreconcilable, the consequences are devastating: "And so there is no reason for hoping for something to happen or for praying that something won't happen; for why should a person hope or pray to avoid something when all things are tied up in unchangeable bonds?" These consequences are the key concern of book 5. The loss of "that single interaction between God and man" stands to destroy all that Philosophy and Boethius have accomplished over the course of their dialogue. Furthermore, the discussion reveals the fact that the final question of the work is whether there is ultimate consolation in God. A detailed examination of divine foreknowledge and human freedom occupies the interlocutors for the remainder of the book.

The conclusion of the work may appear troubling. In short, we could call it the "silence of Boethius". From the middle of book 3, we see a steady increase in the quantity and quality of Boethius' involvement in the dialogue—that is, until the last few pages. His last substantial contribution occurs in the third prose section of book 5, where he has the floor for nearly the entire time; and there Boethius appears to be deeply confused about the relation between divine foreknowledge and human freedom, leading to the conflict and consequences mentioned above. So what should we make of his nearly complete silence thereafter? Is Boethius cured? Or has he reverted to the position he was in at the beginning of the dialogue?

First, we must note that Philosophy thinks she has indeed met the challenge posed by Boethius. In her final remarks, she triumphantly concludes:

> Since these things are so, freedom of the will remains unviolated for mortals, and the laws are not unfair when they propose rewards and punishments, since the will is free from all necessity. And God still remains a watchman on high, foreknowing all things, and the ever-present eternity of His vision moves together with the future nature of our actions and dispenses rewards to the good and punishments to the bad. And not in vain are hopes and prayers placed before God, since when they are just, they cannot be without effect. So

> let us shun vices and cultivate virtues, lifting our minds to
> proper hopes and offering humble prayers on high. (5.pr.6)

Our hopes and prayers are not in vain. Despair has been
defeated, and communication with God has been renewed. Second, we must recall the earlier discussion regarding kinds of
silence. When the strongest arguments against a position have
been raised and met with worthy responses, there is no need
to say more. Philosophy has responded in detail to Boethius'
most astute and incisive objection. At this point, further dialogue would appear unnecessary. Finally, the distinction between
the "two Boethiuses" becomes helpful here.[46] While Boethius
the patient grows silent, Boethius the author speaks to the very
end. In fact, Boethius the author has so internalized the teaching of Philosophy that he has been speaking for both from the
beginning of the *Consolation*, constructing a dialogue that
embodies her teaching in the interchange between physician
and patient. Furthermore, the writing of the *Consolation* is itself
a recollection of her teaching, bearing witness to the extent
to which Boethius the author has brought about in himself
the kind of moral and intellectual recollection that are the
central concerns of the work.

A Consolation of *Philosophy?*

In conclusion, let us entertain one final question: Strictly speaking, is this work a consolation of *philosophy*? In other words,
does Philosophy truly console? Saint Thomas More, in his *Dialogue of Comfort against Tribulation*, has a wise old character,
Anthony, take issue with those who look for comfort or consolation in the "natural arguments" of philosophers:

> For the philosophers never go far enough. They leave un-
> touched, for lack of the necessary knowledge, that specific point
> which is the chief comfort of all, and without which all other
> comforts are nothing: namely, the point of referring the final

---

[46] The inspiration for this final point is McMahon, *Understanding the Medieval Meditative Ascent*, pp. 211–13, although there are a few minor differences.

end of their comfort to God, and of considering and taking as
the greatest cause of comfort that by a patient endurance of
their tribulation they will attain his favor, and for their pain
receive at his hand a reward in heaven.[47]

If Anthony speaks for More, I think Boethius and More may
agree. At various points in the essay, we have noted how
Philosophy's ultimate goal seems to be reestablishing Boethius
the patient's communication with God, convincing him that
"not in vain are hopes and prayers placed before God" (5.pr.6).
Perhaps, then, Philosophy herself cannot console; she can use
her dialectical art only to restore the broken relationship
between God and Boethius so that God, in turn, can truly
console him. So, then, is *The Consolation of Philosophy* not what
its title would imply? It is, but in a qualified, derivative sense.
As a physician cures a patient by assisting the processes of
nature, relying ultimately on the providential care of the great
Healer, so too Philosophy is able, through dialectic, to assist
Boethius in reestablishing his relationship with God, the true
and ultimate Consoler.

---

[47] Thomas More, *A Dialogue of Comfort against Tribulation*, rendered in modern English by Mary Gottschalk, with an introduction by Gerard B. Wegemer
(Princeton, N.J.: Scepter Publishers, 1998), p. 23.

Natural and Supernatural Responses
to Suffering: Boethius and Job

Rachel Lu
University of Saint Thomas

The Consolation of Philosophy is an example of that rare creature, a work that is equally magnificent on both a philosophical and a literary level. If Boethius was indeed "the last of the
Romans", then the empire ended with a flourish. Few men in
history have managed to combine so perfectly the analytic rigor
of the philosopher with the lyricism of the poet. Appropriately, the *Consolation* also stands out as one of the most influential compositions of the ancient world. Appreciation of its
philosophical and literary brilliance began as early as the ninth
century and continued through the Middle Ages and beyond;[1]
great writers who acknowledge a debt to Boethius range from
Dante to Chaucer to John Kennedy Toole. Given the manifest success of the *Consolation*, it is perhaps strange that later
commentators have continued to ask the question: Why did
Boethius write it?

In many ways, both the power and the puzzle of this remarkable work are rooted in the compelling circumstances of the
author. Boethius was led to reflect on the meaning of suffering,
not by a thought experiment, but by the realization that he
personally was likely to face torture and execution in the very
near future.[2] After a lifetime of worldly success and prosperity,

---

[1] See Jacqueline Beaumont, "The Latin Tradition of *De consolatione philosophiae*",
in *Boethius: His Life, Thought and Influence*, ed. Margaret Gibson (Oxford: Basil
Blackwell, 1981), p. 278; Lodi Nauta, "The *Consolation*: The Latin Commentary Tradition, 800–1700", in *The Cambridge Companion to Boethius*, ed. John
Marenbon (Cambridge: Cambridge University Press, 2009) pp. 255–78; and Winthrop Wetherbee, "The *Consolation* and Medieval Literature", in Marenbon, *Cambridge Companion to Boethius*, pp. 279–303.

[2] We cannot be certain just how prescient Boethius was in this regard; given
his many powerful friends, he may still have harbored hope that he might be

he suddenly finds himself betrayed by those he had regarded as
friends and allies. In this dark hour, Boethius puts pen to paper
and allows countless readers of future generations to accom-
pany him as he seeks consolation in philosophy.

His earlier works (especially the *Opuscula sacra*) leave no
doubt that Boethius was—for a time, at least—a committed
Christian. But shouldn't a committed Christian find more
potent remedies in the Bible than in Stoicism and Neoplatonism? Would not the Lord Jesus Christ be a more comforting companion in his misery than Lady Philosophy? The
startling lack of Christian references in the *Consolation* has
led some to conclude that Boethius had apostatized before or
during his imprisonment.[3] But an attentive reading of the *Consolation* renders this solution implausible. Though definitely not
a Christian work per se, it shows none of the bitterness that
one would expect from a recent apostate; quite the contrary,
the *Consolation* explores pagan philosophy in a way that seems
targeted to underscore its harmony with Christian revelation.
This is clearly not an anti-Christian work.

A more credible explanation turns on the distinction, long
acknowledged within Catholic philosophy, between natural reason (which all human beings possess by nature) and divinely
illumined reason (which draws on revelation and supernatural
graces by way of uncovering truths that human beings would
be unable to attain on their own). Although philosophers have
long debated the precise relationship between these, Catho-
lics have traditionally inclined toward fairly optimistic views
about the capacity of natural reason to uncover the truth. Some
seven hundred years after Boethius, Saint Thomas Aquinas
would explore at great length the relationship between natu-

---

rescued from his plight. Still, the general tone of the *Consolation* does clearly
show that he knew his situation was grim.

[3] Although this interpretation has perhaps been more popular in the modern
era, suspicion of Boethius' motives has a tradition of its own. As early as 900,
the Saxon abbot Bovo II was writing warnings to his monks of the dangers of
Boethius. See Henry Chadwick, *Boethius: The Consolations of Music, Logic, Theology, and Philosophy* (New York: Oxford University Press, 1981), p. 247.

ral reason and supernatural faith, and it is his exposition that would have the most obvious and dramatic impact on Catholic doctrine.[4] But although the Dominicans have often been depicted as the champions of human reason, the evidence suggests that Boethius was, if anything, more optimistic than they in his views of what unaided natural reason could do.[5]

It might even be fair to say that Boethius took it as his personal mission to preserve and promulgate the fruits of natural reason. Christian philosophers have long looked to the Greeks as the preeminent examples of what unaided human reason could (and could not) achieve. In the High Middle Ages, the Latin West labored to harmonize the best of the ancients' insights with revealed Christian truth. But Boethius, for his part, had a special dedication to the work of the ancients, owing largely to the circumstances in which he lived. While he himself enjoyed both a superb education and rare intellectual gifts, he knew that he was living at the end of a historical era and that few people in the years to come would be similarly advantaged. Thus, it was from a young age his life's ambition to preserve as much as possible of what he had learned, through a body of translations and commentaries. With remarkable ambition, he aspired to translate *all* the works of Plato and Aristotle and to illustrate through his own writings the underlying harmony between them.[6] Obviously, his early death prevented him from completing this project, but in the *Consolation* we can plainly see that same

---

[4] See, for example, the *Summa contra gentiles*, bk. 1, chap. 3, for a discussion of why some kinds of truths can be known by unaided natural reason, while others exceed its capacities.

[5] This becomes particularly plain in the theological tractates, in which Boethius explores, among other things, the role of logic in philosophy, and the problem of universals, both of which yield insights that Boethius thinks can be fruitfully applied to questions about the Trinity. For a discussion of how Boethius' studies of Aristotle and Proclus led him to a strong two-source view of truth, see Chadwick, *Boethius*, pp. 219–22.

[6] *In librum Aristotelis Peri hermeneias commentarii*, secunda editio, 2.1, cited by Ralph McInerny, *Boethius and Aquinas* (Washington, D.C.: Catholic University of America Press, 1990), p. 3.

zeal to lay the treasures of antiquity before the eyes of future generations.

In light of these considerations, it seems evident that Boethius made a conscious decision to dedicate his final work to *natural* philosophy. Avoiding Christian references altogether was the best way to ensure (and demonstrate to the reader) that his arguments need not draw on supernatural sources of truth. Still, we might reasonably go on to ask: How useful was such a project? Given the gravity of his situation, we would expect Boethius to attack his questions using any and all available resources. Instead, he imposed on himself a severe handicap. For a man facing a death sentence, this was a bold decision. It remains for his readers to consider how much he was able to achieve under such circumstances. In answering that question, we may reach a deeper understanding of the role of natural reason in the Christian life.

I propose to approach the question by setting *The Consolation of Philosophy* alongside one of history's most profound reflections on the subject of suffering: the book of Job. The parallels between Boethius and the afflicted Job are really quite striking. Both lived upstanding lives in service to God, and both prospered. Then their fortunes took a sudden and dramatic turn for the worse, and each found himself alone and seemingly friendless, trying to make sense of the suffering that had been inflicted on him. Their reactions to such adversity are not dissimilar. They bemoan their inability to die and lament that they were ever born. They bristle at the notion that they are being "punished" after having lived so well and faithfully. But in the end, both for Job and for Boethius, personal misfortune becomes a spur to considering the problem of evil in a more general way. This is the intersection that I mean to explore, in hopes that it will throw further light on Boethius' project.[7]

---

[7] Although the *philosophical* parallels will be the focus of this essay, these two works also mirror one another in their literary form. For a revealing discussion of the stylistic parallels and their philosophical and literary significance, see Ann Astell, *Job, Boethius, and Epic Truth* (Ithaca: Cornell University Press, 1994).

Of course, these two men are ultimately quite different in the way that they resolve their personal crises (and, by extension, the problem of evil more generally). Boethius turns to philosophy for answers, while Job addresses God directly; thus, it is reasonable to suggest that Boethius pursues a natural explanation for his anguish, while Job desires a supernatural response. Using these two as case studies, I will discuss what each was able to accomplish, and this, in turn, should yield some insight into the motivation behind Boethius' greatest work.

* * *

The theme of innocent suffering is at the heart of the book of Job. Job is a prosperous man who pleases God with his just and faithful living. When Satan suggests that Job's apparent devotion is merely the by-product of long prosperity, God permits him to torment Job in order to test the depth of his faithfulness.

When Satan destroys Job's children and material possessions, Job responds humbly, bowing down and accepting the divine will. He observes that all his goods were received from God, so that it would be unreasonable of him to complain when they are taken back. "Naked I came from my mother's womb," he declares, "and naked shall I return" (Job 1:21).[8] Thus far Satan's expectations are disappointed.

Things become more interesting when Satan is given permission to inflict Job with horrific boils. Although Job steadfastly repeats his willingness to accept God's will, his wife and friends have other ideas. The book turns into an extended discussion of the meaning of suffering, with Job contending that God does sometimes inflict suffering on the innocent, while his friends remain convinced that suffering is a punishment for wickedness and that Job must have committed grievous sins in order to merit so much affliction.

Job's reaction to this barrage of accusations is complex. Toward his friends he becomes very angry indeed. He accuses

---

[8] Unless otherwise noted, all biblical quotations are from *The Holy Bible: Revised Standard Version, Second Catholic Edition* (San Francisco: Ignatius Press, 2006).

them of tormenting him and reproves them for trying to pronounce judgment on him as if they were God.[9] He maintains
his innocence with increasing vehemence. He continues to
speak of God's wisdom and power and stresses his willingness
to trust God through everything. He maintains with steadfast
conviction that the wicked and the righteous will alike receive
justice, and accordingly, he still affirms faith in God despite
his great affliction: "For I know that my Redeemer lives, and
at last he will stand upon the earth; and after my skin has
been thus destroyed, then from my flesh I shall see God"
(19:25–26).

Despite these powerful affirmations of faith, Job does appear
to alter his stance on one point. Although he is never willing
to take his wife's advice to "curse God, and die" (2:9), he now
wants an explanation for his dreadful situation. "I will speak
in the bitterness of my soul", he declares. "I will say to God,
Do not condemn me; let me know why you contend against
me" (10:1–2). As the book progresses, he becomes increasingly eager to take the matter up with God directly.

Interestingly, it seems that Job is prepared to accept the loss
of his prosperity and loved ones, as well as physical affliction,
but he is infuriated by the injury to his reputation and good
name. He cannot understand why God would allow a just man
to be so maligned, and he begs for understanding and for his
own good character to be made known. Despite his insistence
that he trusts God and anticipates his own eventual justifica-
tion, Job does seem to be implying that he is *prima facie* being
treated unfairly and is owed an explanation.

But when at last God does enter the conversation, he is not
forthcoming with the information Job seeks. Instead, God insists
that Job be the one to answer questions. "Gird up your loins
like a man, I will question you, and you shall declare to me"
(38:3). The battery of questions God produces serves to illustrate a key point: God is the Creator of the universe, and thus
the source of all order, all justice, and indeed of being itself.

---

[9] See chapter 19 for a good example of this.

Job, by contrast, is just a creature. He should not expect to understand how the universe works, and he should realize that he is in no position to dictate the terms of fairness to the very author of justice.

It is important to recognize that the conversation between God and Job amounts to more than just an episode of divine bullying. God's point is not merely that, being all-powerful, he can do whatever he pleases without needing to answer to a pitiful weakling such as Job. God's power has already been acknowledged many times over, both by Job and by his friends, but if this were all God had to say for himself, then the doubts about his justice and goodness would only be intensified. A tyrant is not justified by the ability to annihilate his enemies, though his power is thereby preserved.

What God is showing Job is that his complaint is unintelligible. God's speech furnishes Job with examples, not only of divine power, but also of gentleness and mercy, and of the beauty of creation. The lioness' cubs and the raven's chicks cry for food, and are fed. The stars rise and cast their beautiful light on the children of the earth. These examples show that all good things have their origin in God; God is the beginning and end of all. Thus, there is no external court of appeal to whom Job could theoretically go in order to obtain a judgment about whether his treatment has been fair.

In addition to this, though, God shows Job that Job does not need an answer to his questions about suffering. God offers examples of majestic animals who act without seeking any further reason; they are ordered according to God's design, and there is no need for them to contemplate God's ends in order to participate in their fulfillment. The implication is that, in the division between Creator and creature, Job falls with the horse and the ostrich. He does not need to understand the purpose of everything that happens to him, and it is presumptuous to think that he should. Ultimately Job accepts God's rebuke, humbly submitting, "I lay my hand on my mouth. I have spoken once, and I will not answer; twice, but I will proceed no further" (40:4–5).

At the conclusion of the conversation, Job repents in dust and ashes and is rewarded with a new family and an increase in his prosperity even beyond what he had previously enjoyed. Through his humble submission to the divine will, Job reaps rich blessing and divine protection, as well as the restoration of his reputation among his fellow men. His patient assertion, "Although he should kill me, I will trust in him" (Job 13:15),[10] echoes over the centuries as one of the most perfect and fitting expressions of the virtue of hope.[11] Still, it is interesting to note that his primary demand remains unsatisfied. He is never given an explanation for his suffering.

*   *   *

With these lessons in mind we can now move ahead to a time several centuries after the writing of the book of Job, when another righteous man finds himself overwhelmed by grief. His situation, as previously noted, resembled Job's in many respects. Beyond the superficial parallels mentioned above, we might now add another: like Job, Boethius is tormented by the injustice of his situation. Both he and Job suffer as much from wounded pride as from any physical torment, realizing that outsiders are looking on them as miscreants and evildoers. And although he is not forced to endure the pious speeches of false friends, Boethius has other reasons for feeling that justice has gone egregiously awry. In Boethius' case, there seems to be a causal relationship between his just execution of political duties and his present suffering. It galls him to think that his good deeds should be punished in this way.

Like Job, Boethius seems as much oppressed by his sense of being wronged as he is by the material misfortunes that he suffers. Also like Job, he feels a burning desire to understand

[10] Douay-Rheims translation.

[11] Josef Pieper, in his beautiful essay on hope, meditates on this particular text, declaring that "there are no other words in Holy Scripture or in human speech as a whole that let resound as triumphantly the youthfulness of one who remains firm in hope against all destruction and through a veil of tears as do those of the patient Job." Josef Pieper, *Faith, Hope, Love* (San Francisco: Ignatius Press, 1997), p. 111.

why the universe should be as it is and should allow for such injustice as he is currently experiencing. But Boethius avoids Job's mistake of putting the author and source of justice on trial for a suspected misuse of power. Instead, he writes a work that makes no mention of a specifically Judeo-Christian God, and he approaches the mystery of suffering using the tools of natural philosophy.

Obviously, this project is more intellectual than anything that Job ever undertakes. Still, it should not be forgotten that philosophy comes to the character "Boethius" [12] as a consoler, responding to his overwhelming grief. "Boethius" is not, like Socrates in the *Phaedo*, merely trying to pass whatever time is available to him in the pursuit of wisdom. Rather, from the first book of the *Consolation*, philosophy is presented as a healer, with "Boethius" as a patient in desperate need. It is therefore possible to look at the two works side by side and evaluate the efficacy of each in providing a remedy to the grief-stricken soul.

The Consolation of Philosophy is arranged into five books, but for the purposes of this comparison, books 2 through 4 will be the most relevant. Book 1 is primarily devoted to introducing the characters ("Boethius" and Lady Philosophy) and setting the goal for the rest of the work (to recall "Boethius" to his true self and thus free him from his torment). Book 5 attempts to address a puzzle that is created by the theodicy presented in books 2 through 4. But it is the middle books that give the meat of Boethius' discussion of the problem of suffering. It is necessary, therefore, to summarize the major themes of these books, although it will not be the purpose of this article to describe and evaluate the arguments in all their intricate detail. [13]

Book 2 begins with a description of Fortune, that "monster" (2.pr.1) who

[12] For the remainder of the paper, I will distinguish between the author Boethius and the character Boethius by putting the name of the latter in quotation marks.

[13] For a more thorough discussion of these chapters, with attention to the literary and symbolic elements, see John Magee, "The Good and Morality: *Consolatio 2–4*", in Marenbon, *Cambridge Companion to Boethius*, pp. 181–206.

... encourages the destroyed,
laughing!
at the weeping and groaning
her harshness caused.

. . . .

[P]roving her power—
she revels in her show.
The fortunate she prostrates—
in one hour.

(2.met.1)[14]

"Boethius" is reminded that earthly successes are fleeting and that anyone who tries to find happiness in such goods must be prepared to be bandied about on Fortune's winds. Indeed, there is no injustice in this, because nobody deserves material benefits in the first place. Having basked unashamedly in the warmth of undeserved prosperity, "Boethius" cannot reasonably complain if Fortune has now decided to reclaim what was never rightfully his.

Lady Philosophy continues the argument by detailing some of the specific earthly goods that mortals crave, showing how each in turn is ephemeral and thus unsuitable as a foundation for human happiness. Wealth cannot buy anything that is truly good, and those things that it does buy can always be stolen. Political power never lasts long and at best can be exercised only for one brief moment in one small corner of the world. Fame too is a fleeting thing. And earthly prosperity of any kind brings with it the curse of false friends, who desire our company only for the sake of their own earthly advancement.

In book 3, Lady Philosophy deepens the argument by explaining why it is that people so ardently pursue these false goods. All men, she claims, desire happiness above all else and seek those goods that they think will lead to happiness (3.pr.2). This quest is not utterly irrational, because each of the aforementioned false goods does resemble another, actual good that

---

[14] Boethius, *The Consolation of Philosophy*, trans. and ed. Scott Goins and Barbara Wyman, Ignatius Critical Editions (San Francisco: Ignatius Press, 2012). All quotations from the *Consolation* are from this edition.

could bring happiness. Thus, wealth appears to give some measure of self-sufficiency, which is an actual good. Political office looks as though it would yield the goods of honor and respect, and power is also a good in itself. Human fame is a kind of counterfeit of genuine greatness or glory. In each case, humans mistake the false good for the real thing and pursue it in hopes of finding happiness. Every time, they find themselves disappointed.

Disappointment, however, is not the worst consequence. What is particularly pernicious about all of these "false trails" is that they draw people ever further from the true Good. People seek a modest amount of wealth, power, fame, and so forth, in hopes that this will make them happy. When it does not, they imagine that *more* of the same "good"—a false good— will do the trick. Because the underlying need is never filled, the appetite is simply insatiable and can grow to monstrous proportions. None of these commodities can ever satisfy.

Thus, book 3 ends with a Platonic argument for divine simplicity (that is, for the claim that God's being is one and the same with his attributes). As Lady Philosophy explains, none of the genuine goods (self-sufficiency, honor, power, glory, and so forth) can be lasting or complete unless they are all unified together. Only the most perfectly good thing (that than which nothing better can be conceived) could possibly bring all goods together into one. And that thing than which nothing can be better is what all men call God (3.pr.10). So it must be that God is true goodness, true happiness, and that which brings all other goods together into a unity. Men, for their part, must seek to participate in that divinity if they wish to be happy.

"Boethius" is delighted with this argument, and he exults in the progress they have made. But now, in book 4, he brings forward the question that is nearest to his heart: Why do the wicked prosper while the innocent suffer?

First, Lady Philosophy offers an argument reminiscent of Plato's *Gorgias*, explaining that, contrary to popular belief, the wicked never do truly flourish. Indeed, to speak of a person being both wicked and flourishing is something of a contradiction, since, as established in the previous book, real flourishing comes from participation in divinity, whereas wickedness

is a rejection of the divine. Those wicked men who are empow-
ered to work their evil will are in fact the most grievously to
be pitied, because their evil actions draw them further and
further away from the God who alone can make them happy.

From this narrower argument about the apparent prosperity
of the wicked, Lady Philosophy is able to draw a broader point,
which might be seen as the ultimate balm to the wounded
soul of "Boethius". True happiness comes from participation
in the divine. But, this being the case, the relationship between
earthly prosperity and genuine flourishing is not easy for the
human mind to discern. Some good men may be raised up as
instruments for opposing the wicked; others may prosper because
God knows that they are too weak to withstand adversity. Some
wicked men may meet with hardship as a remedy for their vices,
while others may providentially be granted prosperity as a safeguard against their victimizing others. Given the enormous
diversity of human characters and circumstances, there is no
reason to expect that a single human observer, from the vantage point of one particular time and place, could make sense
of the fortunes of men. Nonetheless, Lady Philosophy assures
"Boethius" that, "just because you don't know the reasons for
such arrangements, you shouldn't doubt that everything is done
rightly, since a good ruler governs the world" (4.pr.5).

*   *   *

Having examined the outline of the *Consolation*'s explanation
of suffering, we can now look back at the book of Job and see
significant thematic parallels. Interestingly, despite the great
differences in their interlocutors, Job and "Boethius" seem to
start and end in more or less the same places. In the beginning, both Job and Lady Philosophy articulate the idea that it
is necessary to take the bad with the good in life; one who has
enjoyed undeserved prosperity must be prepared to accept some
measure of suffering as well. This is, for each, a first attempt
to put suffering in perspective, and for both the argument is
ultimately insufficient to console. But now, flashing forward
to the end, we again find similar themes. "Boethius", like Job,

is led to reflect on how presumptuous it is for him, a mere creature, to expect that he can grasp the full shape of God's providential plan. Ultimately, though, he is assured that everything must happen for good reason, because all is governed by God, who is the author of goodness.

In between these common starting and ending points, the dialectic for each work is somewhat different. Job must contend with nagging friends who think he has committed grave sins; "Boethius" has no such aggravation. Thus "Boethius" is able to use his time more pleasantly, uncovering a Platonic-type argument for God's absolute simplicity and goodness. But even though Job never enters into any such speculation, there is a real sense in which he and "Boethius" are being taught the same lesson. God, through his series of rhetorical questions, teaches Job that it is not merely impious but actually irrational to question the goodness of the supreme being. Lady Philosophy makes a similar point in a philosophical way, by showing that all other things flourish or wither in proportion to their proximity to the absolutely simple God. This precludes the possibility of cosmic injustice.

Given so many parallels, it seems appropriate at this point to ask: Which of the two men benefits more from his "therapy"? Who is ultimately better off? Philosophically, "Boethius" obviously benefits more. Whereas Job's request for understanding is mostly stymied, "Boethius" is offered a rich panoply of arguments that (at least in his own view) successfully address his grievances. Undoubtedly, "Boethius" emerges from his encounter with considerably more perspective on suffering. As an argument for the value of natural reason, *The Consolation of Philosophy* is powerful indeed.

Still, there is also a sense in which Job is ultimately more enviable. (Of course, there is one *obvious* way in which Job is better off: he regains his life of earthly prosperity! But, having seen that material prosperity is not equivalent to happiness, we will disregard this for the purposes of the present discussion.) Whereas "Boethius" is convinced intellectually of the goodness of the universe, Job is asked to submit to God without understanding, in an act of supernatural faith. "Boethius" is given reasons for trusting God's providence; Job is merely asked to trust. Job's act of submission requires him to accept his suffering without knowing the reason for it. No doubt this is doubly frustrating for him, given his friends' insistence that he himself is to blame. Yet it is Job, with his willingness to submit uncomprehendingly to God's will, who is able to articulate the sublime words of timeless faith we quoted earlier: "For I know that my Redeemer lives, and at last he will stand upon the earth; and after my skin has been thus destroyed, then from my flesh I shall see God." No such comfort is available to "Boethius" as his dialogue with Lady Philosophy draws to its conclusion.

Between the two of them, "Boethius" and Job illustrate the natural and supernatural responses to the problem of suffering. Each reaps the reward proper to his response. "Boethius" has greater understanding but is still left to face his impending torment and death in an uncomfortable state of perplexity, having still in his mind many unresolved questions about the universe as a whole and his own fate in particular. Job must drop his "complaint" against God without the satisfaction of an explanation, but his reward is theological hope, with its much more robust assurances of salvation and the eventual renewal of all the earth.

*   *   *

Boethius aspired in his life to translate the full corpus of the ancient world's two greatest minds into Latin. Had he succeeded, the Latin West would have had access to these treasures many centuries earlier than they did. No scholar of medieval thought can avoid wondering, with a tinge of regret, how history might have been different had the project been completed. And yet, despite this interruption of his plans, Boethius nonetheless succeeded in being one of the primary "bridges" through which future generations discovered the riches of antiquity, in large part thanks to his *Consolation of Philosophy*. Realizing that his intended life's work would be left incomplete, he used what time was left to him to leave to future readers this small jewel, in which he took the highlights of ancient wisdom and wove them together in a way that was a credit to the Greeks and, at the same time, brilliantly complementary to Christian faith. He may have hoped that future readers, intrigued by what they found in the *Consolation*, would be motivated to go back and uncover ancient works that inspired it. If so, we can happily declare fifteen hundred years later that his wish has been more than granted.

How Boethius Built a Bridge from Ancient Pagan to Medieval Christian

Louis Markos
Houston Baptist University

Boethius' *The Consolation of Philosophy*, explains C. S. Lewis in *The Discarded Image*, "was for centuries one of the most influential books ever written in Latin. It was translated into Old High German, Italian, Spanish, and Greek; into French by Jean de Meung; into English by Alfred [the Great], Chaucer, Elizabeth I, and others. Until about two hundred years ago it would, I think, have been hard to find an educated man in any European country who did not love it." [1] It is no exaggeration to say that the *Consolation* was one of three books—the other two are Virgil's *Aeneid* and Ovid's *Metamorphoses*—that were responsible for preserving and transmitting many of the key ideas of antiquity.

The *Consolation* served that function throughout the Middle Ages, losing some of its central influence only when the texts of ancient Greece (especially of Plato) were recovered during the Renaissance. In any case, by the seventeenth century, it had suffered the same strange fate that befell the *Metamorphoses*—great writers like Dante, Chaucer, and Shakespeare had so utterly absorbed the contents of these two works that one had less need to read them (rather as many today feel little need to read the *Odyssey*, *Don Quixote*, *Le Morte D'Arthur*, *Hamlet*, or *Paradise Lost*, for they feel they've already read them!).

Boethius (and when we say Boethius, we mean the *Consolation*) continues to serve as one of our chief links to the classical and medieval world; however, he serves perhaps a more

[1] C. S. Lewis, *The Discarded Image: An Introduction to Medieval and Renaissance Literature* (Cambridge: Cambridge University Press, 1964), p. 75.

229

indispensable, if subtler, role to scholars, like Lewis, who desire to draw together the Judeo-Christian legacy of Jerusalem and the Greco-Roman legacy of Athens. Like Augustine, Boethius is one of the channels through which these two great cultural, ethical, philosophical, and aesthetic streams met, mingled, and overflowed to create medieval Europe. This may seem like an odd statement to make about a book that is written in the language and from the point of view of Greco-Roman (that is, pagan) philosophy, but the "pagan" content should not lead us to conclude that its author was a disciple of Julian the Apostate. On the contrary, as many (though not all) scholars have argued, Boethius was not a pagan philosopher writing pagan philosophy but a Christian philosopher writing in a pagan mode.[2] In that, I would compare the *Consolation* to four other great works that, though written by Christians and imbued with a deep Christian morality and world view, are told from and within the perspective of a pre-Christian world: *Beowulf*, Chaucer's *Knight's Tale*, Tolkien's *Lord of the Rings*, and Lewis' *Till We Have Faces*.

Due to his friendship with Theodoric, king of the Ostrogoths and ruler of Italy, Boethius (c. 480–524) became a consul of Rome in 510 and was highly respected as a scholar and philosopher. Sadly, Fortune's wheel, of which Boethius would write so eloquently, turned against him, and the onetime court favorite was accused of treason and thrown into prison. Though the historical record is not fully clear, it seems highly probable that Boethius' falling out with Theodoric was due to the fact that Theodoric was an Arian and Boethius an orthodox Christian. Boethius wrote the *Consolation* shortly before his death as both a theoretical and a practical means of finding solace

---

[2] In *Discarded Image*, Lewis explains it thus: "[W]hat we might take to be the difference between a clearly Christian and a possibly Pagan work may really be the difference between a thesis offered, so to speak, to the Faculty of Philosophy and one offered to that of Divinity. This seems to me to be the best explanation of the gulf that separates Boethius' *De Consolatione* from the doctrinal pieces which are (I presume, rightly) attributed to him" (pp. 47–48). For Lewis' incisive analysis of the *Consolation*, see ibid., pp. 75–90.

in his own chosen calling and profession. By writing his work in the pagan mode, Boethius the Christian (I would emend that to Christian martyr) demonstrated that much solace could be found in pagan philosophy—a belief that does not violate biblical teaching but upholds it. While denying himself, as a writer but not as a believer, the luxury of direct (or special) revelation, Boethius mines the resources of general revelation—that which God has revealed to all men through nature, reason, and the conscience. By so doing, he builds a bridge between general and special revelation, pagan and Christian, ancient and medieval that is particularly relevant to our own age—an age that has been notorious for abandoning, if not indeed burning, all such bridges.

In what follows, I shall survey those sections and passages of the *Consolation* that exerted a particularly strong influence upon the Middle Ages, especially as that period is summed up in the work of Dante and Chaucer, and that helped to unite Christian theology and philosophy with the highest of pagan thought. Though most of Plato's work was lost during the Middle Ages, many of Plato's deepest insights—especially those insights that point the way toward the fuller Christian revelation—were conveyed to the medievals both through Augustine and through Boethius. Let us, then, join the dialogue.

The War between Poetry and Philosophy

Plato's *Republic* is filled with notorious passages that still provoke strong reactions from modern faculty and students. Among the most notorious involve Plato's (Socrates') decision to kick the poets out of his perfect state. In place of poets who arouse our passions, we get philosopher-kings who speak to our reason. As the *Consolation* opens, Boethius is in despair and finds little solace from his Muses (that is, poetry). Philosophy appears in allegorical form as a woman and scolds Boethius for attending to poetry when he should be attending to philosophy:

> As she [Philosophy] caught sight of the Muses of Poetry standing by my bed, giving me words to suit my tearful mood, the

Lady was angry for a moment and her eyes flashed with savage fire. She spoke: "Who let these whorish stage girls come to see a sick man? It's more pain they bring than remedies. No, they make things worse with their sweet-tasting poison. These are the kind of women who choke off a mind's rich fruit, wrapping it up in sterile thorns of passion. They make a mind more used to disease, instead of setting it free from pain. If you were trying to seduce a common man with your enticements, as you usually do, it wouldn't bother me so much. Then you would not be damaging my work—but a man weaned on Eleatic and Academic philosophy? Now go, you Sirens, sweet until you bring destruction; leave him to my Muses to be cured and made whole." (1.pr.1)[3]

Just as the Sirens in *Odyssey* 12 sing their seductive songs so as to drag sailors off course to their doom, so poetry, Lady Philosophy claims, both blinds and poisons us, causing us to fall off the course of reason. This is especially lamentable for men like Boethius who have been partially initiated into the ways of philosophy and who should have progressed up the rungs of the ladder of wisdom (as the true lover-philosopher does in Plato's *Symposium*, *Phaedrus*, and the "Allegory of the Cave", and in the more mystical teachings of Pythagoras).

Exposed by and ashamed because of Philosophy's words, the Muses bow their heads and pass from the room, leaving Boethius to be scolded further by Philosophy, who explains to him exactly what should and should not have happened in his life:

> This man was once free to walk
> under open heavens, familiar
> with celestial courses; he viewed
> the sun's light, the icy moon, and
> wherever stars on wandering returns
> danced through changing circles.
> All these he possessed—

[3] Boethius, *The Consolation of Philosophy*, trans. and ed. Scott Goins and Barbara Wyman, Ignatius Critical Editions (San Francisco: Ignatius Press, 2012). All quotations from the *Consolation* are from this edition. The passages I quote will be taken consecutively from the five books that make up the work.

mastered with numbers.
He understood many causes:

. . . .

He pried into hidden nature's secrets.
This man now lies,
his mind light-forsaken,
neck pressed with chains,
face cast down,
forced to discern nothing
but the ground.

(1.met.2)

Any student of Dante's *Purgatorio* will recognize at once how similar this scolding is to the one that Beatrice gives Dante when she first meets him in the Garden of Eden (canto 30). The young poet-lover Dante had, guided by the beauty and grace of Beatrice, been progressing upward toward truth, but when Beatrice died, he was turned from that path to be inspired by more earthly women who dragged his vision downward. In canto 31, she explains that she had to scold him thus that he might not be tempted again by the Sirens (one of whom he had earlier been tempted by in a dream).

Evangelical Protestants (of which I am one) often forget that Christianity is not just about a moment of salvation but about a spiritual growth toward what the medievals, after Plato and Boethius and Aquinas, called the Beatific ("blessed") Vision. What makes the Christian vision greater than the Platonic, however, is that the end point (or telos) of the journey-vision is not the contemplation of nonpersonal Forms but a great marriage between the Christian pilgrim-initiate and the triune God. In Boethius' allegory, we see this a bit more clearly than in Plato's; in Dante's overtly Christian epic, we see it even more clearly.

But what is preventing Boethius and Dante from completing, or at least staying true to, the vision and the journey? Well, it is, of course, sin, but not sin as we moderns think about sin. Boethius, Philosophy tells him, is "simply dazed, as one would expect of a man suffering under delusion. He's forgotten who he is for a moment. He'll easily remember again soon—that is, if indeed he ever knew me. But first we'll have to wipe away the cloud of mortal cares that darkens his eyes" (1.pr.2). What prevents Boethius is not lust or pride or greed but sloth—a fault that the medievals counted as one of the seven deadly sins. But who, Protestant or Catholic, remembers that designation today? We tend to think of sloth, if at all, as a form of melancholy or depression, as a neurosis for psychologists to deal with, but certainly not as a sin. Yet sin it is: a sullen, lethargic wasting away of our gifts that will cause us in the end to drift away from God and, ultimately, to lose all sense of ourselves as creatures created with a purpose and equipped with gifts to pursue that purpose. The philosophy that Boethius and Dante enjoin upon us is not that vain philosophy based upon human traditions that deceives believers (Colossians 2:8) but a vigorous and humble philosophy that impels us to journey toward Divine Truth and the Divine Presence (two goals that have, incidentally, been outlawed by the modern and postmodern academy).

Boethius gave into sloth when he abandoned his high philosophical calling; Dante gave into sloth when he abandoned his high poetic calling. The real war between poetry and philosophy is not between verse and prose, or imagination and logic, or even passion and reason, but is between that which drags down and that which draws up, that which casts into darkness and that which dispels the darkness, that which is seduced by false images and that which seeks those things that do not change or perish.

The Wheel of Fortune and the Vanity of Fame

Boethius would set our eyes, and his own, on those higher things in which there is no shadow of turning, but he, like the Bible, does not therefore ignore the world of change in which we live. Rather, he helps us to see the world for what it is by using an image that spoke with equal power to the men of the classical, medieval, and Renaissance ages—with Boethius himself as one of the bridges between the three. That image is of Dame Fortune, who ceaselessly spins her wheel, giving blessings to some and curses to others, causing one to rise and another to fall.

At the end of book 1, Boethius casts aspersions on Dame Fortune, complaining to Philosophy that whereas Fortune has fixed the seasonal laws upon which nature runs, she is fickle and unfair with the human inhabitants of the world. In words that rely as much on pagan complaint as on biblical theodicy (Job and Habakkuk), Boethius asks why the just are punished and the ways of sinners prosper.

As readers, we expect that Philosophy will fall into another "cat fight", reviling Dame Fortune as she had the Muses; instead, she comes to the defense of Fortune:

> So what is it, mortal, that has plunged you into grief and mourning? I suppose you've seen something new and strange. You believe that Fortune has changed towards you: you are wrong. These have always been her ways and nature. She's retained her character in her very fickleness towards you. She was just the same when she fawned on you and tricked you with the promises of a counterfeit happiness. You've learned of the fickleness of that blind spirit. Though she still hides herself from others, to you she has revealed herself completely." (2.pr.1)

Why, she asks Boethius, is he so surprised at the fickleness of Fortune, when to be fickle is in her very nature? Indeed, when Fortune changes, she is not being false but true to her nature: it is only in being inconstant that she is constant.

No, the problem is not with Fortune but with those who have trusted themselves to her, who have made her their mistress:

> If you entrusted your sails to the wind, you'd move forward in the direction it was blowing, not where you chose to go. If you entrusted seeds to the fields, you'd expect some good years and some bad ones. Now you've given yourself to the rule of Fortune; you must conform yourself to her ways. Would you try to

hold back the force of a wheel in motion? O most foolish of men! If Fortune began to be permanent, she would cease to be Fortune. (2.pr.1)

Like a man who dates a woman not because he loves her but because she flirts with and is desired by all other men, and then is shocked and dismayed when she shares her favors with those other men, Boethius foolishly thinks he can win the blessings of Fortune while remaining immune to her curses. Jesus warned his disciples that those who live by the sword will die by it as well (Matthew 26:52); the same maxim holds true for those who foolishly place all their faith in Fortune.

Dante, a man who trusted in Fortune and saw her take him to the pinnacle of success (great political power in Florence) and the nadir of despair (exile from his beloved city), was so influenced by the image of Fortune as the arbitress of our world that he created his own myth to explain the powerful sway of Fortune over the affairs of men. He knew from the ancients (particularly from Plato via Boethius) that each of the planets was controlled by an intelligence that drove its sphere. Dante's innovation was to suggest (*Inferno* 7) that Dame Fortune is the intelligence of earth who moves our sphere—a clever image since earth was, according to the medieval cosmological model, the one planet that did not move through space but remained stationary. (Actually, to be more precise, earth was not considered a planet at all, since "planet" in Greek connotes something that wanders!)

Chaucer, who also knew what it meant to dwell in the corridors of power but who was more politic and flexible than the fiery and inflexible Dante, filled the stories that make up his *Canterbury Tales* with cautionary references to Fortune. In *The Knight's Tale* (1.393–402), he directly echoes the passage quoted above, asking why it is that people put all the blame for their woes on God or Fortune when it is so often their yearning for "good" Fortune (riches, freedom, love) that leads them to "bad" Fortune. Such counsel surfaces again and again in the *Canterbury Tales*, though Chaucer was able, where Dante was not, to reflect on Fortune from a bemused distance.

Shakespeare, who knew how to ride and control Fortune even better than Chaucer, fills his plays and sonnets with references to Fortune, investing them now with Dantean gravity, now with Chaucerian humor. To my mind, the most memorable of these references occurs in Act 2, scene 2, of *King Lear*, when Kent, bound in the stocks, cries out to the heavens for Fortune to turn her wheel—the implication being that he is at such a low point that any turn of the wheel can only be for the better! The bittersweet complaint of the faithful and balanced Kent, at once melancholy and comic, captures nicely Shakespeare's use of the image.

If, then, Fortune is fickle, what defense do we have against her? Though Boethius offers a number of answers, the one that perhaps resonated most strongly through the Middle Ages and Renaissance, the wise counsel that Boethius passed down from the ancient pagan world to the newly forming Christian one, can be summed up in four Latin words: *sic transit gloria mundi* (thus passes the glory of the world). Echoing the Roman Cicero's *Dream of Scipio*, Boethius has Philosophy discourse on the vanity of fame and on the physical and spatial (though not spiritual and moral) insignificance of our world:

> Now consider how lacking in substance and empty of weight this fame is. It is established, as you have learned from astronomical proofs, that the entire circle of the earth is comparable to the space of a point when measured against the heavens. The earth is such that we would judge it had no space at all if it were set beside the magnitude of the heavenly sphere. And of this very little part of the universe, only about one fourth is inhabited by living things that we know of, as you have learned from the proofs of Ptolemy. Of this fourth, if you remove from consideration the parts covered by seas and swamps and the vast regions of desert, scarcely the narrowest portion is left to be inhabited by men. And so, when you're enclosed and hedged within this sort of point within a point, do you consider trying

to spread your name around and make your fame known to
all? Do you think that glory confined within such narrow bounds
would have any magnitude or grandeur? (2.pr.7)

In addition to giving the lie to the still-common prejudice that
the medieval Christians were fools who believed themselves
to be living in a tiny little universe in which our earth was of
supreme importance, this passage helps put the ambitions of
man in a cosmic perspective.

For one brief, dazzling moment, Boethius lifts us above the
spinning of Fortune's wheel to show us how small and petty
are our strivings for fame, riches, and glory. It is a vision
meant to inspire awe and humility and to provoke contemplation of our own position, and that of our world, within
the universe. It is a stunning passage that reverberated through
Christendom, but it is surpassed by Dante's tribute to it in
Paradiso 22. Having ascended past the seven planets and
reached the region of the fixed stars, Dante casts a backward glance on the earth (and the whole vast universe)
that he has left behind. And in that moment of supreme contemplation, Dante, whose life had for so long been controlled by the fickle turnings of Fortune, sees how small and
lost in space our globe is, how the Florentine politics that
had so consumed his life are played out, not in a Roman
amphitheater, but on "a dusty little threshing ground" (*Paradiso* 20.152).[4]

Eyes to See and Ears to Hear

A favorite pastime of the medieval Christians was to take pagan
myths from Hesiod, Homer, and Ovid and find in them an
allegory for the moral-philosophical-spiritual life. Such allegorical readings enabled Christians to find (or, better, *access*)
deeper spiritual truths in the pagan classics, thus bridging the
gap between general and special revelation and paying tribute

[4] Dante, *The Paradiso*, trans. John Ciardi (New York: New American Library,
1970), p. 251.

to the presence of God's truth among all people. Oddly, they partly learned this pastime from such Neoplatonists as Philo and Plotinus, who, though they did not embrace the Christian doctrines of the Trinity, Incarnation, Atonement, and Resurrection, also sought higher truths in the often violent and bawdy myths of the great Greco-Roman poets.

It should, by this point in my essay, come as no surprise that Boethius played a key role in mediating between the Neoplatonists and the Christians, thereby helping to enshrine the allegorization of myth as an approach and a devotional method appropriate for believers. (Augustine, who came to orthodox Christianity via Neoplatonism and Manichaeism, also played a mediating role: he even noted in his *Confessions* that although the New Testament alone taught him that "the Word became flesh and dwelt among us", the Neoplatonists *did* teach him that "in the beginning was the Word.") At the close of book 3, and again near the beginning of book 4, Boethius offers allegorical readings of two of the best known myths from antiquity: the tale of Orpheus and Eurydice and the story, told in *Odyssey* 10, of how Odysseus' men were turned to swine by Circe the enchantress.

In the former myth, Eurydice, the wife of the famed musician Orpheus, dies and is carried down to Hades. Impelled by love, Orpheus enters the underworld and, through the power of his music, impels Hades to restore to him his dead wife— but with a condition. Hades will allow Eurydice to follow Orpheus out of the underworld; however, until she has emerged back into the light, her husband may not look back at her. All goes well until, at the very brink of the underworld, Orpheus fears that Hades has tricked him and looks back to make sure his wife is behind him. "Alas," Philosophy recounts, "near the end of his night,/Orpheus his own Eurydice/saw, lost, and killed" (3.met.12).

The story is a moving one, but does it, like the parables of Jesus, contain a moral lesson from which Christians can profit? The answer is yes, but only to those who have eyes to see and ears to hear what the tale is saying.

> This story is for you,
> for those who wish to lead
> the mind into the upper day.
> Since, whoever, having been weakened,
> turns back his gaze to Tartarus' chasm—
> whatever excellence he has gained,
> looking back, he loses.
>
> (3.met.12)

As Boethius is too blinded by his despair to see the meaning, Philosophy kindly explains it to him: as we saw earlier, the lover, poet, or philosopher who would ascend to the Beatific Vision must fix his gaze on things above. Unless we keep our "eyes on the prize", we will, like Dante, fall off course and tumble into that dark wood of error where the poet finds himself at the opening of the *Divine Comedy*.

And the same holds true for those who would live a virtuous life on this earth: they must train their thoughts and actions upward toward the angels, not downward toward the beasts. Since Boethius is not writing in a Christian mode, he does not speak of Heaven and Hell directly as the rewards of virtue and vice. Rather, working within a framework that is both Platonic and Aristotelian, he describes the effects that vice (sin) has on us in this world. By indulging in vice, we, quite literally, dehumanize ourselves. Evil men, Philosophy warns Boethius, since they have turned to evil,

> have also lost their human nature. And since virtue alone is able to make a person surpass his fellow men, it must be the case that those whom wickedness brings down from their human state are sunk so low that they don't deserve to be called human. Thus it happens that if you saw a man transformed by vices, you couldn't consider him human.
>
> Suppose a violent robber burns with desire for another man's riches—you would say he's like a wolf. A wild and restless man, who busies his tongue with lawsuits—you would compare him to a dog. A man who sneaks and lurks about hoping to trip up others by deceit—he's just like a little fox.... And so it happens

that a man who abandons virtue, since he can't become godlike, turns into a beast. (4.pr.3)

Whereas goodness lifts us above humanity toward the angels,
evil sinks us below humanity toward the level of the beast. To
embrace evil is to lose our human nature, to give up that part
of ourselves that was made in God's image and that distinguishes us from the lower animals.

Boethius would have understood this had he paid closer
attention to *Odyssey* 10, had he discerned the deeper meaning of Circe's transformation of Odysseus' swinish men into
literal swine. This much we expect Philosophy to say, for
the link between the Homeric myth and the ethical-spiritual
truth is quite clear, but Boethius takes us a step further in
his allegorical reading. When Circe turns Odysseus' men to
swine, their bodies change, but their minds retain human
memory. In a passage that comes close to being overtly
Christian, Philosophy warns Boethius that there is something
even worse than a sorceress who can change our outward form,
and that is the poison that can effect the opposite state of
affairs:

Oh! Hand [of Circe] too weak!
Your powerful herbs change human limbs,
but potions cannot change hearts.
Within is man's strength: concealed in a hidden fortress.
Those poisons which draw man from himself,
these are the potent ones—dire potions—
which pass deep inside, harmless to the body,
but ravaging with wounds to the mind.

(4.met.3)

The passage surely alludes to Jesus' warning that we should
not fear "those who kill the body but cannot kill the soul;
rather fear him [God] who can destroy both soul and body in
hell" (Matthew 10:28; RSV, Second Catholic Edition). It would
be a grievous thing indeed for our body to take the form of an
animal, but far worse would it be to lose our soul, to have it

sink into subhuman bestiality, to be robbed of that conscience and consciousness by which we reflect the image of our Maker.

Perhaps Dante's greatest insight into the nature of Hell and damnation is partly indebted to this Boethian fusion of Platonic metaphysics/psychology (see especially the "Myth of Er" from the *Republic*), Aristotelian ethics, and Christian revelation. What Dante presents us with in his *Inferno* is a group of sinners who, in losing their fear of God, have ceded their humanity and become a parody of their original God-breathed nature—a vision of Hell and its inhabitants that is further developed in C. S. Lewis' mini-*Divine Comedy*, *The Great Divorce*. Moderns tend to read the *Inferno* as a graphic meditation on punishment-to-fit-the-crime vengeance, but the spiritual and psychological truth is deeper than that: the *Inferno* is not about "poetic justice" but about what happens when sinners become their sin.

Providence and Predestination

Readers of the *Divine Comedy* will not be surprised to discover that Dante the theological poet devotes a great deal of space to the twin issues of providence versus fate and free will versus predestination; they might, however, be surprised to discover that Chaucer the comic poet devotes almost as much space to these issues in his *Canterbury Tales* (even if he does so in a more whimsical fashion than Dante). The classical pagan mind was also troubled by these issues, and the medievals owed a great debt to Boethius for preserving and passing on the highest pagan meditations on the subject of providence and predestination. If truth be told, we who live in the twenty-first century, even those who do not confess a belief in a personal God, continue to be troubled by the interplay between human choice and divine (or cosmic, or evolutionary, or economic, or psychological) determinism. I would like therefore to end this study of Boethius by outlining briefly what the *Consolation* has to say to us about these timeless issues, and how it can help us to resolve conflicts that trouble religious and secular people alike.

The origin, the order, and the forms of all things, Philosophy explains to Boethius, ultimately rest in and proceed from "the stability of the Divine Mind. The Mind, settled in the citadel of its own simplicity, has determined many means for accomplishing its purposes. The means that is viewed in terms of the purity of Divine Intelligence itself is called Providence. When we speak of things that are set in motion and arranged, the means has been called Fate in the past" (4.pr.6). Building on this ancient dichotomy, Boethius the Christian has Philosophy define providence as the divine and eternal reason that arranges and orders all things, and fate as that arranging and ordering as it manifests itself in time and space. All that lies within the realm of fate is subjected to providence, but providence is not subjected to fate.

Very well, Boethius replies, but between fate and providence does any space exist for freedom? In response, Philosophy assures him that free will exists and that all creatures who possess reason have the power both to seek what they desire and shun what is wrongful. But these powers manifest themselves differently in men and angels:

> Heavenly, divine beings have keen judgment and uncorrupted will, and they have within them the power to achieve what they want. Human souls are necessarily more free when they continue to contemplate the Divine Mind, but they are less free when they fall down to human bodies. Their ultimate slavery comes when they are given over to vices and fall away from the possession of their reason. (5.pr.2)

Contrary to those who would say that the great sinners have the most freedom and the great saints the least, Boethius (borrowing as much from Plato as from the Bible) insists that the truth is exactly the opposite. We have the most freedom when we rest in the mind of God (in which dwells that providence that is higher than fate) and the least when we sink to the level of the beast. When the mind turns from the light of truth and sinks into darkness, when it follows the path of vice rather than virtue, it becomes fully subject to fate and loses all freedom.

But for those who do not look back at Eurydice, who do not give in to bestiality and become swine, freedom and reason are twin realities.

And yet a problem remains. How can true freedom exist when God's foreknowledge allows him to know all things that will happen? If God foreknows the future, must he not also predestine it? Boethius' answer to this, an answer that he saves for the end of his *Consolation*, is as simple as it is profound and offers to man a space within which his freedom can thrive without thereby offending the sovereignty of God, who, Philosophy reminds Boethius, does not live, as we do, in time, but possesses a condition both "eternal and abiding" (5.pr.6). God's

> knowledge also surpasses all movement of time and remains in the simplicity of its presence. Embracing the limitless spaces of the past and future, it understands all things simply and considers them as if they were being done now. If you want to examine God's foreknowledge carefully, you'll consider that it's not so much foreknowledge of the future but rather never-failing knowledge of the present moment. And so we might do better to call it forth-sight rather than fore-sight, because set far away from the lowest things as if from the lofty summit of the world it looks forth on all things. (5.pr.6)

God does not foresee the future; he sees it. God's knowledge is ever and always a present knowledge. He sees the future not as we see the future but as we see the present. And just as our seeing of a present event does not necessarily cause that event, so God's present knowledge of what to us is future also does not, of necessity, cause it. Foreknowledge need not imply predestination, for foreknowledge, when used of God, is a misnomer. (Interestingly, just as C. S. Lewis incorporates a Boethian view of the subhuman nature of the damned into *The Great Divorce*, so does he incorporate Boethius' solution to the predestination-foreknowledge conundrum into book 4, chapter 3, of *Mere Christianity*.)

If Boethius could speak to us today, I think he would counsel us to let go of our spiritual sloth, a sloth that is too often fueled by a sense of divine fatalism based on a misunderstanding of foreknowledge, and seek, by means both of divine grace and of those gifts that God graciously bestowed on us, to ascend to that Beatific Vision in which all goodness, truth, and beauty dwell. Just as a good financial advisor will tell you that when you have control of your finances—rather than are controlled by your finances—you will be more (not less) free, so Boethius would teach us that while giving in to our baser (swinish) passions leads us to be enslaved by those passions, learning to properly channel our instincts and desires leads us up out of the darkness of the underworld.

The Death of Boethius: Triumph or Travail?

Regis Martin
Franciscan University of Steubenville

> About suffering they were never wrong,
> The Old Masters: how well they understood.
> —W. H. Auden, *Musée des Beaux Arts*

"Do tell me what you think of life", a woman once asked Henry James. She was not prepared for his answer. "I think it is a predicament", replied the Old Master, "which precedes death." And, to be sure, when the time came for James to face his own death, he rightly called it "the Distinguished Thing". Nothing so wonderfully concentrates the mind, as Dr. Johnson, another Old Master, famously put it, as the certainty of the prospect of being hanged in a fortnight.

Little is known of the circumstances surrounding the death of Boethius, save only that it was exceedingly cruel and unjust— and that he evinced such extraordinary presence of mind during the period leading up to it that, his mind being most wonderfully concentrated, he was able to bring to life a work of unique and unforgettable genius from the experience of it. Without question, here was a very great and enduring Old Master. And the world has never ceased to pay its homage to Boethius for so wise and brave a book as *The Consolation of Philosophy*. Indeed, after the Vulgate Bible that Saint Jerome translated from the original version inspired by the Holy Spirit, no other work during the Middle Ages was read as often as Boethius' timeless classic. Certainly few works have been translated as frequently, from Alfred the Great (who turned it into Old English), to Chaucer (who did the same in Middle English), to Elizabeth I the Tudor monarch (who added her own distinctive touches).

When the status of a work is adjudged sublime, one naturally wonders at the stature of its author. As regards Boethius,

there can be little doubt on that score: his star remains undimin-
ished despite the suddenness and finality of his fall from imperial grace. While not a formally canonized saint, his memory
has yet been revered as such by many—most conspicuously,
for instance, by the pilgrim-poet Dante (whose own creden-
tials as an Old Master would seem to be in very good order
indeed), who has given us, in canto 10 of the *Paradiso*, a glimpse
of the aura of glory that envelops the memory of Boethius. As
Dante is being led by Beatrice into the sphere of the sun, he is
shown a "garland of twelve souls"; these are the holy ones of
antiquity whose light grew so bright as to outshine even the
sun, thus earning them the title of doctors of the Church. And
there, of course, in the midst of the blaze stands Boethius, whom
Dante calls "[t]hat joy who strips the world's hypocrisies / Bare
to whoever heeds his cogent phrases".[1]

So what exactly do we know of Boethius' end? Again, very
little has come down to us in the fifteen hundred years that
separate us from this seminal figure of the Christian West,
widely regarded as both the last of the Romans and the first
of the Scholastics. But we can safely surmise that his last days
must have been unspeakable: protracted torture followed by
a fatal bludgeoning. All done, of course, on orders from Theodoric, the reputedly unlettered barbarian king who presided
over the western half of the empire and who had come to
suspect that Boethius, his chief palace official, was guilty of
treason. The imputation was wholly unjust, to be sure, the
innocence of this man having been established beyond cavil;
indeed, it could hardly have escaped the attention even of
his enemies that here was a man of utter and complete pro-
bity, for whom the Platonic ideal of disinterested government
service had been the hallmark of his life. It was not for nothing that the *Republic* had been a favorite text of his, in whose
pages the reader is recurrently reminded that power is to be
given only to those who disdain its exercise. Boethius, for all

---

[1] Dante, *Paradiso*, trans. John Ciardi (New York: New American Library, 1970),
canto 10, lines 125–26.

that his energies were given over to a deeply felt need to enter the public life, endeavoring thereby to uphold standards of truth and justice, would have vastly preferred a life sequestered among his books.

But the times being out of joint, what other recourse has a man of honor but to come to the aid of the city he loves, inspired by a vision of the *Imperium Romanum* that he sees everywhere in retreat, gravely imperiled by forces of corruption and disintegration? This is an especially exigent calling, moreover, for a man from an old and noble family (among his ancestors were two emperors and a pope) who had become habituated to the life of a Roman consul. And so Boethius, this superbly gifted and admirably situated young man, whose rise had been so swift and sure (by age thirty he had already filled the most important posts in Rome), finds himself suddenly fallen on hard times—"[w]ith hair whitened, and skin trembling loose", a bone-bag hung with flesh, he sadly tells us on the first page of the *Consolation* (1.met.1)[2]—awaiting death by execution for crimes he never committed.

It is Fortune's wheel, of course, that has ground poor Boethius in the dust of obloquy and death: "[P]roving her power—/ she revels in her show./The fortunate she prostrates—/in one hour" (2.met.1). But he need not repine for long. Thanks to the looming and radiant presence of Mistress Philosophia, whom he has long and ardently sought, and on whose sudden and dramatic entrance the gloom begins to lift, thus awakening his soul to memories of forgotten wisdom and joy, Boethius will rally his drooping spirits and so anneal himself to the adversity he cannot otherwise escape. "Wouldn't I help you", the lofty figure tells him, "carry this burden of ours that has been laid upon your shoulders by those that hate me?" (1.pr.3). Thus she reminds Boethius that he is not the first to suffer the ravages of men bent on defiling the temple of truth. Socrates too

---

[2] Boethius, *The Consolation of Philosophy*, trans. and ed. Scott Goins and Barbara Wyman, Ignatius Critical Editions (San Francisco: Ignatius Press, 2012). All quotations from the *Consolation* are from this edition.

was made to suffer an unjust death. And look at others: the
sting of misfortune has left marks on them all. "So don't be
surprised if we're tossed about by storms on the sea of life, when
we ourselves have chosen to be displeasing to the wicked." So
get on with it, she seems to be saying to him, and do not give
way to self-pity.

Boethius finds himself thus in very good company indeed,
which is to say, the roster of the wise whose number shall be
counted among the blessed in Heaven. There, she tells him,
ensconced above in "her fortress", the Furies cannot touch us.
The wise soul remains forever secure: "[W]e, untouched by their
mad confusion, look down and laugh.... Their cunning folly
cannot climb the walls that keep us safe" (1.pr.3). In the mind's
experience of Heaven, she adds confidingly on the final page
of book 1, "[Y]ou will be able to recognize the brightness of
the true light, as the shadows of deceptive desires have been
pushed aside" (1.pr.6).

To ensure the success of the journey, however—the authenticity, as it were, of the consolation conferred by philosophy—
men must first have freed themselves entirely from the tyranny
of Fortune. "I know the many disguises of that monster",
Philosophia tells him, "and her endearing friendliness to those
she tries to deceive—a kindness until she leaves them without warning and overwhelms them with unbearable pain"
(2.pr.1). Those who aspire to the high cliffs, who long to collect the choicest garlands of heavenly grace, must learn to resist
the siren songs of Fortune, lest they keep one from unearthing
the true source of her strategy, which is that her favors are
both fleeting and fickle. "Does the insatiable desire of men",
she asks with mock and almost disarming innocence, "bind us
to a constancy alien to our ways? This is our power, this is the
game we always play. We turn our wheel on its flying course;
we delight in changing the low to the high and the high to
the low" (2.pr.2).

And so the practice of inconstancy remains her one fixed
star, the abiding constant as it were, of the world she runs,
moving remorselessly along lines of pure chance and caprice.

In the circumstance, her flirtations are not to be trusted, and one must never succumb to a single unholy charm, because everything she offers is either false or merely fugitive. But to those who have eyes to see, the myriad duplicities of Dame Fortune may easily be unmasked. Besides, why would anyone wish to hold fast to a standard that evanesces even as one draws near to it? It is no better than the fate of Tantalus, punished by the gods never to reach the fruit that floats always beyond his grasp. It is a frustration, in short, no more infernal than which can be imagined.

So the soul, agreeably armed and accompanied by Philosophia, persisting in purity of heart and poverty of spirit, will thus learn the secret, the fatal germ, in the enemy's heart. Possessed of such saving knowledge, the bewitchments of Fortune cannot but fall to pieces, their very mutability, as Philosophia shrewdly observes, having stripped the enemy of the power to incite either fear or desire. ("The temporary nature of any situation", so she pronounces, "should keep a person from fearing Fortune's threats or hoping for her enticements" [2.pr.1].) Only learn that fact, Philosophia seems to be saying, along with firm adherence of the will to its application, and the soul is set free for the contemplation of those higher things that lead inescapably to consolation: "[Y]ou, settled in your fortress, may live—/and smile at the wrath of the sky" (2.met.4).

In summary, then, what is it that Philosophia would wish for Boethius finally to know and to do? Is there one overarching end toward which he needs to summon all his energies and skills in order to obtain it? Something the possession of which will confer lasting consolation? The answer, in a word, is God. Here is the pivotal truth to which Philosophia herself has painstakingly led her pupil. Were one to pursue only the perfect good, urging every scintilla of the soul to find and possess it, that would surely encompass the most perfect Good of all, which is God. And if to God one wishes to go, then one must never look back upon all that is not God.

Do not, Boethius is warned in solemn and poetic fashion, follow the example of poor Orpheus, who, in one fatal backward

glance, forfeited the love he had gone all the way down into
Hell to retrieve. The law of the underworld may not be gainsaid;
its plunder will not suffer repatriation to the world of light.
As Hades, fearful monarch of the dead, reminds us in passing
sentence upon the pitiful Orpheus:

> Alas, near the end of his night,
> Orpheus his own Eurydice
> saw, lost, and killed.
> This story is for you,
> for those who wish to lead
> the mind into the upper day.
> Since, whoever, having been weakened,
> turns back a gaze to Tartarus' chasm—
> whatever excellence he has gained,
> looking back, he loses.
>
> (3.met.12)

The crowning irony of the book, of course, is that it was
never the intention of Boethius to write it. Nor had it likely
crossed his mind which particular configuration of events would
someday provide a motive for doing so. But history, as T. S.
Eliot reminds us, "has many cunning passages,/contrived corridors".[3] Who can predict the perversities of a fallen race? Had
Theodoric only been wise enough to acknowledge the essential innocence of his first minister, Boethius would have been
spared exile, torture, and death. And we, of course, would then
have been spared one of the truly great and enduring monu-
ments of world literature. Is that the trade-off we are being
asked to make here? (Was it Faulkner who said of Keats' "Ode
on a Grecian Urn" that it was worth any number of old ladies?)
At what precise level of literary and philosophical excellence
are we entitled to say: Here is something so imperishably important to the maintenance of high culture that, yes, in order to
bring the thing off, its author will have to undergo the most

---

[3] T. S. Eliot, "Gerontin", *The Complete Poems and Plays 1909–1950* (Orlando,
Fla.: Harcourt, Brace & World, 1971), p. 22.

horrific tortures and then suffer the death of a traitor? Again, would that be an acceptable trade-off?

But suppose the issue were not like that at all. And, more to the point, would Boethius himself have countenanced such a reading of his own life and death? So what have we got to go on? Only that here was a man for whom the world itself had become his oyster. And that as we watch him perform at the top of his game, this brilliant and gifted young man, flush with power and wealth and every possible worldly success, we suddenly see it all disastrously fall away. All the riches of life, the rewards of work, cruelly pulled out from under him. Leaving him, moreover, not merely bereft of whatever leverage he once exercised at court but moving ineluctably toward a horrific and undeserved death. When you see your fate framed in those terms, only First Questions matter, and, one by one, they take you by the throat.

In the teeth of an absolute certainty of being tortured and killed, what does Boethius do? What does he think about? *Respice finem*, which means "Look to the end", was an ancient pagan motto whose message the faith of Christian men early on embraced. In fact, Jesus himself enjoined his disciples to watch and wait, mindful of their end: "Therefore you also must be ready; for the Son of man is coming at an hour you do not expect" (Matthew 24:44; RSV, Second Catholic Edition). How mindful was Boethius of his end? And did he face it in full view of Christ? Indeed, was he even a Christian? Certainly his family, for at least a century or more, professed the true faith. But did Boethius? And if so, why the silence, why this strangely persisting silence about Christ? For there is not a syllable in the entire *Consolation* that intimates anything at all about Jesus; there is not the least allusion to the frightful events surrounding Christ's Passion, which would seem to be of profound and immediate importance in Boethius' facing his own passion.

What *did* Boethius believe? We will never know what exchanges took place in those deep interior places where Boethius, forced by events he could neither control nor escape, the cruel mesh of an unjust world, found himself at last alone with God. These are intimacies on which it is simply not possible to eavesdrop; nor should we want to. But haven't we got a record already in place? What about the book Boethius wrote—is that not a huge hint of the Mystery before which, helpless and alone, he stood at the last? While we cannot precise the time spent between the sentence of death pronounced by Theodoric, then cravenly confirmed by a senate that would not defy its emperor, and the moment of its execution, it was evidently sufficient to permit Boethius to produce his masterpiece. And what is the organizing principle of the book but a series of dialogues, each driven by a deep and most desperate desire to learn once and for all the meaning of the universe? Does the world make sense? And if so, why is there evil?

Here the questions become existentially urgent. Who am I? Why have I been sent here to suffer? And, most important of all, where do I go when I die? Only God, of course, can reveal these things to him. Which God does in the form of the mysterious figure of Philosophia, the Lady Philosophy ("philosophy" meaning the love of wisdom), who has come in search of her old pupil, who has been "[f]orced by grief" to collect "melancholy measures" instead of the happy poems he used to compose (1.met.1). She comes in order to awaken his mind to a divine and transcendent realm—indeed, a realm whose existence he had for a time forgotten, reminding him that its very indestructibility places it beyond the reach of human wickedness. And she comes to impart real and lasting hope to his heart that, in spite of all that evil has conspired to rob him of his rightful place in the world, a condition of perfect consolation nevertheless awaits him on the other side of death. "A condition of complete simplicity" is how the poet Eliot describes it in the final lines of *Four Quartets*:

> (Costing not less than everything)
> And all shall be well and
> All manner of thing shall be well
> When the tongues of flame are in-folded
> Into the crowned knot of fire
> And the fire and the rose are one.

And so, notwithstanding the terms of a world most cruelly circumscribed by torture and death, Boethius remains a paradoxically free and happy man. Why? Because through his surrender to Philosophia, Boethius has come to know the true meaning of his life. In every circumstance, therefore, moved by the beauty and wonder of the love of wisdom, he will choose only that which draws him yet closer to his destiny, which is the eternal blessedness of Being itself, that is, God. And so on the strength of the faith vouchsafed Boethius by Philosophia, and in light of the sheer certainty of hope she confers, he is happily fortified to face the terror of his own death, and in doing so to vanquish forever the claims and conceits of Fortune.

Every Truly Happy Person Becomes God

Jim Scott Orrick
Boyce College

Just when we were on the verge of appointing Lady Philosophy to be the head of the Ladies' Aid Society, she caught us
off guard. We agreed with her that God is the ultimate good
and that the perfect good dwells within him. Furthermore, we
were ready to shout "Amen!" when she asserted that true happiness[1] is located in this highest God and that the substance
of this highest happiness proceeds from God himself. When
she asserted that "God is happiness itself" (3.pr.10), it sounded
a little strange, but we could not disagree. We nodded our
approval. We began to suspect that Lady Philosophy was a fine
Christian. We began to consider making the *Consolation of Philosophy* the next book we read for our Thursday night prayer
and study group. But it was when she drew her additional conclusion that we felt like she had slapped us in the face and
gone over to the other side. We were ready to initiate excom-
munication proceedings when she impudently said, "Since men
become happy from the acquisition of happiness, and happiness is indeed divinity, it is clear that men become happy
through the acquisition of divinity. But as men become just
by the acquisition of justice, and wise by the acquisition
of wisdom, so it is necessary by the same reasoning that men
who have acquired divinity become gods. Each happy man is

---

[1] In the Ignatius Press edition of the *Consolation* (Boethius, *The Consolation
of Philosophy*, trans. Scott Goins and Barbara Wyman [San Francisco: Ignatius
Press, 2012]), which I have used for the quotations in this essay, the translators
have chosen to use "blessedness" where Boethius wrote *beatitudo*, and "happiness" where Boethius wrote *felicitas* (ibid., p. 32, footnote 3). Most translators,
however, use "happiness" for both words—which is the premise for part of this
essay. For the sake of the essay's argument, I have substituted "happiness" (or
"happy") for the translation's "blessedness" (or "blessed") in this essay.

257

therefore a god" (3.pr.10). Did she really say what we thought she said? Maybe we misunderstood. But a few pages later, in an unmistakably clear statement, she confirms our suspicions: "[S]ince the Good itself is happiness, it is obvious that all good men become happy through the very fact of their goodness, and those who are happy are rightly called gods. This, then, is the reward of good men that the future will never erase, that no man's power can diminish, that no man's wickedness can darken—to become gods" (4.pr.3).

Good people—truly happy people—become gods? That is the sort of statement that leads us to label some religious sects as cults. Religious leaders who make statements like that are likely also to be making end-of-time predictions in which aliens from outer space figure prominently. It sounds unorthodox, to say the least.

But it is not unorthodox. When properly understood, the statement is perfectly consistent with the teaching of the Church Fathers and with the teaching of the Bible.

For us to properly understand what Lady Philosophy means by her audacious statement, two questions need to be answered: What does she mean by "happy", and what does she mean by "god" or "divine"?

What Is Happiness?

In our search to uncover what Lady Philosophy means by "happiness", we must first clear up a semantic problem. In certain circles, a new definition of the word "happiness" has recently arisen, and this new definition presents a significant barrier to understanding what Lady Philosophy is saying. In the redefinition of happiness, a careful distinction is made between happiness and joy, and generally, the end result is that happiness is deemed to be far inferior to joy. More particularly, in the new definition, happiness is dependent on circumstances, whereas joy transcends circumstances. Happiness is primarily emotional; joy is more cerebral or volitional. Happiness is temporary; joy is lasting. Happiness is fun but insubstantial, whereas joy is not necessarily fun but is solid. Happiness is an aluminum Christmas tree, but joy is a bristlecone pine. Happiness is an amusement park, but joy is a river. And so on. The end result is that joy is defined as something like peaceful fortitude or solemn resolve and is a characteristic that seems to be most useful when steeling oneself to undergo a root canal. Happiness is mostly to be avoided by mature persons, but if one occasionally forgets himself and slips into it, it usually does little harm. It is a bit of a jolt to those who have bought into this semantic distinction to read that "every truly *happy* person is God." The blow would have been lightened if Boethius had said "every truly *joyful* person is God."

There are a couple of problems with this distinction between happiness and joy. The first is fairly minor: most English speakers do not make a sharp distinction between happiness and joy. If, however, a writer or a speaker wishes to distinguish between the two, it takes only a few sentences to explain the specialized definitions. There are times when the distinction is useful, and other languages have words that indicate the distinction between temporary, superficial happiness and eternal, substantial happiness. Boethius uses *felicitas* for the former and *beatitudo* for the latter.

A more significant problem with the distinction between happiness and joy is that, in spite of joy's superior standing, it usually gets robbed. The redefiners strip joy of emotional content. There is no emotional delight in the newly defined joy. Joy no longer includes the idea of pleasure. If we should allow pleasure to remain an integral part of our understanding of joy, then I think the new definition of joy is fairly close to what Lady Philosophy means by "happiness". This similarity becomes clear when we allow Lady Philosophy to explain what happiness is not and what happiness is. Happiness is not dependent upon the gifts of Fortune, which are intermittent and fickle. "Do you really value a happiness that will pass away?" (2.pr.1). "Do you think there is any permanence inherent in human things, when the fleeting hour often dissolves a man himself? For even if there is little constancy in the ways of

chance, still, a man's last day is also a kind of death to Fortune, as she lingers with him. What difference do you suppose
it makes then whether you desert Fortune by dying or she
deserts you by fleeing?" (2.pr.3). Fortune-born happiness is
always incomplete (2.pr.4) and is fraught with secret vexa-
tions: "Therefore it's clear how miserable this 'happiness' of
human things is. It won't endure for men who are contented,
nor will it fully satisfy those who are anxious"; "the instability
brought by Fortune cannot hope for eternal happiness" (2.pr.4).
So true happiness is not dependent on the gifts of Fortune,
but is it for that reason bereft of delight? On the contrary,
Lady Philosophy explains in 3 *prosa* 9 that the perfect Good is
alone the repository of the several goods (including pleasure)
that humans seek outside of it: "And whatever needs nothing
outside of itself, and is renowned and revered—wouldn't we
agree that it is most full of joy, too?" (3.pr.9). Lady Philosophy
is not trying to convince Boethius that his new life in prison
can be fun, but neither is she advocating a pleasureless joy.

This exquisite delight, this true happiness—the sort of
delightful joy that leads to participation in the divine nature—
"is the highest Good for a being living by reason" (2.pr.4).
Living in accordance with reason is a human characteristic
that sets us apart from the beasts and makes us like God, in
whose image we are created (2.pr.5). "[H]uman minds are in
no way mortal" (2.pr.4), and therefore, nothing mortal can
ever make humans truly happy. Because of our minds we have
access to true happiness, but few persons deliberately pursue
it. Instead, we persist in seeking happiness through the acquisition of inferior goods such as power, pleasure, wealth, glory,
and fame—the five gifts of Fortune. Yet, a thorough examination of why we seek after the five gifts of Fortune reveals that
we are in fact seeking something that they can never provide.
"Every concern of man, which he pursues in his many efforts
and seeks by various paths, aims nevertheless at the single goal
of happiness. For when a man acquires that good, there is nothing left that he can desire. This is truly the highest of all goods,
containing all good things within it, since there is nothing
beyond it which anyone could wish to obtain" (3.pr.2).

But what is the source of this true happiness? Such a weighty question calls for prayer, and in 3 *metrum* 9, Lady Philosophy addresses God as the one who controls the world by reason and as the one who shapes the world to mirror his image and likeness:

> Father! Flash forth in splendor
> and scatter the mists of earth!
> Permit my spirit to rise—
> and grant light to my mind
> that I might fix clear sight on You,
> Source of all good.
> To the blessed, You are quiet calm.
> To see You is both purpose and end;
> You are the Leader and the Way—
> The First and the Last.

In her request to know the source of true happiness, she reveals that the source is God himself. He is the perfect one, and in contrast to him all imperfection appears. "Since nothing greater than God is able to be imagined, who can doubt that the thing that is surpassed by nothing is good? Truly reason shows that the Good is God, so that He is completely filled with the perfect Good" (3.pr.10). This highest good is essential to God himself—to his very being—and is not something separable from him, so "true happiness must reside in the most high God." It is at this point in her dissertation that she drops her bomb. Here is the logical progression: People become happy by securing happiness for themselves. Happiness is divinity. Therefore, people become happy by securing divinity for themselves. Persons who have divinity are gods. Every truly happy person is God (3.pr.10).

What Is Divinity?

First, and most significantly, anyone who misunderstands Lady Philosophy to be saying that truly happy people become equal with the one God of the universe has not been paying attention. Even if we go no further than the immediately preceding

context of the offending statement in book 3, we see that God
is "the highest Good" and "the Father of all things" (3.pr.9)
and that "two highest goods which differ from each other cannot exist" (3.pr.10). So logically, and unless Lady Philosophy
is contradicting herself, she cannot mean that truly happy people become equal to God.

Instead, she is utilizing a deliberately shocking metaphor,
which, if it were a simile, might be expanded into something
like this: "Every truly happy person is like God in what he
values, loves, and pursues. This happy person becomes a par-
ticipant in the divine nature." So that we will not misunderstand her shocking metaphor, she concedes, "[B]ut indeed in
nature God is one [therefore, we cannot become him]; by participation there is nothing to prevent there being as many gods
as you like" (3.pr.10).

We are still uneasy with the metaphor, but in using it Lady
Philosophy is in good company. The exact same metaphor is
found repeatedly in the writings of the Church Fathers, and it
is overtly used in the Bible by the psalmist Asaph, the Lord
Jesus, and the apostle Peter. The same metaphor is implied in
common Bible words like "godliness" and "godly". And the
metaphor is strongly sanctioned in the biblical language describing humans as having been created in the image of God.

The primary focus of this essay is to show that Lady Philosophy is consistent with Scripture when she utilizes the language of becoming divine, but it is significant that she is also
consistent with the Church Fathers.[2] Saint Athanasius, for
example, asserted that the Word "was made man so that we
might be made God" and that, "[i]f by a partakability of the
Spirit we shall become partakers of the divine nature, it would
be madness then afterwards to call the Spirit an originated
[i.e., created] entity, and not of God; for on account of this
also those who are in him are made divine. But then if he

---

[2] For most of the information summarized in the remainder of this paragraph,
I am indebted to a very fine paper by Michael D. Morrison, "Athanasius's Doctrine of Divinization", posted on the Web site Angelfire.com: http://angelfire.com/
md/mdmorrison/hist/DIVINIZ.html (accessed April 12, 2011).

makes man divine, it is not dubious to say his nature is of God."[3] The language of becoming divine is quite common in the writings of the Fathers: "After Theophilus, Ireneaeus, Hippolytus, and Origen, it is found in all the Fathers of the ancient Church."[4]

The metaphor is overtly used in Psalm 82, which is a stinging diatribe against unjust judges who were showing partiality to the wicked and neglecting to administer justice on behalf of the weak and fatherless. The psalmist Asaph commences his poem with an imaginary court scene. In this imagined court, God himself sits as judge, and the unjust judges are being tried. "God has taken his place in the divine council; in the midst of the *gods* he holds judgment: 'How long will you judge unjustly and show partiality to the wicked?'" (Psalm 82: 1, 2; italics mine).[5] Even though the unjust judges were scoundrels, God still called them gods because they were authorized to exercise judgment—a prerogative that ultimately belongs to God himself. They had been entrusted with the responsibility to act like God, so they were called gods. In this case, their participation in the divine activity did not shield them from God's impartial judgment: "I say, 'You are gods, sons of the Most High, all of you; nevertheless, you shall die like men, and fall like any prince'" (6, 7).

Jesus made reference to this passage when he was accused of blasphemy for claiming to be the Son of God. His offending statement had been, "I and the Father are one." John records the story:

> The Jews took up stones again to stone him. Jesus answered them, "I have shown you many good works from the Father;

---

[3] Athanasius, *De incarnatione* 54.3 and *Epistulae ad Serapionem* 1.24, quoted in Morrison, "Athanasius's Doctrine".

[4] Adolph Harnack, *History of Dogma*, trans. Neil Buchanan from the 3rd German ed. (c. 1900; repr., New York: Dover, 1961), 3:164, note 2, quoted in Morrison, "Athanasius's Doctrine". The note also cites passages from numerous other Church Fathers.

[5] All biblical quotations are taken from *The Holy Bible*, Revised Standard Version, Catholic Edition (San Francisco: Ignatius Press, 1966).

for which of these do you stone me?" The Jews answered him,
"We stone you for no good work but for blasphemy; because
you, being a man, make yourself God." Jesus answered them,
"Is it not written in your law, 'I said, you are gods'? If he called
them gods to whom the word of God came (and Scripture cannot be broken), do you say of him whom the Father consecrated
and sent into the world, 'You are blaspheming,' because I said,
'I am the Son of God'? If I am not doing the works of my
Father, then do not believe me; but if I do them, even though
you do not believe me, believe the works, that you may know
and understand that the Father is in me and I am in the Father."
(John 10:30–38)

Jesus deserves the title "Son of God" in a way that no one else
does; he is the one "whom the Father consecrated and sent
into the world". But in addition to that, he argued that he
deserved the title because he was doing the good works that
God does. He maintained that this alone ought to have been
enough to quell his antagonists' objections to his claims to be
the Son of God. Jesus' argument here is quite similar to Lady
Philosophy's argument: persons who think and act like God
may legitimately be called gods.

The passage in the Bible that sounds most like Lady Philosophy in this line of reasoning is found in the apostle Peter's
second Letter: "His divine power has granted to us all things
that pertain to life and godliness, through the knowledge of
him who called us to his own glory and excellence, by which
he has granted to us his precious and very great promises, that
through these you may escape from the corruption that is in
the world because of passion, and become partakers of the divine
nature" (2 Peter 1: 3, 4). Note several points of similarity
between the teachings of Peter and of Lady Philosophy. First,
both identify God as the originator of these blessings: Lady
Philosophy calls God the *source* of happiness (3.pr.9); Peter
says, "His divine power has granted to us ..." Second, both
emphasize the fullness of the divine blessings. Lady Philosophy calls this fullness happiness; Peter calls it "all things that
pertain to life and godliness". Third, Lady Philosophy teaches

throughout the *Consolation* that it is through understanding—through the mind—that we enjoy true happiness; Peter intimates the same when he says that God "has granted to us his precious and very great promises", which must, of course, be believed to be enjoyed. Fourth, Lady Philosophy asserts that those who are truly happy become gods by participation (3.pr.10). Peter uses nearly the exact same words: "that through these you may ... become partakers of the divine nature". Finally, Lady Philosophy goes to considerable lengths to demonstrate the incapacity of anything short of God to afford true happiness: "[S]ince it is the nature of the mind to put on false opinions when it has cast aside true ones, I will try to clear the mist a little with mild and gentle remedies. This way you will be able to recognize the brightness of the true light, as the shadows of deceptive desires have been pushed aside" (1.pr.6). Similarly, Peter asserts that those who believe the promises and participate in the divine nature have "escape[d] from the corruption that is in the world because of passion".

Anyone consulting a Bible concordance will find that the Bible contains many exhortations encouraging Christians to pursue godliness and to live godly lives. Even a minor etymologist can figure out that "godliness" is a contraction of "godlike-ness", and "godly" must mean something like "god-like". Most readers who take umbrage at Lady Philosophy's shocking metaphor would nod approval had she more mildly said that the truly happy become godly, godlike, or like God. Context indicates that any of these substitutions is essentially what Lady Philosophy means.

Finally, it is well known that the Bible asserts that God created humans in his own image and likeness (Genesis 1:26). The image of God in man was corrupted by the Fall, but "we all, with unveiled face, reflecting the glory of the Lord, are being changed into his likeness from one degree of glory to another; for this comes from the Lord who is the Spirit" (2 Corinthians 3:18). Furthermore, Christians are said to be re-created after the image of Christ, who is himself "the image of the invisible God" (Colossians 1:15): "For those whom he foreknew he also predestined to be conformed to the image of his Son, in order that he might be the first-born among many brethren" (Romans 8:29). If Lady Philosophy were teaching her lesson in a Christian setting, and if she were using biblical language, she might say, "Because of sin, we seek to find our ultimate satisfaction in worldly pleasures that can never truly satisfy us. But when we are born from above, God commences the process of enlightening our minds, redirecting our affections, and renewing our wills. We are therefore enabled to die more and more unto sin and live unto righteousness. In short, we are renewed in our entire human nature. As God continues this process in us, he re-creates us in the image of his only begotten Son, Jesus. We begin to see things from his perspective. We begin to love what he loves and to hate what he hates. We start to find true happiness in what is truly good and truly beautiful. We become more and more like Christ, and therefore we become like God. In fact, it is consistent with biblical language to say that we become participants in the divine nature."

Is that spot on the Ladies' Aid Society still open?

CONTRIBUTORS

Scott Goins is professor of classics and director of the Honors College at McNeese State University in Lake Charles, Louisiana. He received his Ph.D. and M.A. from Florida State University and has published on several authors including Virgil and Boethius.

Mitchell Kalpakgian, professor emeritus of Humanities at Wyoming Catholic College, is contributing editor of the *New Oxford Review* and writes for the *Saint Austin Review* and *Homiletic and Pastoral Review*. His published books include *The Marvellous* in *Fielding's Novels*, *The Mysteries of Life in Children's Literature*, and *The Lost Arts of Modern Civilization*.

Jeffrey S. Lehman teaches at Thomas Aquinas College in Santa Paula, California. He is also a Fellow of the Center for Thomas More Studies and holds a Ph.D. in philosophy from the Institute of Philosophic Studies at the University of Dallas. Presently he is working on a monograph on Saint Augustine's *Confessions*.

Rachel Lu received her Ph.D. from Cornell University and teaches philosophy at the University of St. Thomas. She specializes in medieval philosophy and especially the moral philosophy of Saint Bonaventure. Her interests include the Christian personalism of Dietrich von Hildebrand, the medieval reception of Aristotle's ethics, and college football. She lives in St. Paul, Minnesota with her husband, Mathew, and their son Charles.

Louis Markos, professor in English and Scholar in Residence at Houston Baptist University, holds the Robert H. Ray Chair in Humanities; he is the author, most recently, of *From Achilles to Christ, Apologetics for the 21ˢᵗ Century,* and *Restoring Beauty:*

The Good, the True, and the Beautiful in the Writings of C. S. Lewis.

Regis Martin teaches theology at Franciscan University of Steubenville, where, besides offering courses on God and the Church, opines on such landmarks of literature as Dante, Donne, Eliot, and Flannery O'Connor. He is the author of a half-dozen or more books, including a forthcoming collection entitled *A Baker's Dozen* (Emmaus Road). He is married and the father of ten children and five grandchildren.

Jim Scott Orrick has been teaching Boethius for many years at Boyce College in Louisville, Kentucky, where he is Professor of Literature and Culture and Department Coordinator for General Studies. He also contributed an essay to the Ignatius Critical Edition of *Hamlet*. He is the author of *A Year with George Herbert: A Guide to Fifty-Two of His Best-Loved Poems*. He and his wife, Carol, have six daughters.

Barbara H. Wyman, married to Bruce, teaches English and Latin at McNeese State University in Lake Charles, Louisiana, and is the mother of grown children. Besides Boethius, she has published on George Herbert (*Studies in Philology*, Winter 2000), Hopkins, and others. She attends the Traditional Latin Mass.

BIBLIOGRAPHY

This bibliography consists of three sections. Part 1 includes selected editions, translations, and commentaries on all or parts of the *Consolation*. Part 2 includes works of literature cited in the introduction and notes. Part 3 includes secondary sources cited in the introduction and notes. More complete bibliographies can be found in Obertello, *Severino Boezio* (see part 3 below); Gruber, *Kommentar zu Boethius* (see part 1); and Marenbon, *Cambridge Companion to Boethius* (see part 3). LCL refers to the Loeb Classical Library, which contains the Greek or Latin text along with an English translation.

Part 1: Editions, translations, and commentaries

Bieler, L., ed. *Anicii Manlii Severini Boethii Philosophiae consolatio*. 2nd ed. Corpus Christianorum: Series latina 94. Turnhout: Brepols,1984.

Diels, Hermann, ed. *Die Fragmente der Vorsokratiker*. Berlin: Weidmann, 1954.

Fortescue, Adrian, ed. *Ancius Manlius Severinus Boethius De consolatione philosophiae libri quinque*. Edited by G. D. Smith. Hildesheim: Georg Olms, 1976. Originally published in London, 1925.

Gruber, Joachim. *Kommentar zu Boethius, "De consolatione philosophiae"*. 2nd ed. Berlin: Walter de Gruyter, 2006. Originally published 1978. (This is the most detailed commentary on the *Consolation* and includes a thorough bibliography.)

Langston, Douglas C., trans. *The Consolation of Philosophy*. Norton Critical Editions. New York: W. W. Norton, 2010. (This contains the prose translation of Richard H. Green.)

Moreschini, C., ed. *De consolatione philosophiae; Opuscula theologica*. Munich: Teubner, 2000. (Critical edition of the Latin texts.)

Obertello, Luca, trans. *La consolazione della filosofia; Gli opuscoli teologici.* Milan: Rusconi Libri, 1979.

O'Donnell, J. J., ed. *Consolatio philosophiae.* Vol. 2. Bryn Mawr Latin Commentaries. Bryn Mawr: Thomas Library, Bryn Mawr College, 1984. (This contains notes to the text of Weinberger, which is found in vol. 1.)

Relihan, Joel C., trans. *The Consolation of Philosophy.* Indianapolis: Hackett, 2001. (Here one can find a brief exposition of Relihan's view that the *Consolation* is intended as intentionally ironic, purposely showing the inability of pure philosophy, without Christianity, to console. See also Relihan, *Prisoner's Philosophy*, in part 3 of this bibliography.)

Scheible, Helga. *Die Gedichte in der "Consolatio philosophiae" des Boethius.* Heidelberg: Carl Winter, 1972. (A commentary on the poems of the *Consolation*.)

Sharples, R. W., ed. and trans. *Cicero: "On Fate"; Boethius: "The Consolation of Philosophy" IV. 5–7, V.* Warminster: Aris and Phillips, 1991.

Slavitt, David R., trans. *The Consolation of Philosophy.* Cambridge: Harvard University Press, 2008.

Stewart, H. F., E. K. Rand, and S. J. Tester, trans. *The Theological Tractates and "The Consolation of Philosophy".* LCL 74. Harvard: Harvard University Press, 1973. Originally published 1918.

Walsh, P. G., trans. *"The Consolation of Philosophy", Translated with Introduction and Explanatory Notes.* Oxford: Clarendon Press, 1999.

Watts, V. E., trans. *The Consolation of Philosophy.* New York: Penguin, 1969.

Weinberger, Wilhelm, ed. *Anicii Manlii Severini Boethii Philosophiae consolationis, libri quinque.* Corpus scriptorum ecclesiasticorum latinorum 67. Vienna: Hölder, Pichler, Tempsky, 1934.

Part 2: Works of literature cited in the footnotes

Anselm. *Anselm of Canterbury: The Major Works.* Translated by Brian Davies and G. R. Evans. Oxford, Oxford University Press, 1998.

Aristotle. *Introduction to Aristotle*. Edited by Richard McKeon. New York: Random House, 1947.

Augustine. *Basic Writings of Augustine*. Edited by Whitney J. Oates. Vol. 1. New York: Random House, 1948.

———. *Confessions*. Translated by R. S. Pine-Coffin. New York: Penguin, 1961.

———. *Teaching Christianity: De doctrina christiana*. Translated with notes by Edmund Hill. New York: New City Press, 1996.

Cassiodorus. *Variae*. Translated and edited by S. J. B. Barnish. Liverpool: University of Liverpool Press, 1992.

Cicero. *De senectute; De amicitia; De divinatione*. Translated by William Armistead Falconer. LCL 154. Cambridge: Harvard University Press, 1923.

———. *Tusculan Disputations*. Translated by J. E. King. LCL 141. Cambridge: Harvard University Press, 1945.

Dante. *Dante's "Paradise"*. Translated by Mark Musa. Bloomington: University of Indiana Press, 1984.

———. *Dante's "Purgatory"*. Translated by Mark Musa. Bloomington: University of Indiana Press, 1981.

———. *The "Divine Comedy" of Dante Alighieri*. Vol. 1, *Inferno*. Translated and annotated by Robert M. Durling and Robert L. Martinez. New York: Oxford University Press, 1996.

de Lorris, Guillaume, and Jean de Meun. *The Romance of the Rose*. Translated by Charles Dahlberg. 3rd ed. Princeton: Princeton University Press, 1995.

de Meun, Jean. (See de Lorris and de Meun, *Romance of the Rose*, above.)

Homer. *The "Iliad" of Homer*. Translated by Richmond Lattimore. Chicago: University of Chicago Press, 1951.

Juvenal. *The "Satires" of Juvenal*. Translated by Rolfe Humphries. Bloomington: Indiana University Press, 1958.

Lucretius. *The Nature of Things*. Translated by Frank O. Copley. New York: Norton, 1977.

Macrobius. *Commentary on the "Dream of Scipio"*. Translated by William Harris Stahl. New York: Columbia University Press, 1952.

Martianus Capella. *De nuptiis Philologiae et Mercurii*. In *A Philosophical and Literary Commentary on Martianus Capella's "De nuptiis Philologiae et Mercurii"*, Book 1, by Danuta Shanzer. Berkeley: University of California Press, 1986.

Ovid. *Metamorphoses*. Translated by Charles Martin. New York: W. W. Norton and Co., 2004.

Plato. *Cratylus; Parmenides; Greater Hippias; Lesser Hippias*. Translated by H. N. Fowler. LCL 167. Cambridge: Harvard University Press, 1926.

———. *Euthyphro; Apology; Crito; Phaedo; Phaedrus*. Translated by Harold North Fowler. LCL 36. Cambridge: Harvard University Press, 1914.

———. *Laches; Protagoras; Meno; Euthydemus*. Translated by W. R. M. Lamb. LCL 165. Cambridge: Harvard University Press, 1924.

———. *Lysis; Symposium; Gorgias*. Translated by W. R. M. Lamb. LCL 166. Cambridge: Harvard University Press, 1925.

———. *Republic*. Translated by Paul Shorey. 2 vols. LCL 237, 276. Cambridge: Harvard University Press, 1935, 1937.

———. *The Statesman; Philebus*. Translated by H. N. Fowler. LCL 164. Cambridge: Harvard University Press, 1925.

———. *Theatetus; Sophist*. Translated by Harold North Fowler. LCL 128. Cambridge: Harvard University Press, 1921.

———. *Timaeus; Critias; Cleitophon; Menexenus; Epistles*. Translated by R. G. Bury. LCL 234. Cambridge: Harvard University Press, 1929.

Seneca. *Ad Lucilium Epistulae Morales*. Translated by Richard M. Gummere. 3 vols. LCL 75–77. Cambridge: Harvard University Press, 1917–1925.

Shakespeare, William. *Hamlet*. Edited by Joseph Pearce. Ignatius Critical Editions. San Francisco: Ignatius Press, 2008.

Tolkien, J. R. R., trans. *Sir Gawain and the Green Knight, Pearl, and Sir Orfeo*. Boston: Houghton Mifflin, 1975.

Toole, John Kennedy. *A Confederacy of Dunces*. New York: Grove Press, 1980.

Virgil. *Eclogues; Georgics; Aeneid 1–6*. Translated by H. Rushton Fairclough. LCL 63. Cambridge: Harvard University Press, 1935.

———. *Georgics*. Edited by Richard F. Thomas. Vol. 1, *Books 1 and 2*. Cambridge: Cambridge University Press, 1988.

273

Part 3: Secondary sources on Boethius

Astell, Ann. *Job, Boethius, and Epic Truth*. Ithaca: Cornell University Press, 1994.

Auerbach, Erich. *Literary Language and Its Public in Late Latin Antiquity and in the Middle Ages*. Translated from the German by Ralph Manheim. New York: Random House, 1965.

Barnish, S. J. B., trans. and ed. *Variae*, by Cassiodorus. Liverpool: University of Liverpool Press, 1992.

Barron, Robert. *Thomas Aquinas: Spiritual Master*. New York: Crossroad, 1996.

Benedict XVI. "Boethius and Cassiodorus". General audience, Paul VI Audience Hall, March 12, 2008. http://www.vatican. va/holy_father/benedict_xvi/audiences/2008/documents/ hf_ben-xvi_aud_20080312_en.html.

Bury, R. G., trans. *Timaeus; Critias; Cleitophon; Menexenus; Epistles*, by Plato. LCL 234. Cambridge: Harvard University Press, 1929.

Chadwick, Henry. *Boethius: The Consolations of Music, Logic, Theology, and Philosophy*. Oxford: Oxford University Press, 1981.

———. "Theta on Philosophy's Dress in Boethius". *Medium Aevum* 49 (1980): 175–77.

Chamberlain, D. S. "Philosophy of Music in the *Consolation* of Boethius". *Speculum* 45 (1970): 80–97.

Cherniss, Michael D. *Boethian Apocalypse: Studies in Middle English Vision Poetry*. Norman, Okla.: Pilgrim Books, 1987.

Claassen, Jo-Marie. *Displaced Persons: The Literature of Exile from Cicero to Boethius*. Madison: University of Wisconsin Press, 1999.

Collins, James. "Progress and Problems in the Reassessment of Boethius". *Modern Schoolman* 33 (1945): 1–38.

Copleston, Frederick. *Medieval Philosophy*. Vol. 2 of *A History of Philosophy*. Garden City, N.Y.: Image, 1962.

Courcelle, Pierre. *"La consolation de philosophie" dans la tradition littéraire: Antécédents et postérité de Boèce*. Paris: Études augustiniennes, 1967. (This is one of the foremost works on Boethius' literary tradition.)

————. *Late Latin Writers and Their Greek Sources*. Translated from the French by Harry E. Wedeck. Cambridge: Harvard University Press, 1969.

————. "Le personnage de Philosophie dans la littérature latine". *Journal des Savants* (1970): 209–52.

————. "Le visage de Philosophie". *Revue des Études Anciennes* 70 (1968): 110–20.

Crabbe, Anna M. "Anamnesis and Mythology in the *De consolatione philosophiae*". In Obertello, *Atti del Congresso internazionale di studi Boeziani*, pp. 311–25.

————. "Literary Design in the *De consolatione philosophiae*". In Gibson, *Boethius*, pp. 237–74.

Curtius, Ernst Robert. *European Literature and the Late Middle Ages*. Translated by Willard R. Trask. New York: Pantheon, 1953. Originally published 1948.

Dahlberg, Charles, trans. *The Romance of the Rose*, by Guillaume de Lorris and Jean de Meun. 3rd ed. Princeton: Princeton University Press, 1995.

Dolson, Guy Bayley. *"The Consolation of Philosophy" of Boethius in English Literature*. Ph.D. diss., Cornell University, 1926.

Dronke, Peter. *Verse with Prose from Petronius to Dante: The Art and Scope of the Mixed Form*. Cambridge: Harvard University Press, 1994.

Durling, Robert M., and Robert L. Martinez, trans. *The "Divine Comedy" of Dante Alighieri*. Vol. 1, *Inferno*. New York: Oxford University Press, 1996.

Fuhrmann, M., and J. Gruber, eds. *Boethius*. Wege der Forschung 483. Darmstadt: Wissenschaftliche Buchgesellschaft, 1984. (A collection of important essays, mostly reprinted, on Boethius.)

Gibson, Margaret, ed. *Boethius: His Life, Thought and Influence*. Oxford: Basil Blackwell, 1981.

Gilson, Étienne. *The Philosophy of Thomas Aquinas*. Translated by Edward Bullough from the 3rd rev. and enlarged ed. of *Le Thomisme*. New York: Barnes and Noble, 1993.

Goins, Scott. "Boethius' *Consolation of Philosophy* 1.2.6 and Virgil *Aeneid* 2: Removing the Clouds of Mortal Anxieties". *Phoenix* 55 (2001): 124–36.

Gruber, Joachim. "Die Erscheinung der Philosophie in der *Consolatio philosophiae* des Boethius". *Rheinisches Museum für Philologie* 112 (1969): 166–86.

Jefferson, Bernard L. *Chaucer and the "Consolation of Philosophy" of Boethius*. Princeton: Princeton University Press, 1917.

Joseph, Miriam. *The Trivium: The Liberal Arts of Logic, Grammar, and Rhetoric*. Philadelphia: Paul Dry Books, 2002.

King, J. E., trans. *Tusculan Disputations*, by Cicero. LCL 141. Cambridge: Harvard University Press, 1945.

Klingner, Friedrich. *De Boethii Consolatione philosophiae*. 2nd ed. Zurich: Weidmann, 1966. Originally published 1921.

Lamberton, Robert. *Homer the Theologian: Neoplatonist Allegorical Reading and the Growth of the Epic Tradition*. Berkeley: University of California Press, 1986.

Lerer, Seth. *Boethius and Dialogue: Literary Method in the "Consolation of Philosophy"*. Princeton, N.J.: Princeton University Press, 1985.

Lewis, C. S. *The Discarded Image: An Introduction to Medieval and Renaissance Literature*. Cambridge: Cambridge University Press, 1964.

Liebeschutz, H. "Western Christian Thought from Boethius to Anselm". In *The Cambridge History of Later Greek and Early Medieval Philosophy*. Edited by A. H. Armstrong, pp. 538–55. Cambridge: Cambridge University Press, 1967.

Louth, Andrew. *The Origins of the Christian Mystical Tradition*. Oxford: Clarendon Press, 1981.

Magee, J. "Boethius' *Consolatio* and the Theme of Roman Liberty". *Phoenix* 59 (2005): 348–64.

Marenbon, John. *Boethius*. Oxford: Oxford University Press, 2003.

———, ed. *The Cambridge Companion to Boethius*. Cambridge: Cambridge University Press, 2009.

Matthews, John. "Anicius Manlius Severinus Boethius". In Gibson, *Boethius*, pp. 15–43.

McInerny, Ralph. *Boethius and Aquinas*. Washington, D.C.: Catholic University of America Press, 1990.

McKeon, Richard, ed. *Introduction to Aristotle*. New York: Random House, 1947.

Means, Michael. *The "Consolatio" Genre in Medieval English Literature*. Gainesville: University of Florida Press, 1972.

Mohrmann, Christine. "Some Remarks on the Language of Boethius, *Consolatio philosophiae*". In *Latin Script and Letters, A.D. 400–900*, edited by John J. O'Meara and Bern Naumann, pp. 54–61. Leiden: E. J. Brill, 1976.

Moorhead, John. "Boethius' Life and the World of Late Antique Philosophy". In Marenbon, *Cambridge Companion to Boethius*, pp. 13–33.

Murari, Rocco. *Dante e Boezio*. Bologna: Ditta Nicola Zanichelli, 1905.

Obertello, Luca, ed. *Severino Boezio*. 2 vols. Genoa: Accademia Ligure di scienze e lettere, 1974. (Vol. 2 contains a useful bibliography of Boethius.)

———, ed. *Atti del Congresso internazionale di studi Boeziani*. Rome: Editrice Herder, 1981.

———, trans. *La consolazione della filosofia; Gli opuscoli teologici*, by Boethius. Milan: Rusconi Libri, 1979.

O'Daly, Gerard. *The Poetry of Boethius*. Chapel Hill: University of North Carolina Press, 1991.

Patch, Howard Rollin. *The Goddess Fortuna in Medieval Literature*. Cambridge: Harvard University Press, 1927.

———. "Necessity in Boethius and the Neoplatonists". *Speculum* 10 (1935): 393–404.

———. *The Tradition of Boethius: A Study of His Importance in Medieval Culture*. New York: Oxford University Press, 1935.

Payne, Anne F. *King Alfred and Boethius*. Madison: University of Wisconsin Press, 1969.

Rand, Edward Kennard. "On the Composition of Boethius' *Consolatio philosophiae*". *Harvard Studies in Classical Philology* 15 (1904): 1–28.

Relihan, Joel C. *The Prisoner's Philosophy: Life and Death in Boethius' "Consolation", with a Contribution on the Medieval Boethius by William E. Heise*. Notre Dame: University of Notre Dame Press, 2007.

Robertson, D. W. *A Preface to Chaucer: Studies in Medieval Perspectives*. Princeton: Princeton University Press, 1962.

Robinson, David M. "The Wheel of Fortune". *Classical Philology* 41 (1946): 207–16.

Russell, Norman. *The Doctrine of Deification in the Greek Patristic Tradition*. New York: Oxford, 2006.

Sadler, Lynn Veach. *Consolation in "Samson Agonistes": Regeneration and Typology*. Elizabethan and Renaissance Studies 82. Salzburg: Institut für Anglistik und Amerikanistik, 1979.

Scheible, Helga. *Die Gedichte in der "Consolatio philosophiae" des Boethius*. Heidelberg: Carl Winter, 1972. (A commentary on the poems of the *Consolation*.)

Schmid, W. "Boethius and the Claims of Philosophy". *Studia Patristica* 2 (1957): 368–75. (This is a briefer, English version of the following entry.)

Schmid, Wolfgang. "Philosophisches und Medizinisches in der *Consolatio* des Boethius". In *Festschrift Bruno Snell*, edited by Thomas B. L. Webster, pp. 113–44. Munich: C. H. Beck, 1956.

Shanzer, Danuta. "Interpreting the *Consolation*". In Marenbon, *Cambridge Companion to Boethius*, pp. 228–54.

———. *A Philosophical and Literary Commentary on Martianus Capella's "De nuptiis Philologiae et Mercurii", Book 1*. Berkeley: University of California Press, 1986.

Sharples, R. W., ed. and trans. *Cicero: "On Fate"; Boethius: "The Consolation of Philosophy" IV. 5–7, V*. Warminster: Aris and Phillips, 1991.

Silk, Edmund T. "Boethius' *Consolatio philosophiae* as a Sequel to Augustine's *Dialogues* and *Soliloquia*". *Harvard Theological Review* 32 (1939): 17–39.

Stahl, William Harris, trans. *Commentary on the "Dream of Scipio"*, by Macrobius. New York: Columbia University Press, 1952.

Stewart, Hugh Fraser. *Boethius: An Essay*. Edinburgh: William Blackwood and Sons, 1891.

Tillyard, E. M. W. *The Elizabethan World Picture*. New York: Random House, 1967.

Vann, Gerald. *The Wisdom of Boethius*. Aquinas Society of London 20. London: Blackfriars, 1952.

Vogel, C.J. de. "*Amor quo caelum regitur*". *Vivarium* 1 (1963): 2–34.

Wetherbee, Winthrop. "The *Consolation* and Medieval Literature". In Marenbon, *Cambridge Companion to Boethius*, pp. 279–302.

White, Alison. "Boethius in the Medieval Quadrivium". In Gibson, *Boethius*, pp. 162–205.

Wyman, Barbara Hart. "Boethian Influence and Imagery in the Poetry of George Herbert". *Studies in Philology* 97 (2000): 61–95.